"Could you kiss me good night?"

Jesus. "Sure, kiddo." He leaned over her, intending to kiss her forehead, but she lifted her head at the last moment and her lips pressed against his. He meant to pull back, and did a bit, but she followed him, pressing closer as he jammed one fist into the blanket beside her to stop himself from pulling her against him. It was obvious she didn't know how to kiss, and that was one thing Mitch was thankful for. She kept her mouth closed, but her lips were so damned soft, all he could think about was nudging down her jaw gently and tasting her. But he didn't.

He pulled back slowly and she smiled drunkenly up at him. "Minnie said you looked like a man who could kiss."

More Historical Romance from Jane Goodger

Marry Christmas
A Christmas Scandal
A Christmas Waltz
When a Duke Says I Do
The Mad Lord's Daughter
When a Lord Needs a Lady
The Spinster Bride

Behind a Lady's Smile

Jane Goodger

LYRICAL PRESS
Kensington Publishing Corp.
www.kensingtonbooks.com

LYRICAL PRESS BOOKS are published by

Kensington Publishing Corp.
119 West 40th Street
New York, NY 10018

All Kensington titles, imprints, and distributed lines are available at special quantity discounts for bulk purchases for sales promotion, premiums, fund-raising, educational, or institutional use.

Special book excerpts or customized printings can also be created to fit specific needs. For details, write or phone the office of the Kensington Sales Manager: Kensington Publishing Corp., 119 West 40th Street, New York, NY 10018. Attn. Sales Department. Phone: 1-800-221-2647.

Lyrical and the L logo are trademarks of Kensington Publishing Corp.

First Electronic Edition: August 2015
eISBN-13: 978-1-60183-449-2
eISBN-10: 1-60183-449-7

First Print Edition: August 2015
ISBN-13: 978-1-60183-450-8
ISBN-10: 1-60183-450-0

Printed in the United States of America

To my daughter, Claire, who is turning out to be a wonderful young woman and a great friend. I finally have someone to shop with!

Chapter 1

His little shadow was back.

For two days, Mitch had noticed . . . someone. He wasn't quite sure whether it was male or female, but that didn't matter. Out here in the middle of nowhere, where a man could disappear and never be found, a man had to be careful. A man had to make certain his rifle was loaded, his canteen was filled, and he listened to his gut. And right about now, his gut was telling him whoever had been watching him for two days was up to no good.

"You wait here, Millie." Mitch patted his mule and tied her to a scraggly white pine. If Millie really got in a mind to escape, the sapling wouldn't do much to keep her in place, but he very much doubted Millie would get in the mind to do more than nibble on some grass.

Mitch was no stranger to the mountains of Yosemite. He guessed he knew them better than most. He knew how to walk silently and he knew when to make a noise that might scare a grizzly away. That one creature he wasn't ashamed to admit he didn't much care for. He'd seen the results of a bear attack and was quite certain he didn't want to be on the receiving end of those razor-sharp claws. Other than grizzlies and men with guns, he wasn't afraid of much else. A man who'd seen and done what he had learned not to be afraid.

Whoever was trailing him was high up, likely taking little peeks over the rocks that jutted out above him like crooked teeth. He climbed silently, his boots pressing into the thick cushion of pine needles, until he was pretty sure he was above his prey. He scanned the area, Winchester in hand, fully loaded and ready to fire. And then he saw a movement, a flash of hair.

"Well, damn," he whispered, looking at the girl through his gun sight. At least he thought it must be a girl with that long, pale braid down her back. She was lying on her stomach, no doubt staring at Millie and wondering where the heck the man she'd been spying on had disappeared to. His eyes moved down, following the trail of her braid, until he reached the decidedly feminine curve of her backside. Definitely female.

Now, he didn't like holding a rifle on a woman or a girl, but he'd learned the hard way that women and girls could be just as dangerous with a gun as a man, so he wasn't about to take any chances. If any of his friends back home saw him, they'd probably punch his jaw. But this wasn't New York City and that girl was no debutante, and so he held his gun on her real careful. She turned her head and he saw the delicate curve of her smooth cheek, and seeing that bit of feminine beauty in such an unlikely place did something odd to his stomach. It was like seeing the first crocus after a long and terrible winter. He eased his gun down; the girl didn't have a weapon that he could see, and he relaxed slightly.

"Looking for someone, darlin'?"

It happened so quickly, he wasn't even sure what occurred. She shot up to her feet, took one step back, and a rock beneath her foot slipped—then she disappeared, just like that, over the edge, backward. He heard a sickening thud and then a scream and his blood ran cold.

"Shit." Mitch ran as fast as he could through the rough terrain, his ears filled with the sound of a female crying out in agony. He flew around a cluster of large boulders, grateful at least that she was still screaming. Screaming meant she was alive.

There she was, lying on her side, clutching one leg, which was obviously and grotesquely broken. He swore again and ran over to where she lay. And damn if she didn't try to scuttle away when she saw him, her bright green eyes filled with as much fear as pain.

"I'm not going to hurt you," he said, hunkering down beside her. She looked up at him, eyes wide, her face smudged with dirt, making it difficult to determine her age. "I promise."

She just stared at him, panting like a trapped, frightened animal and he wondered if she could speak. What the hell was this girl doing out here anyway? There wasn't a town for miles, and the only people he'd seen since he'd been in the valley were his own crew. She was dressed in oversized men's clothing, sleeves and pant legs rolled up to accommodate her smaller size.

"My name's Mitch Campbell," he said, softly, looking her over to see if she had any other obvious injuries. Her arm had a nasty scrape, but other than that, he couldn't see anything. "What can I call you?"

She swallowed and looked away. "Genevieve Hayes."

Mitch was stunned. More than stunned. She sounded decidedly British. Upper-class British, like that Lady Something-or-other who'd come to New York when he was a kid to give a speech on abolition. "Where are you from, Genevieve Hayes?"

"Here. I live here."

"Who else?"

She closed her mouth tightly and pushed herself back, then let out another terrible cry of pain.

"Miss Hayes, I swear to you I'm not going to hurt you. I want to help you. You're hurt. Looks like you broke your leg pretty bad, and I can't just leave you out here to fend for yourself. If there's someone nearby who can help, let me get them and I'll be on my way. Please."

She looked away again, no doubt weighing her options. "My father died eight months ago."

"And your mother?"

"When I was eight."

Holy God, she'd been living on her own for nearly a year. "Do you know anyone else? Anyone else living nearby who could help you?"

She shook her head. Hell. She was alone, with a badly broken leg—a condition he was partly to blame for—and Mitch became painfully aware that his plans for the next few days were about to change drastically.

"All right. I need to see that leg of yours. I'm going to have to cut off your pants leg. Just the right one, okay? I've set more than one bone, in case you were wondering." He tried to sound confident, but the truth was, the thought of setting her leg was making him slightly ill. He had set two broken bones in his life, one during the War Between the States and one on the trail not three years prior. But he'd never set a bone so obviously broken and never on a girl. *Hell.*

He took out a wicked-looking Bowie knife and her eyes grew even wider. "Miss Hayes, will you please stop looking at me as if I'm going to murder you?"

Her expression didn't change, but her breath hitched slightly and he wondered if she were trying not to cry. As gently as he could, he cut away the fabric of her pants, revealing her leg. "Holy Mother of God." He had to look away.

She let out a low moan.

"Don't look at it," he said, himself unable to look at her leg for long. "This is good. It didn't break the skin so there's no chance of infection. And I think you only broke the one. Okay?"

She nodded and two tears slipped down her cheeks, leaving clean tracks in their wake.

"I don't have any whiskey," he muttered, mostly to himself. "I'll be right back. I need to get something for a splint." He jogged to where he'd tied up Millie, and without thinking, he grabbed the camera tripod still tied to the mule's back and snapped one of the legs in two. Perfect. In less than five minutes, he was back.

"Good, you're still here," he said, and thought he'd nearly won a smile.

He reached into his pocket and drew out an incongruously clean piece of linen, carefully embroidered with his initials by the sweetheart he'd left at home five years ago. She'd long since married another, but he kept the handkerchief anyway, not for any other reason than it came in handy. It was the last vestige of his New York life tucked in his trail jacket. "It's clean. Put it in your mouth and bite down hard. This is going to hurt like the dickens. I don't want to hurt you, you understand? But I have to set this leg or you'll never walk right again."

"Do what you must," she said, taking the handkerchief from his hand. She fingered the soft cloth, noting the embroidery, before lying back down and stuffing it into her mouth.

"Ready?"

She nodded and closed her eyes.

"Please, God," Mitch said, grabbing hold of her leg as gently as he could just below her knee and wrapping his other hand on her slim ankle below the break. And then he pulled and she screamed, instinctively trying to push away from him with her other leg. Instantly, his skin was bathed in sweat, his hands were shaking. "Hold still. Please, Miss Hayes. I'm almost there." Another pull and then he could feel the bone almost snap back into place. Sweat dripped into his eyes despite the cool late May air, and he wiped at it impatiently with his shoulder.

"How old are you, Miss Hayes?" he asked, trying to distract her from what he was doing.

She pulled the cloth from her mouth, her face pale beneath the dirt. "I'm not certain, but I think twenty."

Placing the wooden pieces on either side of her leg, he carefully wrapped strips of her ruined pant leg around the splint, wincing each time she cried out. "You don't know?"

"Lost track, I'm afraid."

Finally, he was done. He knelt, head down, breathing heavily, with his hands on his thighs, never in his life so glad for a task to be completed.

"It feels quite a bit better now. Thank you."

He smiled. She sounded so damned proper.

"We have to figure out where to put you. You can't stay here and you can't come with me to camp. We move around too much and I don't think that would be good for you."

"There are more of you?"

"Ten of us working for the United States Geological Survey. My job's to take photographs. See Millie over there? She carries around my equipment. Since you've been spying on me for two days now, I'm pretty sure you saw me working."

She nodded. "But I didn't know what you were doing."

"Government wants to know what's out here, to see if there's anything to see." He tilted his head and studied her. "How long you been out here?"

"We moved here after my mother died."

"And where were you before that?"

"Philadelphia. That's where I was born."

"Then why do you sound like you came from England?"

Her face lit up so suddenly, Mitch was momentarily stunned by the change. Despite living in the wilderness most of her life, her teeth were straight and white and not a single one was missing. She was very nearly pretty.

"I do? Truly?"

"Like you're best friends with the queen."

"My parents came from England, so I suppose I talk the way they did."

"Makes sense. So, Miss Hayes, where do you live now?" He looked around. "I haven't seen a house since we came into the valley."

She craned her neck to look back up the mountain. "Up there a ways."

Mitch looked up past the rock hanging and saw nothing but pines and more rocks, then looked back at her. "How far?"

"Do you see that rock that looks like a bear's head?"

Mitch looked up and saw nothing but big pine trees. "To the right. Our cabin is just below it."

And there it was. He cursed. She didn't look like a heavy thing, but he wasn't certain he'd be able to carry her all that way. Putting her on Millie would be far too jarring and he was in no mood to listen to any more female screams. He'd have to carry her.

"I don't suppose you can walk it," he said, anticipating the shake of her head. "All right, then. I'll carry you." He hunkered down by her side. "Put your hands around my neck and see if you can hoist yourself up a bit with your good leg."

"Perhaps I could try to walk?"

"Miss, I'm pretty certain you can't even stand, never mind walk. Now put your hands around my—"

"I could at least try . . ."

"Put your goddamn hands around my neck or I'm going to put them there for you. If I was going to kill you, I would have done it by now."

The look she gave him nearly made him laugh, part anger, part rebellion, part something he couldn't put his finger on, a certain devilishness that was about as unexpected as her being out in the middle of this wilderness. She put her hands around his neck and let out a scream when he straightened, bringing her slowly to a standing position. "Holy Jesus, will you promise to listen to me from now on?"

"Yes, sir," she said, her hands still around his neck. She was shaking like a leaf and he was afraid she was about to faint. Cursing himself a thousand times for frightening her off that cliff, he carefully lifted her into his arms. She tried not to scream, he could tell by the way she clamped her mouth shut and closed her eyes, but it came out anyway. Every time he hurt her, he felt sick. And hell, she weighed nothing. Didn't this poor girl eat?

He began walking, trying to be careful not to jostle her, but maneuvering around rocks and trees made his task nearly impossible.

More than once her broken leg tapped against a trunk or branch and she'd stiffen and cry out as if someone was sticking a knife into her. Or smashing her broken leg. Her arms were tight around his neck, her face buried against his neck. He could tell how much pain she was feeling by how tightly she pressed her head against him.

Mitch had carried more than one woman in his arms, mostly to a warm soft bed, but none had felt like this one. There were no soft curves, no creamy flesh. This girl was hard and pointy. Hell, he could feel the bones of her spine against his arm. She'd been living alone for eight months, through what was no doubt a difficult winter, slowly starving to death.

And she didn't smell like any woman he'd ever held either. There was no sweet perfume, no floral scent. She didn't smell bad, just different. Like clean dirt heating up on a summer day. He nearly laughed out loud at that thought. Imagine telling a woman she smelled like dirt and trying to convince her it was a compliment.

Despite her slight weight, she was getting heavier with every step he took. Just when he thought he'd have to set her down, he saw a tiny building not twenty yards away. A man could walk right by that small cabin without even knowing it was there. "I see it. Almost there." He was looking at the cabin so he didn't see the branch lying across his path. His boot got caught and he started going down, knowing there was nothing he could do.

It was almost worse than the first time, worse than when he'd set the bone. Genny, already dizzy with the pain, nearly lost consciousness as they hit the ground. She screamed, she couldn't help it. But she screamed into his shirt so it wouldn't seem so loud. Even to her own ears, her screams were terrifying. They lay unmoving, with her still in his arms. As they'd fallen, he'd twisted his body so that she fell atop him. His chest worked like a bellows beneath her, his arms were like solid, warm bands around her, giving her comfort as the searing pain began to ebb.

"I'm so sorry, darlin'," he said, his voice low. Then he let out a string of foul words. They lay that way for some time, until Genny wondered if he'd hurt himself. Then what would they do?

"Are you injured?" she asked finally. She felt his chest move, little jerky spasms, and she realized he was laughing.

"I am not injured, Miss Hayes. I'm just scared to death to move in case I hurt you more. I'm not certain I can take hurting you again. I'm about to die from it."

"I'll try very hard not to scream again."

His grip on her tightened slightly. "You go ahead and scream. I'll move real slow and you just hang on as tight as you want. We're almost there. See?"

He pressed his nose against her hair and took a deep breath. Then he chuckled again, though she didn't know why.

"Can you put your good leg down and brace it against the ground? Good girl. Now, I'm going to sit up and get us standing again. You ready?"

She took a deep, shaking breath, knowing what was coming next. She'd never known anything could hurt this much. She'd always figured childbirth was the worst pain. She remembered her mother screaming when she was trying to have her little brother or sister. She was only eight, but she remembered it like it was yesterday, how she thought her mother was being silly for crying so much. In her world, the most painful thing she'd experienced up until then had been a badly scraped knee. Surely having a baby couldn't hurt more than that.

But when her mother died, Genny realized there was a pain much, much worse than a scraped knee. There was pain that could kill you.

"I'm ready," she said, even though she wasn't.

He stood, slightly shaking. She could feel the tremors move through his body like a small earthquake. She held on tight, letting out only a small sound when the pain got too bad. Her father had always said she was too tough for her own good, just like her mother. Genny had never thought of her mother as tough. She was soft and sweet and would sing to her right after her prayers. Genny knew she was nothing like her mother. Her mother had been special and beautiful; she would have known that even if her father hadn't said it.

Then Mitch lifted her up into his arms and she didn't cry out at all. When they got to the cabin, he kicked at the door and it swung open. "We made it," she said. "There's a bed to the right." She still slept up in the tiny loft, but she knew sleeping in her father's bed for now would be more practical.

He deposited her on her bed and stepped back, looking around the one-room cabin. Genny's memories of her home in Philadelphia were vague images of long staircases and red carpeting. She wasn't certain she was remembering her home or some hotel they'd stayed in on the way to California. The ceilings had soared above her head and there were a dozen rooms to explore. At least that's how it seemed to an eight-year-old girl. She couldn't be sure if the memories were real or if she was simply remembering her father's tales of what their life had been like. He got tired of talking about it after a time.

"Homey," Mitch said, but there was something in his eyes that made Genny think he didn't like what he saw. She kept the place neat and clean, but it didn't have soaring ceilings or red carpeting. "Do you have drinking water?"

"There's a stream out back. The dipper and pail are by the door."

He grabbed both and was gone.

For the first time, Genny began to think about her predicament. She knew nothing about broken bones or how long they took to heal. But she figured it would be days before she could walk. What was she going to do? She needed to eat. Already her stomach was rumbling. Her last meal had been a day ago when she'd eaten the last bit of a king snake she'd cooked two nights before.

Mitch walked in, bucket and dipper in hand, and knelt by the side of her bed. "Here." He laid a hand behind her head and helped her to sit so she could take a long drink. "I'll leave it here so you can reach it." He stood and looked down at her, hands low on his hips.

"Listen, I've got to go tell the men what happened. I'll get some supplies and come back. I'll be gone until morning. Do you think you'll be all right?"

No. "Yes, I'll be fine."

He gave the cabin a dubious look. "You have any food?"

"I ate the last of what I had yesterday. I was planning to go out today to look for something."

He gave her a sharp nod, but she had a feeling he was swearing silently. He was a man who liked to swear. "I've got some cornbread and jerky back with Millie. I'll bring that by before I go."

Genny had been alone for eight months in her cabin and it was strange to see another person there. But when Mr. Campbell was gone, it seemed unusually empty, the way it had when her father had first died. It was a small cabin, but it had seemed terribly big and lonely right after it had happened. Her father had done the best he could, but no man could fight an angry female grizzly. When she'd found him, he'd still been alive, torn up pretty bad and weak from loss of blood.

Genny didn't like to think about the way he'd died, but it was stuck in her head like a burr stuck in her hair. He'd made her promise to go home—home to England. She'd promised and had meant it. But winter was nearly on her by then and she couldn't think of leaving. By the time the weather had turned, real fear had sunk in. England? She hadn't the foggiest idea how to get there. She didn't even know how to get to town for certain. Her father stopped bringing her with him when she was old enough to stay alone in the cabin for a few days. It had been years since she'd ventured far from home.

England was a world away, across the entire continent, and then across an ocean of endless water. How would she get there? She didn't even know which direction to start walking. And so, even though it had been warm enough for weeks to travel, she'd stayed put. When Mr. Campbell had shown up, she began getting a niggling of an idea. Maybe she could follow him to a town and then she could ask directions from there. And if he said no, she'd pay him with her mother's jewelry. The thought of going up to a complete stranger, though, had nearly paralyzed her. She hadn't talked to anyone other than her father since the last time she'd been to town. Old Jake didn't count; her father always said he was more ghost than man, though she'd never known what he meant.

She heard the *clomp* of Mr. Campbell's boots outside and turned her head toward the door. When he walked in, his big body blocked out nearly all light from the entry. Her father had not been a big man, certainly not the kind of man who could have carried her up a mountain. This man was like a boulder, big, hard, and solid. Like a big, warm boulder, she amended. When he walked over to her, she could feel the floorboards shaking.

"I've got your cornbread and jerky." He held up a large paper sack that looked like it held enough food for a week, not one night. He looked around for someplace to put it and ended up dragging one of the cabin's two chairs across the room and setting it next to her bed. He stared down at her for a long moment before turning to leave. "I'll be back in the morning," he said, without looking at her, and Genny was certain that would be the last she'd see of Mitch Campbell.

Chapter 2

The men back at camp thought it was hilarious that Mitch Campbell, of all people, would be babysitting a girl for the next few weeks, thanks to his own stupidity. Mitch wasn't particularly known for his warm-heartedness and generosity, so at least some of the men were a bit suspicious of his motives.

"She rich? Got to be. Only thing you care about is money." This was from Will, who teased him relentlessly about his stinginess. True, Mitch would rather drink water than whiskey and it had nothing to do with being a teetotaler and everything to do with the fact that whiskey cost money and water was free.

"She's a looker. That's it." This was from Rainy Talbot, a man Mitch didn't particularly like. He mostly didn't like the look in his eyes when Rainy had asked if she was pretty, and so Mitch told him she was missing nearly all her teeth and her eyes were squinty. While he wouldn't call the scruffy girl he'd left in the cabin a beauty, she might tempt a man who hadn't been with a woman in a while. And Rainy Talbot wasn't the sort of man who attracted women unless he was in a saloon flashing his money.

"Still, she's a human being and injured and I caused it, so I'm gonna have to stick around until she can fend for herself. I'll find you. You all stink so bad, I'll just sniff the air."

Mitch *was* going to miss them. They'd been a team for years now, moving across the country to record what they saw for the government. It was good work and it paid well. Plus, when they were on the trail, they weren't spending money and Mitch had nearly saved up enough to start his photography studio in New York. It would be nice to be back in civilization again. Mitch was pretty close to packing it in, but he'd been having too much fun to settle down in one place just yet. Other than a few visits back home over the years to see his mother, he hadn't been home since he was eighteen years old and joined the Union Army. Fortunately, the war ended before he could get himself killed or maimed, and he'd headed to Nebraska. He'd wanted to get as far away from smoke and noise as he could and Nebraska seemed like a good place to go. For three years he wandered, working odd jobs until he met up with the man who would change his life forever.

William Henry Jackson and his brother had a small photography studio in Omaha, and had been about to head out with the US Geological Survey. Will needed an assistant and Mitch signed on without even thinking. Like him, Will had spent time in the war and the two struck up an instant friendship. Will was leaving behind a new bride, but Mitch wasn't leaving behind anything. The farther he could go from home and all the memories of the war, the better. And he'd be seeing sights no white man had ever seen before.

They'd traveled together during the summer months for the past five years, and Mitch felt sick about missing even a moment of this time. Every winter, Mitch would work for Will in his studio in Nebraska anticipating the next summer's work. Yosemite was one of the most beautiful places he'd ever seen and now he'd be stuck in a cabin taking care of a girl. And it was his own damn fault.

The men had been good about giving him supplies; Genevieve Hayes would not go hungry under his care, that was for certain. He had a sack of flour, corn meal, some bacon, dried peaches and apples, sugar, beans, and more pickled eggs than he figured she could eat. Most important: a flask of whiskey and a small bottle of morphine. Leaving his camera behind hurt mightily, but there was no way Millie could hold everything and his equipment too. That was fine, though, as he'd be able to collect his camera when Miss Hayes was better.

By the time he reached the cabin, the sun was high and he was feeling a bit anxious. She'd seemed fine when he'd left, but he'd seen men who'd looked fine one minute take a turn for no apparent reason. He knew the minute he walked in, she'd taken a turn.

When he walked into the room, she wearily turned her head in his direction.

"Papa. Where were you?"

She was bathed in sweat and her leg had turned an ugly purple.

"It's Mitch, darlin'." He hunkered down beside her bed and laid a hand on her forehead, wincing when he felt how hot she was. She looked confused and shook her head a bit.

"My leg hurts."

"I know. I've got some medicine that will make it feel better." Mitch ran back to Millie and dug out the whiskey—for him—and the morphine for her, swearing under his breath the entire way. He grabbed a spoon from a basket on the table and poured a small dose. "You take this. It'll help with the pain."

Her green eyes were glazed with fever and pain, and she looked at him as if she still didn't recognize him, but she took the morphine without complaint.

"I'm going to let that do its work and then I'm going to loosen these bindings and make your leg more secure."

"The kettle's on if you want some coffee."

"That sounds fine. Thank you."

"Dinner might be a bit late, though."

"That's fine, too."

Mitch grabbed a clean rag and dipped it in the bucket of water he'd given her before he'd left, noting the level hadn't gone down very much. He laid the cool, damp cloth across her forehead and was gratified to see her close her eyes and smile.

"Can I go to town with you this time?"

"Sure. I'm going to get the supplies. I'll be right back."

She opened her eyes sleepily, and Mitch wondered if the morphine was already taking effect. He hoped so, because it was going to hurt like hell when he took that splint off to replace it with a new one. He'd cut some deer hide into wide strips, which he planned to soak in the stream and wrap around her leg. This idea came from one of the men who'd seen that done by one of the Plains tribes when a young boy broke his leg. The leather hardened and made it impossible for the bone to move. At least he hoped that would happen.

Mitch stood up and stared down at the girl, shaking his head. Her cheeks were flushed from fever, her blonde hair dark along her temples, wet from sweat, and that silly long braid hung off the edge of the bed, tied with what looked like a piece of sinew. She had a delicate nose and brows—darker than her hair—that arched above her closed eyes. Her mouth was a soft pink, the sort of color that made a man think things he oughtn't. On another woman, he'd be downright fascinated with those soft pink lips. But the woman lying there was nothing but a problem to him. A big problem, and he couldn't wait until he could leave her alone and head back to his life.

How the hell had he gotten in this predicament? God only knew how long he was going to be stuck here caring for her. As soon as she could hobble about, he was gone.

Genny opened her eyes and there he was, sitting at her kitchen table, making a mess by whittling in the house. He'd come back, so she didn't care that he was making a mess, long curling pieces of wood hitting the floor with every stroke of his scary-looking knife.

Her leg, oddly enough, didn't hurt a bit. She looked down and saw that her entire leg was wrapped in some sort of hard skin.

"Mr. Campbell?"

He turned, frowning at her. "Mitch."

"What is that on my leg?"

"Deer hide. You can cut it off in about two months. How's it feel?"

She sat up, wincing a bit from the pain, but smiled. "Not too bad. When did you do this?" She had a vague memory of him coming back but had no memory of him taking off the splint and wrapping her leg.

"Yesterday afternoon. I gave you some morphine. Too much, I guess, and you slept right through."

He stood up, slowly unfolding and straightening, and loomed over her, still frowning. He didn't look quite angry, but he didn't look happy either. To Genny, he looked just like any other man she'd ever seen. He wore rough clothes and had a thick dark beard, and scruffy hair. Though he was tall, he was lean, and the canvas pants low on his hips were held in place by a thick band of leather with a tarnished brass buckle.

"I'm making you crutches." He held out a long stick, carved smooth of branches and bark, with a Y at the top. "I'm putting another piece here," he said, pointing to the Y. "Padding it up so it won't hurt. When you can stand, I'll measure the crutches for you. You'll be able to get about just fine."

She looked down at her leg dubiously. It was completely covered in hardened skins from her ankle to mid-thigh. Even with the crutches, she knew it would be nearly impossible to get around the forest. But she'd just have to do it, because she had a feeling Mitch didn't want to stick around any longer than he had to. And that meant her only chance of getting back to England would be walking away before she could follow him.

"When do you think I'll be able to use them?"

"Couple days Maybe three. You'll do fine," he said, looking away. Then he sighed. "Listen. I can't stay here and take care of you. I've got a job, and the men I'm with are moving on. You'll be fine. I won't leave until I know you can get about."

Genny nodded, but inside real panic was bubbling up. She'd barely survived when she had two good legs. If she was left alone on this mountain hobbling about on crutches, she'd never make it. She looked toward the door, which seemed infinitely farther away than it had two days ago. The path to the stream was rocky, and how would she be able to bring back a bucket of water if she was holding onto crutches with both hands? How could she hunt?

She had to think of a way to make him stay.

She looked up to see him smiling. It was the kind of smile that came before a lie. "Before you know it, you'll be getting around just fine."

"No, I won't. And you know it. When you leave, I will certainly perish. How can you stand there smiling at me whilst lying? When you saved me, I thought that meant you were an honorable man, a good man."

He stared at her as if she were speaking a language he didn't understand. She thought he murmured something under his breath that sounded an awful lot like "high falutin'" but since she had no idea what that meant, she ignored him.

"Listen, darlin', I'll do my best to make sure you're okay, then I'm leaving. That's the most I can promise. And I might remind you that none of this would have happened if you hadn't been following me around in the first place."

She opened her mouth, then shut it. She'd thought she'd gotten to him when she called him a "good man." Now she'd have to try a different tactic. Her father always told her she could get bears to dance for her if she put her mind to it. "I had a very good reason for following you."

"And what would that be?"

"I was hoping you could help me get home." She plucked at the covers, putting on her saddest expression.

His dark brows drew together, and she knew she had him on the hook. Now she only had to reel him in.

"I thought you said this was home," he said.

"It is. But when my father died, I promised to go back to England. I don't know how to get there and I thought perhaps you could help. I have no idea where it is, you see." When she'd spied Mitch the first time, she'd started to formulate a plan. Of course that plan hadn't included her being injured.

Again, that long, hard stare that made her want to look away, as if he could tell she was trying to manipulate him. "England. You were hoping I could help you get back to England."

She nodded. "Yes."

He started to laugh. "Oh, darlin', you are something else. No, I am not going to take you to England."

"I promised my father." Genny looked up at him with the most pathetic expression she could muster, which wasn't really that difficult because she was feeling fairly pathetic at the moment—and she *had* promised her father.

"Listen, I'm out here doing a job. I can't hightail it off to England just because you were foolish enough to follow me and fall off a cliff."

"Something that wouldn't have happened if you hadn't been pointing a rifle at me," she pointed out darkly.

"True enough. And that's why I'm here now, to make sure you don't die of starvation before you can get around. But you *will* be able to get around soon enough and then I'll be able to rejoin my party."

Genny felt her last chance slipping away. She knew once Mitch was gone, she would never get off this mountain. With her leg still wrapped and using crutches, she'd never be able to follow Mitch when he left. She'd never see her grandparents, never fulfill that promise.

"I could pay you." It was her last strategy, but for the first time, Mitch seemed interested in what she was saying. His expression changed subtly, just enough to give her a small bit of hope that he might actually help her.

"My mother came from an important family, and when she traveled to America with my father, she brought some of her jewelry. She sold most of it, but I still have a ring and a brooch that my father said are worth something. I have no idea what, but surely it's enough to pay you to escort me to New York so I can find a ship to take me home. I don't expect you to accompany me across the ocean, just to New York."

Mitch narrowed his eyes and worked his jaw as if chewing on her idea. "Where are these jewels?"

"In that chest," she said, pointing to her mother's sea chest, a camelback trunk of mahogany and rosewood inlay that held all she had left of her mother. "There are some letters, too, with my grandparents' address. I can't read them, though, because I never learned how to read cursive. I can only decipher some of what it says."

"You can't read?"

"I can read," she said succinctly, earning a strange smile from him. "I simply cannot read cursive. I can read books. I read books all the time." She pointed to her precious collection of books on a shelf on the opposite side of the room.

Mitch went to the chest and lifted the lid.

"The jewels are in a rosewood box. Yes, that's it," she said when he lifted the box out. The jewelry case was on top because she'd frequently take it out to stare at the ring and brooch her mother used to wear.

He opened it up and let out a low whistle, before looking at her with renewed interest. Inwardly, Genny felt a surge of triumph. Her father had always said that food was the way to a man's heart, but maybe for this man, money was. He shut the case and placed it back in the box, and Genny felt a stab of disappointment. Perhaps she'd been wrong about him, and those jewels were not enough to entice him into bringing her to New York.

"That's something to think about, and I'm sure they're worth something," he said, tapping the top of the case with his index finger, every tap bringing more hope. "But not enough for me to take weeks of my life and forgo my wages. Sorry, darlin'." Just like that, hope was dashed.

She watched listlessly as he brought out a small bundle of letters tied together with a velvet ribbon. "Are these the letters?"

"Yes. The ones with the great wax blobs on them." Genny looked away, no longer interested in what the letters said. Unless the letters contained a map to a secret treasure, they were worthless to her

He took the first of them and immediately went to the last page. "Glastonbury," he said, reading the signature.

"My grandfather. For some reason that's not his name, though. His name is Patrick Danforth. Glastonbury is just a title."

"Title?"

"My father told me he is a duke."

Slowly, Mitch lowered the letter and raised his gaze to hers. "Your grandfather is a duke."

"Yes, and my grandmother is a duchess. Apparently they're quite important people in England. At least that's what my father said. Papa told me they could help me. I really have no idea what it all means, their being a duke and duchess. I only know that my father was, as he put it, 'a nothing' while Mama was a lady. I used to say, 'of course Mama's a lady' but he would just laugh and tell me Mama was a different sort of lady. We never really talked about it, but I do know it was important because that's why we were in America in the first place."

Mitch walked over to the table and sat down, laid the letters on the table, and looked at her. "Your grandfather is a duke."

"Yes, as I said. Is that a good thing?"

He took a deep breath, then smiled brilliantly. "Looks like you have an escort to New York. Hell, I'll take you all the way to England. What do you think about that? Can't have you traveling alone, right?"

Genny couldn't believe it. "Truly? That's marvelous. When can we go?"

Mitch looked at her leg and frowned. "Not for a couple weeks yet. Not until you can put some weight on that leg without it hurting." Genny opened her mouth to say she was already feeling fine, but he interrupted her. "And no lying."

She didn't care. She was going home.

Mitch figured he felt much like those old miners when they first stumbled upon gold in '49. When he looked at Genny, all he saw was a nice pile of cash. Piles and piles of it. What would a duke give to the man who put aside his own time and safety to rescue the duke's granddaughter from the wilds of America? Dukes were rich. Dukes could throw a couple of thousand dollars at him and not even feel a pinch. All his scrimping and saving over the years and here he'd gone and found a pot of gold right in the middle of Yosemite.

He made thirty dollars a week, a sum he was pretty proud of. In the last five years, he'd managed to save nearly five thousand dollars. He'd figured in another year or so he'd have enough money to go home and start his own photography studio. Equipment was expensive and so was rent, so he wanted a bit more cash in hand before heading east. And now he'd have it.

Mitch didn't know much about diamonds or rubies, but he knew about gold, and those bits of jewelry were made of gold. That alone would give him enough money to pay for their trip back to New York, with maybe enough left over to get them on a steamship to England. He could picture it now, knocking on the door of a palatial home, producing their long lost granddaughter with a flourish. *Why, yes, it was a terrible sacrifice for me, but nothing is too good for Miss Hayes. What? A reward? Why, I couldn't. I have delivered your granddaughter because she asked. All right, then, if you insist, though I do believe ten thousand dollars is more than generous.*

Perhaps ten thousand dollars was a bit optimistic, but what was that sum of money to a duke? A duke could sneeze out that sort of money.

Only one thing worried him. What if the old duke and duchess were so angry with their daughter for running off with Mr. Hayes that they refused to accept their granddaughter? Mitch took up the letters again.

"Will you read them to me?" Miss Hayes sat up, her eyes alight with excitement, and Mitch felt a small twinge of something in his gut that he didn't like.

"Sure. The first one is dated eighteen fifty-four. Were you born here or in England?"

"In America. I was born the first year they were here."

"That means you're twenty or twenty-one." She didn't look it, but she must be, based on what he knew. Imagine, twenty years old and stuck out alone in this wilderness. What the hell had her father been thinking?

He began to read: "July twenty-third, eighteen fifty-four.

> *"Dearest daughter,*
> *You have broken your mother's heart with your rash decision to leave for America. Your letter was met with great joy and greater sorrow. It is a small death for us, for*

we fear we shall never see you again. I write this with
deep regret over my words, and it is with solemn hope that
I pray those will not be the last words you hear from me.
   Dearest Mary, come home to us. It is not within my
power to judge what you have done, so I leave that to
God's hand and His will.
   Glastonbury."

All the letters that followed held very much the same tone. They were filled with regret and yearning and couldn't have been more perfect. The last of them, written about the time her mother must have died, beseeched their daughter to come home, to allow their granddaughter to live the life which she deserved, to be raised in the bosom of her family. Surrounded by pots of gold and bags of diamonds. Mitch was practically giddy.

As he read the last of the letters, he looked up, and immediately altered his expression upon seeing Genny's tear-filled eyes. They looked, hell, they looked purely beautiful, the color of leaves in spring when the sun is shining through them. Then she blinked the tears away and Mitch was slightly relieved that they turned a more ordinary green.

"I *have* to go home. Don't you see?"

"Yes, I do. We'll get you there. Don't you worry about a thing. But you have to be able to walk; Millie can only carry you so far. It's a good four days to Sacramento, and with your leg, maybe longer."

"Sacramento?"

"Bit west of here. That's where we get on the train. We'll take it to Omaha, then on to Chicago and finally New York." It would cost a pretty penny, likely two hundred dollars for the two of them, but Mitch figured the jewelry would more than pay for the trip. And if it didn't, he could take money out of the bank in Omaha.

"How long will that take?"

"A lot quicker than if we walk, that's for sure. Once we set foot on the train in Sacramento, we'll be in New York in about a week. Maybe we can get one of those Pullman cars and travel first class."

She looked a bit dismayed. "A week? I had no idea it was that quick."

"Could be longer, depending on if you run into any trouble. The problem is that the train stops, you see? And every time it stops, you sit there for a while and wait for people to get on and people to get off. Cattle get in the way. Rails need fixing. Train needs more water. All kinds of things could slow you down."

"How long does it take to get from New York to England?"

Mitch grinned. "That's the easy part. Less than two weeks after we get to New York, you'll be saying hello to your grandparents. Now we just have to get you healed and ready for our big trip." And the prize at the end. It was all Mitch could do not to rub his hands together. Everything he'd hoped for was finally within reach.

Chapter 3

Somehow, and he wasn't certain how it had happened, Mitch had created for himself a sort of living hell.

Mitch saw the beauty in things; it was one of his gifts as a photographer, to see things other people didn't. And at this moment, he was face-to-face with something he'd never seen in his life: a pretty girl's face bathed in the morning sunlight.

They'd left her cabin the day before, allowing her two weeks to heal and get used to her crutches. She could put some weight on the bad leg without any pain, so she hardly even used them now. He figured by the time they got to Sacramento, she'd be ready for a cane or maybe even able to walk about with that cast on.

It had been slow going before they hit some flat ground and a trail. She never complained; never said she was tired or hurting or hungry. But as the day got older, her face got a bit more flushed and her progress slowed. When he couldn't stand it anymore, he stopped to look for a nice place to settle in for the night.

"You need to tell me when you're hurting," he said, more harshly than he'd meant to, but he couldn't stand knowing she was in pain. "It'll do no good if you get hurt and then we have to wait for you to get better."

"I do apologize, but I'm so anxious to get to England, I suppose my enthusiasm overrode my abilities." She smiled as she leaned against Millie.

Fancy talk. "No need to apologize, just be smart about it."

He looked up to see where the sun lay and figured it was only about three in the afternoon. Plenty of time to build a little camp and settle in. Tomorrow would be better because they'd left the roughest terrain behind and going would be easier for the girl.

The next morning, as Mitch let his eyes wander over her face while she slept, he had a terrible feeling in his gut. Call it his conscience, something Mitch hadn't known he had, but he didn't feel quite so good about playing the hero now as he had a few days back. She was so damned trusting, looking at him with those big green eyes, following him no matter where he said to go. Hell, he could be bringing her to a slave trader for all she knew. It was a wonder she'd survived alone for all those months.

They lay not a foot apart, her head resting on a blanket. They'd started off the night three feet apart, settled in by the fire, his back to her. But as the temperature dropped, she'd edged closer and closer until at some point in the dead of night, he'd felt her press against him. He knew she was half-asleep and cold and just wanted to get warm, but his body didn't listen. He had a soft, feminine body pressing up against him and damn if it didn't feel nice.

Now, he was looking at the soft downy hair on her cheek glowing in the early morning light, seeing beauty in every angle. Her eyelashes seemed uncommonly long, brown but tipped with a lighter color that fanned out beneath her eyes. Her brows, so expressive when she was awake, were soft crescents. Her lips. Hell, he shouldn't be looking at her lips, not first thing in the morning when his johnson was saying a hearty hello, but he just couldn't help himself. Her skin was sun kissed, even though she'd worn her father's oversized hat, and her lips were soft and pink. He liked their shape, a little bow on top, fuller on the bottom, with a slight indent in the middle. He had the urge to lay a finger on that little indent but resisted.

She had a square chin with the faintest cleft that didn't seem to go with the rest of her delicate features, but somehow did. He wondered if that was the one thing she'd inherited from her father. She had a nice face, he decided, wishing he could capture this kind of light and beauty in a photograph.

Millie let out a bray, as if protesting his perusal, and her eyes opened. Damn, he couldn't breathe for about two seconds, his breath literally caught in his throat. The color of her eyes—green with shards of gold—was one of the prettiest things he'd ever seen in his life. The kind of beauty you want to hold in your hand and never let go.

It wasn't until she smiled, open and completely innocent, that he started and pulled back, horrified by what he'd been thinking.

"'Bout time you woke up," he said gruffly, sitting up, achingly aware that he was a man who'd just gone a little loopy over a pretty face.

"What time is it?"

"Past time to get on the trail. I'd like to be going in thirty minutes. Think you can do that?"

Genny sat up, every muscle in her body aching as if she'd been pummeled by some invisible giant. Her traveling companion was scowling at her, at Millie, at the sun, but for some reason it didn't bother her. He was like one of those dogs that growled fiercely at you, then flopped down on its back and let you rub its tummy. Not that Genny would be rubbing Mitch's tummy. Just the thought made her laugh out loud, which only made Mitch's scowl deepen.

"I see you are not a morning person," she said cheerfully. "My father wasn't either. He would be a bear, stalking around the cabin, until he had his first cup of coffee. And he'd wait for me to make it because he said I always made it better than he did. It's true. I did." Genny felt a stab of sadness thinking about her father and how he would compliment her every morning on his cup of coffee. "Best cup of coffee this side of the Mississippi," he'd say. And she never got tired of hearing it. It was just one of their little rituals that she missed so much. They'd had to leave the coffee grinder behind, of course, but she'd taken the time to grind some beans for their trip.

"I thought you English liked tea," Mitch had said, a bemused look on his face as she'd ground the last of her beans.

Genny wrinkled her nose. "Perhaps I've never had a good cup of tea, but I much prefer coffee. I do hope they have coffee in England or I shall be quite vexed."

Mitch had seemed amused by her taking the time to bring along coffee, but was apparently glad she had.

"I suppose I could wait for a cup of coffee," he said, rubbing his beard. Genny wondered what he would look like without that full and rather luxurious beard. It was a slightly lighter color than his chocolate brown hair, the kind of beard you could imagine digging your fingers into, soft and a little wavy. He stood, unfolding his long body, and looked around their camp.

"I'll be right back with some water and then I'll take care of Millie. If you could make that coffee."

"Of course."

Genny hobbled about the camp on one crutch, so used to it now it was almost like an extension of her body. In the two weeks since she'd broken her leg, she'd gotten plenty of practice walking about. Mitch, though never mean, had not coddled her. At the time, she'd felt a bit sorry for herself, but was now glad of it. She never would have been able to walk the trail had it not been for him insisting she get up and about as soon as she could.

But, Lord, her body ached this day. She stirred up the coals, glad to see there were enough cinders to heat up the water for the coffee, then stretched, letting out a groan as her muscles protested. She looked up and there was Mitch, frowning at her.

"You're sore?"

She nodded. "A bit, but I daresay a few minutes on the trail and I'll feel better. I might have overdone it yesterday. Perhaps we can take more breaks today."

"Sure. Guess it doesn't matter if it takes a bit longer to get there than I planned."

It took three days longer than Mitch had guessed to get to Sacramento, but by the time they reached the city, Genny had abandoned her crutch and was limping along gamely. Mitch had cut off the top part of the hide just below her knee so she could be more mobile. Each day that had passed, she felt better and stronger and more excited than ever to go home to England. As they entered the city limits, Genny could hardly contain her excitement. One of the first matters of business was selling the jewelry. Though she hated the thought of parting with her mother's things, she had promised, and what better use for them than helping to get her home? She hoped they were worth a great sum, enough to get her to England.

"One hundred dollars? Hell, the gold alone is worth more than that." Mitch stared at the little man, who stared right back at him over his thick jeweler's lenses.

"You won't find a better price. You're welcome to try. But when you come back, it'll be ninety-five." He gave Mitch the smug look of a man who knows he's looking at a desperate fellow.

Mitch looked around the shop, crowded with all sorts of items that people—probably people more desperate than he—had sold for ready cash. One hundred dollars would barely get them to Omaha, never mind New York. He was beginning to doubt his plan, because the jeweler didn't look like the kind of man who could be swayed by a story or a pretty pair of green eyes. Unless he was wrong, Mitch would have to use some of his precious savings to fund the trip, and there was no way on God's green earth that he was going to pay for a sleeper car. If Genny could sleep out on the trail without uttering a single word of complaint, limping along for miles, she could sleep on a train bench.

Mitch looked out the dusty window, saw her standing next to Millie, and recognized how pathetic she looked. "See that girl yonder? The one with the yellow braid down her back?"

The jeweler leaned over to look out his window. "Yes."

"Those two pieces are the only things she has left of her poor departed mama. She needs to get to New York, and one hundred dollars surely won't take her there."

"Sure it will."

Mitch clenched his jaw in frustration. "I'm escorting her. Can't let a woman travel alone all the way from California."

The jeweler gave Mitch a look he didn't much care for but chose to ignore. He needed to get more money out of the man and antagonizing him would not help his cause.

"How about one hundred fifty," Mitch said, smiling.

"One hundred. Take it or leave it."

"One twenty-five. I have to buy the little lady a dress, don't I?" Again, he gave the man a smile that was about as sincere as a wooden nickel.

The jeweler looked out the window again and frowned. "What's wrong with her leg?"

"Lame," Mitch said, shaking his head slowly. "Poor thing." Genny looked up and through the window and Mitch shoved his hands in his pockets, his signal that his negotiations were unsuccessful.

And then, she walked in—or rather limped in—looking like a ragged, unloved orphan. A pretty, ragged orphan. "Have you had any luck, Mr. Campbell?" She stopped still and looked around as if she were standing in the middle of a Paris boutique. "Oh, what a lovely shop. Are you the proprietor?"

The jeweler straightened, trying to make his rather diminutive frame a bit less diminutive. "Why, yes, I am." Funny what a clipped British accent and a pretty face could do to a man, Mitch thought. "Do I detect an English accent?"

Genny smiled, and when she gave a smile like that, she was just shy of stunning. Even in her repaired men's clothes and her hair in a simple braid, there was something about her that just made a man want to lay down his coat across every puddle she encountered. Mitch, who thankfully was immune to her smile and her charm, leaned back to watch the show. He'd seen her do this to three other men and it was fascinating. Her ability to wrap a man around her finger was downright frightening. She had a gift, for it certainly wasn't something she'd learned on the ballroom floor, having never *seen a* ballroom floor.

"I see you've been looking at my mother's pieces. I'm broken-hearted over selling them, of course, but I fear it is the only way I can finance my trip back to England. I'm going to see my grandparents, you see. I do hope you've been fair with Mr. Campbell."

"Oh, yes," the man said, coming round to the front of the counter. "More than fair."

Mitch coughed. "He offered one hundred dollars, Miss Hayes. I'm so sorry."

It was almost comical how her expression went from stunning happiness to dewy dismay. My God, his actress mother would appreciate this performance. He wanted to applaud. Instead, he winked at her, but if she saw that wink, she gave no indication.

"But my mother . . . Oh, I see. I shall never get home now." She gave the jeweler a tremulous smile. "Thank you, Mister . . ."

"Benson," the jeweler supplied.

"Thank you, Mr. Benson. And I am Miss Genevieve Hayes. I do appreciate your time, but I fear I cannot sell my mother's jewels for such a price." She turned to Mitch. "How long would the journey take on foot, do you think?"

Mitch used all his self-control not to burst out laughing, and he feared she might have gone a bit too far. No man, not even one instantly smitten like Mr. Benson, would think she meant to *walk* to New York. What would they do next? Swim to England?

"I think we could buy a couple of horses," Mitch said hesitantly, worrying his hat in his hands. "Though we wouldn't have much left over for food. You don't mind sleeping out under the stars, do you, Miss Hayes?"

Poor Mr. Benson looked beside himself. "If you don't mind me asking, Miss Hayes, who is this man to you?"

Genny looked momentarily confused by the question—not by the meaning, but by the suspicious tone. "Why, Mr. Campbell saved my life and now has offered to escort me to New York. He found me in the wilderness with a broken leg. My poor departed father was mauled by a bear. Ferocious beast. Mr. Campbell slew the bear and repaired my leg, though I fear it will never be the same. Mr. Campbell is a hero, Mr. Benson. A hero."

It was such a ridiculous tale, even if there were some elements of truth to it, that Mitch wanted to groan. No one could be as gullible as Mr. Benson.

"Two hundred dollars. That's as high as I can go, Miss Hayes, though I wish I could do more."

Genny smiled again, brilliantly. "Oh, wonderful, Mr. Benson. I do think that is a much fairer price, don't you think so, Mr. Campbell?"

"Yes, ma'am."

Her smile slipped a tad and Mitch braced himself for what was coming next. She looked down at her clothes and frowned, pulling at a patch in her pants. Then she leaned toward Mitch and whispered, rather loudly, "I suppose that means no dress? That's fine, really. Do you think too many people will notice?"

He looked at her in wonder. What a little scamp.

"Two hundred twenty-five. Then you can buy two pretty dresses," Mr. Benson said, then hurried behind the counter.

"Oh, no, Mr. Benson. That is too much," Genny said, limping over to the counter as if to stop him from throwing cash at her. "I don't want to take advantage of your soft heart. You are a business man and you must be fair."

Mitch was pretty certain Mr. Benson would have laid down his life for her at that moment. He looked at her with pure admiration. Then he made a great show of examining the pieces again, clicking his tongue as he did.

"These are much finer than I first thought, Miss Hayes. I do apologize for the confusion. Two hundred and fifty dollars and not a penny more. But I would ask one favor."

"Yes?"

"Stop by with your new dress before you leave."

Genny tilted her head and gave him a genuine smile. "I will, Mr. Benson. Thank you."

"I could just hug you," Mitch said, shoving the wad of cash into his pocket once they were outside. "Where did you learn to be so charming?"

Genny smiled and shrugged. "I have no idea. I was always able to wrap my father around my little finger and I remember as a little girl going to the kitchen and begging for an extra dessert. It's fun, like a game."

"That game just won us an extra one hundred fifty dollars."

Genny grinned up at Mitch, and he reached over and mussed up her hair.

"What do you say we get you that dress and a bath?" He looked up and down the street, then nodded to a hotel two blocks down. "That looks respectable enough for the granddaughter of a duke."

Genny followed his gaze to the grandest building she could ever remember seeing. Certainly, when she'd lived in Philadelphia as a child she must have seen grander, but the Sacramento Hotel looked like a palace after her cabin in the woods and sleeping under the stars. "I can sleep in a real bed tonight. Will they have a room with two?"

Mitch looked down at her and frowned. "Two what?"

"Two beds."

He immediately turned away and grabbed Millie's lead. "We won't be in the same room, Genny. It wouldn't be proper." He stood silently for a while before turning to her. "We have to be proper from here on out."

"And it wouldn't be proper to share a room?"

Mitch looked like he might choke. "No, of course not. We're not married and we're not brother and sister, so no, we can't share a room."

"Seems silly and expensive to me," Genny grumbled. "Who cares if we're married or not?"

"Oh, good God."

"This is another one of those things I'm supposed to know but I don't, isn't it?"

"Yes."

When they'd passed through one small town, a colorfully dressed woman with bright red hair had asked Mitch if he wanted some company. Mitch had been polite but rather cool toward the woman and declined; Genny had wanted to know why. "'Cause she's a loose woman, Genny, and that's all you need to know."

Genny had been silent for a while before saying, "What's a loose woman?"

He'd sworn under his breath and said, "A woman who gives favors to a man who isn't her husband."

But that didn't clear up things at all for Genny. "Favors?"

"Bed favors. Naked favors. The kind of favors that make babies."

Genny had flushed red, finally understanding what he'd been talking about all along. As exciting as it was to leave her little cabin and head home to England, it was also rather terrifying. And the farther away from the cabin she got, the more lost she felt. She'd grown so comfortable in her world; she knew the smell of pine, the snuffing sound of a bear foraging for food, the way the wind wrapped around her cabin, calming and soothing, as if it added a barrier of protection. Ever since her father had died, all she'd been able to think about was leaving, but now that she'd actually left, she found it hurt to realize she'd never be back.

She knew who she was in that cabin; she didn't know who she'd be in a dress, how she would act, what she would say to her grandparents when she saw them for the first time. In her cabin, she was brilliant. In this world, she didn't even know how to fasten the shoes they'd seen in a storefront window.

Sometimes Mitch would look at her as if she were something hateful, a dark intense look she didn't understand. As they stood on the side of the street, he was giving her one of those dark looks. She put that look on the long list of things she didn't understand.

"Let's see if we can find you a dress. You ever wear one?"

"Of course I did when I was young. But when I started helping out my father more, it made more sense to wear pants. He didn't care for it at first, but when I outgrew my dresses he let it go. It's a bit difficult to hunt in the winter wearing a skirt. The last time I tried to put a dress on, it didn't fit, and there wasn't enough material to alter it."

"When was that?"

"My father's funeral." Genny looked away, not wanting to think about it. It had taken her two days to dig a grave, for the ground had already started to freeze. She'd wanted to look her best when she read the Bible before his grave and said good-bye, but none of her dresses had come close to fitting.

When they walked into the dress store, three pairs of feminine eyes looked at them with something close to horror. Genny smiled. "As you can see, I clearly need a dress."

"Take off your hat," Mitch whispered, leaning toward her, and she pulled it off, her head feeling naked and her whole being somehow more exposed.

Two of the women looked like a mother and daughter, both wearing fancy dresses and fancier bonnets. She curled her fists into the brim of the battered hat that had once belonged to her father. The third woman, Genny assumed, was the shop owner, who stared at Genny as if she'd just heard a pony ask for a dress. The shop owner looked at Mitch, who was standing slightly behind Genny, and suddenly smiled when he pulled out his billfold.

"Oh, you poor, poor dear. Of course we can find something for you."

Mitch nodded his head slightly. "Thank you, ma'am." The words were polite enough, but there was steel behind them that Genny didn't understand.

"I have dresses, of course," Genny said. "But I daresay they wouldn't be appropriate for train travel. My mother brought her best gowns from London, you see, and I hardly would have use for a ball gown, would I? And Mama was much taller than I am at any rate and I haven't had time to alter them."

The smile that the shopkeeper had plastered on her face, softened. "Traveling are you?"

"Yes, to New York and then on home to London. So I'll need something for comfort, ma'am."

"Please, you may call me Mrs. Courtland," the owner said, ushering her over to the dresses.

"I am Genevieve Hayes and this is Mitch—"

"Hayes. Her husband."

Genny nearly burst out laughing, but when Mrs. Courtland narrowed her eyes, she smiled brightly. "*Just* married, as a matter of fact," Genny said, darting a look to Mitch. His lips twitched slightly, and he narrowed his eyes in a subtle warning.

"Oh, lovely," Mrs. Courtland said. "Newlyweds. And you without any pretty dresses." She gave Mitch a look of reproach. "We'll remedy that, won't we? When are you leaving? Perhaps you have time for me to create something for you."

"We're leaving tomorrow," Mitch said, putting an end to that thought. Genny looked at him curiously, wondering why, when Mrs. Courtland was being so kind, his tone was rather tight. Perhaps he felt uncomfortable in a lady's store.

Mrs. Courtland began wading through the dresses, once in a while holding one up against Genny, clucking her tongue as she placed it back on the rod.

"Mrs. Hayes," Mrs. Courtland said, darting a quick look at Mitch. "I'm going to have to measure you. It's impossible to tell if a dress will fit otherwise."

"Stand still," Mitch said, and put his hands around her waist. "Jesus, we need to get more food into you." He smiled down at her and Genny felt that strange warmth that came upon her at odd times. He held up his hands to show Mrs. Courtland, and she gave him a tight smile.

"I thought perhaps a measuring tape?" she said, pursing her lips.

"Ma'am, we just want to buy a couple of dresses and whatever else she'll need and be on our way. We've been on the trail for nearly a week and Mrs. Hayes is still nursing a broken leg."

The shopkeeper's eyes dropped down to the rather hideous-looking wrap on Genny's leg. The two of them had gotten used to the look of the thing over the past weeks, but it was a rather odd sight. "Oh, goodness," she murmured, looking up at Genny with real concern. "Of course."

Mitch moved to the rack and pulled out a blue striped dress. "Too big." Then a red gingham. "Better." He held it up against her and narrowed his eyes as if picturing her in it. "This will do until we get to New York. Let's find one more."

Behind him, Mrs. Courtland was blustering and making small noises of protest, but Mitch ignored her.

He held up a few more, finally deciding on a dark blue dress with a dainty white collar. It was the prettiest dress Genny had ever seen.

He turned to the shopkeeper. "These two and whatever else she'll need. Stockings . . . and whatnot."

Sighing heavily, Mrs. Courtland nodded and retrieved several items, wrapping up the purchases in brown paper and tying the bundle with twine. "The milliner is two doors down," she said, looking with distaste at the old hat Genny still held. "That'll be twenty-two dollars."

Mitch handed over the cash. "A pleasure doing business with you." He flashed a smile that Genny recognized as wholly insincere.

When they left the store, Genny was quiet for a time. It was only after they'd left the milliner's that she spoke what was on her mind. "I didn't like the woman in the hat store. She kept looking at me funny."

Mitch grinned. "She's probably never seen a pretty girl wearing a man's shirt and pants. And with a deerskin splint on. You are a sight, Miss Hayes."

"I am, aren't I," Genny said, laughing.

"And you're used to tying every person you meet around your little finger. 'Bout time someone didn't fall for your charms."

Genny wrinkled her nose. "I suppose I'll just have to try harder. And the dresses and this pretty bonnet will help, I should think."

"Probably too much," Mitch mumbled beneath his breath, then he smiled and she knew he was teasing.

"Come on, let's go check on Millie and get my things."

"Are you keeping Millie here while you're gone?" Genny asked.

"She's not mine to keep. My boss will come fetch her in a day or two."

"How will he know where to look?" Genny asked, worried that the poor mule would languish alone for weeks.

"I told him before they moved on. They knew where I was heading and he sure wouldn't leave Millie behind. I know that. I wouldn't leave her behind, either, if I wasn't sure she'd be taken care of."

Mitch retrieved his pack, which he'd stored briefly in the stables with Mille, before they headed to the hotel. When they reached the entrance to the hotel, Genny stopped. "Are we married?"

Mitch drew back, his expression confused and Genny couldn't help notice that small look of fear in his eyes. Then he took in her impish smile, and shook his head. "No. I'm your brother."

"Good. I think you'd be an awful husband at any rate."

Mitch laughed, as she knew he would, and she walked into the hotel still thinking about Millie and the way he'd rubbed her nose affectionately as they'd left the mule in her stall.

The hotel lobby was small and dark, with rich wood paneling and a carpet that was soft beneath their booted feet. Genny hugged her purchases against her and looked around. It had been so long since she'd been in a fancy building. She looked up at the chandelier above her head, thinking it was nearly dark enough to light the candles even though outdoors it was still bright.

Mitch was back by her side after obtaining two rooms, frowning as usual. "Eight dollars for one night. You might think this was the Grand Central."

"Will we run out of money do you think?" She had felt slightly sick about selling her mother's jewels and sicker still to think selling them still would not provide enough money to reach her grandparents. She'd given everything she had.

"No, we've plenty of cash until we reach Omaha, and I can get more. I'm just not used to buying everything in twos."

Genny nodded, and followed Mitch to the staircase she assumed led to their rooms, her brow furrowed. "Mitch?"

He was trudging up the stairs and turned his head to let her know he was listening.

"Why are you doing all this for me? My money isn't enough to get us both back to New York."

He stopped dead and shifted the weight of his pack, but didn't turn around. "I was heading back home at any rate. Might as well take you with me." He started up the stairs again. "Plus, it's the least I can do after you getting hurt."

Genny looked at him as he climbed, his legs strong, his back straight, even though his pack must have weighed more than a hundred pounds. "I wish we could take Millie with us."

He laughed and shook his head. "Millie's just a mule, darlin', and she'll be fine. Stop fretting."

But Genny couldn't stop. It seemed Mitch was giving up an awful lot to help her, and even if he had planned to return to New York, he hadn't planned to return with a girl in tow. She pushed her guilt away; there was no telling why some people were kind and giving while others were selfish and cruel. Mitch, as her father would have said, was a good bloke, top of the heap.

Giving a small groan, he set his pack down with a thud.

"Okay, squirt, this is your room and mine's next door."

She pulled a face at the nickname he'd given her. She wasn't a child, but she was small—even for a woman. She jammed her hat lower on her head and held out her hand for the key.

He placed the key in her hand and gruffly said, "I ordered a bath for you. Just hang your broken leg over the edge so it doesn't get wet, okay?" He hesitated a moment, his eyes dropping to the bundle she held clutched to her chest. "You know where everything goes?"

It took Genny a moment to catch his meaning; then she looked down at her purchases—and blushed. Even she knew it wasn't proper for a man to mention, well, unmentionables. "I believe it will come back to me."

Mitch watched her disappear behind the door and let out a long sigh. All the hair ruffling in the world, all the cute little nicknames he called her, wouldn't stop her from being a woman. Though God knew he was trying. The only thing he had going for him was the fact he was fairly certain she had no idea how pretty she was.

Those nights on the trail, the long, torturous nights after they'd talked and talked, when she'd snuggle up beside him for warmth, had nearly undone him. He never would have suggested bringing her to Sacramento if he'd known halfway there he'd start thinking of her as a female. She was just so darn cheerful all the time, so full of life and light. He never had been one to stand a woman's chatter, the nonstop blather of a female who talks and talks but never actually says anything.

His old sweetheart had been like that, talking, talking, until one night as she was droning on about how one friend was flirting with a man she oughtn't and how that didn't reflect well on her parents, he had an epiphany. Or rather, he had a daydream of stuffing her mouth full of his cravat. And that's when he'd pictured his days in the years to come, the nights at the dinner table, those times when they wouldn't be naked in bed with him taking his pleasure. When they weren't in the bedroom, he'd still be with her, still have to listen to her. And that's when he'd decided New York really wasn't the place for him. He was heading west.

Genny, though, she was different. She didn't talk just to hear her voice. When she talked, she was giving him little pieces of herself, enough to let him know she was scared to death of what awaited her in London, enough to know that selling her mother's jewelry wasn't as easy as she'd made it seem. The funny thing was, she didn't realize what she was telling him; she never came right out and said it. It was just the things she said, like how she remembered looking at her mother and thinking she looked like a princess, with her pretty ear-bobs and her sparkling necklace.

Then, when they were done talking, the torture would begin. The night would inevitably get cool, the fire low, and as the hours passed, she'd get closer and closer until she was pressed up against him, her head nestled by his arm or his back or his side. Holy God, he deserved sainthood for keeping his hands off her, for never letting her know even a tiny bit how her soft, warm body pressed up against his was making him crazy. He never let her be in front of him, didn't want her to feel just how much she was affecting him, didn't want to be tempted to press even closer to relieve some of that terrible ache that had kept him awake.

And now he faced the wonderful prospect of imagining her in her bath, of hearing her sigh in ecstasy as she lowered herself into the warm water, of thinking how her breasts would look, slick with water and the fancy soap he'd bought for her.

The walls between the rooms were thin, thin enough so that he knew when she stood up from her bath, and he tried, God knew he tried, not to envision how she looked toweling herself dry. And then, blessed silence. She must be decent by now, was perhaps smiling at her reflection in the mirror, seeing how she looked dressed as she ought to be dressed.

Mitch had taken his own bath, a quick dip in tepid water to wash off the trail dust. His bath had cost fifty cents, hers, two dollars, a price determined by the size of the tub and the amount of water, no doubt. Still, he was clean and felt more human again. Funny how a man could get used to his own stink when he was on the trail long enough. When he was in Omaha, he bathed and shaved daily. He looked in the mirror, frowning at his beard, rubbing a hand over it. He rarely shaved on the trail, often returning to Omaha with an impressive beard that was perfect for the winter months.

But he was heading back to New York, where it would be hot and humid, and a beard might not be the best idea. Digging through his pack, he pulled out his shaving kit and set to work, first trimming, then shaving. He always enjoyed the moment when he finished and stepped back to see the stranger in the mirror.

He was turning his face this way and that, when a knock sounded on his door. He couldn't help but smile, suspecting it was Genny on the other side. The two of them would look like very different people from the two who'd walked into the hotel.

He went to the door, then stopped, rehearsing in his head what he was going to say: *You look real nice, squirt, just like a girl.* Yes, that was perfect.

But when he opened the door, what he found on the other side stunned him, and he couldn't utter the blasé words he'd planned. She'd piled all that beautiful blonde hair atop her head in an artless style that suited her far better than the girlish braids she'd worn since he'd met her. And the dress fit her the way it ought, hugging breasts that were surprisingly full and accenting a waist that curved in, making her female figure even more pronounced. Hell, he'd known she was a girl, he just hadn't realized how *much* of one she was. He swallowed on a mouth gone dry.

"Well, look at you," he said, stupidly.

She beamed him a smile as if he'd just told her she was the most beautiful woman he'd ever seen.

He gave a hard jerk of his head. "It suits you."

"Thank you. It does feel a bit strange, but somehow not. And you, look how fine you look with your beard off. At first I thought I got the wrong room."

He brought up a hand self-consciously and rubbed his hand across his clean-shaven jaw. "If we're going to New York, I suppose I should look the part."

"Do men not have beards in New York?"

It was questions like this that made him realize how little she knew of the world. "They do, but they're a bit more neat and trim."

"You look quite respectable," Genny said, tilting her head.

It was a fight not to smile because just those words made him feel as if he was something special, something other than the son of an actress and a father he'd never met.

Mitch suddenly wanted to be in a room full of people, noisy, raucous people. And men. Men who drank whiskey, talked about horses and mules, and bet each other on how far they could spit a watermelon seed.

"Come on, let's go show that jeweler your pretty dress and then go find a place to eat."

Sacramento had two types of establishments—the ones that catered to bankers and the ones that catered to hard-working men. Mitch chose the latter. He was in no mood for polite company, for putting on airs, for making certain he was using the right fork. He'd been in those places, and they were fine, but he needed a place where no one would care if his boots were dusty or his jacket frayed. He hadn't brought his dress clothes with him on the trail; that was one of the beauties of his summers. For a long moment, he felt a sharp twinge of regret. Did he really want to go home to New York, to a life where every day would be the same, where a stroll through Central Park would be the closest thing he found to the wild? He figured he could deliver Genny to her family and then go back to his old life if he wanted to. Or he could start his own studio and settle down. That's what he'd planned all along. That's why even when those girls in Omaha batted their eyes at him, he ignored them. He wasn't about to drag a girl away from her family to New York. If he were perfectly honest, there were times he missed the city, missed the sounds and smells of the place. Hell, sometimes he even missed his mother.

When they entered French's Saloon, Mitch sighed and grinned. Yes, this was exactly what he needed. He cast a worried look in Genny's direction, knowing he was taking her to a place he oughtn't. But she was grinning, her eyes sparkling with excitement. And it was still too early in the evening to bring out the hardcore drinkers and the fancy ladies who took their bills. The two of them would eat and leave, then get a good night's rest before their long train trip back East.

Three hours later, Mitch looked up from his card table to make sure Genny was still fine. She'd been talking to another woman nearly the entire time, taking delicate sips from her teacup. He guessed she hadn't talked to a female in years and seemed to be enjoying herself. God knew he was. He got to slouch and swear and throw back a couple of whiskeys, listen to ribald jokes and tell a few of his own. A fight at a table near the back nearly broke out, and Mitch immediately stood, ready to escort Genny out of the saloon if need be. But the men quickly settled down and a couple of light skirts swooped in to distract them, so Mitch relaxed. He was having fun after being cooped up with a female for so long. Even if Genny was pleasant company, even if she looked prettier and prettier every time he looked up.

It was near ten o'clock when Mitch decided to call it a night. He could tell Genny was starting to get sleepy and he figured he'd had enough of male company to last him until Omaha. When Genny saw him walking toward her, she stood up, a bit wobbly on her feet, and Mitch was instantly concerned. Of course she'd be exhausted. What had he been thinking of, keeping her out so late when they'd traveled so hard? And her still wearing that cast, which was no doubt heavy and uncomfortable.

"Mish, are we ready for beddy?"

His brows snapped together and he gave the woman she'd been sitting with a hard look before picking up the teacup that sat in front of Genny. He gave it a suspicious sniff and jerked his head back. Whiskey. Good God, she was drunk.

"Before you get on your high horse, she only had two," the woman said.

"Three," Genny said happily.

"Is it my fault your sister can't hold her whiskey?"

Close up, Mitch realized the woman Genny had been talking to wore a bit more makeup than was necessary and clothes that were far cheaper than they'd appeared from where he'd been sitting. She took his stare for interest and her demeanor changed subtly.

"You don't look at all tired to me. Why don't you tuck your sister in and come on back here."

He gave her a tight smile. "No thank you, ma'am. We have an early start in the morning and need a good night's rest."

"We're going to England," Genny said, pointing with a flourish in a random direction.

"Your loss," the woman said good-naturedly, before narrowing her eyes. "Hey, why don't *you* have one of them fancy accents?"

"Different mothers," Mitch said without missing a beat.

Genny nodded a bit sloppily. "That explains it," she said.

"I see," the woman said, and Mitch had a feeling she just might see a little too well. "Good night, Genny. It was nice talking to you."

When the woman sauntered away, Genny looked comically sad. "Minnie was so nice. She was the nicest woman I've ever met." Then she looked at Mitch, peering up at him as if she'd never seen him before. "You know? Minnie was right! You *are* handsome. She said you were and I told her I'd never given it a thought and she said that was because you were my brother." She paused and leaned in, whispering, "You're not my brother."

"I know I'm not your brother, Genny," Mitch said, slightly annoyed at the way he was noticing things about her that he wished he didn't notice. Like how soft her lips were and how damned kissable they looked about now. Like the way her dress hugged her body. Maybe they shouldn't have gotten her a dress. She'd been fine with that oversized shirt and pants. At least then it was a lot easier to keep his eyes where they belonged. Genny looked positively adorable at that moment, and drunk or not, if a woman calls a man handsome, it does something to his gut. "Come on, let's get you back to the hotel and in bed."

"Minnie told me all sorts of things," Genny said as she turned, swaying a bit, and walked toward the saloon door. "I feel funny."

"You're drunk."

Genny put a hand over her mouth and giggled. "I know. Drunk as a skunk." She said it nearly proudly.

Mitch took her arm and led her out the door and onto the boardwalk, already thinking about how awful Genny was going to feel in the morning. It was a lesson best learned early, that too much drink was never a good thing.

"You know what, Mish?" She laughed. "I keep calling you Mish. You know what?"

"What?"

"You have a magic pole."

Mitch nearly tripped. "I do, do I."

"Yes. All men do. Minnie said you were handsome and she wanted to ride your magic pole." She started giggling again, and Mitch prayed Genny hadn't a clue what a "magic pole" was.

Genny stopped and looked up at Mitch, and whispered, "She meant your man part."

Mitch let out a sharp laugh. "Yes, I know."

When her unfocused gaze drifted down in the direction of his "man part," Mitch grabbed her arm and marched toward their hotel.

"Where's the fire?" Genny said, sounding annoyed.

Mitch ignored her, not uttering another word until they were standing outside her room. While he dug her key out of his pocket, she stood silently, leaning up against the wall, humming some tune she'd likely heard that night.

"Mitch?"

He slipped the key in the door. "What?"

"Do you think I'm pretty?"

He gave her a quick look. At the moment, even with her green eyes glazed with whiskey and her hair slightly askew, she looked more than pretty. "Sure."

"Did you think Minnie was pretty?"

"No."

"I think she was," Genny said a bit wistfully.

He pushed the door open and Genny heaved herself off the wall to walk into the room. She fell onto her bed, face first. "Tired," she said, the word muffled by the blankets.

Mitch lit a gas lamp, then allowed himself to take her in, her mussed-up hair, her trim waist, her arms akimbo. He shook his head and smiled, then let out a sigh, sat down on the bed, lifted one of her feet and started unlacing her shoe. He tried not to think about her slim ankle or the silk stocking that was so smooth beneath his calloused hand, and so he worked quickly, tossing the shoes one by one onto the floor. When he had her shoes off, she turned around and settled properly onto the bed. He wasn't about to undress her completely, so he stood up. Let her worry about her wrinkled dress in the morning. It would be a good lesson for her.

"Mitch?"

"Yeah."

"Could you kiss me good night?"

Jesus. "Sure, kiddo." He leaned over her, intending to kiss her forehead, but she lifted her head at the last moment and her lips pressed against his. He meant to pull back, and did a bit, but she followed him, pressing closer as he jammed one fist into the blanket beside her to stop himself from pulling her against him. It was obvious she didn't know how to kiss, and that was one thing Mitch was thankful for. She kept her mouth closed, but her lips were so damned soft, all he could think about was nudging down her jaw gently and tasting her. But he didn't.

He pulled back slowly and she smiled drunkenly up at him. "Minnie said you looked like a man who could kiss."

"Yeah, well, most men can."

"Good night, Mitch."

He grunted at her and left the room, closing the door softly behind him. She wouldn't remember that kiss in the morning. At least he prayed she wouldn't. God knew he'd remember, and that was enough for the two of them.

Chapter 4

Genny woke up feeling as if she had cotton in her mouth and an angry grizzly running around inside her head trying to get out. It wasn't until she sat up and the room began spinning that she realized her stomach was aching to empty its contents.

"Oh, God," she muttered, holding her head in her hands and trying to push down the feeling of nausea.

"Train leaves in twenty minutes, squirt. I know you're feeling a bit poorly right now, but I'm not missing that train. I've already packed your things, so let's go."

Mitch sounded angry. And loud. Genny looked at him and saw that, yes, he was angry and she couldn't blame him. She was pretty angry with herself. "I'm never drinking again."

Mitch let out a sound Genny couldn't quite interpret. "You'll start feeling better in a few hours."

"A few *hours*?" She groaned and clutched her stomach.

"You best get that business over with. There's no fighting it once your stomach has a mind to get rid of whatever's in it."

Genny shook her head. "I hate vomiting. I can hold it . . . Oh, no." Mitch lifted the empty chamber pot just in time. When she was done, her head felt even worse.

"Here, drink this," Mitch said, handing over a glass of water. "Small sips or you'll just throw it up again." He pulled out his watch. "Let's go. The train won't wait for us."

Genny pulled on her shoes and took the small carpetbag that Mitch held out for her. "All your new clothes are in there." Then he spun around and walked out of the room, not bothering to see if she was following. Genny took a step to follow, but stopped and gave the bag's contents a quick look to be sure he'd included her father's hat. Her pants and shirt were gone, but the hat was on top, a bit squished but otherwise fine. For some reason, seeing that grungy old hat made her eyes prick with tears and she wasn't sure it was due to seeing her father's hat or because Mitch had been thoughtful enough to include it even though it was unlikely she'd ever wear it again.

"You coming or what?" Mitch called from the door.

Genny closed the bag and hurried toward him, her head pounding with every step. Oh, God, she was going to vomit again for sure before the morning was out.

The Sacramento train station was a bustling place filled with men, women, and children standing on a platform still fresh-looking and new. It had been years since Genny had seen so many people in one place. An older woman caught Genny's eye and smiled. She was wearing a bonnet tied so tightly beneath her chin, Genny wondered if the woman thought they'd be riding in an open car with the wind whipping around her.

"Where are you heading, dear?" the woman asked.

"New York and then on to England," Genny said.

"Oh, yes, I hear the accent. We're heading to Omaha to see family. My sister and her husband and children live there and we haven't seen them in ten years. When we first came out here, it took us more than a month. Can you imagine? And here we'll be there in three days. It's a wonder, is it not?"

"Yes, it is," Genny said. She had few memories of her trip west other than it had seemed like forever from the time they left New York to the time she and her father settled in Yosemite Valley. Her father, mourning the loss of her mother, had been silent for long stretches, letting Genny talk enough for the two of them.

"I'm Mrs. Walsh and that's my husband, Herbert." Mrs. Walsh pointed to a man wearing brown from head to toe.

The train let out a hiss of steam so loud, Genny nearly jumped out of her new shoes. Her head still felt like it might explode at any second, and the noise of the train and the people around her wasn't helping. She felt clammy and out of sorts, and waves of nausea nearly sent her running to the nearest privy. Mitch had disappeared, telling her to stay on the platform; she had no idea where he'd gone and she had the sudden and horrible thought that maybe he'd abandoned her.

Maybe that had been his plan all along, to make sure she was safe and on a train headed east.

"Are you traveling alone, dear? If you are, you can join us for some company."

"Thank you, but my wife and I will be just fine. Perhaps we'll see you at one of the stops."

So, they were married again. And apparently she was married to a man who didn't want company. The train let out another belch of steam and the bell on the engine started pealing loudly, seemingly meant to torture Genny even more.

"All aboard." Right in Genny's ear. She was beginning to wonder if the whole world knew she was sick from drink and was trying to teach her a lesson. The conductor moved down the platform, yelling out again, as if he were trying to let someone in New York City know it was time to board the Sacramento train.

"You have the tickets?" Genny asked.

"Right here," Mitch said, patting his chest.

They stepped up into the car, Genny first, struggling to take the first big step with her long skirts and her right leg still a bit awkward in its half cast. It seemed no matter how she tried, she stepped onto her hem. Finally, with a huff of impatience, she grabbed a handful of skirt in her left hand and a handle with her right and heaved herself up the steps. She was smoothing down her skirts when Mitch, still standing on the platform, spoke.

"Genny, you should have waited for me to hand you up," he said, as if imparting important and grave information. "And next time, try not to lift your skirts quite so high." He looked pointedly at an older man who was grinning at the pair.

Genny could feel her cheeks flush red. "Oh."

"Yeah. Oh." Mitch mumbled something under his breath—probably a curse—and threw first her bag then his up next to her before pulling himself on board.

"You should try taking that step with a skirt on," Genny grumbled.

"When we get to New York, my mother's going to have to teach you how to wear a dress without exposing yourself to every man within twenty feet. At least the deer hide hid one leg."

"I'm certain I can teach myself, thank you very much," Genny said, lifting her chin. Genny turned and smiled, her annoyance with Mitch disappearing quickly. The car looked like a long, narrow parlor with rows of richly cushioned miniature couches on either aisle and green velvet curtains over the windows. In the center of the car was a sitting area, looking much like a miniature of a hotel lobby. At the moment, the car was nearly empty, with only two seats occupied near the back.

"This is lovely," she breathed, touching the seat nearest her. The ceiling was a rich dark wood with gilt molding, and beneath her feet, a thick carpet ran the entire length of the car.

"It ought to be. It was fair expensive."

"We didn't have to travel first class," Genny said, then grinned. "But I'm glad we did."

Mitch's lips twitched. "See this?" he asked, patting the slanted ceiling above their seat. "These here are beds. You pull them down at night and sleep. I'll take the top; you take the bottom. The seats turn into a bed too. The lady's washroom is back there and the men's up front."

Mitch pulled out their tickets and moved down the car until they were near the middle and dropped his pack. "You can sit by the window if you want. See the sights."

Genny sat down and bounced up and down, testing the softness of the seat. "Lovely."

"You won't think it's so lovely in three or four days, but it sure beats sitting on a hard bench."

Genny couldn't remember ever sitting on a seat as soft and luxurious as the one she now sat upon. In her little cabin, the chairs were wood and even the bedding was thin and hard. But this was pure heaven, as if her backside were being cushioned by a hundred downy pillows with gentle springs inside. Mitch sat down beside her, his big body taking up nearly the entire rest of the couch, his thigh pressing up against hers.

He sat there for a few moments before testily saying, "Can't you scoot on over closer to the window? I hardly have room to breathe here."

"I'm over as far as I can go. And it's not so tight as to make it difficult to breathe. Really, Mitch, you do exaggerate."

He mumbled something beneath his breath that Genny thought sounded like he was in for a week of torture. Hmph.

"You know, Mr. Campbell, you don't have to accompany me any farther if this trip is so arduous for you."

"I just don't much care for being cramped up in small spaces for long periods of time," he said, still sounding a bit annoyed. Genny supposed that was an apology. "And do you have perfume on? I don't recall buying perfume."

"You gave me that nice-smelling soap," Genny said, feeling a bit hurt by all his complaints. She liked being with Mitch, and if she was perfectly honest, she liked the feel of his big thigh against hers. It made her feel safe and warm, like when she had cuddled up against him when they were on the trail.

Mitch tried to move over, but it was clear that the seat was too small to accommodate them both without touching. He shifted again, swore beneath his breath, then stood up and glared down at the seat. Then he swiped a hand through his hair and sat down again, stretching out his long legs in front of him.

The car slowly filled up with travelers excited to be on their way, and Genny decided to concentrate on them instead of the cranky man sitting next to her.

Money. Think about the money, Mitch thought as he tried to ignore the heat of Genny's thigh against his. He didn't want to want her. He didn't even want to *like* her. But damn if he could keep his mind from going places it had no business going.

That ridiculous, chaste kiss was still tormenting him. That kiss that hardly had been a kiss was making him think about how lovely it would be to really kiss her, to feel her respond and moan into his mouth. Mitch swallowed thickly, glad of only one thing: that Genny had no idea what she was doing to him. He had to focus on the prize. He had to stop liking her and stop wanting her and just think of her as a means of getting what he'd been dreaming of ever since the day he'd watched Will Jackson take a picture and then turn it into a thing you could hold in your hand and look at forever.

Next to him, Genny touched the carved wall, allowing her index finger to follow a swirl in the wood's grain. He had the uncomfortable feeling that he'd hurt her feelings with his gruffness. Well, good. He didn't need her looking at him with those big green eyes, cuddling up with him as if he truly were her husband. He'd wait until everyone found their seat and if there was an empty one, he'd sit there.

There was no way in hell he'd be able to take being crammed up next to her for a week, smelling her sweet scent, hearing her soft sighs as she slept, and feeling her leg pressed up against his. Money, Mitch thought, think about the money.

"Oh, hello." It was the lady from the platform, trailed by her silent husband. She greeted Genny as if they were life-long friends before giving him a rather cooler look. "It looks like we shall be neighbors for the next three days after all. I never did get your name, dear."

"Genevieve Hayes. Pleased to meet you."

"Campbell," Mitch said, giving Genny a wink before turning to the older woman. "It's so new, she keeps forgetting."

"Our wedding was so exciting, I can't remember a single detail. Not even the ceremony itself," Genny said, looking innocently up at Mitch. He stared at her a long moment, and then his body gave a small jerk from a silent laugh as he shook his head.

"Oh," Mrs. Walsh said, clapping her hands together. "Newlyweds. Harvey, *newlyweds*."

Harvey, a thin man with a thick brush of a mustache, leaned over and gave the two a quick smile before settling back against his seat.

"So this is your wedding trip. How romantic." Mrs. Walsh took off her bonnet, releasing the loose skin beneath her chin, and placed the hat on the floor in front of them. "All the way to England. My."

"My grandparents are the duke and duchess of Glastonbury."

Mrs. Walsh looked a bit startled and glanced at Mitch as if to check whether that could be the truth. "How wonderful," she said, and Mitch could tell by her tone that she'd decided this bit of news was nothing but a tall tale. "Does that make you a princess?" She winked conspiratorially at Mitch.

"I don't think so. I do believe it only makes me the granddaughter of a duke."

Mitch chuckled. "She *is* the granddaughter of a duke, whom she's never met. That's why we're making the trip."

Mrs. Walsh's brown eyes widened. "How exciting for you. I'm certain they're looking forward to meeting you."

Genny bit her lip. "They don't know we're coming yet." She turned to Mitch. "I expect we should tell them. It wouldn't do to simply show up at their front door."

"The front door of their castle," Mrs. Walsh said.

"Do you think they might truly live in a castle?" Genny breathed, awestruck. "Do dukes live in castles?"

"I believe they do." Mrs. Walsh gave Genny a worried look and appeared as though she was about to say something but thought better of it.

Next to him, Genny became silent, no doubt picturing a castle, complete with moat. "We need to telegraph them when we reach New York," she said after a time.

"We will." Another stretch of silence.

"Mitch."

"Yes?"

"What if they don't want me to come?"

"They will. You read their letters. I wouldn't be surprised if they got on a ship the next day and came to you."

The engine let out a loud hiss and the train slowly moved down the track just as the uniformed porter appeared at the far end of the car to see their tickets. Once they were on their way, Mrs. Walsh leaned over saying, "I'm so excited. I haven't seen my sister in years, nor my nieces and nephews since they were babies."

And off they went, the two of them talking, exchanging life stories. Twenty minutes into the conversation, Mitch switched places with Genny to let her and Mrs. Walsh talk without shouting. Genny clearly had missed having the company of a woman. Listening to their prattle, he thought longingly of the men now exploring Yosemite without him. His last summer with the group had been cut far too short.

All around, passengers were settling in for a long trip, taking out books, knitting, crochet hooks, and, thank the gods, dominoes, a cribbage board, and playing cards. Mitch politely excused himself and wandered down the car to the salon area, where he was soon happily involved in a game of cribbage with a gentleman traveling with his wife to visit their children.

Four hours into their trip, they stopped at Truckee for a light lunch and a bit of a break from sitting. Boys had been around their car offering apples and cheese, but Genny was near starving when they stopped, likely because she hadn't eaten anything for breakfast. She was quite recovered from her illness and ate nearly all of her sandwich of thickly sliced ham.

"Isn't this wonderful?" she asked, looking around at the other passengers. "All these people, all heading to visit different places and family. Did you know Mr. and Mrs. Walsh don't have any children? It was something they wanted above all things. It's so sad. I never really gave having children a thought. But I suppose I will, in England, with my husband, the prince."

Mitch lifted a skeptical eyebrow. "You're marrying a prince, are you?"

"Oh, yes, if I'd like. Apparently a duke is the next best thing and Mrs. Walsh said that if I wasn't already married to you"—she gave him an impish smile—"I could have married a prince."

"Instead of the bastard son of an actress," Mitch said, without even a hint of bitterness. "You have surely scraped the bottom of the marital barrel with me."

Genny gave him a face and pulled a small bit of crust from the remainder of her sandwich before delicately putting it in her mouth. "I'm certain you'll make someone a good husband, Mitch. Perhaps I can visit you someday in New York with my prince husband and all our little princes and princesses."

Mitch chuckled and shook his head. "And I can introduce you to my slovenly wife and ill-kempt children. A whole brood of them, barefoot and in need of a bath."

"And I will bestow upon them the knowledge they need to care for themselves properly. Perhaps I'll give your wife some of my old gowns. I daresay I shouldn't have much use for them after I've worn them once."

They laughed, thoroughly enjoying the banter, and Mrs. Walsh walked by at that moment and said, "Ah, young love."

Mitch's smile slipped a bit but he gave Genny a wink. "I do wish we hadn't told them we are married," Genny said softly, leaning forward. "I don't like lying to Mrs. Walsh. She's becoming a friend."

"It's necessary. Otherwise people would think badly of you, think you were the wrong sort of girl. An unmarried woman shouldn't travel with an unmarried man who is not her relative. If Mrs. Walsh knew we weren't married, she wouldn't be your friend."

Genny furrowed her brow. "I can't believe that's true. She's so nice."

"Because she thinks you're a respectable young woman traveling with her husband."

She grinned. "I'm not respectable?"

"Why does that thought make you smile?"

"I suppose I think it's all so silly. I'm the same person she befriended. And you're suggesting she wouldn't be my friend if she knew the truth?"

Mitch drew back slightly. "I hope you're not getting any ideas, Miss Hayes. You've been living in a cabin in the middle of nowhere for most of your life; you don't know about society and how nasty it can be. Just take my word for it, this is a secret that's best kept. Understood?"

Genny sighed. "Understood. But I do think Mrs. Walsh wouldn't retract her friendship simply because I'm not a wife."

"You'll just have to take my word for it," he repeated darkly.

Only six hours into their trip, Mitch could tell Genny was getting a bit stir crazy. Another niggling of worry struck him. Genny had grown up in a cabin, had foraged for food alongside her father, had chopped firewood and cooked on a stove made decades ago. As he looked around at the other women on the train, they were all occupied with various female activities they'd no doubt learned from their mamas. Even he knew women were always busy with something or other—cooking or mending or caring for children. Almost as if on cue, every woman on the train had pulled out some sort of project that involved a needle and gotten started. Heck, the whole time Genny had been talking to Mrs. Walsh, the older woman had been knitting in a frenzy, as if she were trying to get something completed before they pulled in to Omaha.

Genny let out a small sigh, leaned her head against the window, and watched the dry, rolling hills that dominated the landscape go by. There'd be plenty of sights to see later in the trip, but at the moment, there wasn't much more than grass and scrub to occupy the imagination. He had to find something useful for her to do during their trip. He tapped her on the shoulder and she turned to him, a smile on her face, an unexpected bit of cheer that had him grateful she was such a good traveling companion. "Want me to teach you how to play poker?"

And that's how they occupied their time until Chinese waiters, their braids slapping back and forth, served them a dinner of roasted oysters and beef.

As the sky darkened outside, the porter lit their oil lamps, giving the room a cozy feeling of intimacy. One of the passengers took out an accordion and at the first note, Genny moved toward the edge of her seat, flashing him another brilliant smile. Every time she gave him one of those, his gut hurt a little bit more. He was starting to wish she was a bit more ornery so he could relax. He felt on edge, as if he wanted to punch something—like the middle-aged man who kept leering at Genny. Didn't he know she was married? Hell, even if she wasn't really, Mitch still wanted to punch the bastard. What kind of man looked at another man's wife like that? Mitch glared at him until the man's focus shifted to Mitch and the older man started, immediately bringing his attention back to the accordion player.

"Oh, this is lovely, isn't it, Mitch? And to think I was nervous about riding on a train. I barely remember our trip out West, but the time we were on the train was rather frightening. And dirty." She wrinkled her nose at the memory. "I remember my face and hands were completely covered with black dust. And my father's too. I hardly recognized him, and of course, I didn't know it would all wash off." She looked around the room as if she'd never seen anything so delightful in her life. "But this, this is like traveling in a moving hotel."

"That's the point of it. Here, let's switch spots so you can see better."

That grand idea turned out to be one of the worst mistakes Mitch could have made. For as the evening wore on and the accordion player switched to melancholy songs, Mitch could see Genny grow more and more sleepy, until she finally succumbed, her warm body slumping back against his chest. He shifted slightly, hoping to wake her, but she snuggled deeper against him, letting out a small sigh of pure contentment. Mitch was left with one hand awkwardly slung across the couch and the other dangling down. He could smell her pretty soap, that stupid indulgence he'd bought for her, which he now regretted with every fiber in his being. She smelled so damned good and was so soft and warm against him, he thought he would surely burst into flame.

She turned a bit, digging her head slightly into his chest, and put an arm around his waist. *Oh, Lord, help me.*

She started slowly falling and he knew if he didn't put his arm around her, she'd drop to the floor. Part of him thought to let it happen, but he ended up putting both arms around her and pulling her even closer. Why not? Why not let himself enjoy holding her?

The car was quieting down as more and more people had the porter build their beds. The only sound above the clatter of the train was the creaking of the beds as they were pulled down, the gentle murmur of voices, and the occasional snap of a crisp sheet being pulled around the mattresses. One by one, the porter dimmed the lanterns. Mitch figured no one could see him now. Mr. and Mrs. Walsh had settled down a while ago, Mrs. Walsh giving him a smile as she took in the sleeping Genny. Mitch bent his head, pushing his nose into the soft luxury of Genny's hair, and breathed in deeply, feeling his throat ache the same way it had the first time he'd seen the Grand Canyon. Something so beautiful it hurt his heart always seemed to affect him that way. He tightened his arms, just a bit, now afraid to awaken her. He might never get this chance again, to hold her in his arms. Soon enough, she'd be in England and he'd be waving good-bye. He pressed his lips against her head and closed his eyes, his chest burning with something that felt a hell of a lot like regret.

He'd probably be saying good-bye in four weeks. He could picture her, wearing some fancy dress, her hair all done up, grandparents standing smiling behind her. She'd hate to say good-bye, but she'd be smiling, ready for her new life. She'd be where she belonged. He knew that, he had to know that. But as he pictured himself turning away and heading back home, it all seemed so wrong. Funny, in that daydream, he hadn't thought about how nice it would be to have full pockets.

"Sir, would you like me to make up your beds?"

Mitch opened his eyes to see a black man looking at him expectantly. "Yes, thank you." Genny stirred and sat up drowsily.

"I fell asleep."

"Like a log."

She looked back over her shoulder, her blonde hair falling across her face, and gave him a sleepy smile. His gut churned again, because all he could think of at that moment was waking up every morning to see that beautiful face, that sleepy smile. The next four weeks were going to be pure hell.

* * *

Going to the necessary while the train was moving was always a bit of a challenge—and to be honest a bit nerve-racking. Just below the commode, the tracks flew by and Genny, even though she knew it was impossible, was afraid to fall through. Or have something jump up. She sat, her bottom feeling the breeze from the open hole, and as she did her business, she realized the train was slowing to a stop. Oh, goodness, she hadn't realized they were so close to a station. It was bad form to go while in a station. Mortified, Genny quickly finished and peeked out the window, seeing nothing but yellowed grass and birch trees in the distance. Perhaps the station was on the other side of the train? Behind her, the car was strangely quiet. Usually when they pulled up into a station, there was a hubbub of activity. Something was wrong. It was the same feeling she would get out in the forest when all the birds went silent, and the hair on the back of her neck rose.

As quietly as possible, Genny unlatched the door, straining her ears for a sound. That's when she heard a low, rough male voice say, "I'm not gonna hurt none of y'all if'n you politely hand me your wallets."

Genny put a hand over her mouth, fearing the man might hear her breathing. If Mitch gave the man all their money, how would she get to England?

"That better be a wallet you're reachin' for, mister," the man growled.

And Genny knew, she just *knew*, that Mitch had been reaching for his rifle. Most of the other passengers hadn't been the sort to have a rifle, but Mitch had put his beneath their seat. Fear suddenly turned into something else Genny hadn't felt since the day she'd found her father. It was a calmness, a sense of inevitability. She knew that if she didn't do something, Mitch would die.

Silently, she pushed open the door, her eyes wide. She almost let out a sound of surprise, for not six feet in front of her she saw the broad back of a man, his greasy long hair touching the back of his dust-covered red shirt. He had a bandana covering his face and a battered old Cavalry hat jammed on his head. She looked past the man to see the frightened eyes of the passengers but quickly determined, at least in their car, the man was alone. He was standing, all wiry raw energy, with a rifle raised, pointing directly at Mitch.

One of the passengers spotted her, his eyes widening, and Genny shook her head and pressed a finger of warning against her lips. To her right was a cane leaning up against a seat, its owner an older woman who huddled fearfully against her husband. Moving slowly, fearing the outlaw might hear the soft rustling of her dress, Genny picked up the cane, quickly determining she wouldn't have enough room to swing the thing to do much harm to the man. So she did the next best thing.

"Please drop your rifle, sir, I know how to shoot and I shall have no problem shooting you if you continue to frighten these good people." She jammed the bottom of the cane against his back, praying he was too nervous to realize what he was feeling wasn't a rifle.

The man stiffened and several passengers gasped.

"Now, sir. I don't want to shoot you in the back, not very sporting of me, but I will. Drop your gun, if you please."

Genny's voice shook a bit, but she pressed the end of the cane harder against the man's back.

The man raised his arms, but kept the rifle in one hand. "Now, little lady, you don't want to do anything foolish."

"I actually do. Shall I shoot him?" She asked the question politely of the passengers, as if she were really leaving it up to them to decide his fate.

Mitch stood, his face pale, the lines around his mouth deep. Genny had never seen that expression on any man before and didn't know what to make of it. He walked toward the man, his hand extended. "Drop the rifle and she'll let you live."

To Genny's relief, the man sighed and set the rifle down, swearing beneath his breath. Mitch quickly took up the gun and pointed it at the would-be robber.

"On your knees. And put your hands behind your back. Genny, you use Mr. Pitsley's tie and bind his wrists." Mr. Pitsley, the man Mitch had been playing cribbage with the day before, quickly took off his tie and handed it to Genny.

"You said you'd let me go," the outlaw said, outraged.

"And I will. But right now I trust you about as much as I trust a rattlesnake. Hands behind your back or I swear you'll be limping all the way home with a hole in your leg."

"Alright, alright."

The man put his hands behind his back and Genny quickly tied them, pulling tightly and making him curse again. When she was done, Mitch handed the rifle to the nearest passenger and hauled the robber up to his feet. "How many others are there?"

A man's voice from outside called, "Jake, where the hell are you? You know Bobby doesn't want us messin' with the passengers. Get your ass on out here before he finds out, you sorry bastard."

"Ah, one of your friends." Mitch bent over and looked out the window and smiled grimly. "You best get a move on. If I'm not mistaken, looks like you boys are about to get some company." The man looked out the window and swore. On the opposite side of the train where his buddy was waiting, a large cloud of dust was rising up, and in the middle of that cloud were several men on horseback.

"Someone ratted us out," the man said, giving Mitch a look of desperation.

A general cheer rose up from the train when the men on horseback came into view.

"Shit," the man said, and then he repeated that word when he saw the small, blonde woman standing behind him wielding a menacing cane. Genny smiled and Mitch's heart near exploded from his chest. He didn't really care when the man, his hands still tied, made a dash for the back of the train and the still-open door. He heard what sounded like a man falling face first into the dust. But all he saw was Genny standing there smiling at him as if she'd just had the most fun a person could have. He wanted to shake her for doing something so dangerous. When he'd seen her come up behind the robber, he'd just about died, literally feeling the blood drain from his head. He'd heard of such a thing but never felt it, not even in those terrible months in the War Between the States when he'd been just a kid.

And so, he took two strides to her, put his hands on her shoulders and did give her a little shake. "What the hell were you thinking?" he asked, right before pulling her hard into his arms and burying his face against her hair. She was trembling, but she clung to him as if what she'd done had just hit her. He pulled back to see if she was okay, to make sure he didn't see terror in her eyes. He wasn't even really aware of what he was doing when he bent his head and kissed her, hard and long and probably a bit too intimately, given they had quite an audience. When he raised his head, there she was, smiling up at him again.

"It worked," she said, then laughed a bit shakily.

He stepped back, feeling a bit shaky himself, but for an entirely different reason. He'd thought they had an audience, but the passengers, their noses pressed to the windows, were watching as one by one the robbers—five of them—were caught. A collective cheer rose up when the conductor appeared to talk to the lawmen, who handed over heavy canvas bags of what Mitch guessed was gold.

Mitch grabbed Genny's hand and pulled her back to their seats. He suddenly felt weak, and he wasn't certain his legs could carry his weight much longer.

"You were wonderful, my dear," Mrs. Walsh said, then turned to her husband, who looked a bit under the weather. "Wasn't she wonderful? And you, too, Mr. Campbell. You were both so brave."

Mitch nodded, but neither spoke. They sat there, still holding hands, and stared straight ahead for a long while.

"You kissed me." This said when the train began moving to the cheers of the happy and relieved passengers.

"So I did." He shifted away and dropped her hand. "Doesn't mean anything. Just was glad you didn't get yourself killed. Won't happen again."

"Okay." And damned if those two little syllables weren't filled with a trunkful of disappointment.

"Listen," he said, keeping his voice low. "I'm your escort. Just that. Okay?"

She was silent for a long time, her cheeks flushed. "I thought you were my friend, too."

Friend. Hell, if it was up to him, they'd be far more than friends. But it wasn't up to him. They had no future. None. "We are friends. I lost my head is all. I saw you do a dang foolish thing and then you were smiling as if it was nothing, as if you couldn't have been killed, and I kissed you. That's all."

He wasn't looking at her but he could tell from his peripheral vision that she was looking at him. "I liked the second kiss better than the first."

He snapped his head around again and there she was smiling at him again. "You remember that, do you?"

She nodded, her eyes lowering to his mouth. Hell and damnation, if she kept looking at him like that he'd have to kiss her again. And he didn't want to. Didn't want things to get complicated. Didn't like the way his gut was churning, and other parts of his body were reacting. Didn't like that his heart was expanding in his chest.

"Well, you best get both out of your mind 'cause it's not happening again." He settled back into his seat and leaned against the window as if he were about to take a nap, which was highly unlikely given the adrenalin still coursing through his body and the carnal thoughts running through his mind.

"That's too bad," she said finally. "It was rather lovely."

He ignored her, pretended to have fallen into a deep sleep. What the heck was he going to do with her? He'd never been one to fall for a girl. Sure, he'd had a few lady friends back in New York, but none had ever made him want to scream in frustration and pure joy the way Genny did. Surely there must be something annoying about her. He just had to figure it out and focus on that. Not her hair. It was soft and long and he liked the way it smelled. And she was pretty. So he couldn't find fault with her appearance. She made him laugh, and her voice, with that cultured English accent, was soothing and gentle, like a spring rain. He nearly snorted aloud, then, which would have ruined his ruse of sleeping. She let out a sigh. Genny did tend to sigh. A lot. It was getting annoying. If he counted the number of sighs she let out, concentrated on that, he might not think about everything else that wasn't annoying.

She sighed again and laid her head against his shoulder. Damn, that felt nice.

"Your head is too heavy on my shoulder."

She immediately straightened. "Sorry. I'm just suddenly so sleepy. All the excitement, I suppose. You certainly seem tired."

"Listen, Genevieve," he whispered harshly so the other passengers wouldn't hear him, "I'm taking you to England and dropping you off with your grandparents and I'll never see you again. Understand? I'm not your husband and I'm not even your beau. I'm nothing but a man who got himself in a gnarly situation and is trying to figure out a solution. So I don't need your little sighs and your pretty green eyes looking at me like, well, like you shouldn't."

She looked confused and he suddenly had the urge to kiss her again, which made him so mad he had to get away. Or kiss her again. So he stood up and headed to the men's washroom at the end of the car, leaving Genny behind, no doubt hurt and probably a bit angry.

He went to the basin and splashed cold water on his face, looking up and not recognizing the man he saw in the mirror. "Get a grip, man," he told his reflection. He scrubbed his face dry, moving aside as another gentleman entered the small room.

"Your wife is the most daring woman I've ever seen, sir," the man gushed. "Why, I thought we'd be robbed and killed for certain. Imagine, having the courage to wield a cane and pretend it was a gun."

"She's got more courage in her little finger than most men do in their entire body, that's true," Mitch said, feeling that ridiculous swelling in his heart again. Who knew he'd be so quick to go all soft over a woman?

"I thank you both. As do the other passengers." The man held out his hand to Mitch, and the two men shook.

When Mitch went back to his seat, Genny had removed herself to the small parlor area, where she was talking to several other women. No doubt they were thanking her and reliving the events. No doubt they thought she was one hell of a woman.

And, damn, they'd be right.

Chapter 5

Genny's actions were the talk of the train. As she sat there with the women of their car, visitors from other parts of the train came and listened to the story again and again. It seemed that the more times the story was told, the more heroic she became and Genny found herself trying to calm the women, to let them know the only reason she'd done what she'd done was because the outlaw had been holding a rifle on Mitch. Truthfully, she hadn't given the other passengers a thought, a fact that now made her feel a bit guilty given the accolades she was receiving.

She would have told them that if she hadn't been so very angry and confused by the man. Granted, that first kiss had been her idea and her fault, and she had been a bit tipsy at the time. More than a bit, she admitted to herself. But that second kiss, the one that made her toes curl and her stomach all strange, well that had been all Mitch. And it had been rather thrilling. It had been "nothing," he'd said. Well, it hadn't been nothing to her. It had tilted her world on end, made her see Mitch in a different light, made her realize that kissing a man was wonderful and stirring. Made her think of herself as a woman for the first time.

When she'd sat down as the lawmen were capturing the train robbers, still holding Mitch's hand, it hadn't been the excitement of catching the outlaw that had stunned her to silence, it had been that kiss. Although she'd slept beside Mitch for days, snuggling by him for warmth, never in all that time had she *seen* him. Or truly seen herself. He was Mitch, a man who'd saved her, who'd agreed to take her to London. A friend and companion. But suddenly, he was a man. It was all so confusing.

Having grown up in a cabin far removed from society, she had no experience in trying to attract a husband. She found out soon enough that this was a common topic of conversation for most women. They talked about their daughters, their sons, their grandchildren, and many times the focus of their conversation was whether this one would marry that one or that one would be happy with the other one. It was as if she'd entered a foreign world where she didn't know the rules. It was easy to break the rules when one didn't know what they were.

"You've grown quiet, dear," Mrs. Walsh said.

"I'm just pondering things a bit," Genny said, looking back to her seat where Mitch now sat reading a periodical.

"They are a confusing lot," Mrs. Walsh said with a chuckle. "I thought he was going to faint dead away when you came up to that outlaw wielding that cane. Goodness, I've never seen a man so white. That's what love will do, though."

Love. Bah. *I'm not your husband and I'm not even your beau. I'm nothing but a man who got himself in a gnarly situation . . .* Obviously, she was that "gnarly situation."

"And that kiss. My knickers nearly caught fire just watching it."

Genny turned beet red, and Mrs. Walsh laughed. "Oh, my girl, I see that I've shocked you." Indeed, Mrs. Walsh did not seem to be the kind of woman who would say such a thing, but what did Genny know of women? She was just as naïve about them as she was about men.

The porter had come into the car to take their dinner orders, ending the conversation. The two women made their way back to their seats, Genny sitting down at the farthest edge of the couch to avoid touching Mitch. Even that made her sad, but she did it anyway, recalling how grumpy Mitch had been about their close quarters.

"You don't have to do that," he said, low and gruff.

"I have no idea what you mean." Genny stared at the porter as if watching a man take dinner orders was vastly interesting.

Before she knew what he was about, Mitch had wrapped a hand around her waist and hauled her snug up against him before removing his arm from her. She looked at him curiously, more confused now about his actions than before.

"I say things sometimes and they come out the wrong way. Like I'm angry or something. I'm not."

Genny let out a small laugh, for Mitch sounded quite angry at the moment. She lifted a brow and he smiled, sheepishly.

"I want to be mad. Just can't, not at you at any rate."

"Good. I don't like it when you're angry with me."

"I never was angry. I was frustrated and more scared than I've ever been in my life. Don't you ever do such a foolish thing like that again, Genny."

"But it all ended well. The outlaws were caught. No one was hurt."

He let out a gusty sigh. "You could have been killed. The passengers would have given up their money, sure, but they would have been alive. You could have gotten yourself killed."

"But he was holding his gun on you. And, Mitch, he was going to pull that trigger. Maybe all the passengers would have lived, but I had a terrible feeling he was going to shoot you just for sport. You could have died. I had to do *something*. Besides, if he had stolen all our money, how would we have gotten to England?"

He looked at her then, his eyes burning with something she didn't understand. It almost looked to her like he wanted to scream but was holding it in. Then he turned his head sharply away and stared at the back of the couch in front of them.

"I'm sorry, Mitch. I didn't mean to frighten you, but how could I just let him shoot you?" She laid her hand on his forearm and was startled by the knot of muscle she felt, as if he were lifting something impossibly heavy. That's when she saw that his hand was curled into a fist so tight, his knuckles were stark white. "Mitch, what's wrong?"

"You . . ." He swallowed hard. "You are never to put my life before yours. I doubt you'll ever get the chance, but, hell, Genny, I couldn't live with myself if I thought that's what you'd been doing and you got hurt. I thought you were saving the others." He was still staring at the back of the couch, his breathing harsh.

"That was an added benefit," she said, laughing and hoping he'd smile. But his expression only grew grimmer.

He pressed one hand to his chest and rubbed hard and Genny worried that he might be ill. For a time back in Yosemite, they'd had a neighbor, an old-timer who had taught her father what he needed to know to survive in the wilderness. They'd found old Jake dead in his cabin just a day after he'd been rubbing his chest. Her father had explained that Jake's heart had simply given out. Mitch was far younger than Jake, but that didn't mean his heart was strong.

He turned to her, and she saw that his eyes had softened a bit. "I think I just might have to kiss you again, after all," he said. He looked across the aisle and his expression turned regretful. "But not now. Probably not ever. I'll come to my senses, so you don't have to worry."

"I wasn't worried," she said, trying to tamp down the thrill she felt upon hearing his words.

"You're just impossible, Genny."

"I don't mean to be." She couldn't help letting her gaze drift down to his mouth. She'd never really noticed a man's mouth, not that she'd seen that many. Most men she'd known had mustaches and beards and even if they were clean-shaven, she didn't think she would have taken notice of their mouths. But Mitch's was rather lovely. Sculpted and masculine, his bottom lip just slightly more full than his top. She heard Mitch let out a low sound and she looked at him and again saw a heat in his gaze. Oh. That's what that meant; he wanted to kiss her. She thought back to all those looks she hadn't been able to interpret and was stunned.

"Stop grinning at me. And stop . . . just stop looking at me."

Genny let out a laugh. "Stop looking at you? That's going to be a bit difficult in these small quarters."

"You know what I mean. At least I pray to God and Jesus that you do." He said the last mostly to himself.

She leaned forward and whispered, "The porter is taking the Walshs' dinner order. They are quite occupied." And then she leaned in and pressed her lips against his, feeling daring and wonderful. At first, he didn't move, but he didn't pull away, either. And then, he tilted his head, just slightly, and kissed her back, moving his lips in a way that seemed to touch every part of her body—even parts she hadn't really thought existed.

He pulled back, looking as if he'd just hurt her rather than kissed her. "I can't keep doing that, Genny. I can't."

"It was your idea," she pointed out, teasing him. "And I really don't mind. I ought to know how to kiss, oughtn't I, if I'm going to be married to a prince."

Mitch's expression changed subtly, and he dropped his head and let out a small laugh. "Yes, you're right. You wouldn't want to disappoint your prince."

*　*　*

Mitch knew Genny was teasing, but her words couldn't have been more perfect for a man who was in an epic battle with his heart and his head. Genny was the granddaughter of a duke and he was the illegitimate son of an actress. Even in America, a match between them would be unheard of, and he knew the English were much bigger sticklers about such things. In their world, he figured he wouldn't even be hired as a servant. And here he'd been thinking that maybe, just maybe, he could manage a way to keep her.

He'd laugh if he wasn't so angry—with himself, mostly. Her teasing about marrying a prince brought him back to reality. He was a man, just has he'd told her, who had gotten himself into a gnarly situation, who would hopefully end up with some gold in his pocket. If he got a couple of kisses from a pretty girl in the meantime? That didn't make him a villain, just a man who was taking advantage of his situation.

What an idiot he would be to let his heart become more engaged than it already was. That horse was already out of the barn, but he'd do his best in the next few weeks to make certain it didn't get away entirely. And maybe he could coax it back into the barn. He chuckled to himself, winning a questioning look from Genny.

"Just thinking of horses and barns," he said by way of explanation, which only seemed to make Genny more confused.

Omaha, Nebraska was a small but bustling city, seemingly sprouting from the plains in a random way. It had been only twenty years since the first white baby had been born in Omaha, and now it was a sprawling city with brick buildings and paved streets. The train pulled into a station situated in the older part of town with clapboard buildings and fences that looked like a good wind would knock them over. But in the distance, Genny could see a gleaming white church steeple and fine brick and stone buildings.

The Walshes had already gathered up all their belongings and were ready to head to the baggage car when the train groaned to a final stop. Genny stood and bade them a tearful good-bye, feeling as though she was leaving behind a life-long friend.

"You make friends quickly when you travel," Mrs. Walsh said, giving Genny a warm hug. Mr. Walsh patted her shoulder and did something with his mouth that Genny assumed was a smile. As far as she could tell, he hadn't said more than a handful of words the entire way from Sacramento.

After they'd gone and Mitch had collected their belongings, Genny said, "I'll never see them again. I'll never see any of these people again. It's so sad."

"You get used to it. I'll likely never see Will Jackson again and he was the best friend I've ever had. Just part of life."

Just part of life. For the first time, it struck Genny that she would have to say good-bye to Mitch, that after she was safely ensconced with her grandparents, she would likely never see him again either. She closed her eyes briefly and shook her head. She would not think about that until it happened. It would do no good to dwell on their good-bye when they still had weeks left together.

"But I can write. I have their address. Mrs. Walsh did promise to write."

"I'm sure she will," Mitch said, but she could tell he was just trying to appease her.

"You don't think she will?"

"She might. In fact, she probably will. But then your lives will have taken different tracks and you won't have much to say to one another. You'll be a fine lady in England living in a castle and she'll be back here making her own life."

Genny felt she would never forget Mrs. Walsh, never stop writing as long as the older woman continued to write to her. But Mitch? She had a feeling he wouldn't write a word. He just didn't seem to be the type of man who would cling to a friendship. So when they said good-bye in a few weeks, it would be a final good-bye, very nearly like a death. It had been so hard to wrap her mind around the fact that her father was gone forever. It had taken weeks before she stopped looking at the door expecting him to walk in at any time. After Mitch left her, she would never see him again. She would have no reason to return to America and he certainly would have no reason to go to England.

"Are you going back to California after you take me to my grandparents?"

He looked at her and shook his head before staring out at the busy train station and the passengers collecting their bags. "I plan to open up a photography studio and settle down. I always was better at taking pictures of people rather than nature. That was Will's strength. He could capture the beauty and grandness of a tree, but I ended up just taking a picture of a tree. Nearly the same, but to someone who understands photography, it's completely different."

Mitch was going to "settle down." That seemed almost worse than saying good-bye. Settling down meant finding a wife and having children, and the thought of Mitch kissing another woman sent hot shards of jealousy through Genny. It was such an unexpected feeling, such a terrible and painful thing. Yet, she was planning to do the same, was she not? She knew from talking to those women on the train that women were expected to marry, particularly women of rank. One woman on the train seemed to be an expert on the subject and had gone on and on about how the daughter of a lord could never marry someone as ordinary as a banker or shopkeeper. Genny had remained silent on the subject, because, after all, she was supposed to be married to Mitch. But now she wished she'd asked more questions, like why couldn't a woman marry whomever she pleased.

The two had gathered up their rather meager luggage and were waiting patiently as the passengers departed. The Walshes, in a hurry to see their relatives, were the first out the door. Mitch leaned over to peer out the window and gave a satisfied grunt.

"Fine day, but hotter than h . . ." He stopped and grinned. "Hotter than hot. Never did get used to the heat of this place in summer." He straightened, and Genny got the feeling he was nervous about something. "We don't have to catch the train to New York until tomorrow morning, which gives us plenty of time for me to get to the bank so I can close my account. And maybe we can buy you another dress or two."

Genny looked down at the dark blue dress she was wearing, noting a few travel stains she hadn't seen before. "That would be wonderful."

"I know a lady's store near William's photography studio that should have a nice selection."

He was talking more quickly than usual and kept peering out the window, and Genny suddenly wondered if Mitch had a girl here and was worried she would see him with Genny. He scrubbed his chin, which hadn't seen a razor in a few days now, making him look a bit like an outlaw.

"I need to go to the studio to pick up my gear. Will's wife will be there. She's a good woman. You'll like her."

He seemed so distracted, Genny found herself looking through the window to see if she could determine what was making him so antsy.

"Who am I? Genny Hayes or Mrs. Mitch Campbell?"

She knew immediately that she'd hit the right target, because beneath that scruffy beard, Mitch blushed.

"You're Genevieve Hayes."

"That's good. I'm not very good at being Mrs. Mitch Campbell."

He grinned down at her and looked slightly more relaxed. "Mollie's a good woman, but she can be a bit of a stickler, if you catch my meaning. I'm just trying to figure out how I can make her understand that traveling this way was our only option. I'm pretty sure she's going to tan my hide for putting you in this situation."

Genny let out a bubble of laughter. "You're frightened of her."

"Heck yes, I am." He put on an expression of mock fear. "Come on, let's get this over with."

Mitch loved Mollie like a sister, and if she hadn't already been married to Will when Mitch had met her, he might have fallen in love with her. How many women would allow their husbands to go gallivanting off into the wilderness year after year to take photographs? She didn't like it and she let Will know it, but she understood that it was important, that Will was an important man. She was five foot nothing with a huge pile of dark hair, an Irish temper, and other than Genny, had the prettiest eyes he'd ever seen. And she was about to give him a large dose of anger, he was certain of it.

After stopping at the bank to close out his account, a process that made Mitch slightly sick to his stomach, he and Genny headed to the Jacksons' place. The couple lived with their two children across from the photography studio that had been Mitch's refuge. Sick of wandering since the war, he'd been looking for an odd job, and when he walked into that studio, he knew he'd found something that could make him stay. William Jackson recognized a kindred soul, a man with eyes still haunted by the things he'd seen, and immediately offered him not only a position, but a cot in the back room to sleep in.

And that's where he'd stayed for nearly five years, scrimping and saving and dreaming.

The Jacksons' home was a two-story whitewashed clapboard house with a welcoming front porch. As Mitch walked down the street, his arm aching from his heavy pack, he instantly saw that Mollie was out on that porch with her youngest boy, playing jacks. She sat on the second step, while the boy was sprawled out on the porch floor, intent on the game.

And when she looked up and saw Mitch walking toward her, she stood, her face white, one hand going to her mouth as if to stifle a scream. *Oh, shit.*

"He's fine," he said, hastening toward her, leaving Genny behind. "Will is fine, Mollie."

Tears filled her eyes and she dropped her hand, which had now turned into a little fist. "You about scared the life out of me, Mitch Campbell, coming up to me like that, looking all worried." And then she noticed Genny, standing a bit back.

"I'm sorry, Mollie. I can explain. This is Miss Genevieve Hayes and she's the reason I'm here now. Let's go on inside."

Mollie looked at Genny and frowned, then smiled. "Of course. Come on, Seth, why don't you go teach your sister how to play jacks."

"She's too little. She won't be able to."

"Then you can show her how good you are at it. The adults need to be alone."

The boy scooped up the jacks and small ball and moved into the house.

"I think he's grown two inches since we left," Mitch said.

Mollie led the pair to a small sitting room that was hotter than Hades. He wondered, briefly, if Mollie had led them to the sun-filled room on purpose rather than the library, which he knew was far cooler.

"How is Will?" she asked, seemingly composed.

"Just fine, fine. Listen, I'm sorry for giving you a scare. I guess I should have sent you a telegram letting you know I was coming. With Miss Hayes."

Mollie's gaze shifted to Genny and she gave the younger woman a curiously cold look. Genny sat on a small settee, much like the one they'd shared on the train, and Mitch made sure to sit across the room from her. Genny didn't understand that even a casual touch between a man and a woman could seem like something entirely different under the watchful eyes of a woman like Mollie.

Mitch gave Mollie the abbreviated story of how they'd come to be sitting in her stiflingly hot parlor. Genny was uncustomarily quiet, letting Mitch do all the talking. "So after we stop in New York for a short visit with my mother, we're off to England to meet Miss Hayes's grandparents." He smiled, knowing even as he did that Mollie realized he wasn't telling the entire truth. He never had been very good at lying.

Mollie gave him a level look and said, "That's wonderful, seeing your grandparents for the first time. And you, Mitch, taking the time to escort her."

"I figure I owed her after breaking her leg." He smiled, and even he knew how desperate that smile must seem.

"You didn't break my leg, Mr. Campbell," Genny said. "I did that quite on my own. Though I must say I wouldn't have broken it if you hadn't startled me so."

"And I wouldn't have startled you if you hadn't been sneaking around following me."

Genny turned to Mollie to explain. "I was trying to determine whether Mr. Campbell was someone I could trust to escort me to Sacramento. I hadn't any idea how to get there on my own, you see."

"How could you determine his trustworthiness based on observation?" Mollie asked, sounding as if she didn't entirely believe Genny. And to be honest, Mitch had been wondering the same thing.

"The way he treated his mule."

Mollie smiled. "Of course."

"The way I treated my *mule*? You were going to make a decision based on that?" Mitch's blood ran cold to think of how many terrible men treated their animals far more kindly than they treated humans.

"It seemed like a valid way," Genny said, looking to Mollie for agreement. To his shock, Mollie nodded.

Mitch took a deep breath to calm his temper, but he just couldn't keep the image of Genny going up to some ne'er do well and being molested or killed because the man wiped down his horse after a hard ride. Her heroics on the train were still fresh in his mind and though he tried to school his expression, he had a feeling his thoughts were too apparent.

"Miss Hayes, why don't you go freshen up. I'll keep Mitch company. There's a washroom just off the kitchen. I'll show you the way and get you settled."

Mitch knew what was coming. Mollie was getting rid of Genny so that she could give him a piece of her mind. He couldn't say that he didn't deserve it. If he stepped back and looked at his actions—and the reasons for them—he knew he was not going to come out in a very good light in Mollie's eyes. Five minutes after leaving him sweating in the parlor, Mollie returned, shut the door behind her, and stood, glaring at him, arms folded, foot tapping.

"I know what you're going to say, Mollie, and I really am in no mood to hear it."

She stalked toward him and pointed an accusing finger at him. "You have no idea what I'm going to say to you, Mr. Campbell. What are you thinking bringing your lady friend into my house? I have small children to care for. And neighbors." Mitch opened his mouth to explain, but she just kept on talking. "And it's clear that girl trusts you. She looks at you as if the sun rises and sets on your shoulders. And I don't really care much for the way you look at her. You tell me, right now, sir, what is really going on here. Grandparents in England. Honestly, Mitch, how gullible do you think I am?"

"It's the truth, Mollie, I swear. She got hurt, needed an escort, and since I wanted to get home, I agreed to take her to New York."

She narrowed her eyes. "Miss Hayes said you're taking her all the way to England. Are you?"

Mitch couldn't quite meet her sparking blue gaze. "Yes. I am."

"You're a good man, Mitch. But you're no saint. There's only one reason I can think of why you would volunteer to escort a stranger all the way across an ocean."

He tried to appear shocked by her accusation, he truly did, but he ended up chuckling instead. "Her grandfather's a *duke*, Mollie. A duke. I've been saving for my studio for five years and I've got a few more dollars to go before I have enough money to open it. I want to do things right. It's got to be fancy and I have to have the latest equipment. New York is a mite more expensive than Omaha. So, yes, I thought I'd stumbled upon a little treasure."

"Oh, Mitch." The way she said it made him feel like he could crawl beneath an ant—and it was clear she still didn't believe him. "I know you're a skinflint, but a duke in England? You couldn't come up with a better tale than that?"

"I'm telling you the truth, Mollie. On the souls of your children."

Mollie's mouth gaped open and she was silent for so long, Mitch said, "Trying to catch flies, Mollie?"

"You're not fooling me? Are you telling me that she actually is the granddaughter of a duke? And you really did meet her in Yosemite? And that this is all about *money*?"

Mitch shook his head in confusion. "What were *you* talking about?"

She put her hands on her hips and stalked around the room a bit before finally settling down in a chair opposite him. "You're telling the truth? This whole thing is not just some tall tale to make me be nice to your . . . your . . ."

"God, no. Mollie. Hell, what kind of man do you think I am? Besides, Miss Hayes is just about the most innocent woman I've ever met in my life."

She threw her arms out to her sides. Mollie had a way of talking that involved her entire body. "I wasn't sure for a while there. Wait. How was it that you have been traveling? A man traveling with a woman is sure to draw some attention."

Mitch felt his cheeks flush. Again. "We've been traveling as husband and wife." He threw his hand up to stop her tirade. "And before you go getting on your high horse, it's just a ruse so that people are nice to her. Nothing has happened, Mollie. I'm just thinking about the money, that's all."

"Does Miss Hayes know that?"

Mitch shifted in his chair. "No. She doesn't. I'd probably take her anyway, even if I didn't think I'd be getting a reward for my troubles. She has a way of getting under a man's skin."

Mollie looked amused. "Falling for her, are you, Mitch?"

"Her grandfather's a duke, Mollie. I don't even know who my father is. And my mother . . ." He let out a short, humorless laugh. "She's no one's idea of a respectable woman."

Mitch didn't like the expression on Mollie's face right then. If he wasn't mistaken, he'd say it was pity. "You didn't answer my question."

Mitch swiped a hand threw his hair, making the dark strands stand on end. "What do you want me to say, Mollie, that I adore her? That just the thought of leaving her behind makes me crazy? I'm not that man."

"I'm sorry, Mitch."

"Don't be. I made this mess all by myself. And to answer your question, no, I'm not falling for her." Even as he said the words, he could feel a heat come to his cheeks. When the hell had he started blushing?

"Does she know how you feel?"

"Sure she does. We're just friends." Lies and more lies. He rested his forearms against his thighs and hung his head. "And that's the way it's going to stay, Moll."

"If you say so. Just please don't do anything you'll regret."

A tap on the door made them both start. "Come in."

Genny peeked her head into the room. "I'm all freshened up," she said. "I was hoping to get some shopping done while we're here and Mitch mentioned there's a dress shop nearby?"

Mollie practically leaped out of her chair. "Mitch, you stay here and watch the children. I'm going shopping with Miss Hayes."

That night, Genny, obviously feeling more comfortable in Mollie's company, regaled them with story after story, making even the horrifying seem like a grand adventure. She recounted breaking her leg and Mitch tripping with her in his arms as if it were the grandest time she'd ever had.

Mollie wiped her eyes, stilling chuckling, and asked, "When are you taking that god-awful thing off her leg?"

It had been more than a month since he'd set her leg and wrapped it in the deerskin, so it was probably fine to remove it. Mitch was afraid of what they'd find underneath. What if her leg was crooked? What if it hadn't healed all the way? Genny had been walking without crutches for weeks now, but that didn't mean something horrible wouldn't happen when they removed the hide.

"Can we take it off, Mitch? My leg feels fine and the deerskin's quite pliable." She lifted up her leg to show how she could move her ankle back and forth. "It would be so lovely to wear the new pair of boots we purchased today. They won't fit around the skin."

"I suppose we could. But if it doesn't look right, I'm wrapping it back up again." He turned to Mollie. "I need the sharpest knife you have."

Mitch could feel a cold sweat breaking out, even though the evening was still warm. "Let's go out to the back porch. Bring a lamp, will you, Moll?"

Mollie stood back and watched as Mitch carefully cut through the leather, but her eyes weren't on the knife slicing through the thick hide. She was looking at the two of them, the way Miss Hayes laid her hand on Mitch's shoulder, as if comforting him, as if she knew how afraid he was that he was taking the cast off too soon. She watched the way Mitch would look up at Miss Hayes, to check to see if she was all right, the way he forced a smile to comfort her.

Mitch looked up and saw the expression in Mollie's eyes and he felt a small bit of anger. She was feeling sorry for him because he'd let his heart slip down to his sleeve again. He was going to have to get better at hiding his feelings. Turning back to Genny's leg, he slowly peeled the deerskin away, revealing a straight, if somewhat thin, leg.

"It looks as if it had never broken," Genny said. "You missed your calling, Mr. Campbell, you should have been a surgeon."

"It's a fine job, Mitch," Mollie said.

"You'll get your muscle back in no time," Mitch said, frowning at how thin her leg was. The muscle of her calf was like jelly.

Mitch took Genny's hand and helped her to stand. "How does it feel?"

"A bit weak. Let me take a step or two." She did, shakily. "My ankle hurts a bit. Guess it's not used to moving so much."

"Let me go get my grandfather's cane," Mollie said, and when Genny made to protest, the older woman laughed. "He's six feet under, so he doesn't need it anymore."

Once she had the cane in hand, Genny put on her new pair of soft kid boots and practiced walking, back and forth on the porch.

"Why don't you take a break, Genny?"

"I want to build up my muscle. I must say, its gelatinous state is a bit repulsive." She wrinkled her nose as she reached down and touched her calf through her dress.

Mitch laughed. "You're not going to build up that muscle in a day, darlin', so you might as well rest. We can have William's brother drive us to the station tomorrow." Mollie lifted one eyebrow and mouthed the word *darlin'* and Mitch gave her a hard look. He'd had enough of Mollie's opinions to last a while.

"Have you ever been to New York?" Genny asked Mollie.

"The furthest east I've been is Chicago. That's where I grew up until my folks moved out here when I was sixteen. I hear it's something, though. More people in one block than some entire cities."

"We'll only be there for a day or two before heading to England, but you'll have enough time to see the sights," Mitch put in.

He just hoped the sights she saw wouldn't shock her too much.

Chapter 6

Nothing in Genny's past could have prepared her for New York City. It was a cacophony of horses, carriages, newsboys shouting, hammers and saws, horsecars, and people, people everywhere. It was exciting and frightening—and awful smelling. It seemed there were as many horses as people and the paved roads were matted with manure.

Still, riding in a large car crowded with people and pulled along a rail by a horse was something Genny had never done before. They rode from Grand Central Depot on 42nd Street, which didn't seem all that grand to Genny, down Park Avenue, getting off at Bleeker Street. Along the way, Mitch would point out interesting sights and tell her stories, but the closer he got to his mother's home, the quieter he became. Genny did notice that the buildings seemed a bit smaller, the streets more congested with pedestrians and far fewer horses and fine carriages. The shops here had colorful goods spilling out into the street, and many of the people spoke German or had thick Irish brogues.

"My mother lives just outside the Bowery," Mitch said, though Genny had no idea what that meant. "She used to live closer to Niblo's Garden."

"Niblo's Garden?" Genny asked, struggling to walk as quickly as Mitch. In all her time with him, he'd always been conscious of the fact she could not walk as quickly as he could. But now, it was all she could do to stay close enough to hear him.

"It's a theater near Broadway. She was in *Macbeth* there, but that was more than twenty years ago." He stopped suddenly, and she nearly ran into his back. "My mother is . . ." He let out a gusty sigh. "She's eccentric. Very eccentric. She hasn't worked in two years, not since a fire at the theater a couple of years back. I sent money to her for a while until she wrote saying I needn't continue. I haven't been home in a few years, so I don't know what we're going to find."

He turned and stared at a door, painted a cheerful red with a lovely lantern hanging above it.

"Too early for zat, young man," said a woman in a thick German accent. She was sweeping the sidewalk in front of a shop from which emanated the most delicious smell of cooked meat.

"I beg your pardon?"

"You're heading up to Mrs. Campbell's place? Too early."

"Is she not in?" Genny asked, confused by the woman's demeanor. It almost seemed as if she disapproved of them, though she didn't know how that could be.

The older woman, her head covered by a colorful scarf, peered at her with faded blue eyes as if Genny had said something ridiculous.

"Madam, Mrs. Campbell is my mother. Are you saying she's not in?"

The woman's eyes grew wide. Then, without a word, she hurried away.

Mitch swore beneath his breath and didn't bother to apologize; he almost *always* apologized when he swore in front of her.

"If we can't stay here, we'll find a hotel, though I hate the expense of it."

"Perhaps your mother didn't receive your cable," Genny said, looking doubtfully around the neighborhood.

"Come on," Mitch said, and pushed open the door. He led her up to the second floor, and Genny noticed how clean and elegant the entrance was. His mother might be eccentric, but she certainly kept a lovely entry. When he reached the top of the stairs, Mitch waited for her with ill-concealed impatience. Clearly he was nervous about seeing his mother and Genny wondered just how "eccentric" she was.

Mitch lifted a heavy, ornate door knocker, carved in the shape of a mermaid. A rather risqué mermaid. He looked at the figure, his brows furrowed, then stepped back to examine the door again. "I don't think my mother would have moved without telling me," he said, eying the mermaid. He lifted the lady's tail and let it drop again, and Genny had to stifle a giggle.

Mitch gave her a dark look before straightening. Someone was coming to the door from inside the apartment. The door opened to reveal a small woman wearing a maid's uniform. "It's too early," she said in a thick Irish brogue, first looking at Mitch, and then longer at Genny. "Who are you?" The question was directed at Genny.

"Miss Genevieve Hayes. We're here to see Mrs. Campbell," Genny said.

"Well, Miss Genevieve Hayes, if you haven't been here before, you have to make an appointment. You can't just waltz in here and demand to see Mrs. Campbell. Everyone knows that. Besides, we're closed down for a few days."

Mitch held up his hand, stopping any more conversation between the two women. "You work for Mrs. Campbell?"

The maid nodded. "I'm her personal maid," she said, in a way that made it seem as if she expected a challenge to her claim.

"I'm her son," Mitch said, and Genny felt a bit of delight when the girl's eyes widened.

"Oh, Mr. Campbell. That's right, we were expectin' you. Come on in with the both of you. You can't be too careful, you know. Your mother, she's a fine woman, she is. She should be getting up right about now. I'll go check on her."

Mitch pulled out his pocket watch. "It's nearly four in the afternoon."

"Yes, that's about right," the maid said, leading them further into the apartment. "You wait here and I'll be right back."

"Jesus," Mitch breathed. He was standing in the most luxurious room he'd ever set foot in. The walls were rich, carved mahogany, the floor covered with an impossibly soft carpet, the furniture gleaming wood and expensive leather. It looked like a room one would find in an exclusive men's club, not that he'd ever been in one. This could not be his mother's home. Last he'd seen her, her furniture had been shabby and she certainly couldn't have afforded a maid. Hell, she could hardly afford to feed herself. Had she found herself a rich man?

"It's lovely," Genny said, looking up at him worriedly.

"It is that." He knew he'd grown quiet and taciturn, but seeing his mother always put him on edge. He never knew what he was going to find, though she was often more than a little tipsy. In all his imaginings, he had never expected to find himself standing in the middle of a room that actually *smelled* rich. Dominating the ceiling, hanging beneath an intricate medallion, was a spectacular chandelier. It wasn't lit, for sun still streamed through the windows only partially covered by dark blue velvet drapes pulled back by thick gold ropes. He wouldn't be surprised if that was real gold in the ropes' thread.

"Mitchell, I didn't expect you until tomorrow," his mother said as she floated into the room, her robe flowing behind her dramatically.

"We were actually supposed to arrive yesterday."

"Were you?" She was in a dressing gown that even he could tell was expensive. What the hell was going on here? She rushed over to him, kissing him on each cheek. He didn't smell wine on her breath, but that didn't necessarily mean much. She had just woken up, after all. "You look wonderful, darling." She stepped back and smiled at Genny. "And who is this lovely young lady?"

"Genevieve Hayes," Genny said.

His mother looked from Genny to him, the question clear in her gaze. The question of who Genny was hadn't been answered and Mitch knew it.

"I'm escorting Genny to England to meet her grandparents for the first time. We met in California. She'd broken her leg and needed help, so I helped her. We can get more into the story later, Mother. Miss Hayes, this is Madeline Campbell, my mother."

"Pleased to meet you, Mrs. Campbell."

Madeline waved a hand. "Please call me Madeline. Only my clients call me Mrs. Campbell. And I shall call you Genevieve, if you don't mind. We're not so formal here, despite the way the room looks." Her brown eyes sparkled as she made a slow circle, her arms outstretched. "Aren't you curious?"

"As a cat," Mitch said dryly.

His mother raised her chin regally. "I'm a business owner, Mitch, and business is thriving. As you can see."

Mitch was afraid to ask. His mother had struggled for years when it was clear she'd become too old for most parts. When he was very young, they'd lived in a nice apartment, even had a maid for a short time. But for most of his life, they had struggled to pay rent. One thing his mother had never done was have a man friend to pay her bills. She might be eccentric, she might drink a bit too much, but she had principles. When he'd left to fight in the War Between the States, he'd done so knowing he could send his pay back to her. Over the years, he'd worried that their very lives depended on whether she got this part or that part. When the theater burned down, he'd feared she wouldn't have a way to make a living. Apparently, she'd found one heck of a way.

"Here," she said, opening a drawer and pulling out a small pamphlet. "This should explain it."

Mitch took the pamphlet, first reading the title aloud. "The Gentleman's Companion." He began reading and it soon became quite clear what the pamphlet was about. Though it contained a ridiculous disclaimer in the front of the booklet that said the publication was for the purpose of warning men away from houses of ill repute, it was clear that what he held in his hand was a guide of sorts.

His mother could tell from his expression exactly when he realized what the pamphlet was about, and said, "Turn to page sixteen."

This he did not read aloud:

The establishment at No. 79 Houston Street is a private assignation house of the highest standards. It is a first-class operation run by the diminutive Mrs Campbell, a charming lady who only allows the highest caliber of men and women into her establishment. Everything here is arranged in the first style while the pretty girls provide Cupid's services unrivaled by any of the fine ladies of Broadway.

"Good God, Mother. Have you gone mad?" he asked, thrusting the pamphlet back to his mother.

"What is it? What's wrong?" Genny asked, stepping forward as if she feared Mitch might keel over. And at that moment he felt as if he just might.

He couldn't believe what he'd just read. His mother—his *mother*—was operating a brothel. And, if the pamphlet was to be believed, many other people were too.

"First-class establishment," Madeline said, smiling. "Not too many made *that* classification."

He just stared at his mother and shook his head, made mute by the audacity of the woman. "We can't stay here, Genny. Be damned the cost of rooms at a hotel. We'll make do."

"For goodness' sake, Mitchell, when did you become such a prude?"

"Mother, you're running a *brothel*." He darted a look at Genny to see if she was as shocked as he. "Surely you do not expect me to stay here, and certainly not with an innocent single woman?"

Madeline gave him a look that clearly told him she didn't believe the "innocent" part for one second.

"Hell, I need to sit down," Mitch said. Dealing with his mother had never been easy, but he'd hardly thought she would turn into a madam! He sat down on the nearest sofa, sinking onto a cushion of pure luxury.

His reaction to the comfort must have shown in his face, because his mother said, "Nice, isn't it? First class. Everything, from the food to the furniture to the . . ."—she paused for dramatic effect—". . . entertainment." Then she draped herself onto the opposite couch and patting one well-manicured hand upon the leather, invited Genny to sit next to her.

Genny gave Mitch an uncertain look before sitting down. "Oh, it is delightful, isn't it?" she asked, resting her hand on the soft leather.

Madeline laughed. "Wherever did you find her, Mitchell? And that accent, it's perfect."

"I was living in California with my father and was quite alone after he died. I was spying on Mitch and he startled me, purely by accident. I fell, breaking my leg. I was completely helpless, so he brought me back to my cabin and set my leg. And he's agreed to escort me to England to meet my grandparents. You see, my mother and her parents had a falling out years ago, and from their letters they are desperate to see me. I think it's lovely of your son to bring me all the way from California, across an ocean, just so I can be with them."

The entire time Genny gave her speech, Madeline stared at her with a bemused look. And when she finished, she turned that bemused look to her son. "Yes," she said, "it is lovely of Mitch. And so altruistic, too." Genny let out a yawn. "It's been a long day, I do apologize."

"I think we'd better find a hotel, Miss Hayes," Mitch said. Nice hotels in New York were expensive, and he didn't want to have Genny stay in one of the lesser establishments where linens weren't changed regularly and the clients were less than savory. The five thousand dollars he'd taken out of his account represented all the money he had in the world. He still had to book passage to England for the two of them, and passage back for him. If he spent a hundred here and a hundred there, before he knew it, half his money would be gone. But he didn't mind spending a bit of money to avoid having Genny stay at a brothel, even if it was operated by his mother.

"Oh, nonsense," Madeline said. "I've closed down for a month in anticipation of your visit. I'm not worried a bit about losing clients; they'll be back." She smiled serenely. "Do you really think I'd continue operations with you here? What kind of a mother do you think I am?"

Mitch nearly choked, but valiantly remained silent.

"I've prepared a room for you," she said to Mitch. "It's a guest room, so you need not fear about other activities that may have taken place."

"I'll need two rooms, Mother," Mitch said, and almost begged his mother to react. He didn't much care for the women in his life thinking he would corrupt a young girl for his pleasure. Not that he hadn't thought about it, and dreamed about it, and made himself crazy wishing he was that sort of man. "If a room isn't available, I'll sleep on the couch here."

"I've plenty of rooms, Mitchell. I'll have Eileen make one up. I have the rooms cleaned and prepared after every client. No one shares bedding in my establishment. It's something my girls greatly appreciate. It's those little touches that separate us from the others. In the meantime, your friend can take a nap before dinner. I have one of the finest French chefs in the city, and he'd argue he's *the* finest. He wasn't all that pleased to learn I'm shutting down for a month, but I'm planning a few parties with my old friends from Niblo to appease him." She let out a light laugh.

Mitch smiled grimly, begrudgingly acknowledging that his mother looked well and seemed happy—far happier than he'd seen her look in quite some time. Growing up, he'd been subjected to the wild mood swings only an actress can have, moods that depended upon the roles, the audiences, the reviews. He'd spent his boyhood on edge, praying that she would get a standing ovation and dreading the door slamming following a poorly received performance. Still, he loved her. Who could not? She was charming and beautiful, and though she might not be the ideal mother, she'd done far better than some in similar situations.

Madeline rung a small bell and her maid appeared to escort Genny to her bedroom. "And please make up another room, Eileen."

The maid looked from Genny to Mitch in surprise, as if she'd never seen an unmarried man and woman who hadn't shared a bed.

Stifling another yawn, Genny left mother and son alone. And that's when the fun really began.

"Spill it."

Mitch was truly getting irritated by the fact everyone seemed to know him so well. He didn't even bother hiding the truth.

"Her grandparents are the Duke and Duchess of Glastonbury."

His mother smiled smugly. "Ah," she said, drawing out the word. "I see the apple doesn't fall far from the tree after all. I knew it had to be something. And you haven't . . ."

"No, Mother, I haven't. She is completely innocent and a very nice girl."

"That wouldn't stop most men. So, she's rich and you're hoping to collect a sizeable reward."

Mitch slumped back into the couch, annoyed by the fact the piece of furniture was so damned comfortable. "That was the original idea, yes. But now I feel obligated to bring her to her grandparents no matter what."

His mother gave him a look of pure disbelief.

"It seemed like a good idea at the time. Easy money. But it's starting to feel wrong somehow. She thinks I'm some sort of hero and I'm feeling lower than a snake."

"What a delightful drawl you've developed," she said, laughing lightly. "It's not like you're *stealing* money from her." Madeline, if anything, was always pragmatic. "And it is a bit of a gamble. Who's to say she is rich? Not everyone with a title is wealthy, you know. Why, we had a German duke here not six months ago and he tried to leave without paying his due. I had to have Martin rough him up a bit."

"Martin?"

"He's a large fellow I hired to make certain my clients stay in line. I rarely require his services. His presence alone keeps my clients well behaved. The duke claimed he was poorer than a church mouse."

"Perhaps he wasn't a duke, Mother."

"Oh, he was. There was an article in the *Times* about him. I was so honored that he picked my establishment, and then the cur refused to pay. Claimed his girl hadn't performed up to his standards. Well," she said with a scoffing laugh, "I knew that wasn't true. He'd been with one of the best, so he could hardly blame her for his . . . problems."

Mitch closed his eyes briefly. "Please, stop. And yes, I know it's a bit of a gamble, but it could also turn out to be a boon."

"Either way, that doesn't make you a bad person. You see? You *are* a hero, darling."

Mitch chuckled. Leave it to his brothel-running mother to convince him that what he was doing was right and good. "There is one thing I need your help with."

"Oh?"

"Genny, Miss Hayes, was brought up in a cabin in the woods. She has been nearly isolated and sure never spent any time with women. About the only thing cultured about her is her accent. She is a lady but she doesn't know quite how to act like one. You know the kind I'm talking about, those girls who walk up and down Fifth Avenue with their companions, with their fancy dresses and such. And that's New York. I can't imagine what girls are like in England. She doesn't know which fork to use or how to get in and out of a carriage without lifting her skirts up to her knees. She needs polishing."

Madeline looked first stunned, then touched. "And you think *I* can help?"

"You're an actress. You've *played* a lady. And isn't that what it's all about anyway? Acting proper?"

Madeline smiled. "Of course I'll help." She stood and walked over to him, placing a soft hand on either side of his face. "You turned out to be such a good man, Mitchell. I haven't a clue how it happened." Then she kissed his forehead and dropped her hands when Mitch furrowed his brow and shook his head. He had no idea what his mother was talking about.

"What do you care if she's well-received in England?" Madeline asked gently, still looking at him as if he was some kind of hero, not an opportunist. "You'll have done your job. As far as you're concerned, she's simply a package that needs delivering. Right?"

Mitch looked at his mother, his incredibly insightful mother, and shook his head again, but this time in acknowledgment. "So I like her. A lot. That doesn't change a damn thing."

"It changes everything, Mitchell. Everything."

Chapter 7

The next morning at breakfast, Mitch explained a bit of his plan to Genny, who'd spent the night in the most comfortable bed she'd ever slept in.

"My mother can help; she's an actress, and if anyone can help you know how to act around those fancy people, she can."

"Your mother is truly an actress?"

"Yes," Mitch said. "Lady Macbeth was her favorite role. See? She knows what it takes to be a lady."

"But Lady Macbeth was a horrible person," Genny said.

"Yes, but she was still a lady. I'm certain with Mother's guidance, you can succeed." Mitch gave her a dubious look, as if the thought of Genny ever being a lady was a farfetched idea indeed, and Genny wrinkled her nose at him.

"At the very least, I sound like a lady. Father always insisted on it."

"That you do," Mitch said. "With a pretty dress and your hair done up, you'll look like Lady Genevieve, not ordinary Genny. You'll see."

Genny rather liked the notion. At the moment, she was eating an omelet that was so good, she could hardly pay attention to the conversation.

"This omelet is wonderful," she said, slowly chewing.

Madeline smiled. "I'll let Monsieur Letourneau know. He trained in Paris, of course, and was a chef at Delmonico's. Speaking of which, I have an idea, Mitchell."

"I'm certain you do, Mother."

"I thought it would be a good idea for Genny to observe the patrons at Delmonico's. She'd learn far more there than I could ever teach her. Members of high society have a different way of acting, Miss Hayes, and I thought it would be good for you to take note. Of course, dining there yourself would be a good way, but getting a reservation is nearly impossible on such short notice. Unless your name is Vanderbilt or Rockefeller." She laughed, then explained, "They're richer than Croesus."

Genny looked from Madeline to Mitch, not quite understanding the need for her to watch a bunch of wealthy people eat their supper. "I imagine they eat food the same way we do," she said, putting another healthy forkful into her mouth. Mitch was trying not to smile, she could tell. "What?" she asked, the word slightly muffled.

"Your grandparents are rich, Genny, and the rich don't act like you and me," Mitch said. "They have a special way of doing things, a proper way. And they don't eat an omelet in thirty seconds."

Genny looked down at her plate doubtfully. She stabbed the last bit of egg and put it in her mouth. "I don't see how the process can vary all that much."

"It won't hurt to watch. I think those rich ladies wear gloves when they eat," Mitch said.

His mother interjected, "No, that's bad form. Ladies wear gloves at all times *except* when they eat."

"Is that right? Seems I can remember seeing—"

"Does it really matter?" Genny asked.

Mother and son turned to her, looking slightly dismayed.

"Of course it matters. How people perceive you greatly matters. A factory worker doesn't wear gloves. A lady does. And the finer the gloves, the finer the lady. When I walk into a glove shop on Fifth Avenue, I wear my finest pair or they look at me as if I'm someone who doesn't belong in their shop. In this part of town, I can wear any old thing."

Genny didn't own a single pair of gloves, but now that she thought about it, many women on the train had worn them constantly, taking them off only to eat or when they were crocheting. The sales clerk at the dress store had asked her if she wanted gloves and she'd declined, mostly because it was nearly summer and her hands weren't cold. She hadn't realized it was some sort of fashion accessory.

"I need gloves," she said, looking at Mitch.

"There's a lovely shop on Fifth Avenue," Madeline said. "Smythes. She'll have to be measured and the gloves made. If you go today, they should have them ready in a few days."

"See what I mean, Genny? I didn't know about this glove thing.

Who knows how those ladies act when they're eating," Mitch said, and it seemed to Genny that he was getting a bit worried about everything she had to learn.

"I suppose I should go then," Genny said, though she couldn't imagine what she would discover. Spoons were for soup, forks for meat, and everything went in your mouth. She had a sudden and strong urge to head back to her cabin, where she knew everything she needed to know. Although, she thought as she looked at her empty plate, if she went back, she surely would never get to eat another omelet like the one she'd just had.

It turned out that Mitch knew one of the restaurant's waiters and they would be able to slip in and out of Delmonico's easily. Even though they wouldn't be dining, Genny wore her finest dress, a new dress she'd bought on their trip to get her sized for gloves. It was a pretty dove-gray dress with lace at the sleeves, but showed a bit more flesh than Genny was used to. Madeline assured her she was completely respectable, especially as she was going out for the evening. She thought she looked quite dashing and sophisticated, and she knew she looked pretty by the way Mitch stared at her when she emerged from her room.

"The dress is pretty, but don't you need a shawl or something?" Mitch asked, his eyes darting briefly to her *décolletage*.

"It must be eighty-five degrees outside. I hardly think I need a shawl," Genny said.

"She's fine, Mitch. You're simply used to seeing her in those high-necked monstrosities you bought in California. This is New York."

Genny looked down at her rather unimpressive-looking chest and shrugged.

Delmonico's was New York City's premier restaurant. Located in a six-story triangular-shaped building on William Street, it had hosted such dignitaries as the Prince of Wales and Prince Arthur of Great Britain. Genny had never heard of either man, but Mitch explained they were great men from her parents' home country and there was little doubt her grandparents knew them. It was amazing to Genny to think her grandparents likely knew, and were perhaps friends with, two princes. Princes and princesses lived in fairy tales, not in any world that Genny knew.

"I know I've joked about marrying a prince, but do you really think I might get to meet one someday?" Genny asked.

"A prince is just a man in funny-looking clothes," Mitch grumbled.

Genny had wrinkled her nose at him. Ever since they'd arrived in New York, he'd been ornery. There was no hint of the man who'd looked in her eyes and told her he wanted to kiss her. No heated glances, no touching whatsoever; he hadn't so much as offered her his arm since their arrival. It was almost as if that man didn't exist and she was now keeping company with another man entirely. Genny supposed it was for the best. It would be far easier to say good-bye to New York Mitch than the one she'd spent time with on the trail and on the train. But she missed him and wished he'd kiss her at least one more time before she said good-bye. She couldn't help remembering every moment of their too-brief kisses, the way his mouth was somehow both soft and hard, the way he breathed when he lost a bit of control, the low rumble in his chest that she felt down to her toes.

Now, he was simply a man doing his duty—and a duty he didn't seem to be enjoying very much. She'd gone to the glove-maker and dressmaker with his mother while he went in search of old friends he hadn't seen in years and sent a telegraph to her grandparents to let them know she was alive and well and coming to see them.

As they made their way south toward William Street in a horsecar, Genny sat while Mitch stood, clutching a metal bar for stability. The car was not as crowded in the evening, but nearly every seat was taken. The sun was still up, but the sky was beginning to take on a late evening summer glow and the buildings kept them in the shadows most of the time. Mitch pulled the line that told the driver to stop, and they and several others stood to make their way off the car. Mitch went first, turning to hold up his hand so that she could safely descend. When her hand touched his, a shiver went through her so unexpectedly, she nearly stumbled.

"You should have worn a shawl," he said darkly, looking down the street.

"I'm not cold."

He grunted something under his breath and started off down the street, not bothering to see if she was following. She had half a mind to stay put, but she lifted her skirts and followed him, staring daggers at his back.

They walked for a time until they reached the front of the restaurant, where gleaming carriages pulled up and deposited the people from within. Genny had never in her memory seen such finery. The men all wore top hats, the women gowns of such intricacy, it was hard to believe they were made by human hands. Even the horses pulling the carriages wore fancy clothes, and Genny giggled at one particular pair of matching roans who were bedecked with large red plumes. Men in livery stood at attention outside the restaurant and bowed and opened the doors, ushering in the diners.

"The women look like they're floating," Genny said, watching with some awe as a woman about her age drifted from the carriage to the door effortlessly, almost as if she were being smoothly rolled through the door. For the first time, Genny felt a small niggle of worry. She was not like these women. Certainly, if she had a pretty dress and her hair had been done up, she could *look* like them. But she couldn't walk like them. Her skin wasn't white and smooth as porcelain. She'd spent years in the sun, and she had a sharp tan line at her neck. It had faded over the last few weeks, but it was still there, as was the line on her forearm where she'd rolled her sleeves up. She put a hand to her neck as if she might feel the telltale tan line there. These women with their bared arms had no lines, nothing but smooth, white flesh unmarred by the sun or scars. They all wore gloves, she saw, rubbing her own ungloved hands together and hoping no one noticed.

"They don't seem real," Genny whispered.

"They're not."

She looked up to see whether Mitch was smiling, but he looked angry, though Genny wasn't certain what was causing that expression. She started walking toward the entrance, but Mitch stopped her with a small touch to her arm.

"Come on. We have to go in at the back."

"Oh. Of course."

She followed Mitch around the building until they reached a high wooden fence with a locked gate. He knocked three times, and the gate swung open, revealing a dashing young man, his hair parted sharply in the middle and slicked back. He wore a vivid white shirt beneath a jacket and a large white apron that hung nearly to his well-shined shoes, the uniform of the waiters at Delmonico's.

"You owe me one, Mitch," the man said.

"I know, I know. We'll just stay for a bit. This here is Genny.

Genny, Jason. He's a top waiter here and he's doing us a big favor, letting us in."

Genny furrowed her brow. "Maybe we shouldn't do this," she said uncertainly.

"It'll be fine if you stay where I put you and don't wander off," Jason explained. "If the guests see you and complain, you'll be booted out before you can say you're sorry."

Mitch smiled down at her, a smile she knew was meant to relax her but did the opposite. "I really think this is the best way for you to learn. Lord knows I can't teach you anything about proper manners."

Was there really so much about the way rich people ate that was different from how she did? Genny's father had always made an effort to teach her manners, even when it was just the two of them They sat for dinner, said grace, and ate. She knew not to put her elbows on the table or eat with her fingers. And even though the two of them had on more than one occasion broken the rule about not wiping their plates with a thick chunk of bread, she knew not to do that in a restaurant. Mitch and his mother must think she was going to belch or throw food, for goodness' sake.

Jason led the two of them past a large garbage bin, causing several rats to scurry away, their little feet sounding overly loud in the alleyway and Genny pushed down a shiver. She didn't mind woodland creatures, the chickarees and bobcats, but rats with their long, naked tails made her skin crawl. The back door led to a hall, past a large kitchen where Genny caught a glimpse of young men wearing all white rushing about as if they were in a mad race. The smells that emanated from the cavernous room were heavenly, and even though Genny had already eaten, she wished she could sample some of the fare.

Jason stopped at a pair of swinging doors and looked through one of the small round windows. He jerked his head so the pair of them would follow him through the doors that led out into one of the restaurant's larger dining rooms.

"Here. If you don't wander about, no one should be the wiser." He'd led them to a half wall in front of which were several potted plants the likes of which Genny had never seen. Shiny green leaves larger than her head sprang from thick yellow-green stems. Genny peered through the leaves to see several diners quite close. She almost giggled and clapped a hand over her mouth.

"Genny, you stay here. I want to show Mitch our new card room. I'm in charge of a private room that won't have diners until nine and I've already gotten the room ready, so I have some time. You should be fine as long as you don't—"

"—wander about?" Genny said, completing his sentence.

Jason grinned, saying, "I just don't want you to get in trouble. Because if you do, I've never seen you before in my life. Understood?"

"Understood," she said.

"You'll be all right?" Mitch asked, which Genny found slightly patronizing. Why were they acting as if she was a child? She'd survived a winter alone in the wilderness; surely she could handle hiding behind a strange plant and watching people eat.

"As rain."

When Mitch gave her a puzzled look, she said, "Right as rain. It's an expression my father used to use all the time."

"Oh. I'll be back momentarily." He winked. "Don't wander."

Genny pretended to see something interesting and started to walk away, just to be contrary. Mitch wasn't particularly amused by her jest, so she wrinkled her nose and shooed him away.

When they'd gone, she turned her attention to the diners. Though the room was nearly filled, she could hear only a low murmur of voices and the soft clinking of cutlery on china. The round tables were covered with white tablecloths and glittering china and glassware. And the smells; she thanked goodness she wasn't hungry.

Not ten feet from her, two couples, a man and woman with silver hair and a younger pair were escorted to a table so close, Genny stopped breathing momentarily. If she'd wanted to, she could have reached out and touched the older woman's shoulder. As if choreographed, the men pulled out the women's chairs, and the two women sat, then drew off their gloves and placed them on their laps, covering the gloves with a napkin. Genny concentrated on the women, watching what they did, how they acted, thinking this was likely a waste of time. But within a few minutes, she began to get a sick feeling in her stomach, as if she were watching a complicated dance that she would be asked to replicate, knowing she would never be able to do so.

A waiter took their orders and returned quickly with some sort of soup. The women sat ramrod straight, taking delicate sips, bringing the spoon up to their mouths without bending their heads. And they weren't really sipping. They were pouring tiny portions into their mouths. Genny thought back on all the times she'd sat at the dinner table with her father and shoved the entire spoon into her mouth as she leaned over the bowl, and she could feel herself grow hot with something she had no name for.

To the left of their plates were five forks in five different sizes, to the right, three knives and various spoons. Everyone seemed to know which utensil was used for what, as if they were born knowing what they were. Genny watched, fascinated, as the girl, who appeared to be younger than Genny, delicately buttered her bread then took tiny bits of it between her thumb and forefinger and put it into her mouth. It seemed to take forever for her to chew the bread, and Genny wondered if it were particularly tough. It almost seemed to Genny that the young woman was counting out the number of chews each mouthful got. Tiny bite, twenty chews. Pause. Tiny bite, twenty chews. And when she spoke, she lay down whatever was in her hand, as if talking and holding utensils simultaneously was too difficult a task to master.

It was fascinating to watch her eat her dinner without ever bending her head to look at her plate. How on earth did she know what she was putting into her mouth if she didn't see what was on it?

As each course was completed, the four laid the utensil they'd held across the plate, the useful end of the tool facing right. Every diner did the same thing at about the same time. Then, following a course, they all lifted their water goblets and took a small sip. Genny was getting thirsty just watching them.

If this was how her grandparents ate a meal, she was doomed to disappoint them. "Manners separate the classes," Madeline had said, and Genny hadn't truly known what she meant. "If you're going to make a smooth transition into the highest levels of British society, you're going to at least try to fool them, my dear. It's all acting."

Genny couldn't help but think back on all the meals she'd had with Mitch, all the mistakes she had apparently been making. It was not only the way she ate, it was the way she saw the world, how she walked and talked and laughed. No one in this dining room was laughing. They smiled, or if a sound came out, it was quickly stifled with a pristine and starched napkin. When one man did laugh loudly, nearly every head turned, and every face held an expression of annoyance. Just thinking of sitting with her back that straight for so long was making her spine ache.

She was going to be a disappointment to her grandparents, the people who had written such heart-breaking letters. They had no idea of how she'd grown up, of how she could kill a snake, gut it, and eat it and think it was a grand meal. She could cut firewood and she had the callouses to prove it. They were fading, her hands growing softer, but her insides would never be soft. She'd never forget what it felt like not to eat for days simply because she hadn't killed something for her table. She'd been proud of what she'd done—and still was. But the gap between who she was and the girl she suspected her grandparents would expect was far wider than she'd realized. She'd imagined throwing herself into their arms, laughing with delight, but if her grandparents were like these people, she wondered if they'd even crack a smile.

The girl who sat at the dining table, with her intricately coiffed hair and a gown of the prettiest blue Genny had ever seen, was as foreign a creature to her as these strange-looking plants that were hiding her. The girl likely could play the piano and recite poetry, and no doubt had beautiful penmanship. That girl could easily enter the world of her grandparents.

Soft footsteps coming toward Genny startled her from her turbulent thoughts. She looked to her right to see a woman coming toward her, her dress clearly marking her as a guest.

"You, there. Where might I find the powder room?"

"I'm sorry, ma'am, but I'm not familiar with this restaurant."

The woman looked her up and down, obviously trying to assess who she was. "Are you not a servant here?"

"No, ma'am," Genny said, looking around for Mitch.

The woman stared at her a long moment, then turned and left Genny with her heart pounding madly in her chest. She didn't want Jason to lose his job for letting her in. Where was Mitch? The two of them had been gone for nearly a half hour. They'd told her to stay put, but Genny thought it would be best to leave the way she'd come in and was about to do so when a man, dressed in a fancy suit, walked quickly up to her.

"You do not belong here," he said, looking her up and down with obvious distaste. "Leave immediately or I shall call the police."

"I'm sorry, I . . . I was just watching people eat."

"And hoping to attract a customer, no doubt."

"A customer?" She had no idea what the man could mean.

"Don't play dumb with me, miss," the man said, looking pointedly at her chest.

Genny had a terrible feeling the man thought she was a soiled dove. "No, you're mistaken. I was just—"

The man grabbed her upper arm roughly and began leading her toward the back room. "How did you get in here, anyway? This is a fine establishment. A respectable one. And you can tell your friends to stay away, too."

He opened the door and pushed her roughly out, leaving Genny in the darkened alley, listening to the rustling sound of rats.

Hot tears filled her eyes as the man slammed the door shut. Never in her life had she been made to feel such humiliation. It was so beyond her experience, she was stunned. She looked down at the dress she'd thought was so pretty, and realized it was cheaply made and cut in a way that, while flattering, perhaps revealed too much of her shape. She'd thought her breasts were too visible, but Mitch's mother had explained it was quite respectable. Now she felt almost . . . dirty.

Genny pressed her back against the rough brick of the building, feeling angry and hurt. Where was Mitch? What was taking so long? She pressed the heel of her hands against her eyes to stop her silly tears, but they came anyway.

Finally, the door swung open and there he was, all anger and frustration. "Genny, we told you—." He stopped as if someone had placed a gag on his mouth. "What happened, darlin'?"

"Oh, Mitch," Genny said, and threw herself into his arms, letting herself cry against his warm jacket. He brought one hand to the back of her head and the other around her shoulders, pressing her close. "It was awful. A man threw me out. He thought I was a . . . a . . ." she said between hiccuppy sobs. "And the way he looked at me, it was as if I were not quite human. I thought this was a pretty dress, but it's not. It makes me look cheap, and my grandparents are going to think I look like a pro . . . pro . . . prostitute," she wailed.

She felt him chuckle and she made a fist and hit him softly on his chest. "They're not going to think you're a prostitute, darlin'. There's more good in your pinky than in most women's whole bodies. I shouldn't have brought you here."

She pulled back, looking up at him through tear-blurred eyes. "No, it was *good* that you brought me. I'm thankful you did. I can't imagine if I had shown up at my grandparents' door looking like this, thinking I looked p . . . pretty when I really look like a—"

"You don't," Mitch said forcefully. "And you won't."

Mitch wanted to punch something—hard—and figured that the maître d' who most likely tossed Genny out would be a good target. "Wait here, I'll be right back."

Genny grabbed his arm. "No, Mitch, let it lie. We were in the wrong. We weren't supposed to be in the restaurant in the first place. We were trespassing. The man was just doing his job."

Mitch pulled away and stalked back and forth for a bit while Genny watched, half bemused and half fearful he would go inside the restaurant and hurt someone.

"We're getting you nice dresses," he announced. "Like the ones those ladies in there are wearing. No one is ever going to look at you and think you're anything but a lady."

"The money . . ."

"Don't worry about the money. I have money, and dresses don't cost much." He placed two hands on either side of her face, his eyes troubled. "I can't stand to see you cry, darlin'. You know that. It makes me crazy."

"I'm sorry."

She gave him an impish smile, and he knew he was in trouble. He knew he was going to kiss her, right there in that dirty alley with the rats watching them. Hell, what was the point of trying not to when he knew he couldn't stop himself. For two days he'd been trying not to stare at her, not to touch her, not to even talk to her. But right now, with her looking up at him and smiling, tears still in her eyes, there was nothing left to do but lower his head and press his lips against hers. She sighed. God, he loved her sighs. He moved his hands slowly to the back of her head, loving how silky-soft her hair felt, how willing she was to kiss him back. He wanted to taste her, wanted to feel her tongue and deepen the kiss, and he resisted as long as he could. But when she wrapped her arms around his neck and tilted her head, he couldn't resist any longer.

"Open for me, darlin'. Let me taste you," he said, and when she did, even though she probably didn't know what she was doing, he thrust his tongue inside her lovely mouth, letting out a low moan of pure joy. It was clear Genny had never been kissed like that before, clear she didn't know quite what to do, so when she moved her tongue tentatively against his, he pulled her closer, letting her feel exactly what she was doing to him. God, this wasn't the time, wasn't the place, but he'd be damned if he would stop kissing her.

She let out the sweetest sound. He could only describe it as abandon, pure and lovely, and bringing the kiss to a level he'd never experienced with another woman. It was devastating, as though his heart was being torn in two at the same time his body throbbed with a need so strong it was unmanning. A rat scurried over his foot, and he thanked God for that rat, for if he'd continued kissing her much longer, he'd have done things no man should do to a good woman in an alley.

He pulled back, numb except for an insistent ache in his groin. *What the hell was he doing?*

He chuckled and shook his head. "I told you I hate it when you cry. And see? You stopped."

She looked up at him, dazed, eyes glassy now for a completely different reason, her lips slightly swollen from their kisses. It was all he could do not to pull her against him again. What was wrong with him? He'd never been the kind of man to lose control. All these foreign emotions roiling about in his head were making him crazy. He had to stop. It was only going to make it harder for both of them when he left her in England. He didn't like the way she was looking at him, all doe-eyed and woozy. And he didn't like the way he was probably looking down at her, like a man who needed more than a few kisses.

"Come on, let's go home," he said, more sharply than he'd meant. He softened his voice, adding, "We'll go looking for dresses tomorrow."

He held his arm out for her to take and you might have thought he'd handed her the moon, the way she smiled at him.

Louise Brunelle was one of the most sought-after couturiers in New York. She counted the likes of Mary Bishop, Caroline Astor, and Sarah McAllister as her regular clients. They flocked to her store, paid the exorbitant prices, because they all knew one thing: when you wore a gown she designed, you looked as beautiful as was possible. Her gowns were made of the finest silks, the softest wools, the most delicate lace. She embellished her creations with pearls, rubies, and amethysts, and once, for Mrs. Rockefeller, diamonds.

Though she'd claimed to have apprenticed under the famous Charles Worth, she had merely been a seamstress for the fashion giant. But she had learned quickly that her ambitions were nearly as high as her innate talent for knowing in one glance what cuts, colors, and fabrics would look best on a woman. Charles Worth may have been her inspiration, but her creations were all her own. When her husband died, leaving a small inheritance, she headed for America, where she knew she could bring high fashion to the nouveau riche. In the beginning, it was only her and one young seamstress carving their way into the highest levels of society. She rented in the poshest sections of the city and designed the interior of her shop to look like a wealthy lady's parlor. It took years of hard work, but it had now paid off. Her designs rivaled those of Worth and the women of New York were more than happy to pay her exorbitant fees to claim they were wearing a Brunelle.

When her head seamstress, Joanna, came to fetch her, saying that a man had come into the shop demanding an entire wardrobe for the granddaughter of the Duke of Glastonbury, she withdrew from her desk and followed the seamstress to the shop's main room, excitement churning in her chest. Her hopes were high—until she took one look at the pair. Then, she became annoyed. Clearly, this pair wouldn't be able to purchase a handkerchief in her shop, never mind an entire wardrobe.

The young lady, her golden hair braided and twisted into a simple bun, was pretty in a fresh, innocent way. She looked as if she'd just stepped off a train from out West. Even from across the room she could see that the dress she wore was ill fitting and cheaply made, no doubt sewn by a machine and designed by a blind man. The bodice was too tight, the waist too loose and the sleeves looked simply odd. She wore no hat and her hands were bare. He was wearing a linen jacket that had seen better days—and had probably never seen a valet—and pants that looked more suited to farm work than shopping in a store such as hers.

Still, she was bored and dealing with them should make for an interesting anecdote later on; the two country bumpkins on their first trip to New York. *Très amusant.* Trying to maintain a polite façade, she walked up to them.

Walking into that fancy shop on Fifth Avenue took more courage than Mitch would have believed. It was clear from the second he crossed the threshold, he was in the land of frivolous femininity. It wasn't just that he was the only male in the shop; it was that every bit of the place, from the ceiling with the pale pink medallions to the soft creamy carpet beneath his feet was meant to please a woman. It even smelled pretty, although that might have been the co-mingling of ten women's perfumes. And there were women—everywhere. Shopgirls and customers scattered about the large showroom, and no doubt more women were in the back being fitted. The women spoke in low murmurs, admiring lace and fashion plates, all the while casting curious looks in his direction. Mitch felt as out of place as a mouse in a room full of cats. He pulled on his collar, wishing mightily he was back in California wearing his loose-fitting shirt.

With a small squeal, Genny immediately went over to a display of fabrics, and Mitch followed her reluctantly.

"I do believe I've died and gone to heaven," Genny breathed, reaching out one finger to touch a navy blue velvet swatch.

"How may I help you?" The accent was French, the words filled with disdain.

Mitch turned to see a severe woman in her fifties, her black hair streaked with white and pulled up into an intricate design, looking at them in a way that was becoming all too familiar. Her expression was dismissive and arrogant as she moved her eyes over them. He'd worn his nicest suit, the one he wore when Mollie insisted he attend church with the Jackson family. He couldn't wait to show this French woman the wad of cash he had in hand. Then she'd come around and treat Genny the way she ought.

"My name is Mitch Campbell and this is Genevieve Hayes. Miss Hayes requires a complete wardrobe and I was hoping you could accommodate us."

The smallest of smiles touched the older woman's lips, almost as if she were acknowledging his effort to regain his footing. "I am Madame Brunelle and this is my shop."

"Genny, you wait here and look at the samples and I'll talk to Madame Brunelle." Genny nodded happily, excited to get on with the business of buying new dresses. It was all she could talk about that morning at breakfast, making Mitch feel a bit guilty about not getting her fancied up sooner. She looked just fine to him, but after what had happened in Delmonico's, he promised himself Genny would never feel the burning humiliation of feeling unworthy again. She immediately became entranced by the wide array of rich-looking fabrics and a mannequin wearing the most expensive-looking dress Mitch had ever seen. The pale yellow gown was decorated with seed pearls, all painstakingly sewn into a floral design. He might not know much about dresses, but he knew that one cost a pretty penny. He eyed the dress, wondering how many of that type of creation five hundred dollars would buy. Probably not as many as he'd thought.

Mitch led Madame Brunelle to a quieter corner. "That young lady," he said, nodding to where Genny stood, "is the granddaughter of the Duke of Glastonbury. I'm her guardian." He ignored Madame Brunelle's raised eyebrow, which instantly registered her doubt. "See, her mother ran away from home to marry a man and came to America, where Genny was born. She's an orphan now, and she promised her dying father that she would return to England. Thing is, she was living out West, in California, where there isn't much need for fancy dresses and hats and such. She's got a few dresses, but not what she should have. I don't want her grandparents thinking she's dressed like a maid. I want her to look like a lady."

Madame Brunelle stared at him a moment, her brown eyes showing little interest in his story. "You cannot afford my creations. I'm not saying this to be cruel. But it is clear you do not have the kind of money required to purchase even my simplest design."

Mitch smiled politely. He couldn't wait to see the expression on this woman's face when he told her he was prepared to spend five hundred dollars in her shop. It was a big part of his savings, but Mitch didn't care. He'd get it back when they reached England, and even if he didn't, it was worth it to him to see Genny looking the way she ought. He'd bought two dresses and more with twenty dollars. He figured he could outfit her quite nicely with five hundred. "Money isn't a problem," he said confidently, patting his jacket pocket.

Madame let out a beleaguered sigh. "*Tres bien.* What is your budget, sir?"

"Five hundred."

Madame's mouth dropped just slightly, and Mitch enjoyed a small surge of triumph. "Five hundred . . . thousand?" Madame asked, sounding both aghast and excited.

Mitch's surge of triumph started to deflate a bit. "Five hundred. Period."

Madame's polite façade returned, and Mitch had a feeling he'd underestimated the cost of a dress. "While that is a fine sum, I'm afraid in my shop it will not pay for more than one of my simplest gowns. Certainly not an entire wardrobe." She looked genuinely sorry, and Mitch felt like an ass. "Perhaps I can direct you to another shop where the prices are not so high. Of course, the dresses are not so beautiful, either, *oui*?"

Mitch looked over to Genny, who was being served by one of the seamstresses. She was holding up a deep green silk swatch and gazing in the mirror with a look of pure delight. Genny, who'd been wearing an old shirt and a pair of her father's pants when he'd met her, seemed to be taking to being a girl pretty quickly. And that green did amazing things for her eyes.

"Isn't it the most lovely fabric?" Genny asked, turning to show Mitch. "It feels lovely, too."

"The finest silk from China," the seamstress said, clearly trying to make a sale.

Mitch felt like punching something. He'd never seen Genny look so damned happy, and he was going to have to disappoint her. She deserved to have a dress made of that fine material. With her hair all done up, she'd look like a princess. He dipped his head a bit, bringing his attention back to Madame Brunelle, and said low, "How much would four thousand buy?"

Madame raised an eyebrow. "And you have that amount?"

Mitch swallowed and pushed down the sick feeling in his gut. It was a huge portion of his savings, savings he'd been squirreling away for years. If he spent all that, he'd barely have enough money for steamer passage, never mind enough to open his photography studio.

"She is a lovely girl," Madame Brunelle said thoughtfully.

"Yes, ma'am, she is." Mitch looked back at Genny, now delicately touching another sample.

"It would be a pleasure to design for her," Madame said, slowly. There was something in her tone that got Mitch's attention. "She would be spectacular. Of course, you will need to hire a lady's maid for her so that her hair complements the gowns. I assume she doesn't have one."

Mitch tightened his jaw, but had to admit Genny did not have a maid. "I wouldn't even know where to find one."

"I can help with that," Madame said, as if finding lady's maids for orphaned heiresses was something she did every day. "One more thing, Mr. Campbell, and this is most important. Are you truly her guardian? Or something . . . more."

"I guess I am. I found her all alone and hurt and agreed to take her back home."

"How altruistic of you."

Mitch let out a bitter laugh, knowing she saw a kindred spirit. "She's the granddaughter of a duke," he said, as if that explained what he was doing. Sadly, it was explanation enough for Madame Brunelle.

"I wouldn't want to have one of my creations on a woman who, shall we say, was not of the highest society."

Her inference made Mitch angry, but he understood it. "She is the granddaughter of a duke. And I'm a man who needs money."

Madame Brunelle looked him in the eye. "You are telling me the truth?"

"I can show you a letter from the duke himself, if that would help. Now, can you make a few dresses for her or not?"

Madame looked over at Genny again, clearly assessing her. "She's never met her grandparents?"

"No. They sent letters to their daughter, begging her to come home. And Miss Hayes's father's final wish was that she go to England. I even have a telegram from them saying they are anxious to meet her."

A small smile appeared on Madame's lips. "They shall be quite happy to see her, to introduce her to society. They'll throw dinners and balls and . . . yes, Monsieur Campbell, I will make your Miss Hayes dresses. In fact, I will make her the most beautiful dresses I have ever created."

Madame took a deep breath and called Genny over. "Miss Hayes, I have agreed to make your entire wardrobe at a very reasonable price."

Genny looked at Mitch and smiled, clutching her hands together and reminding Mitch of a child who's been promised a special dessert after supper. She looked so damned adorable at that moment, Mitch probably would have agreed to anything.

"I ask only one thing," Madame said. "When someone comments favorably on one of your dresses, you are to say this: 'It was designed by Madame Brunelle of New York City, the premier couturier in all of America.' Can you do that?"

Genny smiled. "Of course I can. And surely if your creations are anything like the one in your window, I'll only be speaking the truth."

Madame smiled fully for the first time. "How delightful of you to say. So, it is agreed. You see, Miss Hayes, more and more British ladies come to New York every year, but my shop has not yet been recognized. They continue to purchase their gowns from Worth or a local seamstress. I want them to come to me. I want them to know that I am the premier dressmaker in the world. And you are my means of achieving this."

Genny looked a bit taken aback. "But no one knows me in England."

"They will," Madame Brunelle pronounced grandly. "You are the lost granddaughter of a duke and duchess. You will be the talk of London, of all Britain."

"I will?" Genny looked more frightened than flattered.

"Don't worry, Miss Hayes," Mitch said. "Your grandparents won't introduce you into society until you're ready."

"But I don't even know how to sit," she said in a small voice.

"We'll get you a tutor. We'll get you ready," Mitch said. He hated seeing her so uncertain. "You're the girl who stopped a train robbery. You sure as hell can learn how to sit."

Genny laughed, and Mitch felt he'd made the world right somehow.

"Miss Hayes, you go on over to Miss Joanna and we can start selecting fabrics," Madame said. When Genny was gone, Madame said, "You do have four thousand, do you not?"

"I do."

"And the letter and telegram from the duke?"

"I'll bring them tomorrow."

"Then I will make Miss Hayes a wardrobe that will be the envy of every girl in England. You will be getting far, far more than four thousand dollars' worth of clothing, Mr. Campbell, but I'm hoping our relationship will be mutually advantageous."

"That is very kind of you, Madame."

"I am not doing this because I am kind, Mr. Campbell. I am doing this because I am the best dress designer in the world. She will be a wonderful advertisement for my shop. We are very much alike, you and I, Mr. Campbell. And if it weren't for the way your eyes soften when you look at her, I might even believe you are only doing what you are doing for the money. Amour, Mr. Campbell. It's a curse."

Mitch just chuckled and shook his head. "I'm counting on getting a nice return on my investment, Madame, and sure as sure, love's got nothing to do with it."

"Perhaps I am wrong," she said with a shrug. "My husband, God rest his soul, was a gambler. A bad one." She gave him another long assessing look, as if she could see into his heart and watch it lurch crazily each time he glanced at Genny. "If I were you, I'd stay away from the cards."

Genny loved dresses. She loved silk and light wools and crinolines and bustles and hats and gloves and lace and everything that went into looking like a lady. It was almost as if she was born to wear such lovely creations as Madame Brunelle was designing. She even loved the corsets that made the dresses look perfect. It was only at night when she was finally alone, that she thought about her old life: the struggles, the hunger. And she thought about what a miracle it had been that she'd found Mitch, who had brought her to this world she was coming to believe she was born to. It was almost as if she had memories of balls and elegance locked away inside her, though that was impossible. Perhaps her mother had told her stories when she was very young, stories she couldn't recall but were buried in her mind. As each day passed, she grew more and more excited about meeting her grandparents. The only thing that darkened her thoughts was the thought of a tall man with piercing blue eyes.

In the days that followed, Mitch kept his distance, allowing Genny and his mother free rein with colors and fabrics. Genny made nearly a daily trek to The House of Brunelle, returning exhausted but utterly happy. If she could have swum in the clothes, she would have done so. And the shoes and the hats and everything else that went along with being a lady. It would not be a complete wardrobe—they'd decided a riding habit was not necessary—but would contain all the basics of what a young British lady should have. Most important was the ball gown, the dress Genny would be wearing when she was introduced into British society. Though Mitch had been absent from most of the fittings, Genny insisted that he be on hand to see this particular gown.

He sat outside the fitting room waiting for Madame to reveal what she called her most beautiful creation. He could hear the murmur of voices in the next room as Genny was put into the dress, and he again was reminded that Genny would require some sort of lady's maid to accompany her.

"*Mon dieu,* Mr. Campbell," Madame said, opening the door to allow him in, "you must force this girl to eat more."

She backed away with a flourish, revealing Genny standing on a small platform, staring at her reflection in a mirror with an expression something between disbelief and awe. Mitch thanked God she hadn't seen the look on his face when he'd first walked in, because he was fairly certain every emotion he'd been bottling up inside for the past few weeks would have shown clearly on his face.

She wore a spectacular gown of deep green with cream lace accenting a tiered skirt and a dark brown velvet underskirt. Mitch wouldn't have thought to put the two colors together, but the results were stunning. Tiny seed pearls decorated the bodice, which exposed the smooth expanse of her chest, just hinting at her décolletage. Holy God, she was beautiful.

Just before she looked through the mirror at him, he schooled his features, trying hard to make certain she didn't see the raw need in his eyes. He chuckled and said, "She's gained a few pounds since I found her." It might have come out hoarser than he'd intended, but he silently congratulated himself on how calm he sounded. Not like a man who felt he was standing on the edge of a cliff with a strong wind at his back buffeting him.

"I wasn't a very good hunter, you see. My father did most of the hunting and I did the cooking."

"Hunting!"

Genny grinned. "I was rather good at catching snakes."

"I think this is something that should be kept to yourself," Madame said, walking briskly over to her and putting a final pin into a delicate cap sleeve. "Ah, *c'est manifique,* no? So beautiful. What do you think, Monsieur?"

Genny turned to show Mitch the dress and she saw he wore the same uninterested look she'd seen for days. All she could think about was that kiss outside Delmonico's, but apparently he had forgotten all about it. Men were strange creatures, Madeline had told her, able to find pleasure without feeling emotion. Mitch had seemed to have emotion that night, but perhaps in her inexperience she'd confused lust with something more. He had apparently forgotten all about it, but Genny couldn't stop thinking about how his tongue had moved against hers, how his hands had captured her head as he drew her against him, how long and strong he'd felt pressed up against her. She couldn't stop herself from looking at his lips, which only produced a frown from him. It was almost as if he were angry all the time. If he hadn't been so attentive during her lessons on comportment, she would have thought him completely uninterested in her. Genny didn't understand how he could so quickly forget a kiss that had been so devastating to her.

Genny knew she was all spoony when she was around him, and though she tried not to be, she couldn't help it. Every time she was near him, she felt strange, as if her skin were fizzy. One time, as he was walking toward the breakfast table, she'd felt such a wave of desire, she'd almost gasped aloud. Just from looking at him!

When she'd first met him, she'd thought Mitch looked like every other man she'd ever seen—big and hairy and a little scary. But now, she couldn't help noticing how blue his eyes were, how thick and wavy his hair was, how the strong line of his jaw looked so much better when he'd just shaved. When she saw him standing next to other men, it was impossible not to notice how much more, well, manly he was compared to everyone else.

"She looks fine," Mitch said, giving her a cursory glance.

"Fine? *Fine?* Monsieur, when a woman this beautiful is standing before you wearing so magnificent a dress, you do not say she looks fine. *Mon dieu.*"

Mitch swiped a hand through his hair and glared at Madame, who had the oddest smile on her lips. "Pretty. She looks pretty. Too pretty, if you ask me."

"A bit better, sir, but still a dismal attempt at flattery."

Too pretty. Why, that was the nicest thing Mitch had ever said to her, though Genny wasn't quite certain what he'd meant.

"She will certainly attract a great deal of male attention," Madame said thoughtfully. "Ah, I wish I could be there to witness it. The men will be in a frenzy to meet her, to dance with her. To *marry.*"

"I sure hope so," Mitch said, though by his expression it didn't look as if the thought pleased him.

Madame chuckled. "I think he will be jealous of all that male attention. What do you think, Miss Hayes?"

"I won't be there to witness it," Mitch said, turning abruptly and walking from the room, not looking back even when Madame let out a light-hearted laugh.

Madame fussed with the dress a bit more before saying, "I think your Mr. Campbell will not like seeing any man dance with you."

Genny furrowed her brow. She hadn't really thought about the dancing part of a ball, and now a small bit of panic flooded her. "I don't know how to dance, so he'll hardly have a chance to see me dance at all. Even if he were to stay on for a while."

"Oh, he will," Madame said knowingly. "But Miss Hayes, this is a terrible oversight. You must know at least some dances. The waltz, the polka, *non*?"

Genny shook her head. "Not one."

"Mr. Campbell," Madame Brunelle called out. "I need your assistance."

Mitch returned, looking as though he wished he were anywhere else but where he was.

"You need to hire a dance instructor. It is a terrible oversight. Miss Hayes does not know how to dance. Standing at a ball wearing this," she said, indicating the dress, "is all well and good, but it is made for dancing." She instructed Genny to turn. "You see? The movement? The beauty. *Mon Dieu*, this dress was made for the ballroom. It would be tragic if she could not dance."

"I'm not going to hire a dance instructor," Mitch said, sounding almost angry.

"It's all right," Genny said. "The expense. I am so indebted already to Mr. Campbell. I could never expect him to spend even more money on a dance instructor."

Mitch muttered beneath his breath. "I don't need to hire a dance instructor because I can teach her to dance."

"Monsieur, while I think this is very generous of you, perhaps you don't realize the intricacy of some dances. She won't be attending a country dance, but a ball in London. You will arrive while the Season is still in full swing, will you not?"

"I know how to dance," Mitch said. "My mother was an actress. She had to dance all the time and I was her partner. Hell, I probably could have made a living teaching debutantes to dance. I can teach Miss Hayes enough to get by."

Genny smiled uncertainly. Mitch was making the offer, but he did it in the same way a man agrees to share his meal when he really doesn't want to. "You don't have to. Certainly my grandparents will—"

"I said I'd teach you and I will. Don't want some stranger teaching you anyway. Likely to do it wrong."

"Well, that's lovely," Genny said.

Madame gave Mitch a look Genny couldn't understand. It seemed to be pity.

Chapter 8

"We can't give the girl a lifetime of polishing in two weeks, Mitchell," Madeline said, looking exhausted, her cheeks flushed from the exertion of showing Genny how to walk across the room. Used to the forest and trails, Genny had a tendency to walk, well, like a man, Madeline explained.

"I suppose I walk like my father."

"Yes, and that is all well and good when you are in the woods, but you are headed to London, where you will be expected to know how to walk like a lady."

Genny gave Mitch, who was looking as if he was trying not to smile, a desperate look.

"Hell, if they can't accept her the way she is, they have no business inviting her in the first place."

Genny stood, hands on hips, and walked over to him, all thoughts of grace far from her mind. "You listen here. You're the one who thought I could use some polishing, and you were right. I want my grandparents to be proud of me, not horrified. Do you remember when I climbed up onto that train? Remember how you said I had to learn how to do all manner of things so I wouldn't be immediately marked as something other than a lady?"

Genny walked over to a settee and slumped down onto it, completely unaware that slumping was completely off limits to a lady. Madeline looked pointedly at Genny, then looked at her son and shook her head. She threw up her hands. "It's impossible."

"No, it isn't. She's smart. She can do this." Mitch turned to Genny, smiling the way a man smiles at a man holding a gun on him. "Darlin', see the way you're sitting there right now?"

Genny looked down at herself, seeing nothing wrong. Her skirts were covering her ankles.

"You're slumping, dear," Madeline said. "Ladies never slump."

Genny immediately straightened, forcing a chuckle from Mitch. "You have to admit she's trying," he said.

"Yes, I try but it's so much to remember. And I can't even walk yet!" Another chuckle from the maddening man. "Stop laughing. I'd like to see you try to walk like a lady and sit like a lady and eat like one. It's more difficult than you think, especially when I'm used to trudging around a forest."

Mitch only grinned at her, then said to his mother, "Should I show her?"

Madeline shrugged, and before Genny's eyes, Mitch changed. It was purely the most amazing thing Genny had ever seen in her life. Mitch was gone, replaced by . . . someone else altogether. His chin went up, his back became rigid, his eyes frosty. He walked to the tea set that Madeline had been trying to show her how to use (apparently pouring tea properly was the mark of a true lady) and expertly poured a small cup of tea before delicately lifting it up to his lips. "Nothing better than a fine cup of tea," he said in a rather high-pitched feminine voice.

Madeline clapped, delighted by her son's performance, and Genny sat there, mouth open. How on earth had Mitch, with all his masculinity, managed to be more of a lady than she was? If he'd been wearing a dress she would have thought him a rather ugly woman.

In seconds, Mitch was back, laughing, his blue eyes crinkled. "See darlin'? It's just acting, just pretend. Now, pretend you're a lady and eventually, it'll be second nature. Ladies don't laugh out loud or show strong emotion or let people know what they're thinking. Pretend you're a statue that can move."

Genny frowned. "That's horrible. If that's what it takes to be a lady, then I'm not so certain I want to be one anymore."

"My thoughts exactly," Mitch said, again sounding slightly angry.

"If it weren't for my grandparents, I wouldn't care. But I do care what they think of me. How could I not? And to be honest, I care what they think about my father. They'll blame him, you know, if I come up short. In a way, they'll be right. He never thought I'd end up going back to England. Learning all this stuff about walking and talking like a lady didn't make much sense in that cabin we were living in. But now . . . now I have to learn. I *have* to. I love my father and he wanted me to go to England. And I want them to be proud of me, to not have a single bad thought about the man who took their daughter away from them. Can you understand that?"

Mitch's gaze softened, and his mother let out a sound of commiseration. "Of course I understand. Now, let's take one thing at a time. Let's practice sitting."

"Sitting?" Genny repeated, and nearly burst out laughing. "I don't *sit* correctly?"

"Not hardly." Mitch thought on it for a while, then said, "Pretend there's a string attached to the very top of your head. The other end of the string goes through a pulley, and I'm holding it. Now, if I were to let go of that string, you'd plop right down on that couch. Just like you did a minute ago. But if I were to gently lower you, you'd go down slow and graceful. That's what you need to do. Pretend I'm holding that string and letting you fall slowly."

"Mitch, you are a genius," Madeline said. "I see you have this well in hand. If you don't mind, I have to go over my accounts to see how much longer I can remain closed. I've started getting some letters from my regular clients and they are quite losing their patience with me."

After Madeline left, Genny stood, then slowly sat, wobbling only a little and clutching the edge of the couch to steady herself.

"Again. And this time when you sit, put your hands like this in your lap." Mitch held his hands together to show her.

Genny stood, then sat, this time without the wobble. "Again." And again and again until Genny could feel her thighs start to ache from all the sitting and standing.

Throughout the afternoon, she practiced walking and sitting, all under the watchful and thoughtful gaze of Mitch. He was patient with her, and the two of them fell into laughter more than one time when he turned into Lady Mitchell and showed her how it was done.

"Pretend everyone you meet is part of the audience and you have to trick them into believing you are a lady. If you never break character, you will never be found out."

"I think I shall very much like it when I finally get to go into my room so I can relax my spine Not that these corsets allow for much bending of the back. Do you know, when I first wore one, the one that goes with that blue gown? I wondered how on earth I'd be able to start a fire. And then it occurred to me that I probably won't have to start a fire ever again."

Suddenly, Genny felt like crying. It was all too much and she missed home. She missed her father and the way he'd smell of the outdoors when he'd come back from hunting. She missed the warmth of the cabin when the fire was high, the way her muscles felt after she'd chopped some wood, the sense of satisfaction she got when she not only hunted for her meal, but returned, prepared it, and ate it. She missed her father's twinkling eyes and the rare times when he'd talk about her mother. She missed the smell of the pines and the sound of the owls hooting mournfully at night.

Genny looked down at her pretty gown, realizing how ungrateful she would sound if she told anyone about her thoughts. Here she was in an exciting city getting ready to travel across the ocean to meet her duke and duchess grandparents, and all she could think about was how she'd likely never eat another bit of dried venison. At least not from a deer that her father had killed.

"Hey, darlin', what's wrong?"

She wasn't crying, but Genny suspected her eyes were getting a bit misty. Then, dash it all, her eyes welled up and suddenly she *was* crying.

"What's wrong?" Mitch asked, real concern in his voice now, and he took a tentative step toward her as if he wasn't certain whether he should embrace her or not. Genny solved that dilemma by launching herself toward him. He held his arms out for a moment before she finally felt them wrap around her, and nothing had ever felt so wonderful and safe in her life.

"I'm just feeling sorry for myself. I'm tired and I started thinking about Yosemite and my father and everything I'll never do again. And I'm wondering if all this is pointless, if they'll take one look at me and send me packing."

Mitch smoothed a hand up and down her back. "Part of me hopes they do," he said so quietly, Genny wasn't certain whether she'd heard him right.

She pulled back. "What do you mean?"

Mitch dropped his arms and stepped away, and the loss of his warmth, even though she wasn't cold, was stunning. "It's just that we don't know what kind of people they are other than the fact they wouldn't let your mother marry the man she loved. Just makes me think. Your mother must have either been very brave or very stupid to do what she did. Love can make a person do things they oughtn't."

"I don't think she was stupid, just in love. Have you ever done anything stupid for love?"

Mitch gave her a long, level look. "Not yet. Haven't been cursed with that particular emotion."

"No?" Genny said, feeling a silly surge of happiness that he'd admitted to never being in love. A surge that was just as quickly replaced with disappointment when she realized that meant he didn't love her, either. Which was a silly thought and useless. What would be the point of either of them loving the other when they would say good-bye in a matter of two weeks?

Mitch had booked passage on the steamship *Oceanic*, which would reach London on July nineteenth, weather permitting. They would depart New York on the eleventh, only five days away. Mitch explained he would purchase her a first class ticket and that she and her maid would be two floors above where he would be sharing a room with three other men in third class. It would be difficult, he said, for them to see one another, for third class passengers weren't allowed on the first class deck and first class passengers would never venture to third.

Which meant she really only had five days to spend with Mitch. What would be the point of letting her heart do what it so desperately wanted to do? Not that she'd been very good at stopping it. Genny had never been in love and couldn't recall her parents together. She had vague memories of laughter, of her mother playing a piano and her father singing by her side. But she'd been so young, she didn't think of them as a couple in love; rather they were her parents who loved her.

What did one feel like when one was in love? If it was this silly, spoony feeling she got whenever Mitch walked into a room, then perhaps, yes, she was in love. She didn't want to think about saying good-bye, knowing she would likely never see him again.

Mitch walked over to a window that overlooked the back garden. It was raining, the wind making the drops splatter against the pane, disrupting the smooth rivulets that streamed down to the sill. His face held the shadows of those drops. "Love isn't always a gift," he said finally.

"I suppose it can hurt. When someone dies or leaves."

"Yes, like that."

Madeline returned, stopping at the entrance and looking at the two of them curiously, noting they were on opposite sides of the room. "Have you two been quarreling? I'll have none of that. We've too much work to do."

"Oh, no," Genny said. "We're simply getting philosophical about the meaning of life."

Mitch looked at her curiously, wondering why she hadn't said what they were really talking about. He'd been so wrapped up in his own troubling emotions, he really hadn't thought about her. He knew she was likely developing a crush on him, but he figured it was something fleeting, as fleeting as their time together. Now he wondered if she was feeling as torn as he was about saying good-bye. And he was torn. He'd die before saying anything aloud, but he was at least man enough to admit to himself that he loved her. God, he loved her so damn much it hurt just to be in the same room with her and not be able to tell her, to show her. It was futile and maybe that's what hurt the most. He'd never be able to tell her how much he loved her, never be able to show her. Never hold her all night, feel her move against him. Never hear her come, never know what it was like to slide inside her and find heaven on earth.

Never marry her. Never see what their children would look like.

Damn, it hurt. Nothing had ever hurt like this. Love, a blessing? Hardly. It was a curse and one he wished he had the strength to vanquish. Lord knew he'd tried. He'd tried to stay away, but apparently he was a weaker man than he'd thought. He'd hear her laugh and be pulled into the room where she was, and he'd be tickled about something that he'd hadn't thought was even funny. Until now.

"I think she's worn out. I was going to start our dance lessons today, but I guess we're both done in. Genny, why don't you walk over to that couch and take a seat." He gave her a wink so that she knew she should act like a lady.

She lifted her chin slightly, then moved over to the settee as if gliding upon the carpet. With a graceful turn, she slowly lowered herself onto the seat, gently clasping her hands in front of her and smiling just enough to look pleasant.

"Oh, brava," Madeline said, clapping. "A wonderful performance, Miss Hayes. Mitch, I swear, you missed your calling. To have produced a performance like that in such a short time." Madeline walked over to her son and kissed each cheek. "All of this makes me wish I could still be in the theater, but alas, I fear that ship has long since sailed. Do you know I actually found a whisker on my chin the other day? A whisker! It's a curse to grow old."

"You're not old, Mother."

"I'm nearly fifty."

"You don't look a day over forty," Mitch said grandly. The truth was, his mother did look young for her age, but that was likely because she knew how to apply makeup artfully.

Madeline waved a dismissive hand at her son, but she was clearly glad to hear his flattery.

"Are you certain you want to put off the dance lessons?" Madeline asked. "That only leaves four days until you depart, and that's hardly enough time."

"It'll have to do, Mother. She's exhausted and her leg's been bothering her a bit today. Probably the rain."

Genny looked up, no doubt surprised that he'd noticed. He noticed everything, from her flushed cheeks to the slightest wince when she stood too quickly.

"I have the most delightful news," Madeline said. "I've found you a maid."

Mitch loved his mother, but he also knew her well enough to know that the slight tingling of unease he was feeling was completely justified. "Where did you find her, Mother?"

"Oh, stop looking at me like that. Do you really think I'd hire one of my girls to be her maid? Really, Mitchell, have more faith in your dear mother."

"I apologize," Mitch said, not meaning a single syllable. "Who is she?"

"She works at the Niblo in the costume department." Madeline threw up a hand to stop him from protesting. "She's a genius with hair, she can dress Miss Hayes in a trice, and she's an aspiring actress."

Mitch had to admit the girl sounded as if she could do the job, at least until Genny's grandparents got her a real lady's maid. But something about his mother's demeanor was still making him nervous. "There's more. Tell me, Mother."

"You can imagine a young girl doesn't want to be away from home. She is doing me a huge favor. She wants one hundred dollars."

Mitch felt a slight sick twist in his stomach. When he returned to New York, he'd be dead broke at this rate. "One hundred. For a maid? That's more than a year's salary."

"For a woman *pretending* to be a maid. That's much more difficult to find."

"Then I'll just hire a *real* maid," Mitch said.

"I don't need a maid," Genny said.

"Yes, you do," Mitch and his mother said in unison.

"Darling, you'd never find a real maid on such short notice, not one willing to move to England, for goodness' sake. Tillie is perfect. She knows it's a short-term role and she's excited about seeing London. She has an adventurous spirit and is perfect to play the part."

Mitch took a deep breath. "It's not a part, Mother, it's a job."

Madeline waved her hand as if it didn't matter, and Mitch was starting to believe it wouldn't.

"I'll introduce you to her tomorrow. She wants half now and half when she's in England. And you have to pay her passage, of course."

"I know." Mitch wasn't much a praying man, but he was starting to pray that Genny's grandparents were very grateful to see their granddaughter delivered safe and sound.

Mitch sat at the piano, pounding out a polka as Madeline attempted to teach Genny the basics of the dance. As a child, he'd often played the piano while his mother's friends danced, so even though he hadn't played in years, his skills came back quickly.

The two women stumbled across the makeshift dance floor, Genny's face full of determination, Madeline's full of amusement. Finally, Madeline stopped, her face a bit red.

"It's no use, Mitchell. I don't know how to lead and I'm already tired. I'm not used to this type of activity, you know. I've become a lady of leisure. You're going to have to take over. I don't understand why you didn't dance in the first place."

Mitch folded his arms over his chest and looked at his mother skeptically. "Because I'm a better piano player," Mitch said. Though it was a true statement, it was nowhere near the real reason he'd sat behind the piano rather than dance. His mother was either completely oblivious to his feelings toward Genny or, worse, was trying to foster them. Either way, it would be painful to dance with Genny, knowing he would never truly have the privilege. That would go to men with "lord" before their names. And that's the way it should be, he reminded himself brutally.

"Shoo. I'll play," Madeline said, waving her hands at him.

Mitch reluctantly stood and stared at Genny, who looked at him expectantly. God help him, he just couldn't stop his heart from picking up a beat every time he looked at her. What would it be like to hold her in his arms?

"The polka simply requires you to keep up with your partner," Mitch explained. "It's one and two and one and two." He demonstrated by taking a step with his left foot, then bringing his right foot even with the left, and taking another step with his right.

"See? It's almost like skipping."

Genny watched, a small furrow between her brows. She looked positively adorable as she gazed up at him as if he'd just shown her something terribly complicated. She wore one of her simplest new gowns, a high-necked soft blue muslin that fastened up the front with mother-of-pearl buttons. Madame Brunelle was a genius, for even this simple and chaste creation showed off Genny's figure to perfection, making her waist seem even tinier and her small breasts somehow larger. He tried not to let his thoughts go in that particular direction, but it was nearly impossible, especially when he laid his hand at her waist and instructed her to place her left hand on his shoulder.

"Go on and play, Mother."

What Madeline lacked in skill, she made up with enthusiasm, and the two were soon dancing across the large living room where they'd pushed aside the furniture to create a makeshift dance floor. Genny stumbled, his firm hand on her back keeping her steady, but before long, she was dancing rather than being dragged around the floor.

"Oh, this is fun," she exclaimed, bouncing along with him as if she'd been dancing all her life. He twirled around the floor, and she kept up with him easily, her right hand gripping his tightly. And then she started laughing, so hard, she could no longer continue to dance.

He couldn't help it; he started laughing too, even though he didn't know why the two of them were laughing like a couple of people gone mad. Madeline sat back with a bemused expression as Genny wiped at a tear, still trying to control her mirth.

"A much better reason to cry," Mitch said softly, dropping his hands. "What did you find so funny?"

"It wasn't that something was amusing. It's difficult to explain. I've never danced in my life and there I was, dancing across the floor as if it were nothing. It just made me so happy it bubbled out as laughter."

"All the dances won't be nearly as easy," Mitch said.

"The waltz is next, I think," Madeline said. "Coming from America, she can decline to dance the quadrille or some of the more complex dances; no one will think badly of her if she doesn't know them. But she must know the waltz and perhaps a reel. A *schottische*?"

"Not a *schottische*. It's too complicated. If we have time and she's mastered the others, we can move on to that."

"Oh, posh. Look how quickly she took to the polka."

Genny adored the waltz. She'd never felt so feminine in her life as she did in Mitch's arms as they moved around the small dance floor. The way he made her go in the direction he wanted by applying the slightest amount of pressure to the small of her back was thrilling.

"When you waltz, you are expected to have some sort of conversation," Madeline called out. "Something to draw a man's interest. I played a part once where I had to speak dialogue the entire time I was dancing. Do you remember that, Mitchell? He was just twelve years old and I made him practice and practice so that I could get my lines in before the song ended."

Mitch smiled at his mother while continuing to lead Genny around. "I remember how frustrated you were. 'Mr. Browne, please tell me how you like our fair town?'"

Madeline laughed, and ceased playing, shaking her hands out as if they were sore. Mitch stopped dancing and immediately dropped his hands and stepped back.

"You remember that play?" Madeline asked.

"I do believe I could recite not only your lines but Mr. Browne's as well. Perhaps Genny could memorize a play to help her along." He gave her a wink, but that did nothing to allay a new worry. She moved off the dance floor and sat down, twisting her hands together. She was going to have to talk to these men while she danced? Wasn't dancing difficult enough? Now she'd have to be interesting and witty. What on earth should she say to them?

"What sorts of things does one talk about?" she asked Madeline.

"Ask them about themselves. Men adore discussing anything that has to do with their lives. Watch." Madeline moved in front of Mitch. "Tell me about your country home, Lord Campbell."

Mitch smiled slightly. "Why, it's ten million acres of the finest farmland in the world," Mitch said grandly, putting on a cultured English accent. "My home, or should I say, my palace, has five hundred bedrooms and my stable houses one hundred of the finest steeds in all of Britain."

"My goodness, Lord Campbell. How on earth do you manage such an estate? Quite impressive."

"I daresay, I cannot do it alone. My one thousand servants do help out a bit."

Madeline dissolved into laughter, clearly delighted with her son's banter. Genny laughed too, but she was not finding their play nearly as amusing as they did. The closer she got to actually making the trip to England, the more nervous she felt. Lately, she would lie in bed at night and try to recall anything her mother had said about her life before America, but all Genny had were vague memories of stories that might not even be true.

As a child, Genny had adored tales of princesses, and her mother would indulge her nearly every night. It was one of the few strong memories she had of her mother, of those drowsy moments before sleep when her mother would read to her or make up stories as she went. The made-up ones had been her favorites, for she liked to think they weren't just stories, but adventures that had actually happened. She knew that sometimes her mother would talk about people she'd known, as well as her parents, but now Genny couldn't separate the stories from the true tales of her mother's youth. All she did remember was that her grandparents lived on a large estate in Cumberland with a big lake where black swans swam during the summer. She remembered this only because her mother had been afraid of the swans and Genny had thought a black swan was such an exotic creature. All the swans she had ever seen had been white as snow. After her mother had died, Genny had tried to get her father to tell her more about England, but the conversations always left him so sad, she stopped asking after a time.

Genny could hardly bring herself to smile; their banter only show-cased how little she knew of what was to be her new life. She walked over to one of the couches pushed up against the wall and sat, chin on her hands, the fun of dancing suddenly gone. It was almost as if the re-alization of why she was learning to dance suddenly hit her. It wasn't for fun, it was so that she would not embarrass herself or her grandparents when she was living in England. Though Genny knew and accepted the why of it, she was suddenly and inexplicably sad. For the first time, she wished her father hadn't made her promise to go home to England. Home was her little cabin, not some palace in England, not with two people she had never met whom she might not even like. She knew Mitch was exaggerating, but just how much she didn't know.

"Does everyone in England have more than one home?" she asked.

"Only the men you'll be meeting," Mitch said, sounding far too jovial to Genny's ears.

Madeline walked over to where Genny sat and dropped down next to her. "A lady doesn't rest her chin on her hands," Madeline said gently, making Genny feel even more miserable.

"I know it's a wonderful thing that my grandparents want to see me. And I know my father did the right thing making me go to Eng-land, but it's all getting a bit overwhelming." She looked down at her dress and lifted the material slightly. "This doesn't feel as if it's mine. I feel like I'm a little girl playing dress up."

"Oh, posh," Madeline said. "In no time you'll feel completely yourself."

Genny forced a smile. "I know I sound ungrateful, but I'm not. I truly appreciate everything that you both are doing to help me." She *did* sound ungrateful, she realized. Here she was, wearing a pretty dress Mitch had purchased for her, practicing dancing, learning com-portment, and all she could do was complain. Genny gave herself a strong mental shake. "From now on, I shall take this as the adventure it is. I shall charm everyone I meet in England."

"Including all those lords?" Madeline said, obviously teasing her.

"Why, especially the lords. If I'm to marry a prince, I shall have to charm them, won't I?" Genny looked up at Mitch, hoping she might see some sign that the idea of her marrying a prince was disagreeable to him, but he was smiling down at her as if he thought it the best of ideas.

"Are we done with our dance lesson for the day?"

"I know I'm done," Madeline said, rubbing the knuckles of her right hand. "Tomorrow I'll introduce you to your new maid, Tillie. You two will get along famously, I'm sure."

Chapter 9

The next day after breakfast, Tillie arrived, smiling brightly as she walked into the main parlor, as if she were walking into a party being held in her honor. She had the blondest hair Genny had ever seen in her life, like sheep's wool, though her brows were considerably darker. Oddly, she wore a shapeless dull brown dress, which didn't seem to match the rest of her at all, for even at first glance she seemed far livelier than the clothing she had on.

"Oh," she breathed as she looked around, brown eyes wide. "This is the prettiest room I've ever seen." She turned quickly to face Genny. "And you must be Miss Hayes. Such a pleasure to meet you. My goodness, how pretty you are."

Genny had to smile, for the girl was a whirlwind of enthusiasm, her face animated, her smile bright.

She spun to face Madeline, and it seemed to Genny that this girl was incapable of moving slowly. "Madeline, I know I thanked you before, but I want to thank you again for this opportunity. England. Goodness, I never thought I'd be traveling across an ocean. I wrote my dear mother as soon as I got the role."

"Position," Mitch corrected.

Her smile faltered a bit. "Yes, position," she said with slightly less spirit. Then, she smiled again, so abruptly Genny was taken slightly aback. "Look at your hair," she exclaimed, coming up to Genny and circling around her. "You were right, Madeline. I can't wait to get my hands in it." She laughed, and Genny joined her, though a bit uncertainly. "Not like mine," she said, and to Genny's shock, she removed her hair and held it up like a prize. Where her hair had been was a tightly pinned mass of dark brown hair. Seeing Genny's expression, she laughed again, rather a braying sort of laugh that made one cringe. "It's a wig, you silly girl. Ha! I do believe she thought I'd just scalped myself. I decided I would wear this ugly brown dress but I fear I didn't want to part with my lovely hair just yet."

Genny looked from Mitch to Madeline, uncertain how to react to this strange creature claiming to be her maid. She had no experience of how a maid should act, but she was fairly certain this was not it.

"Mother," Mitch said, softly but with an authority that Genny had come to recognize. It was his "tone of steel," the one he used when he was very upset but not willing to let it show. "May I have a word with you?"

Madeline simply waved a hand at him. "Tillie, do please get into character. *Really*, child."

Instantly, Tillie changed. It was fascinating; almost as if another person had entered the room, a girl who looked like Tillie but . . . wasn't.

"Yes, ma'am. If there's nothing else, I'll go and mend your stockings," Tillie said, adding a deferential little curtsey.

Madeline clapped her hands in appreciation. "Marvelous, marvelous." Tillie made a deep curtsey, accepting the accolades with grace.

Mitch actually let out a sound that reminded Genny of a large dog's growl. "It is *not* marvelous, Mother. If she doesn't stay in character, it could be disastrous. These English, they're sticklers for such things and staying in character every day all day is more than I could ask of even the best actress."

"I can do it," Tillie said, full of affront. "Besides, how do you know how the English are?"

A tick showed just below Mitch's left eye, a sure sign he was about to lose his temper. Genny had only seen it one other time, the night she'd been thrown from Delmonico's. "I don't know," Mitch said through gritted teeth. "But I do know that maids do not take off their very blonde wigs and hold them up like some sort of prize."

Tillie stuck her tongue out at Mitch, and it was all Genny could do not to laugh. He gave Madeline a withering look, then threw up his hands in apparent surrender. "Wonderful. She has a bad actress for a maid, a bastard for a guardian, and a madam for a mentor. This is all fine. Just fine."

"Who's calling me a bad actress?" Tillie said, fisting her hands and jutting out her chin. The mood changes this girl made were dizzying.

Madeline held up her hand again, and Tillie instantly became subdued. Perhaps his mother should have been a director, not a madam.

"Don't be so dramatic, Mitch," Madeline said. "Everything will be fine if we all remember our parts."

"Parts?" Then Mitch, who had been doing quite well about not swearing, let out a rather foul curse. And didn't apologize.

"Pardon me," Genny said to Tillie. "I don't mean to be critical, but how do you know the way a maid acts? Having never seen a maid, I wouldn't even know if you were doing it wrong."

Tillie shrugged. "I've seen enough plays with maids to know how to act like one. Basically, you act real polite, do as you're told without any complaint, and keep everyone happy."

"See?" Madeline said. "It's settled."

Genny looked at Mitch, who seemed to have turned to stone. Nothing moved. He didn't breathe. He didn't twitch. He just stood there for a good ten seconds before stalking from the room, muttering under his breath. Genny couldn't make out what he was saying, but she was fairly certain it was curses.

The next few days went by far more quickly than Mitch would have liked. Though he had his doubts about Tillie, he had to admit she knew how to dress hair and, when she bothered, could actually sound and act like a maid. Every day when Genny appeared, her hair was in a style more intricate than the day before—and every style looked stunning on her. Between the new gowns and her hair, Genny looked like a completely different woman from the one he'd met in Yosemite. It hurt to look at her, she was that beautiful. And he never wanted to forget her, never wanted to wake up one morning struggling to recall the shape of her mouth. He might forget the soft lilt of her voice, but he'd be damned if he forgot her face.

Genny arrived at the breakfast table wearing one of her old dresses, her hair in a simple braid down her back. Tillie liked to sleep in in the morning, and Genny could think of no reason not to let her. She could dress herself and braid her own hair just as she'd been doing for more than a decade.

Like her, Mitch was an early riser, and there were many mornings they shared a quiet breakfast. Madeline often didn't make an appearance until very late morning or early afternoon. Mitch wasn't much of a talker, but that suited Genny just fine in the morning. Her mind was always a bit foggy before she had her nice strong cup of coffee. Madeline had urged her to try tea because apparently the English were mad for the stuff, but Genny had been drinking strong black coffee since she was fourteen and nothing else could replace it.

"I have a surprise for you today," Mitch said, setting down his own mug. "After breakfast, have Tillie do your hair all fancy and put on your ball gown."

"Are we practicing dancing?"

"Something far better. At least as far as I'm concerned."

Genny laughed. "I can't imagine what could be better than dancing." She finished her breakfast and dashed toward the bedrooms in a way she knew was completely unladylike, but she didn't care. She could be ladylike for the rest of her life, but today Mitch had a surprise for her and she couldn't wait to see what it was.

She went to Tillie's room, which was across from hers, and knocked on the door. She thought she detected some movement, but when there was no answer, she knocked again.

"Go away."

Lady's maids likely didn't tell their employers to "go away" and Genny had to smile. What a pair they made, trying to fool everyone around them into thinking they were a fine lady and her maid. She pushed open the door and Tillie pulled the covers over her head.

"What time is it?" Tillie asked, clearly disgruntled.

"Just past seven."

"Has the sun even come up yet? Why on earth are you in here?"

"I've been up for more than an hour already," Genny said, sitting at the foot of the bed and tugging at Tillie's feet. "I do believe servants are supposed to be up before their employers."

"And employers are supposed to sleep until noon. That's what I heard," came the muffled reply. Tillie dropped the blankets and glared at Genny, revealing dark brown hair falling out of its braid. "Why are you here, anyway?"

"Mr. Campbell said he wanted my hair done up pretty and said for me to wear my ball gown. He has a surprise for me."

Tillie immediately sat up. "The green one with the pearls?"

Genny nodded, and Tillie whipped off the covers. "I'll be dressed in a few seconds and we can get started. I have the most wonderful idea for your hair just for that dress." As if she'd never complained about being awoken, Tillie smiled and began rushing about.

"I'll get the dress ready," Genny said, rising and moving toward the door.

"And take out that hideous braid."

Genny's hand flew to the offending braid, but she grinned before closing the door behind her.

Mitch carefully set up his camera and tripod, positioning it to face a leather wingback chair. The light in the morning was bright and perfect for the photograph he had in mind. He'd used some of his quickly dwindling savings to purchase new chemicals and plates so he could produce the photo he wanted. In one corner of the room, he'd set up a dark room where he would prepare his glass plates. He'd learned the hard way that the plates had to be prepared right before taking the picture or they were useless. Out in the field, plates tended to dry out quickly. He remembered several occasions early on when his pictures failed as a result of improper preparation. Will had groused for weeks about those wasted plates and chemicals.

Just setting up his camera equipment again after so many weeks served to remind him of his dream of opening up his own studio. With funds so low, he was glad he'd decided to take his studio camera from Will's studio when they'd stopped in Omaha. He certainly couldn't afford to buy a camera now.

The smell of the collodion never ceased to transport him back to the field or to Will Jackson's photography studio. To some, the smell might offend—two of the ingredients in collodion were alcohol and ether—but to Mitch it was the sweetest perfume. He'd douse himself with collodion if it would make him forget Genny and remember the original reason he'd agreed to bring her to England. Somehow he'd forgotten about the money, money he now needed more than ever. He wasn't certain how he'd allowed himself to go all soft on a woman, but he had. And taking a picture of her just so that he could look at her face when she was gone sure as heck wasn't going to help.

He was giving the chair another small adjustment, when Tillie rushed into the room.

"Presenting Miss Genevieve Hayes," she said with a flourish and then pretended to play a trumpet fanfare. Genny entered the room, head held high, as if floating on a cloud. Somehow, the ball gown he'd first seen her in back at Madame Brunelle's looked even more beautiful on her now. Perhaps it was her hair, upswept and curled, with one long bit artistically flowing down and resting upon the creamy expanse of her upper chest. She nodded serenely to Tillie, then dissolved into laughter—stopping abruptly when she saw the camera equipment.

"You're taking my picture?"

"I thought I might. I want to stay in practice."

"I've never had my picture taken," she breathed, going over to his camera. "How long before I see it?"

"Later this very morning. Now, when I'm ready, you have to stay still for twenty seconds." He walked over to the window and peered out, smiling when he saw a pure blue sky and no danger of clouds ruining his light. "We've nice bright light, so it shouldn't take too long. Do you think you can stay still for that long?"

"I believe so. Should I smile?" She pulled a rather maniacal-looking happy expression. "Or look dour." She frowned. "It seems every picture I see of people, they look miserable. I shouldn't like to look miserable."

"Then smile. It's what I had in mind. Now, come here and stand by this window." Genny walked over, followed by Tillie. "Rest your left hand like so " He took her gloved hand and draped it over the back of the chair. "Turn a bit, so that you are facing the window, now without turning your body, look at the camera." He stepped behind the camera and focused the lens, then placed the lens cap back on. "Perfect. I'm off to prepare the first plate, so you can relax a bit, but don't move."

He rushed back to a side table near his dark tent, and held the spotlessly clean glass up to the light just to make certain it was free from dust. "This is where your image is going to be," he said, showing Genny the glass. "I'm going to put some chemicals on it"—he held up a bottle of Mawson's Collodion—"then let it soak for a bit in silver nitrate and we'll be all set."

He gently poured the collodion over the glass so that it flowed to all four corners. Then he lifted the plate and let the excess pour back into the bottle; no use wasting perfectly good chemical. Ducking beneath the tent, he placed the plate in a container of silver nitrate, then returned to where Tillie was fussing with Genny's hair.

"Just a few minutes and I'll be ready to take your picture."

"I'm so nervous. Can I blink?"

"It'd be better if you didn't."

Several minutes later, Mitch returned carrying a case from which dripped a bit of silver nitrate. As he looked around the room, he noticed that Tillie had disappeared. "Where's Tillie?"

"She said she was bored. I don't think she's going to fool anyone into thinking she's a maid."

"Probably not," Mitch said, slipping the holder into his camera. "We have to take the picture while it's still wet. Are you ready?"

"Yes."

"All right, then, look beautiful."

Genny immediately made her face go completely slack, so she looked rather like a simpleton.

"Very funny. Smile please or at least try to look like you have a thought in your head."

She did, but she crossed her eyes at the same time, just enough to be noticeable.

"Genny, stop it," he said, trying to sound stern but laughing instead.

She gave him a look of complete innocence. "Didn't I look pretty? What an awful man you are."

"The plate will dry and I'll have wasted all the chemicals."

Genny shook herself as if to throw off her mischievousness. "I'll be good. Promise." And then made another face.

Mitch couldn't help it, he laughed again, only serving to reward her for her bad behavior. "If you don't stop, I'm going to go over there and kiss you silly." As threats went, it wasn't a very good one, because Genny's face lit up and she smiled, a perfect smile, and he thanked the man who had invented photography for allowing him to preserve this moment as he removed the lens cap and allowed the light to flood the glass plate.

"Hold that, Genny, please God." And she did.

"I still want that kiss," she said, not moving a muscle in her face.

He pulled out his pocket watch to mark the time. "If you stay still, I just might give you one." Mitch looked at his watch, then assessed the amount of light hitting Genny, and at twenty-five seconds, he covered the lens again, blocking any more light from hitting the plate.

"You can relax," he said, and walked over to her. He gave her a quick buss on the cheek, nearly laughing out loud at the disappointed look on her face. "Someday you'll thank me for not taking advantage of you. Do you have any idea how improper it is for me to kiss you?"

"You kissed me before."

"Yes, and it was a mistake." The biggest mistake he'd ever made, but he wasn't going to tell her that. Those kisses had stayed with him and haunted both his waking and sleeping hours.

Genny put on a pout as he went over to the camera and pulled the container with the glass plate out. "I'm going to prepare the negative now. You can relax. It will be several minutes before I'm done."

Mitch ducked beneath the black cloth of his tent and immediately set to work. Creating a negative in complete darkness had become second nature to him and his hand went unerringly to the bottle of developer, which he carefully poured over the plate. A few seconds later, he placed the plate into a bath of water, rinsing the developer off.

"Are you almost finished?" Genny asked from directly behind him. She so startled him, he nearly dropped the plate.

"Finished," Mitch said, pulling back the black cloth. He immediately held the negative up, examining it with a practiced eye. "Lovely. But I'm not done yet."

"More chemicals?" Genny asked, wrinkling her nose at the smell.

"More chemicals. Come here, you can watch this part. See? I have to soak the plate in this solution for a moment. That washes away the extra silver. Then water." He held the glass plate by the edges, never touching the actual surface of the negative for fear of leaving a fingerprint. He'd done that a time or two when he was learning.

"Now to dry." He lit a small lamp and held the negative over it, moving it so that the entire surface dried. "And now, varnish."

"Goodness, you do all this outside?"

"It's a bit more difficult, but yes. Once this dries, I'll make the print. But look here," he said, studying the negative. "See this dark area? That's going to be the light area of the picture. It's difficult to know precisely how the photograph is going to look until I make the print, but it looks sharp."

Genny leaned over to study the glass plate, and Mitch found himself looking at her, at the gentle curve of her jaw. He wished he could take a hundred photographs of her so that he would never forget how soft her skin looked, the way her lashes, thick and long, framed her eyes. "Tillie made your hair look real nice," he said, nearly wincing at the gruff way his voice sounded.

"She said my braid was awful."

Mitch chuckled. "Not awful, but not as pretty as this."

"She has so many pins in my hair I feel as if my head is made of metal. Braids may not be pretty, but they're far more comfortable. So much about being a lady is uncomfortable."

Genny sounded so disheartened, Mitch laughed again. "You'll get used to it all. And you'll be glad you went through all this when you have one of those fancy lords dancing with you." Mitch forced himself to say that last, just to remind himself that he had no claim over her and never would. *I'm just an escort, nothing more.* But, damn, it was hard to stay focused on that reality when she was standing so close he could smell the floral soap she'd used to wash her hair.

"I can hardly breathe in this dress. I shall become one of those ladies who faints from lack of oxygen."

Mitch furrowed his brow. "Tell Tillie not to make everything underneath so tight."

Genny laughed. "How ferocious you look, Mitch."

Mitch took a deep breath. She was right, he likely did look like a man bent on murder—just from the thought that someone had made her feel a bit uncomfortable. "It'll be a while before the plate is dry enough to make a print. I'll come get you when I'm done. You can get out of that dress now. And put your hair in a braid, if you'd like."

Genny tilted her head a bit, studying him. "You know, sometimes you sound angry, but I don't think you are."

"Just go change, Genny. You'll ruin your new dress."

"There you go again, sounding angry," she said in a singsong way.

"I am angry."

"Ha. No, you're not. I don't know what you are, but you're not angry." She gave him a saucy look before leaving him alone to stew over the fact that she was right. He wasn't angry. He was in love.

When Genny saw the picture, it was the oddest thing. It was almost like looking at someone else, someone she didn't recognize. She looked regal and sophisticated, and the expression on her face was one of suppressed joy. "Is that what I truly look like?"

"You really do look like a princess," Tillie said.

The two women, heads close together, were looking down at the print, studying it as if it were a painting by a master. It was that beautiful, and Genny couldn't stop the surge of pride she felt that Mitch, grumpy Mitch who swore too much, could have produced something as beautiful as this. It wasn't vanity that made her think that; she had a good idea what she looked like. The woman in the picture was not the woman she saw when she looked in the mirror every day. The woman in the picture was almost lovely beyond words.

She looked up to see Mitch studying her, no doubt looking for her reaction. "It's lovely, Mitch. Really. I don't know how you made me look so pretty."

"You are pretty," Tillie said, laughing.

"Not *that* pretty," Genny said.

"That's true," Tillie said, then turned to Mitch. "You think you could take a picture of me and make me look that good?"

"Of course."

Tillie shot him a look of disbelief.

"It's so strange," Genny said, staring at the picture again. "When I'm an old lady, I'll know just what I looked like. I'll remember this day, and you, and I'll have this image to hold forever. It will almost be like going back in time."

"That's why so many people take pictures of their children, so they can remember them always," Mitch said.

"Even the dead ones." Tillie said dramatically.

"Dead children? Why would they do that? It seems so macabre," Genny said.

"So they can remember them," Mitch said, coming around to look at her photograph. "It gives the parents comfort. William took one picture of a young woman holding her little dead baby. It was the saddest thing I've ever seen. We were all a little shaken up by it. But when she got the picture, days after the little one was put in the ground, she was so happy she cried. She held that picture almost like she was holding her baby. Near broke your heart to see it."

Tillie's eyes flooded with tears, and when Genny saw Tillie cry, her eyes started burning too. "That's the saddest thing I've ever heard," Genny said.

"It is sad, but that picture made her happy. That's why I like photographing people, not things. You're giving someone something they can hold onto forever, almost as if you have a piece of them." Mitch stopped talking abruptly and looked away. "Anyway, I'm glad you like the picture."

"I do," Genny said, wondering why Mitch's eyes had momentarily looked so bleak. She knew so little about his past. Did he have someone he wished he had a photograph of? Someone now gone? She wished suddenly she had a picture of Mitch or even one of the two of them. She thought that was a wonderful idea.

"We should have a picture of the two of us, Mitch. Tillie can take off the lens and put it back on. Then I'd have a memento of our time together. And so would you."

Mitch's jaw tightened and he shook his head. "I don't have enough chemicals left for another negative."

Genny nodded, but had a feeling he wasn't telling her the true reason he didn't want a picture of the two of them. She swallowed her disappointment and forced a smile. "At least I have this photograph."

Chapter 10

Two days before Mitch, Genny, and Tillie were due to board the ship, his mother and Tillie disappeared on an errand of "finding costumes for Tillie's role." Mitch couldn't recall the number of times he counted himself the biggest of fools for getting caught up in this scheme. He was out nearly all of his savings, had fallen in love with a girl he could never have, and was facing the prospect of preparing her to attract another man.

It was a cruel irony that when Mitch finally found himself in a place where he thought he could give a woman what she needed, he'd found one he could never have. Mitch had grown up in a world of misfits, so the idea of not being good enough hadn't really entered his mind until he reached adulthood. But he understood it now. His mother's friends had welcomed everyone into their fold, and as a boy Mitch just figured that's how people were. It wasn't until he reached the Army that he realized rank and privilege had anything do with respect and authority.

It had been a hard lesson for a seventeen-year-old kid who'd spent his life practicing lines and dance steps with his mother. The first week of his training had nearly destroyed him. Sgt. Baker had seen his weakness the first day of training. He saw a kid who had no business putting on a uniform, a kid who had never really been in the company of other men. Something inside Mitch wouldn't let him give up, wouldn't let the sergeant break him, though God knew the older man had tried. Or maybe he'd seen something in Mitch that he hadn't even known was inside him. Either way, the Army changed him.

In the end, he'd survived the war, Sgt. Baker had died in Petersburg, Virginia just seven days before Lee surrendered. Mitch hadn't seen the man fall, but he'd seen plenty around him die. It was only dumb luck Mitch had survived the fighting. He learned later that more than seven thousand men had died; it was easy to believe given the bodies he'd seen. Mitch had been part of the New York 40th Infantry regiment, trying to take back a city that had fallen early in the war. He was wiry and strong, a tall target for the Confederates. A bullet grazed his head and he went down. That bullet saved his life, for when he came to, it was all over. He was in a ditch surrounded by dead men, and for a while Mitch wished he'd been among their number.

Mitch had only been in the fight six months before that day, but he came back to New York a changed man, one who saw everything his mother and her friends did as frivolous and silly. He'd tried to return to his old life, but the war had reshaped him into a new person, though he didn't know who that person was until much later.

Years of wandering led him to Nebraska and Will Jackson, a man Mitch came to think of as a big brother. Mollie and Will took him in, let him heal, showed him what a normal life could be like, made him realize that what he wanted more than anything was peace and a soft place to put his head each night.

Now he was twenty-seven years old, and he'd let his heart destroy that dream of peace he'd been working so long to achieve. All those years, all that focus on one goal—to save enough money to start his own studio—would be gone if his gamble did not pay off.

What had he done? What had he *allowed*?

He looked down at the photograph he'd taken of Genny and felt as if his chest was on fire. This was all so wrong. This was not supposed to have happened. Part of him wanted to rip the picture, to throw the negative into the fireplace and smash it. She was his peace. She was his soft place. But she was going to England and he was coming back to New York to start a business he no longer even had the heart to care about.

The morning of July ninth, Mitch took a long, hard look in the mirror and saw a man he wanted to hit. Hard. He was aching for a fight and only wished he was back with his crew in California, for certainly one of them would have obliged him. As it stood at the moment, he was left feeling he wanted to hit something, but there was nothing to hit.

It was this dark mood in which Genny found him. He was in what his mother called the library, but was really nothing more than a dark room on the north side of her apartment with over-large leather furniture and not a book in sight. He didn't even know why he'd gone there, except perhaps it was a room Genny rarely visited. It was warm, stifling, actually, for the windows in this particular room didn't open wide. The room felt the way he did. Like hell.

"There you are," she said, and with just those innocuous, cheerfully spoken words, a sweat broke out on his brow that had nothing to do with the New York July heat.

"Here I am." He stiffened at the sound of her voice and calmly turned the photograph over, hoping she hadn't seen what he'd been staring at.

"We're leaving in two days."

He took a deep breath, feeling impatient and in a foul mood. "So we are."

"Are you looking at something interesting?"

He slowly turned toward her and saw that she was wearing one of her ready-made dresses from Nebraska; her hair was in a simple braid down her back. The sight of her, looking as she had when they'd first met, nearly made his knees buckle. He'd thought that girl was gone.

"Just staring at the bricks." He knew he sounded put out but couldn't stop himself. He *was* put out.

Genny's smile faltered a bit. "Are you angry with me?"

She said it in such a small, un-Genny-like voice, his heart lurched a bit. "No, Genny. I've never been mad at you and I don't expect I ever will be."

"Then why . . ." Her voice trailed off. "It just seems as if you are."

"I'm not."

A long silence, and then, "Could you dance with me?"

He jerked slightly before he could stop himself, and he gave himself a mental shake. Innocuous words should not hurt, but it seemed that almost everything she said felt like a blow to his gut. "There's no one here to play the piano. Besides, you know all the dances well enough."

"I'm a bit worried about the waltz."

Mitch closed his eyes briefly, his entire body on fire with needing her. He wanted to bury his face against her hair, breathe her in, hold her, kiss her. Oh, God, did she even have the smallest idea what she was doing to him? If she did, if she knew the dark thoughts coursing through his brain, she'd run.

"No piano," he said, almost desperately.

"I could hum. Or you could."

She was worrying her hands together and he hated that he was hurting her. He couldn't allow her to know just how difficult this had become for him. God knew, he had only a hair's breadth of control left. If she took another step toward him, if she smiled again, he doubted he'd be able to stop himself from kissing her. And if he started kissing her, God knew whether he'd be able to stop at that. Not when he lay in bed each night and dreamed what it would be like to see her next to him with that sleepy grin of hers, not when he could still recall the earthy-sweet scent of her hair.

"Listen, Genny. I'm tired and not feeling too good. I just want to be left alone, all right?"

She nodded but didn't leave. "I miss you," she said with a little shrug. "It seems these last few days you've already left me behind."

"I guess that's about right."

She dipped her head a bit, and it seemed to Mitch she was almost trying to duck his words. "I wish you wouldn't. I wish—"

"Don't matter what you wish, Genny. The only thing that matters is what's happening. I'm taking you to England and I'm saying good-bye. That's what's happening. Get it? That's what has to happen."

She looked as if she was trying not to cry; she knew how much he hated it when she did. "I understand," she said, and he could hear her voice tighten. *Damn it to hell.*

He walked up to her and gently grabbed her upper arms, giving her the smallest of shakes. "Look at me. I'm trying to do the right thing, Genny," he said, hating the way his voice broke, the way she looked at him as if her heart were shattering, as if she knew his was too. "Please, let me do the right thing."

"I can't." She leaned to kiss him, and Mitch didn't know how he had the will to push her away. It would kill him, that kiss.

"If you won't leave, I will," he said, and stalked from the room.

Genny let him go. When Mitch was in a foul mood, she found there was nothing she could do but let him stew a bit. She looked around the gloomy, hot space and walked to the window that Mitch had been staring out to see if there was anything of interest outside. Craning her neck, she looked down at the bricks, but saw nothing noteworthy. Leaning out further, she rested her hands on the narrow table that stood beneath the sill and felt a piece of thick paper.

It dawned on her suddenly what Mitch had been looking at; she wondered if it would be a terrible violation of his privacy if she were to turn the paper over. Biting her lip and feeling rather guilty, she looked. "Oh."

It was her picture. He'd been staring at it, his hands braced on either side, his body tense.

Genny wrapped her arms around her waist and turned away from the photograph. *Please, let me do the right thing.*

Genny suddenly closed her eyes and sagged against the table. She had no experience with love, but she had a pretty good idea that's what she felt for Mitch. And now . . .

"Does he love me?" she whispered, feeling none of the joy she should with such a thought. The minute she said the words aloud, doubt filled her. He didn't act like a man in love; he acted like a man who wanted to kiss her and knew he shouldn't. That wasn't love. Then again, she had no idea what a man acted like when he was in love. Didn't they write poetry and send a girl flowers? Or maybe they took your picture and made certain you had pretty clothes.

Genny pressed her fingertips against her temple. This was all so confusing, not at all like the fairy tales she'd read where the princess knew immediately that she was in love. If this was love, it was nothing like in the books. This *hurt*.

Genny sat down in one of the big leather chairs. Nothing was as it was supposed to be. Other than the day her father died, she'd never felt quite so miserable in her life. She sat there for several minutes before she heard Tillie calling out for her. Part of her wanted to remain silent, to pretend she hadn't heard, but she ended up shouting, "In here."

In a few moments, Tillie peeked around the corner, her blonde wig seeming to glow in the gloom of the room. Other than that first day when she'd taken it off and the morning of her photography session, Genny hadn't seen her without it on. "There you are. What are you doing in here all alone in the dark?" Tillie's smile faded slightly, as if sensing something was troubling her. She peered at Genny's face. "Oh, honey, what's wrong?"

Genny's throat closed up so suddenly, she couldn't speak, so she just shook her head. Clearly, the desperation she felt was easy to read, for Tillie rushed over to her, went down to her knees and grabbed her hands.

"What's happened?"

Genny swallowed, willing the lump in her throat to disappear; she would not cry in front of another person. "It's just that nothing is the way it was supposed to be," she said, barely getting the words out. "I promised my father to go home to England, but . . ."

"It's not home, is it?"

Genny shook her head. "No, it's not. And it just occurred to me. I've been so worried that they won't like me, but what if I don't like them? My mother had to run away to marry my father. What kind of parents would be so awful that a daughter would do that?"

"You say your grandparents are a duke and duchess?"

Genny sniffed, still desperately trying not to cry. "Yes."

"And your dad, what was he?"

Genny furrowed her brow, trying to remember what he'd been doing before her mother escaped with him to America. "I think he was a land steward for my mother's neighbors."

Tillie's face cleared, as if everything was dropping into place. "That explains it then. Why, your mother falling in love with a steward would be like you falling in love with a jailbird. Daughters of dukes marry sons of dukes or earls or some such. It's just not done."

Her father had never spoken of the precise reason he'd run from England. Genny had only known it had something to do with her grandparents' not liking her father. "How do you know all this?"

"Jane Austen," Tillie said with a nod. "Well," she equivocated, "not quite, but her books gave me a general idea that class is a very important thing in England. It's important here, too. Do you think John D. Rockefeller would let his son marry me? Not hardly."

"I know my grandfather was terribly upset by my mother leaving. Then he wrote the dearest letters begging her to come home."

Tillie dipped her head, forcing Genny to make eye contact. "Please don't take this the wrong way, but I know about a hundred girls who would take your place in a second." She snapped her fingers. "What's happening to you is the stuff of dreams. Look at this dress, your hair," she said, flicking Genny's long braid. "Is this the girl you want to be or that girl in your picture?"

"I'm not certain. I know who *this* girl is. I haven't the foggiest idea who that girl in the picture is."

Tillie's expression became fierce. "I'll tell you who that girl in the picture is. She's a girl who isn't going to ever wonder where her next meal is coming from or deal with some masher trying to take things he oughtn't. She'll have a warm house and a soft bed and a place to stay for the rest of her life. And that girl ain't ever going to have to do something she doesn't want to just to survive. That's who that girl is."

The more Tillie said, the worse Genny felt. She knew she should be grateful, but she couldn't tell Tillie the real reason she was feeling so low. Even she knew how foolish it would sound to tell Tillie she had fallen in love with Mitch. "I do have one question," Genny said. "What's a masher?"

Tillie let out a gust of air and rolled her eyes as if everyone knew what a masher was. "A masher is a man who doesn't show respect for a woman. I've had more than a nodding acquaintance with a few mashers. They'll treat you like a queen, then steal kisses and sometimes more, but do you think you'll get a ring afterward? No, ma'am, you won't."

Genny straightened abruptly. That sounded a lot like Mitch. "So men aren't supposed to kiss you unless you are engaged?"

A slight blush touched Tillie's cheek. "Well, it depends. I suppose it's something you feel in your bones. But I can't always trust my bones," Tillie said, laughing. "Plus, there're kisses and then there're *kisses*, if you know what I mean."

"I haven't any idea at all what you mean," Genny said. "I've only kissed one man in my life."

Tillie's jaw dropped. "You're such an innocent," she said. "But I suppose that's to be expected. To be honest, I've never been kissed by a man who loves me." Again, her cheeks turned pink. "But it can still be lovely."

"How do you know if a man loves you?"

"He tells you, I suppose. You can't go by how much he wants to kiss you or even if he gives you flowers. My mother told me one thing, though, and I never forgot it. Why would a man buy a cow if he gets the milk for free?" At Genny's blank look, Tillie laughed. "You can't let a man under your skirts unless you have a ring on your finger. If they want to do it, they've got to do it proper."

Genny knew what "doing it" meant and knew that what she felt when Mitch kissed her, or even looked at her, meant she wanted to "do it."

"Men are such odd creatures. We can't understand them and they can't understand us. It's a wonder we get together and make babies." Tillie stopped abruptly. "Hey, you, um, know about that, right?"

Now it was Genny's turn to blush. "I understand the mechanics of it. One tends to, living in the wilderness."

"Thank goodness, because I don't think I'm up to a talk on the birds and the bees."

Genny laughed. "I'm glad you found me in here. I was feeling sorry for myself and I really oughtn't. I know I should be grateful. I just have a tendency to wish things were different than they are. Sometimes I wish I was back in my cabin, but I know that I couldn't survive there alone."

Tillie's happy expression turned to worry. "Other than your grand-parents, do you have anyone else in the world?"

"An uncle, I believe. He was my mother's older brother. I think he actually came to America looking for my parents when they first ar-rived but I don't know if he found them."

"What about here? Anyone?"

Genny shook her head. Of course, she'd realized she was alone in the world, but she hadn't dwelt on it. When her father had died, she'd set her sights on finding her grandparents; there had been no other choice. Now, she realized having no other choice wasn't a very com-fortable feeling. "I don't have anyone here except for Mitch and Madeline. And you."

"See? If you don't go to England, what will you do?"

Genny didn't like the feeling of helplessness that came over her. She had no money, no relatives, no home. She couldn't impose upon Madeline forever. She had no other choice but to go to England. "I could get a job," she said uncertainly.

"You could, but it's awfully hard getting a job when you're a fe-male, unless you want to work in a factory. And I'll tell you one thing, you don't want to do that. It'll kill you and you likely won't even make enough money to pay a decent rent, never mind food.

"I worked for a year in a textile factory. Some of those women, they'd been there for years and their lungs were so full of dust, they could hardly breathe. It does something to you, working so hard for nothing. And honestly, how silly would that be when you have rich relatives who could give you the world?"

Genny, with no formal education and no skills, would likely be forced to work in such a place. Either that or work as a servant, and Genny just couldn't picture that life. "You're right, of course."

"Madeline is a lovely woman, but given her new occupation, I don't think this would be such a good place to live for an innocent girl. You wouldn't be innocent for long, that's for sure. You can't stay here and you can't go back to your cabin, so looks like you'd best accept that England is the best place for you to be."

Genny nodded. "I was just being silly. England is my only option. And it's a good one."

Tillie laughed. "Unless Mr. Campbell proposes to you. Ha!"

Genny forced a laugh, because Tillie's words had the oddest effect on her heart. It gave a little painful lurch that she recognized immediately as hope.

That night at dinner, Madeline walked into the lavish dining room, spread her hands out wide and announced, "I have the most wonderful surprise. A reporter is coming over tomorrow to interview us all about Genny."

Her announcement was initially met with stunned silence. Mitch, whose mood had only darkened since he'd left abruptly earlier that day, calmly placed his fork and knife back on the table and the women—except for Madeline—watched him warily. "I think that isn't the best of ideas, Mother."

"Oh, posh, it's a wonderful idea. And by the time the story runs, you'll both be long gone. Besides, it's not as if the reporter is from the *Times*; he's from the *Herald*."

Mitch hadn't been able to look at Genny directly since he'd returned, but he looked at her now, taking in her pale complexion and the circles beneath her eyes. She still wore her simple dress and a long braid and it hurt to see her like that. He wished she was all fancied up because her finery reminded him what her life was going to be like when she was in England. Yet as beautiful as she was in her new gowns, he found he preferred her as she was now, a girl a man like him might be able to keep.

He wondered if she was ill, and whether they should postpone their trip. He could always send a telegram to her grandparents explaining the delay. She was a shell of the girl who had walked miles with a cast on her leg. So many times he wanted to draw her into his arms, but as the old adage said, 'If wishes were horses then beggars would ride.' Holding her, kissing her, would only make saying good-bye all the harder—for both of them. He would do the right thing, even if it killed him, but he longed to kiss her, hold her, let her know that everything was going to be all right.

But how could he do that when his gut told him that nothing would ever be right again?

Genny took a small sip of the excellent burgundy, as if to give her courage to question Madeline's plan. "I'm afraid I don't understand why a newspaper article would be a good thing. I am sorry, Madeline, because you seem so pleased."

Madeline pursed her lips. "Fine," she said, looking at each of them in turn. "It will help my career immensely."

"Mother, you cannot possibly be thinking of linking Miss Hayes to your business," Mitch said, putting telling emphasis on *business*.

"I'm not doing it to help my business, I'm doing it to help my career. Having Tillie here has made me miss the stage. I know I seem happy, but there's something about being in front of all those people, hearing the applause. My soul is dying. And I'm not so old."

Mitch sighed. "There's a part, I take it?"

Madeline closed her eyes and said, "Mrs. Rich in *The Beau Defeated*. Oh, I was *meant* for this role. It's perfect for me, but I've been out of the limelight for so long, no one will even let me audition."

Mitch felt that old surge of protectiveness toward his mother. "They've denied you an audition?"

Madeline looked slightly chagrined. "Not quite. Auditions don't start until next week. But if this article appears in the *Herald*, I'll be on everyone's mind. The reporter can call me the great stage actress Madeline Campbell. Oh, it will be perfect. So, yes, my idea is completely selfish and I admit it." She turned to Genny. "What do you think, dear?"

Genny looked from Madeline to Tillie, skirting over Mitch.

"No, Mother."

Genny lifted her chin. "If it will help your career, and as long as your business isn't mentioned, I'm perfectly fine with a story."

Mitch could tell his mother was trying not to show too much triumph, but she wasn't *that* good an actress. "Then it's settled. Mr. Tish will be here tomorrow at the ungodly hour of eleven, so please, everyone, be ready. Genny, I want you to wear that darling violet day dress Madame Brunelle created for you. Tillie, have her ready, please. And I think it would be a good idea to get into character." She ignored Mitch's growl. "Eileen can bring us tea, of course, but you may be needed for something."

"Genny," Mitch said, looking at her intently. She was concentrating on her food—a perfectly baked duck—and did not look up even when she answered him.

"Yes?"

Wonderful. He *had* hurt her this afternoon. He'd thought perhaps it had been his imagination that she hadn't looked in his direction all evening. "Are you certain you want to do this?"

She lifted her head and looked at him, her green eyes snapping. "Absolutely." She turned toward Madeline, and her expression softened considerably. "What shall we talk about?"

"My dear, your story is so exciting. A lost heiress, rescued by *my* son, foiling train robbers, taken in by *me*, traveling to England to meet your grandparents, the duke and duchess. It's positively delicious. I wouldn't be surprised if it inspires a play. And of course, I can play myself. The best part is, by the time the article appears, you'll be long gone and won't be hounded by the public."

"I suppose that will be your job, Mother?" Mitch asked dryly.

"What?" Madeline asked, seemingly confused.

"To be hounded by the public."

"Of course," Madeline said, ignoring her son's tone. "Who else to expound on the story but me? You'll all be gone."

Mitch knew there was little he could do to stop his mother once she got something into her head. And frankly, if she was back on stage, perhaps she'd stop running a bordello. The realization that few other sons in the world would be glad to have their mother on stage was not lost on Mitch. If helping his mother to get this role would aid her career and not hurt Genny, how could he possibly argue?

Tillie, who as Genny's maid had no business at all sitting at the table with them, clapped her hands. "Oh, tomorrow will be a bit of a dress rehearsal. What could be more perfect?"

Mitch stifled a groan, reminding himself that at one point in his life, this would have been a normal thing to say. "I do wish you would stop thinking of this as a performance, Tillie," he said, knowing his words would fall on deaf ears.

"That's precisely what it is," Madeline said. "All the world's a stage; don't ever forget it."

Robert Tish took out his handkerchief and wiped the sweat off his brow. It was deathly hot in the city this day, the sun making the brick around him an oven. He wondered if he would literally cook should he remain on the streets too long. Robert had grown up in Rhode Island in a little fishing village called Galilee. As a boy, he'd spent his days fishing and clamming and generally being on the water. He'd never in his life experienced this sort of unending, dead heat. No breeze. No cool ocean air wafting over him. God, he hated New York, but if a man wanted to learn the newspaper business, if he wanted to be any kind of success at all, this was the place to do it. At least that's what he'd told his father, who'd been rather angry when Robert had announced he didn't want to grow old stinking of fish and brine, he wanted to go to the big city and write. Yes, that was grand news for his father and older brother to hear.

How stupid could a man be? He was in the city, but working for one of the smaller newspapers and generally writing stuff that was mind-numbingly boring. City ordinances about taxis and the new rail system, endless meetings. So when his editor told him about some lost heiress who was supposedly living with an aging actress, he had not been particularly enthusiastic. Probably a bunch of bunk anyway, a stunt to increase public interest in some play.

It was beneath him. He was the best writer on the paper and here he was heading to the Bowery to interview a supposed princess or something.

Robert trudged up the stairs to number seventy-nine Houston Street, noting with slight interest how clean and fine the entrance was.

The door opened wide and he set eyes on a middle-aged woman with auburn hair, smiling as if he was some sort of dignitary.

"You must be Mr. Tish," she said, sweeping an arm back to allow him to enter. "I am Madeline Campbell. Perhaps you've heard of me? I've been at the Niblo for years."

"I'm not much for plays," he said, looking around the room, mildly surprised at the rich furnishings.

"Let's go into the main parlor, shall we?" She walked toward a large room where a maid was laying out some refreshments, and he prayed they had something cold to drink. If he had to drink another drop of tepid water, he just might die.

He smiled when he saw a pitcher, sweating in the heat of the parlor, and obviously filled with something cold.

"Lemonade? It's the best in the city, I assure you. Eileen, please pour Mr. Tish a glass while I go fetch Miss Hayes and Mr. Campbell." She turned to leave, then stopped in a way that seemed planned, almost as if he were part of a play. "Mr. Campbell is my son and the hero of our little story."

Story. He prayed it wasn't just a story, that he wasn't here simply to advance some aging actress's career. He thanked the maid for the lemonade and took a small sip. Oh, heaven. It didn't matter if the entire story was false and he was wasting his time, for he'd just had the best lemonade of his life.

He was alone in the room only a short while before a man returned with Mrs. Campbell—a man who didn't look all that pleased to be participating in the drama. Mr. Campbell looked at his watch then snapped it closed, sending the message that he was a busy man, too busy to be spending it talking with a reporter. Robert was a bit heartened by that; people tended to be less likely to speak to a reporter when they were talking about something that actually happened rather than making it up.

"And here is Genevieve Hayes," Madeline said, almost as if she were the narrator of a play introducing the main character.

Robert tried not to let his jaw drop to his chest, but never in his life had he seen a woman quite as lovely as the one he was looking at. She smiled brilliantly at him, full of poise and grace as she walked toward him and extended one gloved hand.

"I'm so pleased you could come today, Mr. Tish. I must admit I was a bit reticent about sharing my story. It's such a personal thing. But I'll be leaving tomorrow for England and Mrs. Campbell assures me the story won't run in your newspaper until long after we're gone. Is that correct?"

Robert swallowed. "Yes, ma'am."

She smiled again and Mr. Campbell chuckled, as if he knew what was happening to Robert. He gave himself a mental shake, reminding himself why he was in the room, and pulled out his pencil and pad. When everyone was seated, Robert dropped onto a large ottoman, which was positioned so that he could see all three at once.

"What would you like to know, Mr. Tish?" Miss Hayes asked, her head tilted slightly in curiosity. She had the loveliest voice, her accent cultured and clearly British.

"Why are you going to England? My editor gave me only the barest details, you see."

Miss Hayes looked at Mr. Campbell before saying, "It's a long story. I do hope you have time."

Two hours later, the lemonade long forgotten and diluted by the last of the previous winter's ice, Robert put his pencil down. He'd heard the story, he'd seen the letters from the Duke of Glastonbury, obviously authentic, and he had the best tale he'd ever heard, never mind had the privilege to write. They'd even shown him the telegram they'd received from the duke, expressing his happiness that he'd soon be seeing his granddaughter for the first time.

And more amazing? He had actually read the account of the train robbery in the *Times*. Here he was, sitting in the same room as the woman who'd helped to foil the crime.

"Do you have everything you need?" Mrs. Campbell asked, the smile on her face telling him that she knew what a wonderful story he had.

"Yes, ma'am, I do. I want to thank you all for your time and for sharing your story with me."

"I'll walk you to the door, shall I?" Madeline asked.

Robert was nearly giddy. He could not believe what he had stumbled upon. Just as Mrs. Campbell was closing the door, she said to him, "I know this is a story about Miss Hayes, but if you could give me a prominent role, I would greatly appreciate it."

"I'll certainly see what I can do, Mrs. Campbell. I know I wouldn't have gotten this story without your help. I'll make sure it's clear I'm grateful."

She smiled, and it struck Robert at that moment that in her day, this woman would have been a rare beauty. "Thank you. I look forward to reading it."

Robert had a definite bounce in his step as he walked toward the corner where he could get a horse car. This story was going to make his career, and it was far too good to run in his tiny rag of a newspaper. To hell with the *Herald*. He was going to the *Times* with this one.

Genny slumped back into her seat as soon as Mr. Tish left the apartment. "I'm exhausted," she said to no one in particular.

Madeline came back into the room, beaming a smile. "My goodness, Genny, you were wonderful. So charming. So amusing. Where did you get such talent? You would be wonderful on the stage, my dear, just wonderful."

"Genny has a way about her, that's for sure," Mitch said, but it didn't sound like a compliment. "She can wrap a man around her little finger without his even knowing it."

Madeline laughed. "I've never seen a man fall in love so quickly as Mr. Tish. You shall do very well in England," she said. "Who knew you had that in you? It was like watching a performance."

Madeline was looking at her as if she'd never seen her before. And Mitch? He was frowning. "I do have a talent for putting people at ease," Genny said, and even she knew it was false modesty. She had a talent for making men do what she wanted. Every man with one glaring exception. As soon as she had that thought, she felt bad. Mitch was right. She *knew* he was right, but it still stung, the way he'd walked away from her when all she'd wanted was to dance.

Liar. She'd wanted a kiss. She'd wanted him to hold her, to feel his large, warm body wrap around her. Just the thought made her flush.

"How'd *I* do?" Tillie asked, hands on her hips.

Genny chuckled. "Oh, don't be like that, Tillie. It's a lot easier to have a man go all spoony on you if you're wearing a dress like this and have such pretty hair, thanks to your extraordinary talents."

Tillie seemed appeased. "You do have a way about you," she said, then laughed. "Did you see his face when you were talking about the train robbery? I thought he was going to drop down on his knees and propose, right then and there."

Genny laughed, too, but it was a forced laugh. She'd made light of the robbery when she was talking to Mr. Tish, but it had been terrifying. And wonderful. It had been the first time Mitch had truly kissed her.

"My adventure continues tomorrow," Genny said. "Who knows? Perhaps the ship will be boarded by pirates. Or it will go down in a terrible storm and we'll be stranded on an island with nothing to eat but clams."

"Oh, don't talk about shipwrecks, Genny, please." Tillie looked genuinely frightened. "I'm scared to death as it is."

Genny looked surprised. "You are? Then why did you agree to come?"

"I have one hundred reasons," she said with an impish grin.

Mitch stood, and Genny was struck, as she often was, by how much room the man took up in even a large space. "You're all packed?"

He was staring at her and for some reason she still couldn't meet his eyes. Perhaps it was because the memory of throwing herself at him was still so raw. "Yes. Tillie has been a great help."

"I learned a lot about packing dresses in the wardrobe department," Tillie said, looking pleased with the compliment.

"Weather looks calm. Should stay that way this time of year. Too early for hurricanes and the like." Genny gave Mitch a curious look. He almost sounded . . . nervous.

"Have you never been on a ship, Mitch?"

"Unless you count a canoe as a ship, then no."

He *was* nervous, she could tell. For some reason, that made him even more endearing. "I've never been on a ship either," Genny said. "It'll be grand, you'll see."

"Grand for us up in first class," Tillie said, her voice shaking just slightly. "For poor Mr. Campbell, perhaps not so grand."

The *RMS Oceanic* was the pride of the White Star Line, a four hundred twenty-foot iron ship that carried more than one thousand passengers and was powered by both sail and steam engine. One great smoke stack, painted a bright orange, dominated the deck, which was crisscrossed with ropes and cables, reminding Genny of a cat's cradle. Her hull was black, the structures built on the deck a pristine white that almost hurt the eyes in the bright morning sun. An American flag, snapping in a stiff breeze on the most forward mast, reminded Genny that she would likely never set foot on American soil again.

Everything about the ship was intimidating—its size, its hulking black hull, even the uniformed crew standing at attention as the passengers boarded. She had never seen anything so impressive in her entire life. She looked at the ship doubtfully, wondering how anything so large could possibly stay afloat.

"It's really big," Tillie said, looking up at the ship, which seemed to stretch on forever. "And those masts don't look like they could carry much sail."

"I suppose they're only used when the engine fails," Genny said doubtfully.

"The engines fail?" Tillie's voice had taken on a high-pitched tone Genny had never heard before. Without her wig and wearing her plain maid's dress, Tillie looked completely different, and Genny found she liked the looks of this girl far better. She had a wholesome, fresh quality now that her face was free of makeup. But Tillie was clearly out of sorts. It was almost as if the blonde wig and flashy clothing she'd worn after her initial appearance had given her more confidence. No one would doubt her role as a lady's maid as they stood waiting for Mitch to return from wherever he'd disappeared to. He'd looked decidedly pale when they'd arrived at the port and gotten their first look at the *Oceanic*. Genny looked around her, but no one seemed at all concerned about the ship's seaworthiness. Indeed, there was a festive air to the passengers, who were already standing at the rail waving good-bye to family or friends.

Not twenty feet from the two women, an older couple stood waving and smiling at someone on the ship even as tears streamed down their faces. Genny nudged Tillie and nodded to the couple, who looked about as heartbroken as a pair of people could.

"It must be awful to say good-bye to someone, knowing you'll never see them again. I've a feeling that's what's happening there." Tillie said softly so the couple wouldn't overhear.

Genny's heart squeezed painfully in her chest. The couple was a stark reminder of everything she was leaving behind. Her parents were gone, but America was home. Everyone she knew was here. She wondered how her mother had gotten the courage to leave behind England and her parents all those years ago. It must have broken her heart, though she had no memories of her mother being sad.

Because her mother had been in love; she'd had Genny's father.

"We might as well board," Mitch said, coming up behind them, his eyes on the ship. "I've been talking to some of the crew. The *Oceanic* is the safest ship on the seas and built to luxuriously accommodate its passengers. We'll be fine. And the saloon staterooms are first rate."

Genny studied his face and decided he seemed more relaxed than he had been before he'd spoken to the crew. The crowd near the boarding plank was thinning out, and it was clearly time for them to go on board. Just as they were about to walk up the gangway, a shout from behind caused them all to turn around. Madeline, who had tearfully told her just that morning that she couldn't bear to bid them farewell at the ship, was hastening toward them, already dabbing her eyes with a handkerchief.

She threw herself into Mitch's arms, sobbing against his chest, while Mitch, looking more bemused than embarrassed, hugged her closely.

"I'll be back in less than a month, Mother," he said, chuckling.

Madeline lifted her head, as if trying to determine whether he was speaking the truth. Ships did sink; not one year ago the *Oceanic's* sister ship, the *Atlantic*, had collided with another ship, killing sixteen souls on board. She nodded, turned, and her face crumpled again as she stumbled toward Genny to embrace her.

"You're almost like a daughter to me," she said dramatically. "And I'll never see you again." This last was squeaked out, as if she could hardly get the words past a throat clogged with tears.

"She'll write, Mother. Now get your hug over with Tillie. We have to board before they pull up the gangway."

Madeline sniffed and gave Tillie a hug. "I'll see that you have a place in the cast when I get that part," she said. "Bon voyage." Then, as only Madeline could, she turned and walked stoically away. Genny almost wanted to applaud, even though she knew the woman's feelings were sincere.

Mitch let out a gusty sigh. "Every time I see my mother, I'm reminded why I left home when I was seventeen," he said, but he was smiling fondly at his mother's departing back. "Let's get on board, ladies. You all have your tickets?"

They both produced them and headed toward the porter, who stood impatiently waiting for the last passengers.

Once on board, they headed to the deck to look out and wave, even though they were all fairly certain Madeline was no longer at the pier to wave back. When the dockworkers pulled in the bridge connecting the pier to the ship, Genny felt a sense of finality. The only way to go back would be to jump, and that was hardly an option. A few minutes later, a gunshot rang out, the ship gave a shudder as the screws began to turn, then slowly it began moving away from the pier.

"This is it," Tillie said as she clutched the railing. The ship moved slowly, but eventually, the pier was out of sight and the passengers began to move about the deck, some to their staterooms, others to sit on deck chairs to watch the land slowly move past.

"Shall we go see our rooms?" Genny asked. It had been decided, mostly at Madeline's urging, that Genny should stay in first class accommodations "just in case someone on board should later recognize you. It wouldn't do for the granddaughter of a duke to be seen in steerage."

And so, she and Tillie headed to their stateroom while Mitch, taking out his watch to check the time, departed to the men's section of steerage at the bow of the ship, where the sea was felt more readily They agreed to meet again on deck after supper.

"This certainly is first class," Tillie said, glancing around the luxurious room. "Look, they've already delivered our baggage." Indeed, Genny's steamer trunks and Tillie's two smaller carpetbags were stacked neatly on the floor.

The room was small but well appointed, with carved wood paneling, and a soft carpet beneath their feet. Tillie's quarters, just off the main room with its bed and small sitting area, was tiny, holding only a narrow bed and small side table.

"Guess I know whose room this is," Tillie said with remarkable cheerfulness, given her tiny room didn't even have a porthole. She sat on the bed, giving it a little bounce and grinned up at Genny. "I can't believe I'm on a ship headed for England."

"I can't believe it either," Genny said, with slightly less enthusiasm.

Tillie lay back with exuberance on her bed. "I'm not nearly as nervous as I was, and these are posh accommodations. Did you see the sink? Hot and cold running water! I don't even have that in my flat. Do you know I've never even been out of New York? Now I'm sailing to England. Maybe I can see the queen. You're probably going to meet her."

It did seem likely from what she'd learned about dukes and duchesses. She wished she felt half the enthusiasm that Tillie seemed to grab from thin air. Genny knew she'd be acting far more eager if she weren't feeling quite so awful about saying good-bye to Mitch. She was in love for the first time in her life with a man she would say good-bye to in just a handful of days. A man, she reminded herself cruelly, who likely hadn't given their good-bye a second thought.

"Have you ever been in love?" she asked Tillie, who took the rather random question without pause.

"No. Well, I thought I was, but no."

"What happened?"

"Remember I was telling out about mashers? How they'll kiss you and make you feel like you're the center of the world, and the next thing you know, you see them walking about with another girl on their arm, looking at her the same way the bounder looked at you?"

Genny nodded.

"I was a lot younger then. Maybe eighteen. And he was the first boy who ever kissed me. I was stupid and naïve and thought when a boy kissed you, it meant he loved you. And I thought I loved him right back. Maybe I did," she said with a shrug. "But I'm not so stupid and naïve anymore. I know a kiss don't mean a thing to a man."

Tillie sat up and studied Genny for a long moment. "You ever been in love? With that gent who kissed you?"

Genny flushed, but shook her head. "No. I haven't really had that much opportunity to be with men, so I was just wondering. I'm going to be meeting a lot of men in England and I suppose I just want to be prepared."

Tillie nodded, accepting Genny's lie without argument, then said, "I thought maybe you liked Mitch a bit."

Genny schooled her features as best she could. "I do like Mitch and I'm very grateful for all his help. But, goodness, I don't think about him *that* way. He's a friend."

"Really?" Tillie asked, raising one eyebrow. "He's awfully good looking."

"I suppose some would find him so."

Tillie laughed. "Anyone with eyes, you mean."

Genny allowed herself a laugh, but her heart hurt more than she could ever admit. She felt a wash of humiliation and embarrassment, thinking about how she'd sought Mitch out and asked him to dance, all the while hoping he'd kiss her again.

How stupid of her to read more into his kisses than was there. He'd only kissed her on the train and again outside the restaurant, just that. He'd teased her about kissing her, acted as if he wanted to kiss her, but when she'd given him the chance, he'd reminded her he needed to do the right thing.

Now she understood. He'd been trying to protect her, trying to let her know that nothing could ever come of their kissing. He was no doubt mortified by her awkward attempt to seduce him. No wonder he'd been so distant over the past few days—he was trying to avoid her. When he'd rebuffed her, she'd been hurt and angry, but now all she felt was a hot shame, remembering how he'd gently pushed her away. Now that she thought of it, she was certain that had been pity in his eyes, not the regret she'd originally thought she'd seen.

Oh, God.

Despite everything, she knew she was still in love with him, knew if he tried to kiss her, she'd let him.

Two days into their trip, Genny was still looking at land on the port side, wondering if they were ever going to start heading toward England. She and Tillie were walking on the promenade deck, enjoying a sunny afternoon, when she spied Captain Spencer leaning on the railing and surveying the passengers. He was an imposing man, tall and with a back so straight it looked as if a plank was tied to his spine. His salt-and-pepper beard, thick and wind resistant, dropped to the top of his chest. He wore a uniform of dark blue with insignia that marked him as a man of command—though given his stern countenance, it was doubtful he'd ever be taken as anything but the captain.

Genny held up her hand, shielding her eyes from the sun, and called up to him, ignoring Tillie's urgent shushing next to her.

"Hello, Captain."

He looked down as if surprised to be addressed. "Yes, miss?"

"May I have a word with you?"

Tillie let out a low groan, but Genny walked toward a set of stairs that led up to where the captain stood, now looking faintly put out that a passenger was venturing toward the wheelhouse.

"You stay here, Tillie, if you'd like, but I'm going to talk to the captain."

Tillie let out another small sound of protest, but followed Genny as she climbed the metal stairs, her shoes sounding like dull bells against the steps.

"Miss, I don't let passengers on the bridge," the captain said, in what Genny suspected was his attempt at being polite. But with a voice as subtle as a foghorn, it rather sounded as if he were shouting at her.

"Of course you don't," Genny said, smiling. "You've more important things to do than talk about navigation to your passengers."

A young sailor stepped out of the wheelhouse. "Sir?" That one word spoke volumes, such as "should I escort the ladies down to the promenade deck or throw them overboard?"

"Thank you, sir," Genny said to the young officer. "But I think Captain Spencer can answer my questions adequately."

Five minutes later, Genny was in the wheelhouse, holding the wheel as Captain Spencer explained why the ship followed the shore for so long before heading out to the open ocean. Genny was completely oblivious to the sensation she was creating until after she bade the Captain a good day and was walking down the stairs with Tillie. She was stepping down from the stairs onto the promenade deck when Tillie, just in front of her, turned and with hands on hips said, "How do you *do* that?"

"What?"

"How do you manage to charm every person you meet into doing anything you want? I was there. I watched it happen, and I still don't know what you did. One of the officers told me that no one had ever touched the wheel of Captain Spencer's ship without years of training, and there you were, your hands on the wheel, making the old curmudgeon laugh. You didn't only make him smile, which apparently they've never seen him do, he actually laughed."

Genny shrugged. "I have no idea what you mean."

"While you were talking to the captain, I was talking to the crew. No one has ever, *ever*, been invited into the wheel house, never mind put their hands on his wheel, and certainly not a woman." Tillie studied her a moment. "You are pretty, but I'm sure the captain's seen plenty of pretty women in his day." Tillie looked at her, exasperated and confused. "How do you do it?"

"I'm still not certain what you mean. I suppose I was genuinely interested in what he had to say."

Tillie grinned. "That's the secret. Pretend everything a man says is fascinating."

"But I wasn't pretending," Genny protested. "I *was* interested. Imagine, setting out into a vast ocean with no road, no paths, just water and the sun and stars. It's amazing to me these ships can navigate so accurately."

Genny looked at Tillie, who seemed momentarily distracted by a pair of gentlemen walking by, and Genny couldn't help but notice Tillie's sudden interest. The younger man caught Tillie's eye and winked.

"Do you know those men?" Genny asked.

Tillie's cheeks turned pink. "I met the younger one last night. Figure he's a real masher, but he has the sweetest smile."

Genny watched as the two men disappeared. "You should stay away from him then."

Tillie looked at the shore and hugged herself as if she were cold. "Yes," she said, "I really should."

"I can't find Tillie."

Mitch, trying to shield Genny from the view of the other three men in his tiny cabin, stepped out into the narrow corridor, snapping his watch closed as he did. It was nearly ten o'clock at night, and the passages were only dimly lit by lamps, but Mitch knew his roommates would take one look at Genny and know she didn't belong in third class.

"Come on, let's go up to the deck to talk." Mitch hadn't seen Genny except from a distance since they went their separate ways after boarding the ship, and he wasn't all that happy to see her now. Just ten more days and he would deliver her safely to her grandparents, collect his reward, and be on his way. Over the past few days, he'd nearly convinced himself that saying good-bye was the right thing—the only thing—he could do. The gut-wrenching ache that kept him awake at night would go away eventually. It had to, for he wasn't certain he could continue to go on feeling the way he was, day after day, for the rest of his life. No one had ever died from just loving someone too much, but damn it, sometimes it felt as if he just might.

Like now, with her looking up at him as if he could save the world and smelling like a bit of spring sunshine in this shadowy, rather unpleasantly scented place.

The deck was dark, holding only a few crewmembers on watch. No passengers were in sight, likely because the temperature had grown quite cool. Genny stood, her feet slightly braced, for with the cool air had come a bit of a wind and an unsettled sea. Her hair whipped about her head, her dress flapped like a signal flag, revealing the slim outline of her legs. And she was smiling.

"You feel alright with the sea getting rough?"

"Perfectly fine. But I am worried about Tillie. She was feeling a bit poorly and the seas were still fairly calm."

He'd felt only the slightest effects of the motion, but two of his cabin mates had complained of feeling ill.

"When did you see her last?"

"This afternoon. She—" Her mouth snapped shut.

"She?" Mitch prompted.

"She was with a man who winked at her. I think he might have been a masher." She said this last on a whisper.

Mitch smiled at her use of the slang she'd no doubt learned from Tillie. "And how do you know that?"

Genny shook her head and slumped a bit. "I've no idea," she admitted. "I only know that she was worried he might be."

"I doubt she's fallen overboard. Wherever she is, I'm sure Tillie can handle herself. She has that way about her. But let's take a look in the saloon. I doubt this time of night anyone would mind my being there."

Genny gave him a look of exasperation. "I doubt very much that anyone would mind at any time of the day if you went into the saloon. And if they did, I'd . . . well, I'd shoot them."

Mitch let out a burst of laughter. "I've no doubt you would. But these folks, you've seen them, they might take exception to my stepping into their world."

Genny stopped dead and turned, pointing a finger into his chest. It actually hurt. "The only thing separating you from the toffs on this ship is the cut of your clothes. If you'd spent a dime on yourself instead of buying me all these fancy things"—she fluffed up her skirt—"then they'd accept you as one of their own."

"Maybe I don't want to be a toff," Mitch said, leaning in close.

"And maybe I don't want to be one either," Genny said, leaning in even closer.

Mitch jerked back, irritated by how much he'd wanted to kiss her. It came on him like a wave he couldn't stop. "Let's just go find Tillie," he said, knowing he sounded annoyed. He hated this feeling of being out of control every time he was near her.

In the end, Tillie was pretty darn easy to find. She and her masher were both in the saloon, suffering by varying degrees from seasickness. Of the two, Tillie was much the worse off.

"I want to die," she moaned, clutching the young man's sleeve. He was valiantly trying to appear stalwart, even though his complexion had taken on a bit of a green tone.

"You're sick?" Genny asked, perplexed, even as the ship took a rather nauseating plunge.

Tillie's answer was only to nod. "A crewmember said the best way to avoid seasickness . . ." She swallowed heavily, as if just saying the word made her ill. ". . . was to look at the horizon. But it's dark now and there is no horizon." She moaned and her masher hugged her tightly.

Mitch introduced himself.

"Nathan Paulings," the young man responded. He was perhaps twenty-two and trying to grow a mustache that looked a bit sparse. And he didn't look at all like a masher, at least not to Mitch's eyes. He looked more like a young man who was smitten for the first time in his life.

Genny stepped up and looked at the pair of them. "Mr. Paulings," she said in a tone Mitch had never before heard. For the first time since he'd known her, she showed just a bit of the blue blood in her veins. "Do you think it's appropriate for you to be here in the saloon by yourselves?"

To his credit, the young man blushed and said, "No, ma'am. But Tillie's sick and I'm just trying to comfort her. I've already asked if I could court her."

Mitch suppressed a laugh as Genny's mouth opened slightly in surprise. Clearly, Nathan Paulings was no masher, just a young man falling for a lively girl.

"Do you think it's all right to leave them alone?" Genny asked Mitch.

Mitch glared at Mr. Paulings for good measure, then nodded. "I think he'll behave."

"Yes, sir, I will."

"I'm glad you're in good hands, then, Tillie," Genny said. "I do hope you feel better. If it gives you any comfort, I'm sure you're not the only one on the ship bothered by the rough seas."

"You're not ill?" Tillie asked, clearly envious of Genny's iron stomach.

"Not yet, at any rate."

The ship took another dive into a trough, and Tillie clutched her stomach. "Oh God, I think I'm going to . . ." And Nathan produced a small spittoon just at the right moment, saving the fine carpet on the floor of the saloon.

Mr. Paulings grimaced as Tillie retched. "I had an inkling that would happen," he said, rubbing Tillie's back.

"Come on, Miss Campbell. I think Tillie will be fine, and you have to get back to your cabin." Mitch led Genny out of the saloon and toward her stateroom, but instead of walking directly there, as a sensible girl would do, she stopped and looked out over the rail at the quarter moon.

Reluctantly, Mitch stopped and stood next to her, far enough away that even if he were tempted, he couldn't touch her. He stared at the moon as if it were far more interesting than gazing at how beautiful she looked in the moonlight.

"I owe you an apology."

Mitch whipped his head around. "Apology?"

Even though there was scant light on the deck of the ship, he could see her nod. "Remember when you kissed me on the train? And again at the restaurant?"

Heat flooded Mitch's body. "Vaguely."

"Those were the only times anyone has ever kissed me," she confessed in a rush. "I think I put more meaning into those kisses than there was. And I made you feel awkward. So I apologize." She paused and took a breath and Mitch couldn't stop staring at her, wondering how a woman could so completely misread a situation. "I know now that those kisses really meant nothing and I feel rather foolish for thinking about them the way I did."

Mitch swallowed. "You thought about them, did you?"

"Constantly." Genny let out a small laugh. "Tillie said girls tend to misinterpret a man's intention and I expect that's precisely what I did. And then to go to you and . . ." She stopped, mortification in every syllable. "I suppose that in a year or two, when I've been out in society, I will be used to such kisses."

His entire body rebelled at the idea and it suddenly became too much for Mitch. Genny kiss other men? Make love to some toff who didn't even know who she really was? By God, he wouldn't let it happen. "I don't want you to get used to being kissed," he said, before he could even think about how she would respond to such a statement.

Her breath caught, and he heard it, as clearly as if she'd shouted to the world that she wanted him to kiss her again and be damned with the consequences.

"I embarrassed you," she said, persisting in the lie she was building.

Oh, to hell with it. He was done fighting it, done pretending he didn't care, didn't love her, didn't want her. "No, you didn't. You tempted me. You made my heart hurt." He stopped, knowing that what he said next would seal his fate, but, by God, he just couldn't help himself. He crossed the distance between them and made her face him, made her look at him as he laid his heart at her feet. "Genny, I can't let you go. I can't. I thought I could. A better man might have let you go, let you live the life you were meant to live. But I'm not that man. I thought I could deliver you to your grandparents' doorstep and go on my way and let you live your life, but I can't. I'll die if I have to."

She looked up at him, and even in the moonlight he could see her eyes filled with tears, giving him crazy hope. "What?"

He swore and she smiled. "I love you, damn it. I love you and it'll be a cold day in hell when I get back on a ship to America without you next to me." He looked down and shook his head, as if shaking off the demon that had possessed him. "I'm asking you to marry me. I'm begging you." He didn't even care that his voice broke, not when his heart had been breaking for weeks at the thought of losing her forever.

Genny placed two soft hands on either side of his head. "Goodness, Mitch, you don't have to *beg*. All you had to do was smile at me and I would have said yes."

He let out a sharp laugh and she joined him, tugging at his head as if she were trying to shake some sense into him.

"Does that mean I can kiss you without feeling like a . . . masher?" he asked. He'd never in his life felt such utter relief, such airless happiness. For weeks, he'd been trying to do the right thing, only to realize the right thing was standing right in front of him.

Genny got up on her tiptoes and planted a soft kiss on his lips. "You can do more than that," she said, giving him a look he didn't even realize was in her repertoire.

Chapter 11

Genny pulled back and searched Mitch's face, wondering if she had imagined the conversation they'd just had. He loved her, wanted to marry her. Had loved her for some time, apparently. Men were such strange creatures. Every time he'd looked at her with a scowl took on a completely different meaning now.

"How much more do you think, darlin'? 'Cause I got to tell you, saying that to a man gets him pondering all sorts of things." He chuckled and kissed her again, this time longer and more deeply. "God, you taste good."

Just then the ship took a steep dive between growing swells, throwing the two of them off balance. Genny clutched Mitch, laughing as they tried to right themselves.

"Not the best place to kiss a girl," Mitch said over the sound of the growing wind. "Looks like we might be in for a storm. We should get you back to your stateroom."

Genny clung to him, her arms wrapped around him as he leaned back against the bulkhead to wait for the ship to level a bit more before setting out to her stateroom. "Come on," he shouted, and pulled her toward the nearest door, the wind nearly whipping it from his hand. When he closed the door, it seemed as if everything had gone quiet.

"I don't think I would have made much of a sailor," Mitch said, leaning back against the door, clearly relieved to be off the deck.

"Are you sick?"

"No. I'm scared out of my mind," Mitch said, but he smiled when he said it.

"I didn't think anything scared you," Genny said, holding him close, liking the way his clothes, damp from the sea, smelled.

"I'm scared of lots of things, but I think this"—he stopped as the ship made another dive into a trench—"may be nearly as bad as a battlefield."

Genny leaned up and gave his beard-roughened jaw a kiss. "I spoke with the captain earlier today. He told me this is the safest ship ever built so I don't think we have to worry. Please don't worry."

Outside, the howling wind seemed to calm a bit, but the seas were still rough. "Just a squall," Mitch said, sounding relieved. "It's too early for a hurricane. Come on, I'll take you to your room."

He began leading the way, but Genny stopped him. "Can you stay?"

He studied her a long moment and Genny held her breath. "You're sure?"

She nodded. "We'll be married soon enough."

A slow smile appeared on his face and his eyes grew so heated, she nearly moaned. Her entire body flushed in a delicious way.

When they got inside, he whipped her around and kissed her again, one hand going to the back of her head, the other to the small of her back.

"I have some rules," he said after he'd made her all drowsy with desire.

"Rules?"

He nodded solemnly, then kissed her again, slow and deep, the entire length of him pressed against her. "Everyone is different. What pleases you may not please someone else. So this time, this first time with you, I'm going to find out what pleases you. Next time, you find out what pleases me."

Genny furrowed her brow, and he chuckled.

"For example," he said, moving his mouth to her earlobe and sucking gently. Her knees nearly buckled. "You like that. I can tell because your breath hitched. But I don't want to guess. You need to tell me."

"So far I like everything you do to me."

She smiled up at him and he tightened his jaw and swallowed. "When you smile like that, you do something to me. Did you know that?"

"What do I do?"

"I'll tell you later. After." He eyed the door worriedly. "You think Tillie will be coming back to the room?"

Genny turned and set the lock. "There. If she knocks, we'll just stop whatever we're doing and answer the door."

"Pray God I don't have to stop." He took a step back from her and muttered something beneath his breath. "Now, this making love stuff, it requires you to be, um, naked." The most charming blush stained his cheeks.

"It does? What about you? Are you also required to be unclothed?"

"I'll be naked soon enough, don't you worry. But for now, this is your turn, remember?" He put a hand on each shoulder and gently turned her around, and Genny realized he was going to unbutton her dress. She stood, her breath getting more and more jagged as he revealed first her corset cover, then her bustle and petticoats.

"You sure do have a lot of stuff under here."

Genny turned her head. "Haven't you ever undressed a lady before?"

"No. At least not one wearing such a complicated get-up." He pressed a kiss to her neck and brought his hands around her waist, pulling her backside up against him. She felt his arousal and closed her eyes, aware of everything he was doing to her, the way he sounded. When he brought one hand up and skimmed one breast, she arched against him and let out a low moan.

"I like that," she said, shocked by how breathless she sounded. His index finger circled one nipple, sending bolts of pleasure from her breast to between her legs, even through layers of cloth. "Oh, and that."

He chuckled, taking her now-erect nipple between his thumb and forefinger and twisting gently, creating even more sensation. It was almost unbearable, and he hadn't even touched her skin yet.

"All right, darlin', turn around."

When she did and looked up into his eyes, his expression nearly seared her skin. She'd never in her life seen Mitch look at her with such a heated gaze, and another flood of desire washed over her. "I like the way you're looking at me now."

He smiled, his eyes crinkling and losing that heat in an instant, but she liked this Mitch too. He brought one hand up to her jaw and brought her close, kissing her at first gently, and then with a groan, deepening the kiss, pushing his tongue into her mouth. This kiss was unlike the others she'd shared with Mitch. Those were out of control, filled with passion and urgency. This kiss was slow and all consuming, as if he had all the time in the world to explore her, and she found herself kissing back, with just as much passion, not thinking, just feeling, as if she couldn't control her own body. His other hand captured one breast, and Genny found herself holding onto him, her hands clutching his sea-dampened shoulders or surely she would melt like wax to his feet. When he moved a thumb across her nipple, she actually sagged. She could hardly breathe, but she wanted more, even though she wasn't quite certain what more was.

Mitch pulled back and that heated gaze returned. "I want to go slow, and I will, at least I'll try," he said with a chuckle. "But if I don't see what's under all these layers pretty soon, I think I'm going to go a little crazy." He began undoing the tiny ribbons that held her corset cover together, slipping it off her shoulders when the last was untied. "Turn around."

Genny laughed. "I'm going to get dizzy with all this turning."

"It's not my fault you're wearing all these damn clothes."

"Language, Mitch," she said, though she secretly liked the way he cursed. "I must say, I sometimes miss just wearing a pair of pants and shirt. It certainly made getting ready for bed far easier."

Behind her, Mitch groaned. "Are you trying to torture me? Just the thought of having such easy access..." He groaned again, pulling her against his erection, putting his hot mouth against the nape of her neck, before starting on her laces, cursing beneath his breath. "My hands are shaking," he said in disbelief. "If I had my knife, I swear I'd slice right through these strings."

"You wouldn't dare. This is my favorite corset. It's so pretty. Did you see the little florets around the top?"

Mitch grunted something that sounded like a negative response. Genny gradually felt the corset loosen, so apparently Mitch was having some success. "When we're married," he said, "your maid is going to do all this and when I come in, you'll already be naked."

"I can't walk around naked," Genny said, laughing. "I'll have on my nightdress."

"One that's easy to take off," he muttered, just as he completed the task.

"The rest is simple," Genny said. She undid her petticoat, letting it drop unceremoniously into the growing pile at her feet. Tillie would be horrified by her treatment of her clothes, but at the moment, Genny didn't much care. Right now, she was watching as Mitch made quick work of his own clothing. He wore only shoes and socks, a jacket, a collarless shirt, pants, and underclothes. In a flash, he was naked and Genny found herself staring at what had to be male perfection. Heavy slabs of muscle covered his chest and stomach, which were lightly covered with hair, just enough to run her fingers through if she had the inclination—which she did. She flattened one hand against his chest, marveling at the strength of him, the heat emanating from his body. His stomach was taut and ridged, a dark line of intriguing hair trailing downward. She followed the line, fascinated by how different his body was from hers, and he laid a hand on hers, stopping her exploration.

"Darlin', if you keep that up, I'm afraid all my good intentions of taking it slow are going to go flying right out that porthole."

She dropped her hand and continued her visual exploration, skipping past the middle part rather quickly, to note that his legs were long and muscular. Slowly, she made her way back up, allowing her curiosity to overrule her shyness, and finally looked at his man parts.

"What shall I call that?" she asked, staring at the hard length of him. It twitched and she let out a small, "Oh."

"It's a penis," Mitch said, clearly suppressing a laugh, "but I figured you knew that already."

Genny felt the warm rush of a blush stain her cheeks because she *hadn't* known what it was called. If she thought about it at all, which was rare, she didn't have a proper name for it. Why would she? She didn't have a brother, and her father had certainly never enlightened her.

"I just call it my johnson."

"Your johnson."

"That's when I'm being polite. When I'm not polite, I call it other things."

Genny knew what making love entailed. Mitch was going to put his johnson, his large, long, thick johnson, inside her. And that's about all she knew about making love, for whatever she did know she'd learned only from watching nature.

Mitch was naked, standing unabashedly in front of her, hands on his lean hips, and Genny had on only her chemise and bloomers. Not long ago, the thought of another person seeing her naked had seemed so strange. Madame Brunelle and Tillie, with their cavalier attitudes, had done away with any modesty she'd had. But Mitch was a different story altogether. Biting her bottom lip, she shimmied out of her bloomers, then pulled her chemise over her head. Naked. She closed her eyes and took a deep breath, feeling the cool air wash over her body.

"My God, Genny. My God."

The ship rolled a bit, and Genny stumbled toward Mitch, hitting him square in the chest. Immediately, his hands went around her and he held her against him. "The ocean is finally cooperating," he said against her hair.

Oh, skin on skin was the most exquisite sensation. She might get used to this naked thing for it felt rather wondrous. Mitch let out a low sound, then kissed her, wrapping his arms fully around her, pulling her up and against him so that her feet no longer touched the floor. Within seconds, she was on the bed, Mitch on top, resting on his forearms so as not to crush her beneath his weight.

"Remember I said that wherever I touch you, I can kiss you," he said, moving one finger from her jaw, down her neck, to the slope of her breast, and then, oh, finally, finally, to her sensitive nipple. She arched her back and let out a sound that had never escaped her lips before. She couldn't help it. Never could she have believed that anything would feel as good as Mitch touching her.

"I wish I could tell you how beautiful you are."

She smiled. "You just did."

He bent and kissed her jaw, moving slowly down, following the path his finger had traced, and Genny felt her insides clench in anticipation of what was next. He'd said he would kiss wherever his hand had been, and it seemed as if he was moving . . . oh, goodness, there, to her nipple. He kissed, then licked, then suckled and she cried out, brought her hands to the back of his head just in case he got the idea that her crying out meant stop when she never, ever wanted him to stop.

Then he kissed the other breast and slid his hand down her body, resting it on her thigh, inches from where all sensation seemed to pool. "Mitch," she said, stunned by how her voice sounded. Even more stunned by the way she lifted her hips, inviting, begging, for him to touch her, to somehow relieve the exquisite pressure that was building inside her.

"I know," he said, bringing his lips to hers. "I know."

What do you know? Genny wanted to ask, would have asked, had he not touched her at that moment, right at the center of her.

"Yes," she sighed. And then it seemed as if she lost control, lost sense of everything except his finger, moving against her, making her feel things she couldn't have imagined just a few minutes earlier. She began moving her hips, unaware of why, but just knowing she had to, had to. "I need . . . oh, Mitch, I need . . ." And then it happened; her body grew taut, and a flood of such intensity enveloped her, and she was lost.

Slowly, she came back down, aware that Mitch was looking down at her and grinning. "I hardly got started, darlin'. You are a pure wonder."

"What was that? It was wonderful."

"You climaxed."

"It was quite nice."

He put his hand between her legs, the heel of his hand pressing lightly, and she lifted her hips experimentally, gasping at the sensation. "I'm going to make love to you now. Are you sure you want to do this? We could wait until we're married. It just might kill me if you say no, but I'll stop."

"Why would I want to stop?" she asked, and pulled him down for a kiss, feeling his smile against her mouth. Mitch moved between her legs, touching her, inserting a finger, his eyes closed. She tensed at the invasion, but relaxed when he kissed her. "I love you," he said, and she felt something larger there. He pushed inside, just a bit, and it felt as natural as breathing, so she shifted her hips. Mitch, shaking above her, let out a curse and pushed all the way inside her, letting out a long, low moan. It hurt, a burning sensation that she hadn't expected, for everything else about making love up to this point had been only pleasure, and she let out a small cry.

"I'm sorry, darlin'. I tried to go slow. I tried." Then he started moving slowly, in and out, in a way that she understood. "Wrap your legs around me. Oh, Jesus." He kissed her breasts, her mouth, her neck, thrusting, filling her. The burning sensation was replaced by another, far better one, and Genny started moving with him, trying to again reach that peak that had made her cry out. His thrusts became frantic, faster, right before he arched his back and let out a hoarse cry.

He rested his head next to hers, his breathing labored, his heart beating wildly. "I can't wait to get married," he said, laughing out loud.

"Is this what married people do all the time?"

"It's what we're going to do all the time." He kissed her before slowly withdrawing from her. It was so odd; she hadn't realized how much he'd filled her until he pulled away. "Are you all right? Did it hurt too much?"

"Just a bit," she said. "And then it started to feel good again."

"It's only the first time, you know. It won't hurt again."

"That's good. It really was lovely, Mitch."

"It really was."

Mitch was drifting off to sleep, lulled by the movement of the ship and the best love-making he'd ever experienced, when a loud knock sounded on the door to Genny's stateroom.

"Shit. Tillie."

The two of them scrambled as best they could to dress, though any thought of having Genny climb back into her gown was immediately dismissed. Genny ran for the small wardrobe and pulled out a nightgown, slipping it over her head in a frenzy of movement, as if the cotton gown were attacking her. Mitch would have laughed if he hadn't been so busying looking for his shirt.

"Miss Hayes," Tillie called out. "Are you all right? Should I get the steward?"

Before Tillie could do anything as foolish as that, Mitch flung open the door. The look on Tillie's face was priceless. In a matter of seconds, it was clear she had accurately assessed the situation and it was just as clear she was livid.

"You *bounder*," she said, coming into the room, poking his chest with surprising strength. Damn, that hurt. "How could you, you snake. I trusted you. *Genny* trusted you."

"Hold on a minute, Tillie, we're getting married."

Tillie looked at Genny, who stood like a frightened deer staring down the barrel of a rifle.

"We are," Genny said.

Tillie crossed her arms. "Oh? Really? And where is the ring?"

"This wasn't exactly planned," Mitch said.

"I'll bet it wasn't. Are you all right?" Tillie said, rushing over to

Genny to embrace her, then turning as if Mitch would pounce on Genny and have his way with her again.

"I'm perfectly splendid, Tillie. We're engaged."

Tillie snorted, and Mitch felt his temper start to slide. He took a deep breath. "Listen, Tillie, I know you're upset, but please know I only have Genny's best interests at heart."

Another snort. "So, you're going to live in a palace with her and her grandparents."

Mitch was taken aback He hadn't really thought that far ahead. "I expect we'll head back home and live in New York."

"And make her give up on everything she's entitled to? That's having her best interests at heart?"

Mitch felt his cheeks flush. "We really haven't had time to discuss the future beyond the fact we are getting married." He pointed a finger at Tillie. "And if you snort again I'm going to plug your nose."

Obviously, that was the wrong thing to say. Tillie, her dander already up so high it was likely floating above her head, stood up and marched over to him. Then she snorted like a bull in heat.

"Tillie, look," Genny said, holding up the watch Mitch had left on the small side table near the bed. "He loves me." Tillie looked at the opened watch, her expression softening slightly when she saw his watch case held the portrait of Genny he'd taken.

Tillie harrumphed, which was better than a snort, Mitch supposed. He was a bit embarrassed that she'd seen the picture and would no doubt recall the many instances when he'd pretended to be checking the time. He held out his hand and Genny gave him his watch with a cheeky little grin. Mitch knew when to leave best alone, so he looked past Tillie to where Genny stood, a smile still tugging at her lovely mouth. He wanted to go over and kiss her silly, but thought better of it when Tillie stepped into his line of vision. "I'll see you in the morning, darlin'."

"Bye, Mitch. I love you."

"I love you too," he managed to get out just before Tillie pushed him out the door and slammed it shut.

A sharply cold blast of air hit Mitch as he stepped out on the deck into a gray early morning. The seas were almost eerily calm after the storm the previous evening, and Mitch took a deep breath of salt-tinged air. He went to the railing, bracing himself against it, and looked out, letting the peace of the sea wash over him. She wasn't leaving him. Every morning for the rest of his life, he would look over and see her smiling sleepily at him, and he'd be able to draw her into his arms. If he wasn't the luckiest man on earth, he didn't know who was.

Mitch, his steps lighter than they'd been in years, went down to third class, not even bothered by the sight of a rat slinking away in the gloom. He quietly entered his room and sat on his lower bunk, waking one of his bunkmates, a large Irish fellow named Ross McFadden who was visiting his family after being away for six long years.

"And where might you have been all night?" Ross asked, turning on his side to face Mitch. The two had become chums of a sort since the trip began, mostly because the other two men couldn't speak much English. "These two," he said, "had a rough night. Sorry for the stink."

Mitch lay down on his bunk and flung his hands beneath his head, grinning like a fool. "I'm getting married," he said.

"You don't say," Ross said, sounding as if such a thing were a commonplace announcement. "And who is the lucky lady? Don't tell me it's that girl you've been mooning after, the one in the fancy dress."

Mitch frowned a bit, but refused to let the Irishman's doubt lower his mood. "It is. She's not what she seems."

Ross let out a sound that reminded Mitch of the snorts Tillie had been emitting with such regularity. "All right. Who is she, then? Or didn't you notice that you're here in third class and she's got a stateroom up top?"

"I noticed because I'm the one who paid for her room," Mitch said good-naturedly. "It's a long story and one I'm not inclined to go into right now. Just say congratulations and stop talking."

Ross sat up. "This sounds like the kind of yarn my daddo used to tell. Let me guess. You're the knight in shining armor, disguised as a poor slob, and she's a princess who doesn't realize she's a princess until the knight rescues her."

Mitch chuckled. "It actually is something like that."

"Won't end well."

"It already has ended well. We're getting married."

"I'll tell you what, boyo, I'll give you that happy ending when I see her walk down the aisle holding a bunch of pretty flowers and you're there waiting at the other end. Until then, you ain't got a happy ending."

Mitch's mood could not be lowered by one skeptical Irishman. "I'm going to try to get some sleep."

"You're askin' for trouble, my friend. If she likes pretty things and pretty dresses, you're either going to be a very poor man trying to look rich or a middling poor man with a very unhappy wife."

"Shut up," Mitch said lightly, but the truth was, that last did bother him a bit. Genny *did* like the beautiful dresses he'd purchased for her. Who wouldn't like the latest fashions and traveling in first class? On their trip home, there would be no stateroom for them unless her grandparents gave him a sizeable reward. And would they reward him at all when he was going to be taking her away from them soon after they'd been reunited?

Hell. He hadn't thought of that. He was very nearly broke. He hadn't considered paying the return passage for two of them, only himself and Tillie. He'd thought they would stay at a nice hotel when arriving in London, but he'd have to look for far lower accommodations. Though the ship had rooms for married couples, they were tiny and windowless, a far step down from the luxury of Genny's current stateroom.

"She's used to being poor," Mitch said into the silence. That was true. She'd been starving when he'd found her. Surely she wasn't a woman who would resent being poor after such a brief stint of living as if she weren't. He smiled in the darkness. Genny wouldn't give a fig.

"Mebbe you're right. But I'll tell you somethin'. Once you get a taste of how the other half lives, it's awfully hard to go back. You think I'd like to live in the hovel I grew up in? In New Jersey, I've got myself my own farm, my own house. It's mine. I got fifty dairy cows. Fifty."

"Then why are you in third class?"

"Because I worked damned hard for every penny I have and I sure as hell ain't going to waste a dime of it for some fancy bed. This is just fine. But would I live in a shack again, eatin' rotten potatoes and bowin' down to some landlord? The hell I would."

Mitch pictured Genny back in the tiny cabin she'd been living in and smiled. Genny would be happy there. She'd be happy wherever the two of them were together. He was as sure of that as he was sure he loved her.

"You want to live in my old cabin?" Genny asked, slightly dismayed. They were standing on the deck watching as the land they'd been following for so many days began to slip out of sight until it was only a dark smudge on the horizon. When she'd seen Mitch standing at the railing looking so handsome, the wind buffeting his wavy brown hair, she couldn't help but hug herself in pure joy. This man, this beautiful, wonderful, kind man was going to be her husband. She truly didn't care where they lived as long as they were together. But her cabin? Why on earth would he want to go back there?

"I thought you loved your cabin." He seemed surprised by her reaction, as if he'd forgotten how lonely the cabin was, how isolated. She would always think fondly of the time she'd lived there with her father—it was home—but she'd nearly starved to death. And she and her father had had more than one lean winter when they'd been only a few empty traps away from not eating. She would never wish those years away, but she would also never want to go back to them. Perhaps Mitch thought she missed it?

"I do love my cabin, but I also love eating a meal without having to hunt or trap it." She let out a small laugh. "Did you have your heart set on returning?" Genny tried to keep the dismay out of her voice. "I thought you planned to open a photography studio in New York."

Her response seemed to bother him, though she didn't know why. More than once Mitch had talked about his dream of opening his own photography studio. He'd never once talked about giving up that dream to live in the wilderness.

"It was only a suggestion. We have to live somewhere when we get back."

"I hadn't really given the future a thought beyond our wedding," she said. Mitch let out a gusty breath, and Genny noticed his hands clenched tightly on the rail, his knuckles gone white. "Mitch, what's wrong?"

"I don't have any money, Genny. Other than a few hundred dollars in my bank back in New York, all I have is what's in my pocket and that's hardly enough to get us back to the States, never mind rent a studio and set up a business. I'm broke."

"Oh."

"So I can't open my studio and I can't buy you a house or even rent a nice place." He snapped his head around to look at her and swallowed, looking sick.

"I don't need a nice place or all these silly clothes. Is that what this is all about?" And then she realized something horrible and felt a rush of hot shame for being so utterly blind. She was traveling in first class with a maid. She was wearing clothes that she knew were expensive. Mitch hadn't batted an eye. She hadn't had any idea how much all those luxuries had cost, and to her dawning horror, she hadn't even thought of it beyond feeling grateful. She'd figure if it was too much, Mitch would have simply refused. Goodness, he'd grumbled about paying two dollars for a room back in San Diego.

"Why didn't you tell me? Why did you spend all your money on these clothes, my stateroom, when you didn't have it to spare?" She stared at him but he remained silent. "And this entire time you believed you were going to just drop me off and say good-bye. Why would you do that?"

He looked back out to sea. "I couldn't stand the thought of you standing there outside your grandparents' mansion and having some butler look at you as if you were anything less than what you are. It drove me crazy thinking you'd be hurt. You know that. That's why we got the clothes, taught you to dance."

"To save my pride," she said, feeling the knot in her stomach grow. "Oh, I'm such a selfish, horrible person. None of this mattered two months ago. None of these things."

"But you like them."

"Of course I do. Who wouldn't? But I don't need them, Mitch. You spent all that money, you gave up your dream. For me. I'm not worthy of such sacrifice."

Mitch turned to her and gripped her upper arms. "You are worthy of it." He dropped his hands as another passenger walked by, giving them a curious look. Genny nodded and smiled, silently reassuring the older man that she was fine. "I'm no saint, Genny, so don't paint me as one. I'm just a man who fell in love with the wrong woman." He swiped a hand through his hair. "That's not quite what I meant. I don't think you fully understand the sacrifice you'll be making when you marry me. I know you said yes, but I want you to realize you can change your mind."

She placed her hands on his lapels and gave him a little tug, not caring who might see. "Never."

"Now hear me out. You have to understand what you're giving up. I want you to take a good hard look at the life you would have been leading if last night had never happened. I'm the selfish one here, Genny. I'm the one who's asking you to give up the kind of life most people dream of. To be with me. A dead broke, second-rate photographer."

Genny grinned up at him. "A very nice, very handsome, dead broke, first-rate photographer."

He shook his head, looking miserable. "I love you. I'll never stop loving you no matter what you decide."

"I've already decided, you silly man. Do you really think I'm so shallow as to allow my head to be turned by some pretty lace? And silk so smooth against your skin it feels like a warm bath? And wool so soft you could wrap a newborn in it?" She let her voice go all wistful, then laughed at Mitch's expression. "Goodness, Mitch, I was only jesting. You're worth a thousand pretty dresses."

"Just promise me, Genny. If you come back to New York with me, I want you to do it without regret. We'll have some lean years, darlin'. I'll never be able to buy you the things you deserve."

Genny looked down at her dress. "When I think of what you gave up just to make sure I was accepted, it breaks my heart."

He grinned down at her. "Honestly? It breaks my heart a bit too. I worked years to save that money, and all it took for me to give it away was your pretty smile." He shook his head as if he couldn't believe what he'd done. "It's just when it comes to you, I don't have much sense. I don't think I'll ever do what's right."

Do what's right. Was she doing the right thing? She'd made a promise to her father, but she would be breaking it. No doubt her grandparents would be excited at the prospect of having a bit of their daughter back, of presenting her to society. She would likely break their hearts just as her mother had. She pushed her thoughts away but not before Mitch saw her small frown.

"What's wrong?"

"I was just thinking about that promise I made to my father. I'm going to break it."

"Your father asked you to make that promise because he was scared you'd be left alone. He wanted you safe, taken care of. And that's what

I'm going to do. Besides, did your father make you promise to *live* in England or just *go* to England?"

"Go. He made me promise to go." She grinned, then leaned forward, wishing she could give Mitch a hug, but they'd already attracted too many stares. A few weeks ago, she wouldn't have noticed the looks of near hostility other passengers were giving Mitch, as if he wasn't worthy of speaking to her. Just because of their clothes! She wondered what they would have thought had they seen her traipsing around the wilderness in her father's old cast-offs. Once Mitch and she were married, she'd be sure to wear simpler clothes. Or buy Mitch nicer ones.

"See? Sometimes you can have your cake and you can eat it too," he said, laughing.

"Are you the cake?"

"Your grandparents are the cake you have. I'm the cake you get to eat."

Genny didn't care what people thought of a very fine lady kissing a man sleeping in steerage. She pulled him down by the lapels and kissed him, right there on the deck, not giving a fig what anyone thought. She was almost disappointed when she looked up and realized no one had seen.

For the next two days, Tillie hung on Genny like a burr. An angry burr. It didn't matter how many times Genny told her she and Mitch were getting married, Tillie would not let the two of them alone. She'd turned out to be the perfect chaperone for a young, single lady visiting family in England. Genny resigned herself to reading in the main saloon and visiting with the other first class passengers on the ship while Tillie, with great skill, crocheted. Genny pretended interest in learning, but her attempts to replicate what Tillie was doing were nothing less than disastrous.

"I can repair a boot or sew on a patch better than anyone," Genny grumbled, looking at what was supposed to be the beginnings of a doily. "I can set a rabbit trap, skin the rabbit, and prepare a stew. How many women can say that?"

"Thankfully, not many," Tillie said, wrinkling her nose.

Apparently, crocheting a round using a chain and slip stitch was the easiest thing to do, but for some reason, Genny's stitches were uneven and her results were more misshapen than circular. Her abysmal attempts were drawing the attention of a young woman Genny had noticed before.

When she put aside her crochet impatiently and took up her book, the young lady crossed the saloon to introduce herself. "Hello. I couldn't help but notice your struggles. No matter how many times my governess tried to teach me, I failed. I have an entire collection of those," she said, pointing to the tangled mess beside Genny. "My name is Miss Sylvia Marshall."

Genny held out her hand. "Genevieve Hayes. I'm so pleased to meet another woman who is a crocheting failure."

Miss Marshall laughed. "I fear I'm also rather awful at needle work, but I do continue to try." Miss Marshall, a tiny woman with sharp brown eyes, had a warm smile that completely transformed what was otherwise a rather plain face. "May I?" she asked, nodding to the spot on the couch beside Genny.

"Of course," Genny said, a bit nervous that somehow this woman would immediately know she was completely out of her element.

"What did you think of America?" Miss Marshall asked, and Genny had to laugh.

"Since it's the only country I've ever lived in, I'd say it's lovely."

"But your accent . . ."

"My mother and father were from England, but I've lived in America my entire life," she said. "I'm actually on my way to meet my grandparents for the first time."

"You're an American?" the other woman asked, and something about her expression and tone put Genny on alert.

"I am."

Miss Marshall darted a look to her mother, but the older woman was occupied with her own conversation. "You must be excited about visiting your grandparents."

"Yes, but also a bit nervous. I'm not used to living in a very grand style and I fear I'll seem a bit of a country bumpkin."

Miss Marshall gave her a cool assessment, one Genny did not understand. "Your dress is lovely," she said. "My mother and I thought perhaps it was Worth?"

"No, though my couturier did study with Mr. Worth. It's from the house of Madame Brunelle. I'm certain you've heard of her. She's the premier dressmaker in America." Genny hoped she didn't sound too rehearsed, but she was secretly thrilled she could talk about Madame Brunelle so early in her trip. "She was such a dear; she created my entire wardrobe in less than a month."

Miss Marshall's eyes widened. "I do know of her. Your entire wardrobe? Are they all as lovely as this?"

"Not quite so plain, but yes."

Miss Marshall stood abruptly. "If you'll excuse me." She walked directly over to her mother, who had been watching the pair of them with interest.

Genny watched curiously as Miss Marshall spoke with her mother. They'd apparently come to some conclusion, because after their brief conversation, the younger Marshall waved her over.

"This is my mother, Mrs. Harold Marshall. Mother, this is Miss Genevieve Hayes."

"My daughter and I have been admiring your dress, Miss Hayes. It was designed by Madame Brunelle, I believe?"

Genny nodded. "She's quite accomplished, isn't she?"

"I should say so. We were unable to get an appointment. Of course, we were only in New York for two weeks," she hastened to add. "We were visiting my sister in Pennsylvania, you see, before going to New York. Sylvia mentioned that your entire wardrobe was created by her?"

The three women sat at a small table by the large open windows where a cool breeze filtered in. It was so warm in the saloon, the air felt wonderful against Genny's face. "Yes. I feel so privileged."

A steward immediately came to their table, notepad in hand.

"A pot of tea, please. And a small selection of pastries. And sandwiches. And chocolate." Mrs. Marshall looked at Genny. "I find the sea improves one's appetite."

"I've found it can have the opposite effect for many," Genny said, making the two women hide their mouths with their hands lest anyone see them smile. Genny furrowed her brow. She hadn't realized that showing ones teeth whilst laughing wasn't done. She'd have to make a note of that.

When the tea arrived, Miss Marshall said, "Shall I pour, Mother?"

Genny put a hand over her delicate teacup. "None for me, thank you. I have to confess, I know I'm supposed to like tea, but I haven't developed a taste for it. I was raised on strong, black coffee."

"Oh, dear. That's something you're going to have to remedy at once," Mrs. Marshall said, nodding to her daughter to fill Genny's cup despite her protest.

Genny smiled wryly and let her pour, before proceeding to take two sugar cubes and plopping them into the steaming liquid, causing tiny drops to splash onto the nearly translucent saucer. She stirred, liking the way the small spoon made a gentle clinking sound, then took a sip, trying not to grimace. It wasn't until she raised her gaze to the other two women that she knew she'd done something wrong. They looked, well it could only be said that the two women looked horrified. Genny paused, the cup in midair, before she gently placed it back onto the saucer.

Mrs. Marshall's smile was tight. "And where were you raised?" she asked.

In a cave. "In the West. We had a lovely place with a view of the mountains." Why she was embellishing she couldn't say, but it felt like the right thing to do at the moment.

"And your family? I noticed your accent. Why, it sounds as if you never stepped out of England, and yet my daughter was telling me you were born in America?"

"My mother and father moved there before I was born, but they're both gone now," Genny said.

"And you're visiting relatives in England?"

"Yes. The Duke of Glastonbury is my grandfather, and, of course, my grandmother is the duchess. I think I may also have an uncle, but I've never met any of them, and my father never made mention of any relatives on his side."

It was Mrs. Marshall's turn to pause with her teacup in midair. She looked as if she'd swallowed the cup whole, rather than just taken a small sip. "Your grandfather is the . . ."

"Duke of Glastonbury." Genny was somewhat used to people being stunned by such a revelation, but the expression on the two ladies' faces was nothing short of astonished. "Is that very good or very bad?" Genny asked, laughing.

"Very, very good," breathed Miss Marshall.

"Sylvia, manners," Mrs. Marshall said harshly. Then she smiled beatifically at Genny. "Glastonbury is quite well regarded in England. *Quite* well regarded. A very important man from an esteemed family. You didn't know?"

"I only know that whenever I tell anyone that my grandfather is a duke, people seem interested."

Mrs. Marshall clutched her daughter's wrist, as if trying to stop herself from fainting. Genny looked from one woman to the other. "Do you realize who you are?"

"I think so." Genny let out a small laugh.

"You, my dear, are the luckiest young lady in all of England."

"I am?"

"And to think, you're sitting here with us, completely unaware how very important your family is. How unlikely it would be that you would even speak to us. Share tea . . ." Her voice drifted off. "No wonder Madame Brunelle designed for you."

Genny could feel her face grow more and more heated as the two women stared at her. "I expect I would share tea with anyone who asked me to."

Mrs. Marshall shook her head adamantly. "You were living in America and now you're going to be living in England in a palace. A *palace*. Why, we toured that home two summers ago. Do you remember, Sylvia?"

"Remember, Mama? Of course I do. Remember how wonderful we thought it would be to live in such a place?" Miss Marshall turned to her. "And you will be. Oh, my. Perhaps we can visit."

"Sylvia, really," her mother said. "We could hardly presume such a thing."

Genny shook her head. "I'm afraid I won't be living with them, or staying. I'm going back to America. I'm engaged, you see."

The two women looked utterly crestfallen. "To whom?"

"I daresay you wouldn't know him. He's a photographer from Nebraska."

Mrs. Marshall looked slightly ill. "A photographer?" The two women exchanged glances. Mrs. Marshall cleared her throat. "Congratulations. Your grandparents, they approve?"

Genny smiled. "I hardly think they could. It just happened on this trip."

"On your way to see your grandfather, the duke," Sylvia said mysteriously. Another glance exchanged. "And does this photographer know who your grandparents are?"

"Of course. He agreed to take me to them all the way from California. It's a long story, but along the way we fell in love and we're to be married when we return to New York."

Mrs. Marshall gave her a look of what almost seemed like pity. "Please forgive me, but you seem to be quite alone in this world and I can't help thinking you are, perhaps, a bit naïve. What do you really know of this man?"

Genny sat back, finally understanding what the exchanged gazes had been about. "I know he's a fine man who loves me. Honest and honorable."

Mrs. Marshall pressed her lips together. "I'm certain he is. As I said, please forgive me. So you've known him for how long?"

Genny furrowed her brow as she thought. "Oh, it must be at least two months now."

Mrs. Marshall gasped. "Two *months*?"

"It seems longer," Genny said in a small voice. If she wasn't mistaken, these two women were implying Mitch had some ulterior motive, when in fact he had sacrificed everything to bring her to England. He'd even spent nearly all his savings to buy her clothes befitting a duke's granddaughter. She would have loved to have told these two that, but Tillie had warned her that a young, single girl should never accept such a large and personal gift such as an entire wardrobe, not if she didn't want to set tongues wagging. Though she wouldn't be staying in England, she didn't want to do anything that would reflect badly on her grandparents.

"You say he escorted you from California? Why?"

"I asked him to, and at the time, my leg was broken and he felt it was his fault." Genny took a deep breath. "I know you two ladies mean well, but I also know Mitch would never do anything untoward. He may not have a title, but he's a gentleman."

Mrs. Marshall gave her another look of pity. "I'm sure you know best," she said, but her meaning was the opposite. Genny realized she was seeing just a small bit of what her mother had gone through. How terrible must the pressure have been on her mother not to marry Genny's father.

"I know you mean well," Genny repeated. "And I also know I am ignorant about English society. Frankly, the more I learn, the more it baffles me. I grew up thinking that one person was as good as the next, and I find it a bit strange that someone is thought less of just because of their occupation or their parentage. I'm trying to understand, truly."

"I do see what you mean," Miss Marshall said, warming to the subject. "In America, a man can build his own life, create his own dreams. In England, if you are born a farmer, you will die a farmer. I find it fascinating." She looked at her mother to gauge the older woman's reaction. "Did you know that Mr. Vanderbilt grew up poor and was a ferry pilot? Now he's one of the wealthiest men in the world."

"Sylvia," Mrs. Marshall said, as if her daughter were blaspheming.

"It's true, Mother. In America, you can be whoever you want to be. You may not have a title, but if you gain wealth, you're respected and considered aristocracy."

Mrs. Marshall shook her head sharply. "That may be, but they are *not* aristocracy and they never will be. It's in the blood."

"What's in the blood?" Genny asked, not impolitely.

"Good breeding," Mrs. Marshall said with a sniff. "You, my dear, despite your unfortunate circumstances, cannot deny your breeding. You are the granddaughter of a duke. You are young and perhaps do not realize the importance of this, but mark my words, someday you shall."

"You're so old-fashioned, Mother," Miss Marshall said lightly. "Is he very handsome?"

"Sylvia Mary Marshall," Mrs. Marshall said, but something in the way she said it made Genny realize she wasn't nearly as bothered as she was putting on. Mrs. Marshall raised one eyebrow, and asked, "Is he?"

Genny grinned. "The most handsome man I've ever met." She didn't bother telling them that Mitch was one of only a handful of men she'd formally met. "Shall I introduce you?"

The two women looked at each other and nodded.

Mitch was feeling a bit antsy. It'd been two days since he'd made love with Genny, and since that time he hadn't been able to talk with her, never mind make love to her the way he wanted to. He knew he probably shouldn't have made love to her, not without a ceremony, and in hindsight he was beginning to regret his actions. Genny was about as innocent as a girl could be and his damned conscience began to nag at him about four hours after he'd left her. But still, he wanted her, conscience be damned.

Ship life was bloody boring. Since he really wasn't a drinking man—plenty of the men on board were—he had little to occupy himself except reliving those wonderful hours spent with Genny. He would imagine a lifetime of nights, of how beautiful she would look in the morning. Of their children, gathering around them. Of how she would look, heavy with their child.

He stood near the bow of the ship, watching some of his shipmates play a game of craps. He would have joined in if he had any coin to spare. That was where Tillie, sullen and clearly unhappy with her task, found him.

"She wants to see you," she said in a near snarl.

"I assume you mean Miss Hayes."

Tillie simply turned on her heel, obviously expecting him to follow, which he did. When it was clear she was headed toward the first class saloon, Mitch stopped dead.

"I can't go in there," he said, spreading his hands to indicate his rough attire. "They'll throw me out in a minute."

Tillie shrugged. "She wants to introduce you to some friends she met."

Mitch took a step back. "I don't believe you." He knew Tillie disliked him and he wouldn't put it past her to try to humiliate him. What the hell was she trying to do?

Tillie stared at him a long moment, hands on hips, then sighed and walked over to him. "She doesn't know. She doesn't know that a man like you shouldn't even look at her, never mind . . . God, Mitch, she's the nicest girl I've ever met in my life and I know she loves you. And I know you love her. But she doesn't have the foggiest idea how other people think. She told me to fetch you, nice as you please, so she could introduce you to some of those fancy ladies she's making friends with." Tillie took a deep breath. "Look, Mitch, you're a swell fellow. But I don't think either of you knows what you're doing. Especially Genny."

Mitch let out a curse.

"That's about right," Tillie said. "What should I do?"

If regret was something you could hold in your hands, Mitch would have two fistfuls of it. He couldn't take back that night they'd shared, and he probably wouldn't even at gunpoint. But he knew—he *knew*—he'd made a terrible mistake. A selfish one. Genny deserved better. It didn't matter what she said because, dammit, she just didn't understand. Genny had no idea the life she was throwing away. Hell, he didn't even know. Someday, when things were lean and they couldn't afford all the things she deserved, she'd think about everything she could have had and she'd start looking at him in a way he wouldn't like. He fully believed she loved him. But how long would that love last when they were hungry? Or their children were hungry?

"Maybe she needs to see this," Mitch said finally, silently adding, *and maybe I do too*.

"It's your funeral," Tillie said, with one of her characteristic shrugs.

Mitch walked into the room and watched in amazement as twenty pairs of eyes turned his way—and froze. The saloon was a long narrow room with a sitting area at one end, complete with what looked like a well-stocked bar, and a series of small round tables with delicate, padded seats at the other. In the middle were four sofas, set up in a square, where three elderly women sat looking as if they'd all eaten something sour. Two younger men, standing across from him with brandy snifters in their hands, literally looked down their noses at him and narrowed their eyes as if trying to determine what sort of being had just walked into their midst.

Hell, he might not be wearing his nicest jacket and trousers, but he didn't look like a loafer. Genny sat with two women at one of the small tables, and she immediately rose when he spied her. She stood gracefully, and he had to smile thinking about how many times they'd practiced just that movement. She walked over to him, smiling as if nothing at all was wrong.

She held out both hands, and he grasped them automatically, feeling a bit like a man clutching a lifeline.

"I'm glad you came," she said warmly, and gave him a wink. And just like that, he knew that she knew exactly what the disapproving stares meant and that she didn't give a damn. That she was actually having a bit of fun and allowing him to be an accomplice.

"Come over and meet two new friends," she said, pulling him over to where she'd been sitting. "Mrs. and Miss Marshall, I'd like to introduce you to Mr. Mitchell Campbell, one of the finest portrait photographers in America," she said.

The two women, looking a tad uncomfortable, stood and nodded. "Pleased to meet you, Mr. Campbell. Your fiancée is charming."

Mitch darted a look at Genny and drawled, "She sure has a special way about her, doesn't she?"

"Oh, Mother, a cowboy," Miss Marshall gushed.

If Mitch had had a hat on, he would have tipped it. "No, miss, I'm not a cowboy but I spent time with some."

As they were talking, a steward approached the small group, discreetly, and went up to Mitch. "I do apologize, sir, but this saloon is reserved for first class passengers only." Mitch had to give the steward some credit, he could have been a bastard about it, but he was giving Mitch a modicum of respect.

Genny immediately came to his rescue. "Oh, no, Mr. Dunn, it's perfectly fine. I've invited Mr. Campbell. You see, we're to be married and he didn't think it proper for both of us to be on the same level. Such a stickler, you know. But I am so glad to see you are performing your job with such ferocity. I'll have to mention this to Captain Spencer, as I'm certain he'll be more than pleased to know his crew is so capable." She flashed a smile that produced such an idiotic reaction in the poor slob, Mitch almost laughed out loud.

The steward wasn't a complete fool, apparently, because he looked over Mitch's attire and said, "Mr. Campbell is more than welcome to stay, but we do have a dress code in the saloon."

"I see. And under normal circumstances, he would comply. We must maintain standards, mustn't we? But how silly would Mr. Campbell look if he wore his regular attire while in third class? I think he might draw a bit too much attention, don't you? I think it was awfully clever of Mr. Campbell to dress like the other third class passengers so as not to attract undo attention or make the others uncomfortable. There is nothing worse than a snob, whether it's a rich man or a poor one, and I'm sure you agree."

"Of course I do, Miss Hayes, but—"

"Thank you, Mr. Dunn. I'll be sure to mention your stalwart behavior to the captain. I'm meeting him on the bridge right before dinner, you know. He's promised to show me how to navigate using the moon."

Mr. Dunn let out a small sigh, and Mitch knew it was a sigh of defeat. "Yes, miss." He nodded to Mitch, giving him a curiously long look before moving back to his station near the bar.

Genny gave Mitch another smile, one that could only be described as saucy, and he chuckled. "What you've seen, ladies, was a small miracle and one of the reasons Miss Hayes managed to ensnare my heart. She could sell snake oil to a traveling salesman."

Mitch knew how to charm a lady, and he gave his best smile to Miss Marshall, who looked like she might swoon, and Mitch congratulated himself on at least ingratiating himself with the younger Marshall. The older one was still looking at him as if he might take out a knife and rob them all.

"Do you have a studio, Mr. Campbell? I was thinking I should have a portrait of my daughter done."

"I've just returned from out West, ma'am, but I do hope to set up a studio in New York when Miss Hayes and I return to the States. I'd be more than happy to accommodate you when you visit again."

Mrs. Marshall sniffed, as if she could tell by his scent whether he was telling the truth, which he decidedly was not. There was no way in hell he'd be able to afford to set up his own studio now, but he didn't want to appear a pauper. "I'll make certain to look for your studio on our next trip."

"He does take the most beautiful portraits," Genny said. "You should see the one he did of me. I hardly recognized myself. You have it in your watch, do you not, Mr. Campbell?"

In a hundred years, Mitch knew he would never meet another girl like Genny. Anyone looking at him at that moment would see he was likely the most smitten man on the planet. He couldn't even try to stop what he was feeling from showing on his face. Mitch drew out his watch and snapped it open, revealing a miniature of the larger portrait, which was carefully packed away for their trip, a gift for her grandparents.

The two Marshall women leaned over to look at the portrait, the younger giving a small gasp; she did seem prone to them. "It's lovely," she said. "Oh, Mother, we must have my portrait done."

"Yes, Sylvia, we most certainly must."

With a smile filled with satisfaction and just a smidgeon of smugness, Genny said, "I'm so glad you took the time to meet my new friends, Mr. Campbell. I'll walk you out." Genny calmly took his arm and they walked sedately to the door and onto the deck. She continued walking until they were far out of sight, then burst out laughing, clutching her stomach as if it hurt.

"Did you see their faces? Oh, what horrible women. No, not horrid, but victims of their beliefs. You should have heard what they said, Mitch, how I was making a terrible mistake and was too naïve to know better and how could I possibly think of marrying you when I was the granddaughter of a duke. Goodness, the way they were acting, one might think *I* was a duke."

"Duchess."

She waved a hand as if the title didn't matter, which apparently it did not. At least to her.

"I have to admit, I was a bit nervous walking in there," Mitch said. "It was a little bit like throwing a mouse into a room full of hungry cats."

"I know and I'm sorry, but I wanted to put them in their place just a bit. I know I lied, but I just couldn't help it." She pulled his arm closer against her. "You know, I am naïve, because I just don't understand the fuss. I'm just me, the girl who grew up on the side of a mountain in a one-room cabin. I may like pretty things, but that doesn't mean I'm a different girl from the one you met. You do know that, don't you, Mitch?"

He looked around and seeing no one about, pulled her in for a long, slow kiss. He wanted more, but forced himself to draw back. "I'm starting to, darlin'."

Chapter 12

As scenery went, it wasn't much, but Mitch supposed there was some beauty in the endless blue. The ship cut through the waves at a small angle, for a nice breeze had come up and the captain had ordered the sails hoisted to aid the steam engines. The only other time Mitch had seen the sails up was during the storm; apparently the canvas helped stabilize the ship and keep her on course.

Far more fascinating was watching the crew, who worked well together, obeying orders quickly and efficiently with a sharp nod and an *aye-aye*. Still, Mitch would rather look out over the plains of Nebraska than out to the endless sea. He liked the sharp division between land and sky, the way the sun sent shadows and light over the plains, the subtle sound of the grass moving in the wind. At sea, it seemed there was endless noise—the wind, the sails, the ropes, the engines, and the sea itself. A man's ears couldn't get a rest, even at night, at least not in steerage. The men's steerage was set next to the engines and there'd been nights he'd thought he'd go mad if he continued to hear that continuous pulsing sound. More than one night, he'd headed to the deck to lie out on the deck chairs, at least until one of the crew came along and told him to go back to his cabin. It could get mighty cold, but Mitch would rather be cold than hear the engines. His roommates found that large quantities of liquor was a good solution to dealing with the noise on board, so not only was he hearing engines, he was also suffering through a chorus of manly snores.

The voyage would soon be over. He'd overheard one of the crew say they'd be in Liverpool by the next afternoon. A quick train to London and they'd finally reach their destination—only to do it all over again in two weeks. Genny and he had decided that two weeks was plenty of time to see the sights and have a nice visit with her grandparents, and that was about all he'd be able to afford anyway.

Mitch gripped the rail and leaned back, stretching unused muscles. He wasn't used to being so sedentary, and found himself walking around the deck in endless circles. He'd just spun to take another turn around the deck when he spied Tillie walking toward him on the arm of Mr. Dunn. He was still struck by how different she looked without her wig and rather outlandish dresses. She looked, in his opinion, far prettier. She was smiling up at something Dunn said, but that smile instantly disappeared when she saw him.

"Miss Parks," Mitch said, doffing an imaginary hat. He'd taken to leaving his own hat in his cabin, tired of the struggle to keep the damned thing on his head in the wind. Mr. Dunn had pulled his hat down so far, he looked rather misshapen, as if his head was half the size it truly was.

"Where is Miss Hayes?" he asked, looking behind the couple in hopes of catching a glimpse of Genny behind them. He hadn't seen her in nearly a day and, frankly, he missed her.

"She had trouble sleeping and was up most of the night reading so I let her rest," Tillie said with forced pleasantness. "I don't suppose you'd like to join us for breakfast?"

It was clear she didn't want him, so Mitch politely declined and let them go on their way. And then a wicked and wonderful thought struck him: Genny was alone in her cabin in her nightclothes. Nightclothes that were easy to remove. He was instantly aroused, thinking of her lying naked beneath him, her slim legs wrapped around his torso, her eyes closed in ecstasy.

He debated with himself whether he should take advantage of this rare gift, all the while walking toward her stateroom. Looking up and down the hall and finding no one about, he tested the door, thanking God and all the saints that it was unlocked, and let himself in. He closed the door and locked it.

When he turned to look into the room, he found Genny sitting up in bed, her hair streaming down her back, and looking worriedly at the door until she realized who it was. She let out a small sound, threw back the covers, and was in his arms in seconds, kissing and laughing.

"You're such a clever man," she said, placing her hands on his cheeks. "A clever man who needs a shave. Are you growing your beard again?"

He shook his head, still celebrating the miracle of being able to hold her, to feel her warmth through the thin cotton. "I tried shaving the first day and nearly cut my throat," he said, nuzzling his lips against her hair. He loved the way she smelled, all fresh and Genny-like.

"Tillie's at breakfast," she said, stepping back and holding one of his hands. Then she pulled him toward her bed and Mitch swallowed hard. He hadn't wanted to presume—actually he *had* wanted to presume—but he sent up another quick prayer thanking the Lord for giving him such a willing woman.

"It's your turn, I believe," she said.

"My turn?"

"Or rather it's my turn. To find out what you like." She blushed and looked away, losing a bit of her sauciness. "You said—"

"Darlin', you are a pure miracle. I think that, you know. Every time I kiss you or hold you in my arms, I think that I don't deserve a miracle like you." He hissed in a breath when she touched his chest, growing painfully hard at that simple caress.

"This should be easy," Genny said, grinning.

"Men are far less complicated than women," Mitch managed to say. He made quick work of his boots and clothes, and in just a few minutes, he was standing before her naked, feeling her gaze as if she were touching him. God, he wanted her, *burned* for her. "Come here," he said, hardly recognizing his own voice, which had gone low and rough as if he could hardly get the words past his throat. She stepped toward him, suddenly shy, and he smiled at her reassuringly, adoring her charming mix of courage and nervousness.

"Hands over your head," he ordered.

She complied, grinning, all shyness gone, and he lifted her gown over her head and tossed it to the side so he could drink in the sight of her, the perfection. Her arms were still lifted, her breasts thrusting up, nipples hard, waves of blonde hair flowing down her back. Slowly she lowered her arms to her sides, and the desire he saw in her eyes made him groan. Mitch reached out, bringing one hand behind her head, then pulled her toward him, swallowing hard when he felt her luscious softness and heard that small, heady sound she made when she was flush against him.

"I could stay like this forever," she said against his chest, then kissed him just below his clavicle, her lips so damned soft.

He let out a low rumble of agreement, but his body was screaming for something more. "I'm going to lie down on my back and you're going to get to know me better."

She giggled. "I already know you quite well, Mr. Campbell."

"You know what? I can't wait to call you Mrs. Campbell. But for now, I'll settle for Miss Hayes." She gave him a look. "We have to maintain a certain level of propriety, you know." He lay down on the bed and she knelt next to him, her breasts swaying tantalizingly. He knew he was breaking the rules, but he couldn't stop himself from lifting his head and taking one perfect nipple in his mouth and sucking gently. He loved the way she arched her back, the sound of pure pleasure that escaped her mouth. She splayed one hand on his chest and gave herself up to his caresses. His hand found her other breast and he rolled the hardened nipple between his thumb and forefinger, his cock responding to the harsh breath she let out as if she'd touched him there.

"Oh, Mitch," she breathed.

He brought her down for a soul-stealing kiss, thrusting his tongue against hers, thrusting his hips in time to his strokes. He wanted to be inside her, *now*, their little agreement be damned, but she pulled away, a determined look in her eye.

She touched his shoulders, her eyes following her hands as she moved them over him, intent and so damned beautiful. The morning sunlight streamed through a crack in the thick velvet drapes, making her eyes seem almost ethereally beautiful. "You're very handsome," she said, moving her hands down his arms and trailing them to his chest. Everywhere she touched him felt so damned good, and he knew she could feel how fast his heart was beating. She must know the power she had over him. If she stopped, he'd cry like a baby.

She moved her hands over his stomach, smiling at the muscled ridges, and he felt like a king. When she lowered her hands, near his thrusting arousal, she bit her lip and darted a look to him, and Mitch let out a low chuckle. "You can touch it. Here," he said, taking her hand and gently wrapping it around him. God, her hand on him felt so good. He was breathing as if he'd just run a mile on a hot day. "God, Genny, don't stop."

He moved her hand, up and down. "It's quite amazing, isn't it?" she asked, and he grinned at her proper accent. "It's like velvet, so soft, and yet . . ."—she gave him a squeeze and he nearly lost control—". . . so very firm. I suppose that's so it goes in more easily."

He groaned. "I never really thought about the biology of it. Touch the top." He sounded like he was begging, and he was, his pride be damned. If she didn't touch him now . . . She did, two fingers moving over the sensitive tip, and he threw his head back, losing himself in the pure pleasure of her caress.

"You like this." It was a statement.

"God, yes."

She changed her grip, holding him as one would hold a thick stick, but moving her thumb over the tip. Oh God. "Okay, that's good You can, God, you can stop, darlin'." He was close to coming, and when he did that, he wanted to be inside her, surrounded by her tight heat. Mitch clenched his jaw and thought about the sea, the sound of rain, anything to distract him from his impending release.

He opened his eyes to find her looking down at him, smiling prettily and with a bit of triumph. "This is lovely, isn't it, finding what we like."

He could only nod. He took a deep breath. Another. "Get on top of me, darlin'." She did, straddling him, and he couldn't help but thrust his hips. "Ease yourself onto me." She lifted her head, her eyes wide.

"Truly?"

"Only if you want to," he said, hoping against hope she wanted to.

She smiled and lifted her bum, and grasped him in her hand. He helped guide her, slowly, achingly slowly, until he was fully in her. She was more than ready for him, slick and hot.

"You all right?"

She nodded, but seemed a bit uncertain. "Here," he said, and showed her what to do, lifting her hips and guiding her, up and down, until he saw desire make her eyes drowsy, until she let out that small sound she made when she felt her own release building. He put a thumb against her hard little nub, and made small circular motions, hearing her breath hitch, feeling her tighten around him like a vise.

"Oh," she breathed, her body moving in frantic thrusts as he gave himself up to his own desire. When he felt her convulse around him, he found himself in a place he had never been before, a place he hadn't known existed. He was unaware of anything but the way she felt, pulsing around him. He let out a shout, losing himself in an orgasm so powerful he thought he just might die.

He didn't. When it was over, he realized he'd never felt so alive in his life. "I'm the luckiest man on earth," he said, and she collapsed on top of him, her body slick from sweat.

"I do believe we are both quite fortunate."

He chuckled at her formal way of speaking, then kissed her deeply. "I love you so damned much."

"Language, Mr. Campbell." But she was smiling as she said it.

Chapter 13

"Will you look at that. Do you think it's for us?" Tillie stood, mouth agape, looking at a deep-red carriage with an impressive crest on the spotless door. Four matching black horses with matching red plumes stood patiently in front of the carriage, held in place by a footman wearing a uniform in gold and that same deep red.

"It can't be," Genny said, looking at the gilt trim and shining brass lamps at the front of the vehicle. They had cabled her grandparents to let them know approximately when they would arrive from Liverpool, but Genny had hardly expected them to send a carriage, never mind one so well appointed.

Mitch stepped forward and spoke with one of the uniformed men, nodded, then waved Genny and Tillie over. "Your carriage awaits, miss," he said, sweeping a bow and making both women giggle. The footman immediately pulled down a step and motioned for another man to take their baggage and load it onto a smaller, less luxurious carriage behind theirs.

Genny stepped aboard with the assistance of the footman, who kept his eyes trained forward, never making eye contact, though he did move his head slightly when Genny thanked him, the way one would if one were pinched.

When Tillie made to climb aboard, the footman moved in front of the steps. "The other carriage for the two of you," he said.

Already inside the carriage, Genny overheard and immediately went to the door. "No, they are to ride with me."

The footman hesitated only slightly, then nodded and stepped aside, seeming unhappy with the situation.

"Oh," Tillie said when she climbed in, drawing out the word. "This is far too nice for the likes of me." She'd put on an exaggerated cockney accent and Genny had to laugh despite the fact she was more than a bit bothered that neither Tillie nor Mitch was expected to ride with her.

Quilted padded black leather lined the walls, and the roof was a rich dark wood that Genny suspected was mahogany, with an intricate inlaid pattern of a lighter wood. The floor was the same, shining wood, with more inlay. It was so fine, Genny hardly wanted to put her shoes down on it. The carriage rocked slightly when Mitch pulled himself aboard, and he sat down heavily across from the two women, looking too large for the small space.

"This isn't half as nice as a New York City cab," he said, laughing. He looked around and let out a low whistle. "If this is their carriage, I can't wait to see their house."

Genny was terribly nervous and could feel her hands sweating inside her infernal gloves. She wanted nothing more than to take the fine kid gloves off and wipe her hands on her skirt, and would have if she wasn't worried about staining her peach-colored dress. Madame Brunelle called it a "travel costume" though to Genny it was like any of the other dresses she had in her trunks. The only difference was the smart little bolero jacket that went over her bodice, making it unbearably hot to wear. Mitch gave her a look that she suspected was meant to calm her, but he appeared none too calm himself, so it had the opposite effect.

"They'll love you," he said, shifting in his seat and looking out the window.

Genny did the same, marveling at how crowded the streets were. It seemed as if all of humanity was gathered around the Victoria train station.

The carriage moved forward and Genny gripped the seat, her stomach giving a little nervous flip. After months of longing and dreaming, she was about to meet her mother's parents, the great duke and duchess, the authors of those heartfelt letters. It seemed as if they'd only traveled a few minutes before the carriage pulled into a circular drive, stopping before a huge building, precisely symmetrical, with marble steps leading to enormous, whitewashed double doors. Mullioned windows stretched along each side of the doors, perfectly matched by second floor windows. The only buildings Genny had seen that were this large were hotels. Surely this couldn't be their house. Why, it nearly took up an entire city block and then some.

The steps were lowered and the same footman who had handed her up into the carriage stood at attention, one hand extended, as he waited for Genny to descend.

"Welcome to Glaston House, miss," he said, giving a bow.

"This is the home of the duke and duchess of Glastonbury?" Genny asked.

"Yes, miss."

Genny stepped down onto a drive paved with smooth stones laid in a circular pattern. Tillie came up beside her and said, "Time to get into character," and Genny nearly laughed aloud. The front door swung open at that moment, and a man, his silver hair slicked back, his clothing impeccable, opened the door and stepped back. At first, Genny thought it must be her grandfather, but then realized the dignified gentleman was the butler.

Genny looked back at Mitch, giving him a small smile. She must look terrified, for he held out his hand and grasped hers tightly, going up the stairs with her; Tillie following meekly behind, as a good maid should.

As they passed through an entry so high two men standing upon one another wouldn't have touched the top of the door, a sea of uniformed men and women emerged from a door off the massive, marbled foyer. With military precision, they entered the foyer, shoes pattering lightly on the floor, heads up, giving her curious glances before getting into a severely straight line and staring directly in front of them. It took Genny several moments before she realized she was looking at the staff of Glaston House. The women all wore gray dresses with white aprons and caps, and the men all wore deep red uniforms that had an almost military look. Finally, an older woman and the man Genny had presumed was the butler came forward, the woman wearing a fine dress of the deepest green and the man in a formal suit. Genny's heart nearly beat out of her chest. Her grandparents. It must be—and to think she'd thought her grandfather was the butler.

She very nearly stepped forward to greet them, then Mitch tugged at her hand as the two of them stepped into line with the other servants, leaving Genny confused. She was still looking at the pair when a sound down what seemed an endless hallway drew her attention, and she knew immediately she was looking at her grandparents. The woman wore a gown that dripped opulence, her granite-gray hair swept up in an impossibly intricate style that must have taken her poor maid hours to create. The man, his nearly bald head shiny in the muted sunlight coming through the mullioned windows, held himself with military precision.

Genny watched, with a sense of anticipation, as the pair walked toward them before her grandmother stopped sharply, gave a quick intake of breath, then proceeded forward, stopping perhaps six feet in front of Genny. "Genevieve?"

"Yes. Ma'am."

Her grandmother's nostrils flared almost imperceptibly. "Your Grace."

Genny felt her cheeks flush, for she had no idea what the older lady was saying to her. "Pardon?"

"You are to call us 'your grace.' "

"Both of you?" She looked from one to the other.

Beside her stone-faced grandmother, her grandfather coughed, and Genny suspected he was trying not to laugh. He had a twinkle in his eye as he looked at her, though he didn't do anything so gauche as to smile. Or speak a word.

"It is the proper address. I would have thought your parents would have instructed you on that at least," the duchess said.

Genny ignored the unexpected criticism, swallowing down a retort. "I thought I might call you Grandmother and Grandfather, Your, um, Graces?" Genny said, trying to squelch the disappointment coursing through her. Though they were strangers, they were her relations, and she had envisioned a warmer welcome. She'd even thought her grandmother would open her arms and she would rush in for an embrace. But it was obvious such a display of emotion would never be tolerated, at least not with her grandmother.

Her grandfather's mouth twitched, but he remained silent.

"And who is this?" her grandmother demanded, staring at Genny and Mitch's still joined hands as if Genny were holding a dead animal.

"My name is Mitch Campbell."

Genny looked up at him, sensing a small bit of hostility in his tone.

"Yes. Your name is not as important as the reason you are holding my granddaughter's hand."

He squeezed her hand and Genny got the distinct impression he was growing angry. "Ma'am," he said, and she had a strong feeling he addressed her incorrectly on purpose, "your granddaughter has been through one hell of a journey to reach you. I think the lessons in decorum can wait until another time."

Genny rushed to explain. "Mr. Campbell is my fiancé, Your Grace."

"Your—" And then her grandmother smiled warmly, quickly recovering from whatever shock she had felt. "Of course. You are the man who has been corresponding with us. And you're engaged. How wonderful." She looked at each of them, her expression welcoming at last.

"You must both be exhausted. I've prepared a room for you, Genevieve, and of course, Mr. Campbell, you are staying at a nearby hotel? The Langham obviously. There really isn't another hotel that would be suitable."

"I'm to stay here?" Genny asked. She had assumed she would visit with her grandparents and stay at a hotel as well. "I have a maid." She'd been under the impression that as long as she had Tillie with her, the demands of propriety would be met.

"We can accommodate another servant," her grandmother said, misunderstanding. She turned to the older woman in green. "Mrs. Parsons, would you please have one of the girls escort Miss Hayes's maid to the servants' quarters."

"But—"

Her grandmother turned back to Genny, giving her an icy smile. "Yes?"

Genny shook her head. "Of course. Tillie, go on."

"You weren't thinking of staying at the same hotel as Mr. Campbell?" The duchess let out a small laugh. "You'd start tongues wagging before you are even introduced."

"I hadn't given our accommodations much thought," Genny said, feeling completely out of her element and more than a little terrified of being left in this house of strangers without Mitch nearby. It seemed her powers of charm were at least temporarily gone.

A maid stepped forward then and curtsied, first to her grandmother and then to her. "Tea is ready in the blue parlor, Yer Grace."

Her grandmother pursed her lips, as if the fact that it was teatime was unexpected. "Can you stay for tea, Mr. Campbell? I'm sure you are weary after your trip . . ."

"I'd be delighted," Mitch said, his smile just a tad effusive.

Another tight smile. "Very well. Mrs. Parsons, you may dismiss the servants. Thank you." When her grandmother turned to her, the old woman's smile warmed considerably, putting her at ease. "Let us remove to the blue parlor, shall we?"

Genny nodded, and looked around for her grandfather, who had apparently disappeared with the servants. He hadn't uttered a single word. Genny looked at Mitch and tried to convey in her expression what she'd thought of her first meeting with her grandparents. Mitch chuckled silently, but Genny could feel the subtle shake as they followed the duchess down the long hallway into the bowels of the mansion.

The ceiling soared high above them, painted to look like a cloud-filled sky, with small cherubs looking down upon them every so often. It was such a whimsical touch, Genny wondered at her grandmother allowing it.

The blue parlor was, indeed, blue—the carpet, the ornate, flowered wallpaper, the cushions on the furniture. The only other color in the room was the brown wood and white ceilings and trim. In the center of the room, a sitting area and small table with a silver platter placed atop it was set up for afternoon tea.

"Shall I pour?" the duchess asked.

"Yes, please. I fear my education on tea pouring was sorely lacking." Genny laughed aloud, but quickly stifled her mirth when her grandmother gave her a sharp look. Goodness, was she not allowed to laugh? She was suddenly and fiercely glad that she would be returning with Mitch to New York. She was not certain she could live in a world where laughter was not allowed.

After they'd all settled with their tea, Mitch looking rather uncomfortable holding the tiny teacup, the duchess said, "Now, Genevieve, give me your life story."

"I'm not certain how much you know of our time in America, but when I was very small, we lived in Philadelphia. I don't remember much about that time, just snippets of memories. My mother reading bedtime stories to me or making them up as she went. I always liked the made-up ones best because I imagined she was talking about her own life."

Genny watched her grandmother carefully to make certain talking about her dead daughter wouldn't evoke too much emotion, but she might have been talking about the weather for all the reaction she saw.

"She was a wonderful mother, and when she died, my father was quite devastated."

"Was it a boy child?"

It took her a moment to understand what her grandmother meant. The baby who'd died with her mother. "We never knew. It was never born, you see." Genny paused. "After that, my father and I traveled by train and wagon to California, where my father and I lived in a small house quite far from the nearest town. I have your letters, the ones you wrote to my mother."

The duchess lifted her chin. "I never wrote."

Genny furrowed her brow. Now that she thought of it, all the letters had been signed by the duke. "Where is his grace?"

"He dislikes emotional scenes."

Genny started to laugh, then quickly covered it by coughing. *Emotional scene*? She'd seen more emotion from a rock.

"And how did Mr. Campbell enter the picture?" her grandmother asked before taking a sip from her teacup. Genny had no doubt the tea they were drinking was excellent, but she longed for a cup of nice, strong coffee. Her teacup was so delicate, she feared it might chip just from the pressure of her lips on the edge. Genny took a tiny sip of tea, then carefully replaced the cup on the saucer, taking extra care not to make a sound.

"When my father died, I was left quite alone. One day I saw a man near our home and thought perhaps I could ask his assistance in getting to a train or a town."

"Mr. Campbell?"

"Yes. You see, winter had just passed, and I was nearly out of food, so—"

"Out of *food*?" her grandmother asked, clearly shocked. "I had no idea you were in that type of circumstance."

"Only after Father died. I knew if I went the wrong direction and a storm came up, I'd die. So I stayed put to wait for spring. It's much easier to find food when the weather's fine. And that's when I met Mitch."

"Find food?"

"Of course. How else would I eat?" Genny knew she was shocking her grandmother, but for some reason she couldn't explain, she was enjoying herself immensely. She told the rest quickly, noting with some satisfaction that the horror on her grandmother's face seemed to grow exponentially with each word.

"That was my life," she said when she'd finished, and took a rather too large bite of cucumber sandwich.

"You traveled *alone* with this man?"

Of all the things her grandmother could have been shocked by, such as Genny's foiling a train robbery, *that* was what had struck her? Genny was a bit dumbfounded that her traveling with Mitch would be the one thing the duchess commented on.

"We were mostly in the company of other people," Genny said. "The train was quite crowded. Mitch was very clever and told everyone we were husband and wife, so as not to cause a scandal." Her grandmother drew in her breath sharply, and Genny had the distinct feeling she was not appeasing the old woman.

"And when we got to New York," Genny hurried to add, "of course we stayed with Mr. Campbell's mother." She knew enough not to disclose Mitch's mother's occupations. The duchess's face had gone quite pale, her lips compressed so tightly, they appeared flesh-toned. "I have a maid," she added softly.

"This is a story that must not—*ever*—be told beyond the walls of this house. It would ruin you. It would ruin *us*." Her grandmother's voice shook, and Genny felt awful for causing such distress. Everyone else she had told the story to had been enthralled; she'd never expected this sort of reaction.

Genny looked at Mitch, who was staring at her grandmother as if he wanted to cold-cock her.

The duchess looked from one to another. "This engagement. Is it . . ."—she closed her eyes briefly as if what she was about to say was exceedingly painful—". . . necessary?"

"I'm not certain I understand the question, Your Grace."

"Could you be increasing, girl?" she said sharply.

Mitch leaned over and whispered, "She means with child."

"Oh!" Genny's face turned scarlet. "No. I'm blee—" She was stopped cold by the look on her grandmother's face. "That is to say, no."

Her grandmother appeared only slightly relieved, for Genny realized her answer had told the duchess all she needed to know about her and Mitch's relationship. An untouched woman would have been appalled by such a question.

"I don't think you fully understand the consequences of what you've done, Genevieve."

"No, Your Grace." She didn't know what else to say.

"We have failed you," her grandmother said. "We should have done more to find your mother. And you, once we heard of James's death. We had no idea that you were being raised like a heathen without morals, without an education, without guidance. A girl's virtue needs to be protected at all cost. *All cost*. And we failed." She took a calming breath. "I apologize for my hysteria, but this interview has been exceedingly upsetting."

How foolish to think pretty dresses would be all Genny needed to fool her grandmother into thinking she was worthy.

"Ma'am," Mitch said, "Miss Hayes is the finest woman I know."

"I have no doubt that is true," the duchess said, and Genny wasn't certain whether she was being kind or insulting them both.

Mrs. Parsons walked into the room then and announced that Genevieve's room was prepared and a bath drawn.

"Genevieve, why don't you follow Mrs. Parsons to your room and get settled in," her grandmother said, standing gracefully as if the conversation they'd just had had never happened. She sounded calm and pleasant. "Your maid—Tillie was it?—has been shown to your room so she could unpack your things. We'll talk more later tonight at an informal dinner. Just the three of us."

"Couldn't Mitch stay for dinner?"

The duchess gave Genny a smile that edged on warmth. "You must be tired from your trip, after all. Mr. Campbell, you are invited to dine with us tomorrow evening. We dine at eight. Thank you so much for escorting Genevieve to us, sir. I'm certain she is terribly weary after her journey." Her grandmother nodded to the butler, who had silently entered the room and was apparently waiting for Mitch to depart.

"But . . ."

"Yes?" her grandmother asked, as if questioning her orders was so completely foreign she could hardly guess why Genny would object.

Mitch turned and grasped Genny's hand, giving it a squeeze. "It's all right, darlin'. I won't be far, and I'll see you tomorrow night." He winked at her and she smiled, wishing she could throw herself into his arms and kiss him good-bye. Instead, she nodded and swallowed away the sudden tears that threatened. It was ridiculous, of course.

She would see him the next day. It was just that everything was so odd and she was very tired.

After Mitch left, the duchess came up beside her. "He seems like a pleasant young man."

"He is, thank you. I know you perhaps thought I might stay in England and I had planned to until, well, until Mitch proposed."

"Such is love, my dear. We dine at eight. And, as I'm certain you know, we dress for dinner."

Genny nodded and smiled and wondered what dressing for dinner meant. Surely it couldn't mean that they sometimes were *un*dressed for dinner.

She followed Mrs. Parsons to her room, overwhelmed by the size of the house, the endless marble, the cold elegance of everything. But when she reached her room, she gasped. Never in her life had she seen anything prettier, more feminine, more wonderfully luxurious. She supposed if she had to stay in the house rather than in a hotel, this was a lovely place to be. The four-poster bed, its sheer curtains tied back to reveal a pristine white quilt, was so high a small set of steps was required to get in it. A large bank of windows opened to a little balcony that overlooked the garden. Even from inside the room, she could smell the roses below.

"This is lovely," she breathed, going immediately to the balcony to look down at the profusion of flowers below. A gardener was there, trimming a bush with severe precision, and she called down. "You've done a wonderful job, sir."

The man looked up, surprised, then gave a little bow acknowledging the compliment.

Genny spun back around and reentered the room, her feet sinking into the impossibly soft carpet, beaming a smile at Mrs. Parsons. "I think I shall be quite happy whilst I'm here," she said, and Mrs. Parsons looked inordinately pleased.

"We all do hope so," the housekeeper said, then looked pointedly at a portrait hanging on the wall. Genny followed her gaze, drawing in her breath.

"Your mother, miss. The resemblance is, well, no less than amazing."

No wonder her grandmother had let out that small gasp. Looking at the portrait of the regal-looking woman was nearly like gazing in the mirror. Her mother's hair had been slightly darker, her eyes more hazel than green, but other than those small differences, they could have been twins.

"It's so good to have a young lady in the house again," Mrs. Parsons said warmly.

"Thank you. I do wish I could stay longer. Everything is so lovely here."

Mrs. Parsons's smile faded slightly. "We all wish you were staying, miss, your grandmother most of all."

Mitch looked critically at his reflection in the mirror in the hotel room at the Langham, accommodations he would change that night when he returned. Living at the hotel was extremely expensive and he'd be out of cash long before they set sail in two weeks' time. For a few pence a day, he could stay at a boarding house he'd found in a decidedly less fancy part of town and get a full dinner included. What did he need with running water and a toilet in his room? A wash basin and chamber pot would be just fine.

He wore his best suit, which admittedly wasn't much, but at least it fit him. He'd had it pressed (for three shillings!) and his shoes, while not new, had been freshly polished. He'd even bought a hat to replace the rather battered and stained one he'd had and thought he looked downright respectable. Hair slicked back, freshly shaven.

He moved his head back and forth, studying his appearance and feeling slightly ridiculous about how nervous he was. He positively felt ill about this evening and resented the fact. Those pompous asses of grandparents grated on his nerves. For Genny's sake, he'd try to keep his mouth shut, but they'd best stop looking at her as if she were some sort of mistake.

Still, he'd get to see Genny. Even if he couldn't touch her, which he had no doubt would not be allowed, he could talk to her. If someone had told him just four months ago he'd be so head over heels and idiotic for a woman, he would have punched them. Hard. Men like the one he'd become, well, they were pathetic creatures. Funny thing was, Mitch didn't give a damn. If loving Genny meant he was pathetic, then he was pathetic. He chuckled aloud and shook his head at the stranger in the mirror, that well-groomed man about to eat dinner at the table of a duke. He wondered if they'd be sipping from golden goblets and eating beneath a chandelier dripping real diamonds.

It was a fine evening and St. James Square wasn't all that far from the Langham, so as he'd done the previous evening, Mitch walked, heading down Regent Street to Glaston House. He pulled out his watch, grimacing at the time. It had taken a bit longer to walk than he'd thought and it was very nearly eight o'clock. With a quick check to make certain his shoes were still as shiny as when he'd left the hotel, Mitch stepped up the stairs with the happy bounce of a man about to see the woman he loved.

After a brisk knock, his stomach a jumble of nerves, he stepped back and waited for the door to open.

It was Mr. Blackwell, the butler. "Yes?"

Perhaps the man had forgotten what he looked like, and it *was* getting dark. "Mr. Campbell, here for dinner."

"I regret to say their graces are not in."

That was about the last thing he'd expected to hear. "I beg pardon? I was invited. To dinner. This evening. I can't have been mistaken."

Mr. Blackwell, his face devoid of any expression but perhaps resolve, repeated, "I regret to say their graces are not in."

"What of Miss Hayes? Is she in?"

"She is not."

"When are they returning?" Mitch asked, bewildered and more than a bit annoyed. He craned his neck to look past the stalwart butler, but saw nothing but a bunch of marble and an empty foyer.

"I couldn't say, sir. I am not privy to their schedule," he said.

"May I wait?"

"You may not. I do apologize, but I am not authorized to admit visitors when their graces are not in. Good night, sir." And as he closed the door, Mitch thrust his hand to stop the door's progress. Mr. Blackwell raised one brow, but otherwise did not react. "Will there be anything more, sir?"

"Could you tell Miss Hayes I was here?"

"I could," the butler said, in a way that left Mitch feeling completely unsatisfied. "If you have a card, sir."

"A card?"

"A calling card."

Mitch felt his cheeks turn ruddy and hated it. Hated being made to feel that he was something less, that he was only the bastard son of a second-rate actress-turned madam. Damn, but he hated the truth of who he was.

"Just tell her I was here," he said, allowing the butler to successfully close the door, leaving Mitch on the doorstep, angry and disappointed.

Why would they have invited him if they hadn't planned on being home? Perhaps they'd sent a note to the hotel; he hadn't checked at the front desk before he left. Suddenly Mitch felt foolish. Of course they'd changed their plans. Perhaps they were dining out and expected him to join them. But now it was nearly eight o'clock and by the time he got back to the hotel, it would be half past. Wherever they were, Mitch was going to be embarrassingly late.

Genny looked at the clock, an ornate gilded piece that had struck the hour of eight five minutes earlier. And Mitch had not yet arrived. They sat at a table that could have comfortably seated twenty people in a room that could have easily fit three more tables. The gaslight was bright, making the fine crystal and silver sparkle, though several large candelabra had been placed in the center of the long table, incidentally blocking her grandparents' view of one another.

"I'm afraid we can no longer wait for Mr. Campbell, my dear," her grandmother said, eyes etched with concern. "I'm certain there is a good explanation for his absence. I can see you are worried."

Genny forced a small smile. Her grandmother had been wonderful all day, exclaiming over her wardrobe, inquiring about her childhood. She supposed that the coldness she'd seen when she'd first arrived perhaps was her grandmother's nervousness. The duchess did kindly point out small things that Genny should know, such as when she pulled her gloves off, she should always start with her index finger. "It's a small thing, but it's these types of things that separate a lady from one who is not."

Genny didn't dare tell her that until a few weeks ago, the only gloves she'd worn on her hands were to protect her from the elements.

Her grandmother had even asked about Mitch, putting to rest any concern Genny had that her grandmother was less than pleased with the engagement. When Genny brought out the portrait he had taken of her, her grandmother seemed truly moved and immediately ordered it placed in the gallery where all her ancestors' portraits were.

"A pity it is not a painting, but perhaps we can have an artist do a rendering from this. You are lovely in it."

"I saw the portrait of my mother in my room. We look quite a bit alike, don't we? Father never mentioned it."

The duchess pressed her lips together, a movement Genny was beginning to recognize as distress. "It likely pained him to talk about her."

Her days while she was in England would be full, her grandmother explained, as it was the height of the Season. Dinners, the opera, Covent Garden, art exhibits, a horse race, and a ball—all before she left for America.

"I do wish you could stay a bit longer. You've already missed the Henley Regatta. It's always so entertaining and all of the *ton* was there, including the queen, you know." She'd let out a sigh. "I suppose you are eager to begin your new life as a married woman."

Genny smiled. "I am. New York is an exciting city and not so far away from London."

"I fear many a young swain will be terribly disappointed to learn you are off the marriage mart. Why, I've a stack of letters from several mamas hoping for an introduction." She'd paused and studied Genny for a long moment. "You are quite sure of your young man? You have only known him a short while, and we know virtually nothing of his family. And he is an American."

Genny let out a laugh.

"I know this is difficult for you, but do try not to show your teeth whilst laughing. It's so common." The words had been said kindly, but Genny blushed beet red.

"I love him, Your Grace."

The duchess smiled. "Then all is well."

All day Genny had been on the edge of anticipation, feeling almost desperate to see Mitch. They hadn't been so far apart for weeks, and she missed him, missed knowing she had only to call to him and he would be there. Even on the ship, she'd felt their separation, and they'd only been separated by a few decks.

Now, after waiting all day, checking each clock as she passed by, it was finally, finally time for him to be here. And he wasn't.

Had he gotten lost? Injured? Robbed? Surely he would have sent round word if he had been delayed.

The duchess nodded at a footman, standing at attention near one of the room's doors, and he disappeared silently. Within a few moments, two other footmen entered, carrying with them a silver soup tureen and a ladle. This was tantamount to acknowledging that Mitch was not coming. Genny swallowed down a thickness in her throat and watched as the footman put one ladle of thin-looking broth into her bowl before stepping back and returning to wherever the kitchens were.

Genny had put a single spoonful of soup in her mouth, pleasantly surprised by its rich, beefy taste, when the butler, Mr. Blackwell, entered the room, apologizing for the interruption. He had a slip of paper resting on a small silver platter.

"Your Grace," he said, bowing as the duchess removed the slip of paper, annoyance on her face. She unfolded the note, read it, then placed it back on the platter.

"It seems Mr. Campbell will be unable to attend," she said.

"Why ever not?" Genny asked, wanting to grab the note off the tray before the butler disappeared.

"I'm afraid the missive didn't say. He said only that he extended his apologies but would be unable to attend. I'm sorry, my dear, I'm sure you are disappointed."

Genny nodded, feeling hot tears threaten. "I am disappointed. Terribly so."

Genny laid down her spoon, her appetite gone. It seemed so strange that Mitch had not come to dinner. Perhaps he'd gotten caught up in the excitement of being in a strange city. Or perhaps he'd made a friend and . . .

No. It didn't make sense. Perhaps he simply hadn't wanted to come, to sit down at a formal dinner and be grilled by her grandparents. That made more sense. And "dressing" for dinner, she found out (thank goodness for Tillie, though she couldn't imagine where she'd learned such a thing), meant wearing formal clothing. It seemed silly, given it was just the three of them, but it was simply what was done. Genny was already getting a bit tired of doing what was done.

Mitch walked quickly back to the hotel, cursing the uncomfortable shoes he wore and wishing he had on his well-worn boots. By the time he got back to the Langham, he was hot and sweaty and had lost any polish he'd had when he'd marched up the Glaston House steps. The sun had long disappeared behind London, and with it most pedestrians but for the gaslighters who were making their way down Regent Street. His stomach churned at the thought that Genny was sitting with people she didn't know, feeling lost and wondering where the hell he was, her idiot fiancé.

He sharply hit the bell at the front desk, satisfied by the resounding sound it made, and waited what seemed like an eternity for the clerk to arrive. When he did, Mitch tried to be polite, tried not to let the man know the small panic beginning to grow in his chest. "Sir, would you mind checking to see if I have any messages?"

"Of course. What is your room number, sir?"

"Three twenty-five."

The clerk, his black hair parted precisely in the middle and tamed with pomade, went to the boxes where keys were stored, but even from where he stood, Mitch could see his room box was empty. "No, sir," the clerk said, turning back. "Is there anything else I can do for you this evening?"

No message. Mitch furrowed his brow. Could he have gotten the wrong evening? No, he remembered precisely the conversation, the duchess inviting him for dinner the following evening. It made no sense to him. The invitation, while not effusive, had been issued; did British peers often issue invitations only to renege on them?

"I'd like to check out, actually," Mitch said.

The clerk pulled out a thick leather-bound ledger, opening to where a green satin ribbon marked the correct spot, flipped a page, and made a notation. "I see your account is paid, sir. Would you like to leave a forwarding address?"

"You do that?"

"Certainly, sir. We have many foreign visitors who like to receive their mail whilst traveling."

Mitch nodded. "All right. Twenty-two Great Russell Street."

The clerk paled. "No, sir. No gentleman is safe in that part of London at this time of night. I would very much like to dissuade you from taking such a course of action."

Mitch was in no mood to be thwarted. "I think I can handle myself," he said with quiet confidence.

The clerk looked at him as if considering his words. "No gentleman, sir. There's cutthroats and hoodlums who lie in wait for well-dressed blokes foolish enough to cross their paths. While I don't doubt your ability to defeat one man, if you are accosted by several, which is not uncommon, you could be severely injured. Or killed.

And I cannot in good conscience sentence a man to that fate. If you're to stay in London, sir, you should stay at the Langham."

Mitch let out a sigh. "I appreciate your concern, sir. The truth is, I can't afford to stay here. I'm sailing back to New York in two weeks' time and don't have the money to pay for this hotel *and* our trip home."

"Our trip, sir?" He looked back at the ledger. "I wasn't aware we had another guest under your name."

"My bride-to-be is staying with her grandparents at Glaston House, but they thought it would be improper for me to stay, too, so here I am. Just put down that address, will you? Twenty-two Great Russell Street." He could feel his patience slipping and would be mighty disappointed if he had to use physical force on the clerk. Now that he knew he could leave a forwarding address, doing so became important.

"Your bride to be is . . ."

Mitch could feel his temper rising, hotter than a July day in New York City. "The granddaughter of the damned duke. And if she wants to know where the hell I am, I'd like to leave the damned address for her to find me," Mitch said, his volume and frustration growing with each word.

The clerk swallowed and took a step back. "Why did you not tell me who you are?"

"I did. Mitch Campbell." He let out a foul curse and the clerk had the nerve to look affronted, his skinny little mustache twitching.

"As a guest of the Duke of Glastonbury, you are welcome to stay here as long as you wish," the clerk said primly. "In fact . . ." He opened his ledger again. "We'll have your things moved to the Regent Suite, shall we?"

"Are you saying that I get to stay here for free?"

"As a guest of his grace, yes. He often hosts dignitaries and they *always* stay at the Langham. Always." He pulled on a velvet rope and in a few moments, a uniformed bellboy appeared. "Please follow Mr. Campbell to his room. Three twenty-five. And remove his things to the Regent Suite. I daresay you'll find accommodations there far better than in St. Giles." He smiled.

Mitch turned to follow the bellboy, when the clerk called out to him. "All inclusive, Mr. Campbell. Simply charge everything to your room."

Mitch stopped and turned slowly, looking the clerk straight in the eye so the man would know he meant what he was about to say. "Thank you."

The clerk nodded, closed his ledger, and disappeared into the back office.

"Their graces are not at home."

It was the fourth time Mitch had heard those words from the mouth of the butler who, each time he opened the door, seemed to not recognize the man on the other side. Mitch had told himself the last time he'd walked away, frustrated and ready to hit the first man who gave him a funny look, that this time he would not accept that same answer, delivered in that same emotionless way.

"You're lying," he said, the frustration of the last four days apparent in his voice. He hated it, but he'd be damned if he'd let something happen to Genny while he did nothing. It made no sense that he hadn't seen her, hadn't heard from her. The second time he'd arrived at the door, he'd been ready with a note, which the butler assured him would be delivered. And every time after that, when Genny "was not at home" he'd ask if she'd left him a message. She hadn't. And that was mighty suspicious to Mitch.

"What have they done to her?"

"I assure you Miss Hayes is well."

"Prove it. I want to see her. For four days I've been coming here, and every time you tell me she's not at home. Where the hell could she be?"

The butler looked behind him, then slipped out the door to stand with Mitch on the stoop. Dipping his head as if he were about to divulge the greatest of secrets, Mr. Blackwell said, "Sir, when I say their graces are not home, I do not necessarily mean they are *not at home*."

Mitch reared his head back. "You mean to say you've been lying to me from the start?"

The butler raised his chin. "I am doing my duty."

Pure rage filled Mitch, for the way he was being treated, for the way it made him feel, for the way Genny likely felt wondering where he was. He wanted to kill someone. "You've been lying," he spat. "And I'm not going to take it anymore, not from you, not from the goddamned duke, and sure as hell not from the duchess." Then he physically lifted the man—no small feat, for Mr. Blackwell was not a slight man—and put him to the side.

"Sir, unhand me."

Mitch turned on him and grabbed the older man's lapels, pulling him up to his greater height, fueled by a rage he hadn't felt in years. "You do not tell me what to do, do you understand? I'm going in there and I'm going to find my fiancée and then I'm going to take her away from this damned house and never come back."

"Sir, no!"

Mitch ignored him, pushing the door open with such force, it slammed against the wall with a resounding crack, frightening a maid so greatly, she let out a blood-curdling scream. She stood there, eyes wide, a feather duster trembling in her hand.

"They truly are not in today. They're at the Botanical Gardens." Mr. Blackwell hurried after him as Mitch barged into the house and began his search.

"I don't believe you. Genny!" He moved down the hall, calling her name over and over, drawing servants to the ruckus from all over the house. He ignored them, ignored their frightened faces, the way they cringed when he stormed by, opening every door he saw, slamming it closed when Genny wasn't there. He moved systematically, looking in rooms, closets, alcoves, becoming more and more frantic with each empty room he saw. He got the terrible feeling the duke and duchess had kidnapped Genny, had taken her away where he would never find her again. All the while, Mr. Blackwell followed him, trying to convince him that Genny wasn't in the house when Mitch knew she was.

"Genny!" he screamed, his voice becoming raw. He ran up the long, curving staircase, taking two steps at a time, calling for her constantly. And then, room by room, he searched, as the butler, and now the housekeeper, Mrs. Parsons, followed him. He heard the housekeeper urging all the other servants to get back to their posts, most likely thinking a madman was among them. Well, they were right. He felt crazed, filled with longing and fear and anger that they had kept Genny from him. She was alone in a strange city with purely awful people who didn't love her, didn't understand her.

After he'd searched every room and Mr. Blackwell's pleas had sunk in, he stood in a long hall, bent over, hands on his knees, panting, sweating. Defeated. He slumped to the floor, pressing his back against the wall, raising up his knees and pressing his eyes hard into his hands.

When he found a bit of control, he glanced up at Mr. Blackwell, knowing he looked like a broken man, knowing his eyes were burning with unshed tears. "Why are you doing this to us?" he asked, and the butler winced and looked at the housekeeper, who stood there wringing her hands.

"They are our employers," the butler said, clearly upset by the entire scene.

"Is she all right?" he asked, not caring that his voice cracked. He swallowed. "Miss Hayes, is she harmed?"

"No," the butler said hastily. A pause.

"Yes," Mrs. Parsons said, sounding fierce. "I can't take this anymore," she said, turning to Mr. Blackwell. "It's wrong. The poor girl is broken-hearted. She doesn't sleep, hardly eats. I can't watch it anymore without doing something. And now this." She waved a hand at Mitch.

"Mrs. Parsons," the butler said harshly, "both of our positions depend upon our *not* doing anything. Perhaps you don't need this position, but I do."

Mrs. Parsons shook her head. "I saw what they did to Lady Mary and I'm not going to allow it to happen to that poor girl." She pointed at Mitch. "Look at what they've done."

Mitch got an inkling of just how pathetic he must look to them, so he stood even though he could have sat there forever.

"Does Genny know I've been coming each day?"

"She does not," Mr. Blackwell said.

"You told me you delivered my notes. You lying sonofabitch."

Mr. Blackwell stepped back, clearly afraid of the rage that Mitch knew was burning in his eyes. "I said only that I delivered the notes, not to whom. I did not lie."

"Genny thinks I've not come? She must be worried sick."

"They've told her—"

"Mrs. Parsons," the butler said sharply.

"It's wrong. And you know it is." Mrs. Parsons turned to Mitch, her expression softening considerably. "They've told her that you left, sailed back to America. Without her."

Mitch fell back against the wall, shaking his head. "And she believed them?"

"Why would she not?"

Mitch swiped two hands through his hair. "Why do this thing? I know I'm not a duke, but, hell. What kind of person does such a thing?"

"Come with me," Mrs. Parsons said, and marched down the hall, the keys at her waist jingling in time to her precise steps. At one room, she stopped and beckoned the two men to follow her.

Stepping into the room, Mitch got the overwhelming feeling that this was Genny's room. Her bed. Her brush. Her scent.

Mrs. Parsons stepped before the fireplace and looked up. "There is your reason, Mr. Campbell."

Mitch looked up directly into the face of Genny—or at least a very close representation in oil.

"That is her mother," the housekeeper said. She turned to Mitch. "Do you know the story of Lady Mary?"

"She married a man her parents thought she shouldn't."

"A steward. It was such a scandal. It broke her father's heart and humiliated her mother. We all thanked God she didn't have a sister, for such an elopement would have ruined any girl's chances of marriage. Her grace believed Mr. Hayes was a fortune hunter, but I believe to this day he was devoted to Lady Mary."

"So, it's because Genny reminds the old bat of her dead daughter? That's what this is all about?"

"Please refrain from using such derogatory terms when speaking of their graces," Mrs. Parsons said sternly. She took a bracing breath. "It is either Miss Hayes's uncommon resemblance to her mother, or the money." Mrs. Parsons was looking up at the painting, so she didn't see the look of confusion on Mitch's face. But Mr. Blackwell did.

"What money?" Mitch asked.

Mrs. Parsons turned to him. "Miss Hayes is an heiress, Mr. Campbell."

Mitch just laughed and shook his head. "That's where you're wrong, Mrs. Parsons. She doesn't have a penny to her name. The only thing of value she had when I met her was a few bits of jewelry her mother left. We got two hundred dollars for them. She was living alone in a one-room shack."

The two servants looked at each other curiously.

"She doesn't know," Mr. Blackwell said, sounding stunned, then turned to Mitch. "How did her father die?"

"He got mauled by a bear. Before he died, he made Genny promise to go back to England. That's all I know."

"She doesn't know," the housekeeper repeated with certainty. "You see, Mr. Campbell, Miss Hayes's great-grandmother was a very progressive woman. She did not believe that it was fair a woman could not own property, that she was completely under the control of her husband. I think also she knew her granddaughter was of the independent ilk, so she created a fund for Lady Mary—a fund that would come to her, and only her, upon her marriage. And of course, upon Lady Mary's death, it would have gone to Miss Hayes."

"It was an enormous sum," Mr. Blackwell said.

Mrs. Parsons leaned forward and whispered, "I think the idea of that money going into American hands bothers the duchess."

Her grandparents, in more ways than one, were desperate to keep Genny by their sides. All the pieces fell into place, like a puzzle that seemed impossible to solve. "You have to help her," Mitch said.

Again the servants looked at one another and seemed to come to a silent decision.

"Sir, if we lose our positions, and without a reference, it would be disastrous for us both. If we do help you, their graces can never know we had any part in it."

Mitch took a deep, shaking breath, knowing everything depended upon these two people in front of him. "I need to see her, to let her know I'm here and waiting. That I would never leave England without her."

"Tonight. Nine o'clock. There's a narrow lane that runs behind the property, where the mews are. Go to the second gate and wait."

Mrs. Parsons smiled and gave the butler the warmest of looks. "Mr. Blackwell, you do have a heart, after all."

"Quiet, woman!" The harshness of his words was considerably diminished by the red stain on his cheeks.

"Have her ready to leave," Mitch said, and was surprised when the servants, in unison, rejected that plan.

"She can't leave tonight," Mrs. Parsons said. "Neither one of us will have a chance to forewarn her of your visit. Surely you will not ask her to leave with only the clothes on her back. This needs a bit of planning; they watch her like a hawk, you see."

The butler furrowed his brow. "The night of the Medford ball, then. He could attend, then bring her back here. We'll have her packed, a carriage ready."

"He can't go skulking around Medford's estate," Mrs. Parsons said, rejecting the plan. "What if he gets arrested as an intruder?"

"After the ball then?"

"I'm leaving with her tonight."

Two heads swiveled Mitch's way and they both looked at him as if they'd forgotten he was there.

Mitch felt slightly overwhelmed by their kindness. "Thank you for your help, it's greatly appreciated. But I'm leaving with Genny tonight. I thank you for any assistance you can give me and I promise I'll do whatever I can to make certain the duke and duchess never suspect you helped me."

The two looked at each other again, and Mrs. Parsons said, "Lady Mary once thanked us, too. We'll do whatever we can."

Mitch walked back to the hotel, his steps lighter than they had been in days. He tipped his hat to ladies, young and old, earning blushes from all generations. He would see Genny tonight. He was going to hold her in his arms. When he got to the hotel, he went to the front desk to retrieve his key, giving the clerk who'd insisted he stay at the Langham a hearty hello.

The clerk, who'd been reading a newspaper, placed it on the counter and smiled at Mitch. "A fine day, I take it?"

"The finest," Mitch said, unabashedly happy. He looked down at the newspaper, his grin turning into a laugh. "The finest day ever."

Chapter 14

Even her father's death had not been as devastating as hearing the news that Mitch had departed and sailed back to America.

Without her.

It was inconceivable. Gone. Without her. A death, but worse. When her father had died, of course she had been devastated, but despite her deep grief she'd had the knowledge that she would go on, that death, as difficult as it might be, was simply part of life. She'd lost one parent and survived. She *knew* that pain. She'd known she would survive her father's death.

This was far, far, worse. Death was final, and after a while, one could accept it. But this, this pain was laced with disbelief and horrible hope that somehow he'd come back. Realize he loved her.

He hadn't even said good-bye.

Two days ago, her grandmother had given her the news, the older lady's eyes watering slightly in sympathy. She'd held Genny as she'd sobbed against the duchess's breast, for the first time acting the part of grandmother. As comforting as the embrace had been, Genny had been aware there was a brittleness to that embrace, as if her grandmother was so unused to affection, she instinctively held back.

Genny still couldn't believe it. Couldn't accept the idea of Mitch packing his things, catching a hack, going to the train station, and leaving. *Leaving.*

They were to be married, to live in a little flat in New York as he established his photography business. To have children. Dozens, he'd joked. It simply didn't make sense.

Could she have been so blind? How could she not have seen that he didn't love her as he'd claimed, that his proposal was just a way to get her to . . . *oh, God!*

It didn't help that Tillie, though sympathetic, had that look in her eyes, a look that said *I told you so*.

She tortured herself, remembering their time together, from the moment they'd met to the moment he'd said good-bye, promising to see her the next day. No, he hadn't promised. *I won't be far and I'll see you tomorrow night.* And he'd winked.

His words, the night they'd made love, mocked her now. *I love you and it'll be a cold day in hell when I get back on a ship to America without you next to me. I'm asking you to marry me. I'm begging you.* Why would he say such a thing if he hadn't meant it? He'd never broken a promise before. All that traveling with her, protecting her, buying her lovely things, all for the chance to bed her? No. It couldn't be. Something else had happened.

Had she disappointed him? He'd seemed pleased, but perhaps he had not been. Had she done something that angered him?

Had he thought, upon seeing her grandparents' house, that he would play the martyr and let her live the life he thought she deserved? Of all explanations, only that one seemed to ring true. *A better man might have let you go, let you live the life you were meant to live. But I'm not that man. I thought I could deliver you to your grandparents' doorstep and go on my way and let you live your life, but I can't. I'll die if I have to.*

She needed an explanation. She needed . . .

Mitch.

If he had done that stupid thing, thinking he was saving her, she'd throttle him if she ever saw him again.

Her grandparents had tried to keep her busy, to keep her mind off her misery, but tears were always close to the surface. They'd returned from visiting the Botanical Gardens, and as soon as she walked through the door, tears began streaming down her face. She could tell from her grandmother's expression that the old woman was beginning to lose patience with her.

Genny knew that Mitch's leaving was a good thing from the duchess's perspective. Her granddaughter would now be able to marry someone more appropriate, someone more in keeping with her station. Just that morning she'd gone on and on about a young lady they'd met at the gardens who was destined to marry a duke. Lady Rose Dunford was everything she was not; born to a life so far removed from the one Genny had led it didn't bear thinking about. The girl was pleasant enough and beautiful and apparently the pinnacle of what a young girl should be. Genny knew she'd never be like Lady Rose and never want to marry any of the young men she'd been introduced to. The thought of marrying anyone other than Mitch made her want to vomit. She loved Mitch. She loved him even though he'd left her, betrayed her. Crushed her heart.

Genny walked to the gallery, entering the long, narrow room to gaze up at her photograph. He loved her. She felt it in her heart. Believing otherwise was unbearable. Nearly as unbearable as believing he'd left *because* he loved her.

That night at dinner, Genny picked at her food, letting her grandmother drone on about this or that she had planned for them. Apparently, she'd asked Genny a direct question, which Genny had not heard, because her grandmother said sharply, "Genevieve, I am speaking to you."

Genny lifted her head. It felt thick and heavy, as if she were covered in thick molasses. "Yes, Your Grace?"

"I was discussing the Medford ball tomorrow evening. It will be your debut into society. Lady Rose will be there. I think you should befriend her. She is an excellent example for you to follow. I want you to try very hard to remember all that I've taught you these last few days."

"No smiling. No laughing. Look sedate and vaguely interested in everything that is said but never offer my own opinion. Do I have it right?"

The duke let out a laugh, sharp and brief, and was rewarded with a scathing look from the duchess. "Don't be impertinent, Genevieve."

"I prefer Genny." She knew she sounded sullen, because, frankly, that's how she felt. If her grandparents weren't quite so wealthy and highly placed, perhaps Mitch wouldn't have felt the need to leave. If, indeed, that was why he'd left. It was far easier to place the blame on her new position than to think he'd left because he didn't love her, because his profession of love was merely a way to get her into his bed.

"And I prefer that you not have a name that sounds like a guttersnipe, Genevieve," her grandmother said precisely.

"I'm sorry, Your Grace. I am quite tired this evening and have a slight headache." This was true. She hadn't slept well since arriving at Glaston House and she did have a headache, likely caused by lack of sleep.

Her grandmother's expression went from annoyance to concern, as if she'd somehow forgotten that her granddaughter's heart had been broken just two days before.

"I'm truly not hungry. May I be excused?"

As they were only on the second course, it was highly unusual to leave the table, but her grandfather said, "Let her go." And the duchess nodded in agreement.

Genny left the dining room, relieved to be away from them, their suffocating interest and concern. She had one foot on the stairs leading to the second floor, when Mr. Blackwell called out to her.

"Miss Hayes," he said, looking around, as if to make certain they were alone. "There's a full moon this evening."

Genny furrowed her brows, confused at this pronouncement. "Thank you, Mr. Blackwell."

"You can view it in the garden. It's quite spectacular."

Genny gave him a curious look. "I'm certain it is, but I'm not feeling particularly well. I'm afraid I'll have to forgo the pleasure this night."

"By the back gate. The best place to be tonight at nine. To view the moon." He spoke with strange urgency and it took a moment to realize the older man was speaking in some sort of code. The breath left her.

"At nine?" she asked.

He looked immensely relieved. "Yes, miss."

Hope bloomed, painful and fierce. Could he be saying what she thought he was saying?

"Mr. Blackwell. Do I love the moon?" She smiled, tears pressing, throat closing.

"Very much so," he said with utter kindness.

Genny knew that when questioned, the butler could say with complete honesty that he hadn't told her a thing, that he had mentioned in passing that the full moon would be lovely that evening. Impulsively, Genny grabbed his hand and gave it a squeeze. "Thank you, Mr. Blackwell. You've no idea how happy you've made me."

He leveled a meaningful look at her before saying quietly, "You should, perhaps, shroud your joy."

His meaning was clear: don't let their graces know. And it dawned on her that her grandparents had told her Mitch had sailed for America. She felt sick inside that they had practiced such subterfuge. It hurt. And made her spitting mad. For now, she'd go on as she had been, as if her heart was broken.

Just before nine o'clock, Genny slipped out of the house unnoticed and into the gardens. It was dark as pitch, the promised moon nowhere in sight, and Genny smiled. What a silly excuse Mr. Blackwell had come up with to get her to go outside. Anyone who had overheard the strange exchange and who looked outside would think the butler daft. The garden was dark, lit only by muted light coming from the house, which didn't penetrate more than ten feet. Over the last two days, Genny had spent enough time in the garden to be able to navigate the brick path that led from the house to a high wall thickly covered with vines.

The garden was her favorite place. She wasn't used to being cooped up and longed for a day walking in a forest without seeing another human. She didn't want to live in a forest necessarily, but walking in one would be fine. The smell of roses was strong, almost cloying, but nothing could really bother Genny this evening. Looking back at the house to be certain she wasn't being watched, Genny headed directly to the gate and pressed her ear against it just to be certain no one was in the lane before she opened it. She imagined she could feel him on the other side and nearly screamed when, a moment later she heard, "Genny." A low whisper.

Without hesitating, Genny threw open the gate and immediately found herself in an embrace that took her breath away.

"Mitch," she cried, pressing herself against him, loving his familiar strength as he picked her up and held her against him, his arms wrapped completely around her. "I thought you'd left me. I thought you were gone."

He tightened his embrace, spinning slowly, his face buried against her neck, and let out a low, wretched sound. "Never," he said, his voice raw. "Never, darlin'. Don't ever think it. I was going insane worrying about you. I thought they'd taken you away." He let her down and put two large hands on either side of her face. "Are you all right?"

"I am now," Genny said, laughing and crying, all her pain and joy combining in a flood of tears. "They told me you'd gone and I didn't want to believe it, but you didn't come and there were no notes."

"I came every day. Aw, darlin', don't cry. It's almost over." He kissed her cheek, her lips, her nose and drew her against him again, as if he were afraid to let her go even a few inches away from him.

"It was awful. Oh, Mitch, I thought I'd lost you. That you had decided to be some sort of hero, that you actually thought I'd be happier without you. I wanted to throttle you."

Mitch chuckled. "I'm afraid I'm not much of a martyr, darlin'. I'm not letting you go. Not ever. I'll never leave you."

He drew her to a bench and sat down, pulling her onto his lap and putting his arms around her waist in such a wonderfully possessive gesture, Genny laughed again. She pressed a kiss to his jaw, loving the roughness of his beard.

"I'm quite angry with my grandparents," Genny said. "They lied to me over and over. Directly to me, looking me square in the face." The entire time she spoke, he was nuzzling her neck and she let out a happy sigh. "I still cannot believe you're here." And she started crying all over again.

Mitch held her close, pushing down the anger he felt toward her grandparents for putting both of them through this pain. His own throat was thick, and he swallowed heavily as he wiped the tears from her cheek with his thumb.

"We're leaving tonight," he said fiercely. "Mr. Blackwell had a plan that I should fetch you at some ball, but we're leaving tonight. Is that all right with you, darlin'?"

She nodded, still so overwhelmed with emotion, she couldn't find her voice.

"We'll go back inside. Both of us. Tillie can pack and we can say good-bye to your grandparents."

She hiccupped, then giggled. "I hate the hiccups," she said. "But I love you."

Mitch grinned, then dipped his head for a long, heady kiss. "God, I missed you."

"I can tell," she said, wriggling a bit on his lap, making him go hard. He let out a moan, thrusting up his hips, and he imagined she blushed.

"Time for that later." He pushed her off playfully so that she sat on the bench beside him. "I don't think my poor body can take you sitting on my lap a minute more."

"Are you calling me fat?"

"No, darlin', I'm calling you far too tempting."

She leaned her head against his shoulder. "Mitch?"

"Yes, darlin'?"

"I don't understand them, my grandparents. To be honest, they don't really even seem to like me all that much. My grandfather, perhaps, but he rarely says more than two words. My grandmother would have made a much better duke."

"You've seen your mother's portrait?"

Genny nodded. "I have. *You* have?"

"Let's just say I stormed the castle earlier today. Scared the living daylights out of the staff. When I finally realized you actually weren't home, Mrs. Parsons showed me the portrait. I think your grandparents wanted their daughter back, only this time, they were hoping she would stay."

"Perhaps you are correct. I do look an awful lot like her."

Mitch kissed her again. He couldn't stop himself. She was in his arms, finally, soft and warm, her silky hair brushing his jaw. Tonight, he would make love to her, he would kiss every inch of her beautiful body, make her sigh and scream and shout for joy. And tomorrow, they would leave for Liverpool and head home. Never had that word held so much meaning. It didn't mean his mother's apartment or his small room in Omaha; it was an intangible thing, a place where he and Genny could be together.

"Did your father ever mention that your mother had money?"

Genny pulled back and looked at him. He couldn't see her features, but he could imagine her puzzled face. "No. Why?"

"It was something Mrs. Parsons said. She said the reason the duchess was so protective of you was either because she wished for her dead daughter or to protect the money."

Genny laughed. "Oh, yes. I've pounds and pounds of it hidden in my corset."

"May I look?" Mitch said, pretending to search and making Genny laugh. And then she stiffened, so sharply Mitch stopped. "What's wrong? You remember a buried treasure back at your cabin?"

She batted him on the chest. "No. But when my father was dying, after he made me promise to go to England, he said, 'The box.' At the time, I assumed he meant the box where my grandfather's letters were kept, so I could find them. But . . ."

"What?"

"There's a false bottom. I remember finding it when I was young. It held papers that I didn't understand, so I put them back and completely forgot about them until now. I wonder if they have something to do with the money my mother had."

"Wouldn't your father have told you about it?"

She shrugged, then laughed.

"What's so funny?"

"I shrugged. Do you know how many times I've heard in the last four days that 'Ladies do not shrug, Genevieve,'" she said, doing a fine imitation of the duchess. "My father didn't like talking about my mother or their time in England. Every once in a while, I'd pull out that box to look at the letters from my grandfather or look at my mother's jewels, and I could tell it hurt him. So I stopped looking."

He pressed a kiss against her temple. "It doesn't matter. Rich or poor, we'll still be happy."

"But would it not be better to be happy and wealthy rather than happy and poor?" She let out another light laugh.

"Especially since you seem to like pretty dresses," Mitch said, winning another light bat on his chest. "Let's go get Tillie so I can start absconding with the lost heiress, shall we?"

"They can't stop me from leaving, can they?"

Mitch let out a laugh. "They can try, darlin', but I guarantee you they won't be successful."

Anne Danforth, the Duchess of Glastonbury, had to acknowledge that her high hopes for her granddaughter were diminishing as each day went by. She was beautiful, yes, and charming in her rustic way, but other than her clothing, she was wrong. All wrong. Even her diction had suffered under the influence of her lowborn father. She shrugged. She burped. And when she was trying not to laugh aloud, she let out the oddest noise. It was disconcerting to say the least.

"She's hopeless," she said to her husband, not expecting any sort of reply.

"I rather think she's wonderful."

Anne turned her head slowly to look at her husband, annoyed that when he did speak, it was usually to contradict her. They sat together, as they did most evenings, in the blue parlor. It wasn't that they enjoyed one another's company; they did not. It was more of a habit, something they did mostly because the old duke had done so. "Then you are blind. It will take months to bring her up to snuff. I'm send-ing my regrets to the Medfords. Clearly, she's not ready for the ball. She told me today she only knows three dances. Three!"

"But I imagine she does those three famously."

Anne closed her eyes, trying to gain control of her emotions. Her granddaughter was nothing like she'd expected. It was cruel of God to create a child who looked so much like Mary only to have her be so completely unpolished. Mary might not have been an obedient daughter, she might have been foolish enough to marry the wrong sort of man, but she had always been the epitome of a fine English girl. Genevieve didn't seem to know the first thing about how to act properly. She had been completely Americanized. It was dreadful, but in time perhaps Genevieve could be molded into the woman she should have been.

"You've always been so blind, Glaston. And weak. If you'd stopped Mary from eloping, none of this would have happened. Mary might be alive today."

She was gratified to see her words had hit their mark. "She died in childbirth," he said, the pain of his guilt clear in his voice.

"It doesn't matter—"

She stopped, interrupted by the sight of her granddaughter enter-ing the room on the arm of her fiancé.

"Who let you in?" Anne asked, feeling her face flush from impo-tent rage.

"I did. We're leaving. Tonight." Genevieve didn't seem to know that she was supposed to be meek. Her granddaughter lifted her chin, resembling Mary so much at that moment, Anne felt like screaming at the unfairness of life. She took a calming breath and forced a smile.

"I see. I suppose it's not unexpected."

"You lied to me, Your Grace. He came every day to see me. You told me he'd left."

"Every day?" Anne asked. "I don't think so. And we were in-formed that he had left. I do apologize for the misunderstanding."

"The only misunderstanding, ma'am, was Genny, here, thinking you have her best interests at heart."

Anne gave the American her coldest smile. "Very well. Before you rush off, Mr. Campbell, could you spare a moment please? Out on the veranda will do."

The two young people exchanged a look. "All right," Mr. Campbell said, with a confidence that Anne found exceedingly irritating. He turned to Genevieve. "I'll be right back." The way her granddaughter looked at the man, as if he could stop the earth on its axis, was sickening.

Anne, her back ramrod straight, her emotions in turmoil, walked through the French doors to the small veranda that overlooked the side garden. When the two were alone, Anne turned to the young man, trying to maintain her composure. Everything about him was abhorrent to her, from his American accent to his working-man's clothes. He was so far beneath what Genevieve should have, it was unimaginable that they should marry.

How could Genevieve be so blind? She could almost understand Mary running off with James; they'd known each other since they were children. But this man, he hadn't even met Genevieve until a handful of weeks ago.

Ever since she'd heard his story, something hadn't rung true. Why would a man go out of his way to escort a girl he didn't know all the way across the country? It made no sense. And when things made no sense, it meant there had to be another, better explanation. Anne was quite certain she'd solved the puzzle of Mr. Campbell.

The American leaned negligently against the railing in a way that made her want to grind her teeth together. "Are you truly in love with my granddaughter, Mr. Campbell?"

"Yes, I am." How convincing he sounded.

"That is unfortunate for you. But it should be comforting to know that love is a fleeting emotion. Once you're back in New York, you'll soon forget all about Genevieve."

He straightened off the railing, but if he thought to intimidate her, he was sorely mistaken. "I don't think so. I don't think I'll be leaving here tonight without her. And if I did, I sure as hell wouldn't forget her anytime soon."

Her nostrils flared at his coarse language. "You will. And she will forget you. We've already heard from several families with eligible sons. She'll be married within the year. There's no reason she cannot marry as befitting her station. Mr. Campbell, look around you. Could you ever give Genevieve the kind of life she deserves?" She looked him up and down. "Of course you cannot."

Mr. Campbell shook his head, looking at her with what almost seemed to be pity. "I can't give her a mansion, no. But I can make her happy. I'm as sure of that as I'm sure you're a conniving old biddy."

Anne smiled, ignoring his insult. "I wonder," she said, "what your real reason is for wanting to marry Genevieve. I do hope you're not under the misapprehension that we will give her money. We will not. She has nothing, Mr. Campbell. I can't help but think that a young man who drops everything to escort a girl to England is after something more than, let us say, special privileges. You didn't love her when you met her, yet you left your position, spent hundreds of dollars of your own money, and for what? Because you are a kind and good man?"

When she saw him dip his head and his cheeks redden, she knew she had him pegged correctly.

"Ten thousand pounds."

His head snapped up. "What did you say?"

"I'll give you ten thousand pounds tonight if you leave and never return. You have to promise only one thing: no one must ever know the circumstances of her journey here, nor how she was living in America. Her chances of a good marriage depend upon it. If word got out that she spent days alone with a cowboy"—she held up a hand to stop him from explaining that he was not a cowboy—"she would be ruined. In your world, appearances are not important, but here they are everything. No man would want her and no family would accept her. I just wanted you to understand the importance of this."

"I understand. And you should understand that I've no interest in your money."

"Have you told anyone about her history?"

"No, ma'am." He smiled, and something about that smile made her blood run cold.

Her eyes sharpened. "You hesitated."

"There may have been an article in the newspaper. My mother talked to a reporter the day before we left. I didn't think any harm could come of it, especially since the article wouldn't run until after she'd left."

The duchess felt herself grow pale. "What newspaper?"

"The *New York Times*. To be honest, the reporter said he was from a small newspaper. I have no idea how the story ended up in the *Times*."

"Oh my God." She staggered slightly.

"It came today. I had no idea the hotel would carry American newspapers. Fascinating reading, by the way." He opened his jacket and removed a folded newspaper. "Would you care to take a gander?"

Anne took the newspaper, feeling numb, and let out a small sound of dismay at what she saw—the perfect likeness of her granddaughter on the front page beneath the headline: Duke of Glastonbury's Long Lost Granddaughter Found.

"Oh my God."

"You want to read it now or save it for later?" Mr. Campbell asked, all affability.

Anne moved blindly into the parlor, her eyes scanning the article. With every word she read, her dread only grew. "She's ruined." It was over. Genevieve would not save them, could not replace Mary. And it was obvious her daughter and that scoundrel she'd married had spent every dime of Mary's sizeable inheritance. Why else would he have left what had been a rather opulent home in Philadelphia to live in the wilderness? In a shack. She shuddered just thinking of it. The cad had likely gambled the fortune away.

God, how she loathed him. James had not only ruined Mary, but his actions had also ruined Genevieve.

And Anne had had such hopes that Genevieve could somehow turn back the hands of time. How foolish her hopes seemed now.

Given what the article contained, Anne knew she was being almost eerily calm. The article detailed Genevieve's trip from a one-room shack in California, where she'd lived alone of all things, to New York in the company of a single man. It mattered not that they were now engaged. Just the fact that a newspaper article had been written at all was scandal enough, but that it contained such a disgraceful story and that it was entirely true . . . There was no hope for Genevieve now. No man would want her; no family would welcome her.

And *this man*, whose mother was apparently an *actress* (that was, perhaps, the worst revelation found in the article), had the audacity to claim he could make Genevieve happy.

"It certainly is detailed," she said, throwing the offending article to the side.

"What's this?" the duke asked, picking up the newspaper. He scanned the headlines, stiffening when he saw the likeness of Genevieve. "Oh, good God."

Anne waited, livid beyond reason. The joy she'd felt when she'd heard that her granddaughter was not only alive but coming to live with her was replaced by utter desolation.

"Our granddaughter certainly has lived an interesting life," the duke said, winning a scathing look of derision from his wife.

"I think it's past time we left," Mitch said. "We'll go as soon as Tillie is finished packing."

The duchess sat, her legs suddenly unable to hold her, and she turned her head until her eyes rested on the newspaper and the damning article. A wash of humiliation made her almost ill.

"Genevieve, you are no longer part of this family."

"Anne, no," Glastonbury said, finally getting his gumption up. How *charming*.

"You have no say in this. If it wasn't for you, none of this would have happened. She is ruined and this article has humiliated us all. She is a whore, just like her mother."

Anne should have known her granddaughter, hoyden that she was, would object.

"How dare you speak ill of my mother! At least she was married to a man she loved. I feel sorry for you. For both of you."

Genny had never in her life been angrier at another person, and to think this anger was directed at her grandmother, a woman she'd dreamed of meeting for so long. What a horrid, horrid person she was.

"Miss Hayes, you're all packed," Tillie said, still in character.

"Tillie, call me Genny. We're leaving."

Tillie looked slightly confused, then gave a little whoop. "Can't get out of this stuck-up place fast enough," she said, smiling.

The three of them turned to go, Genny holding Mitch's arm like a lifeline.

"Genevieve, wait."

Genny looked back, surprised to see her grandfather coming toward her.

"Yes?" Beside her, Mitch squeezed her hand, giving her courage.

"Wait, Genevieve, please. I . . ."

To Genny's surprise, the old man's eyes teared up.

"I made a terrible mistake with my daughter. She left and I never saw her again. You have my blessings. Someday I hope to see you again. Perhaps I can come to America?"

"For goodness' sake, Glaston, get a backbone," the duchess sneered.

The duke nodded. "Yes, dear, you are correct. Now if you would be quiet so I might say good-bye to my granddaughter, it would be greatly appreciated." He turned back to Genny. "Let me call the carriage. At least let me do that. Your trunks won't fit in a cab at any rate."

"Thank you."

Her grandmother stood and picked up the newspaper again. "You cannot think to allow them to use our carriage after this," she said, slapping one hand against the paper. "If someone sees, it will be interpreted as approval of her behavior. Which I certainly do not."

The duke ignored the old woman and gave instructions to a footman who hovered outside the door to fetch the carriage and have another sent round for Genny's trunks.

"Is the article that bad?" Genny asked her grandmother.

"No," Mitch answered. "It's actually one of the best things I've ever read."

Her grandmother let out an odd sound, then seemed to lose her bluster all at once. "It doesn't matter. Leave. You're ruined. This article made it a certainty."

Genny furrowed her brow. "The article appeared in the *Times*?" she asked, walking over to where the newspaper lay. "Oh, and my picture, too. They drew it from my portrait."

"A wonderful likeness," her grandmother said, sitting. "I had such high hopes for you."

"As I had for you," Genny said softly. "I thought you might even like me a bit."

Her grandmother, face completely devoid of expression, said, "You may leave," as if her permission was necessary.

"Your carriage is ready, miss," the footman said.

Genny looked around for her grandfather, but he had disappeared. "Good-bye, Your Grace."

The duchess stared straight ahead, silent.

Despite everything, Genny felt sad about leaving her grandparents in such a manner, but what choice did she have?

"Let's go, Genny," Mitch said softly, holding out his arm to her before she walked out of the parlor and down the long hall to the entryway and the front door. Behind them Tillie was fairly skipping.

Mr. Blackwell was there, as dignified as ever, and when they approached, he pulled the door open.

"Thank you, Mr. Blackwell," Genny said, then whispered, "Your name was never mentioned."

She was about to walk through the door when she heard her grandfather calling out to her. When he reached them, he was slightly out of breath.

"Good-bye, Genevieve," he said. "Try not to judge either of us too harshly. Losing your mother was difficult. For us both."

Genny smiled sadly and embraced her grandfather, something he obviously wasn't used to, for he stiffened and patted her back a few times before stepping back. "Here," he said, taking her hand and pressing something into it. "A wedding gift."

"Thank you," Genny said, then turned and walked out the door to the waiting carriage.

When they were in the carriage, Genny began laughing so hard that Mitch became concerned. "What a strange journey this has been," she said.

He grunted in agreement. "What did your grandfather give you?"

Genny held it up in the glow of a passing gaslight. "Money. Quite a bit of it, actually." She handed it to Mitch, who let out a whistle as he began counting.

"There's a thousand pounds here."

"Truly?" Genny asked, and clapped her hands together. "We can use this toward your studio."

Mitch smiled. "That and first class passage on the ship. I'm already thinking about that bed you had."

"The beds *are* larger in first class, I expect," she said, her voice low, and just the way she said it, just the way she *meant* it, made him instantly hard.

"Definitely first class."

Chapter 15

The ship was still within sight of Liverpool and Genny and Mitch were in bed, naked, and feeling quite pleased with themselves.

Genny stretched out on top of Mitch, drowsy and completely sated. The things he'd done . . . with his hands, his fingers. His wonderfully talented tongue. He had brought her to a place she hadn't imagined, where wave after wave of ecstasy engulfed her body in the throes of such complete pleasure, she finally understood why the French called it *la petite morte*.

She kissed his jaw, loving the way his chest vibrated when he moaned in appreciation. "Am I too heavy for you?" she asked, for her entire body was on him, a human blanket.

"I never want you to move," he said.

"We shall starve."

"There is that. I suppose I can let you up briefly, to eat and such."

She giggled and kissed him. Lord, she could kiss him for hours and hours and never get tired of it. If they never left their stateroom, that would be perfectly fine with Genny. Considering what they'd paid for the suite, they might as well stay inside. In bed.

Tillie had been given her own room in first class on the other side of the ship, no longer needing to pretend she was a maid and glad of it. Genny and Mitch, of course, told everyone they were married, because nothing wags more than the tongues on a ship. Mitch had purchased a simple gold band for Genny to wear, promising a much lovelier ring when they were Mrs. and Mr. Mitchell Campbell in fact.

She looked at it now, liking the way it felt, foreign and yet perfect. "Mrs. Mitchell Campbell," she said. "I do believe I shall like that."

"I do believe I shall like it too," Mitch said, kissing her deeply.

Genny let out an irritated sigh, and Mitch turned his head so he could better see her expression. "What's wrong?"

"I'm famished."

"Ah."

"Which means I'm going to have to get up, get dressed. I suppose we should unpack. We'll be on this ship for days and days."

"Not just yet," Mitch said, moving his hips. Genny's eyes widened, and she smiled.

"No," she said, her lips against his. "Not just yet."

When Genny got out of bed some time later, her limbs strangely loose, she walked over to her trunks, unabashedly naked, and started to unpack.

"Darlin', if you don't get some clothes on, I'm afraid you're never going to eat."

She turned back to him and smiled. "As wonderful as that sounds, if I don't eat soon, I will perish." Mitch turned on the bed so that his head was at the foot, his chin propped up on one fist as he watched Genny go through her trunks in search of something to wear. A short time later, wearing one of her simpler gowns, she came back to the bed and sat, laying one hand on his bum.

"You're very pretty," she said, making him laugh.

"Men aren't pretty. They're handsome."

"This part of you is pretty," she said and leaned over to kiss one firm buttock.

He growled and reached for her, but she dashed off the bed and beyond his reach. "Get dressed, Mitch. I truly am famished. They always have some sort of food in the saloon."

"All right," he grumbled and heaved himself off the bed.

"While you get dressed, I'll start unpacking. I do wish Tillie were still a maid. It was lovely having help with this," she said, dragging one of her dresses out of the trunk. She stilled, her eyes on her rosewood box that contained the letters from her grandfather. She carried it to the bed, where Mitch sat tugging on his stockings.

"Do you think it's possible I am an heiress?"

He kissed the tip of her nose. "No. But let's find out anyway."

She opened the box and took up the letters, setting them aside carefully. Then she slid the bottom until an opening appeared, just large enough for one of her slim fingers to slip inside and take up the false bottom. She started to lift it, then looked at Mitch. "I do hope I am. It would be rather nice, wouldn't it? Imagine if it's enough for you to start your photography studio. I feel simply awful that you spent all your—"

Mitch pressed a finger against her lips to stop her. "Just look, will you? And don't get your hopes too high."

She lifted the false bottom out of the box and set it aside, revealing several documents beneath.

She unfolded the first and read, "Girard Bank." Her eyes scanned the document, but having never read a bank statement, she had no idea what all the notations meant. She handed the thick vellum to Mitch.

"Let's see how rich we—" He stopped dead, his eyes widening. And then he swore.

"Oh," Genny said, disappointment washing over her.

"No, darlin'. If this is correct. My God, you're rich."

"What?" she said, getting excited. "How much is there? And what if it's not still there? What if my mother and father spent . . ."

"This is dated March fifth eighteen sixty-five," he said. He looked at the dates and entries. "Nothing was added or withdrawn since the eighteen sixties." He looked up at her, excitement in his eyes. "I don't want to get your hopes up too high, darlin', but I think this money is still there, and if it is, it's yours."

"How much?" she whispered.

"Two hundred thousand thirty-two dollars and fifty-eight cents."

"What?" It was an enormous sum. An outrageous one.

He repeated the number, and Genny squealed, "We're wealthy!" She stood up and hopped up and down. "We're wealthy. Oh, Mitch, it's wonderful!"

"Whoa, darlin', you don't know for sure if this money is still there." He studied the documents again, shaking his head as Genny looked on hopefully. "We'll have to wait until we get to Philadelphia to be certain. Anything else in there?"

Genny began taking out the rest of the papers. "My birth certificate. My parents' wedding license." She looked up and smiled. "This is all so lovely to have." Then her smile faded. "My father's will." Her eyes immediately filled with tears and she handed the document over to Mitch.

"Do you want me to read it?"

She nodded.

Genny watched Mitch's eyes, for they always told the story of what he was looking at. But this time, she just couldn't tell. "What is it, Mitch?"

He shook his head. "I don't know. It talks of the money in the Girard Bank, but not how much, and it talks about, let's see. 'All stocks and bonds as listed in addendum two'." He flipped through some pages. "There's a list, but I have no idea if any of these stocks have value. With the panic last year, they may just be pieces of paper with no value at all."

"Panic? What does that mean?"

"It's complicated, but it was mostly about silver and gold. Used to be that silver was also used to back paper money. You can't just print money with no backing. So for every dollar in your pocket, there's a piece of gold or silver of the same value in a vault somewhere. Then they decided to back money with only gold, and everyone who had silver, well, it wasn't worth as much, you see? Bunch of other stuff happened, too, men spending money they didn't have, and all of a sudden, everything went a little crazy. Banks closed, businesses closed. People lost jobs. That was all last year and it's still pretty bad now."

Genny felt foolish for getting so excited about the money. "So it could all be gone?"

"If this bank is closed, then yes. And the stocks? I don't even know if any of these businesses are still around. I'm sorry, darlin'."

She sat down next to Mitch and rested her head against his shoulder. "Poor and happy suits me just fine," she said, and smiled when she felt Mitch kiss the top of her head.

Mr. and Mrs. Mitchell Campbell stepped from their cab on South Third Street and looked up at the imposing structure of Girard Bank. The marble building, stark white against the blue September sky, dominated the street with its six columns that rose three stories, ending at a portico decorated with an eagle and a cornucopia.

Several people walked in and out of the building, causing Mitch to remark, "At least it's open."

After returning to New York and learning more about the financial devastation wrought by the panic, they had little hope that any money was left from Genny's once sizeable inheritance. They'd married within a week of returning to New York and had been staying with Mitch's mother, who'd welcomed them effusively. Her career, it seemed, had been greatly aided by the *New York Times* article about Genny in which she had been prominently featured.

"If I ever start up my business again," she'd said grandly, "Mr. Tish may enjoy all services free of charge."

Mitch was grateful for his mother's generosity—to them, not Mr. Tish—but he wanted nothing more than to set up a home for just the two of them. Unfortunately, all they had was a few hundred dollars left in his accounts and a few hundred more from the duke's wedding present.

Mitch had worn his best suit and Genny one of Madame Brunelle's creations. "It won't do to look like poor church mice when we go into the bank," she'd said, fixing his tie.

In just a few minutes they would know whether they were, indeed, poor church mice or something a bit better. Since they'd discovered the will, Mitch had taken care not to let Genny get her hopes too high. He couldn't count the times she'd said, "But wouldn't it be nice if there is money?" And he'd always say, "I wouldn't count on getting a dime, darlin'."

Genny tugged at her kid gloves, a gesture Mitch recognized as nervousness, and the two walked up the shallow marble steps to the door, which Mitch swung open, saying, "After you, Mrs. Campbell."

She smiled, as she always did when he called her that. The interior of the bank was just as impressive as the exterior, with marble columns that soared from the brilliantly polished black-and-white marble floor, to the arched sky-blue ceiling. They walked up to a teller, who gave them an assessing look Mitch was beginning to recognize, a look that was meant to discern in a few seconds whether they were important or not.

"How may I help you?" he asked.

Mitch pushed Genny forward gently, a hand on the small of her back. "My name is Mrs. Mitchell Campbell, formerly Miss Genevieve Hayes, and I believe we may have funds in this bank."

The man drew out a piece of paper and took up a pencil in an efficient manner. "Genevieve Hayes you said?"

"Yes. The account may be in the name of my late father, James Hayes, or my mother, Mary."

The man stopped writing and looked up sharply, giving them a strange smile. "One moment please," he said, and disappeared behind a windowed partition that separated the tellers from a series of offices.

"What's happening?" Genny asked, sounding almost frightened.

"I think they recognize the name and the teller is too cowardly to tell you all the money is gone," Mitch teased.

"You're likely right," Genny said, sounding forlorn.

As they watched, an older man peered at them through the window, then stood and came out from behind the glass partition.

"Mrs. Mitchell, welcome to Girard Bank. My name is Arnold Dwight. I'm the manager here. Please do come into my office."

Genny and Mitch looked at each other and, when the teller lifted a portion of the counter, they slipped through and followed the manager to his office. He sat in a tufted leather chair behind a large desk, completely covered with stacks of paper, sunlight from a high window streaming down upon his nearly completely bald pate. When they sat down, he cleared a spot by shoving a few stacks aside and folded his hands in front of him.

"How can I help you?" he said.

Genny explained that her father had died, then presented to the manager all the documentation she had, which Mr. Dwight looked over silently and thoroughly while Mitch and Genny sat, getting more and more nervous every minute.

Then Mr. Dwight let out a short, heavy sigh, which sounded like regret to Mitch's ears.

"You are aware of the panic last year," he said, and Mitch felt any hopes he'd harbored drop to his feet.

"Yes, sir." Mitch looked at Genny, whose expression told Mitch she was feeling the same sense of hopelessness he was. They were poor. They would likely stay poor. He reached over and squeezed her hand and she turned and smiled at him, understanding exactly what Mitch was trying to say: it didn't matter. Not really.

The clerk entered the office and handed Mr. Dwight a slip of paper and a long metal box. "If you'd give me a moment," he said, starting with the slip of paper and moving on to the contents of the box, which Mitch recognized as stock certificates. Likely worthless ones. The manager began putting the certificates in two separate piles, working as if he and Genny weren't in the room.

Finally, after several minutes, he looked up. "The panic," were his first words. So, that was that. "I'm very sorry. Your father, Mrs.

Campbell, was an intelligent investor. He couldn't have possibly predicted what happened last year." He took a deep and tragic breath. "At one time, Mrs. Campbell, your inheritance was sizeable. Quite, quite sizeable."

Mitch looked over at his wife, noting that her hands were clutched together in her lap. "And now?" she asked. Mitch hated the way she sounded and wished with all his might that he could give her a better life than the one facing them.

"I'm afraid there are only two left." Mr. Dwight looked positively ill.

"Dollars?" Genny asked, bewildered, shocked. Bitterly disappointed

Mr. Dwight's eyebrows shot up. "Oh, no, Mrs. Campbell." He let out a laugh as if she'd said the most delightful thing. "Two million."

Genny's hand shot out and clutched Mitch's thigh. Hard.

"Million? Two million *dollars*?"

Mr. Dwight smiled, obviously realizing that two million dollars was a happy surprise. "Yes. As I said, your father was an intelligent investor. At one time, his portfolio was worth considerably more. Considerably more. But I take it you are pleased with the result?"

"Pleased? More than pleased, Mr. Dwight. You see, I had no idea I had any money, never mind . . ."

"Two million dollars," Mitch added, when it became clear Genny was so overwhelmed she could hardly say the words.

"Of course, it is not all liquid funds. Only approximately fifty thousand is readily available. But I'm more than happy to liquidate some of these stocks for you so that you have more cash available."

Genny let out a laugh. "That would be wonderful, Mr. Dwight. I do think fifty thousand should tide us over for a bit." She laughed again.

Genny signed some papers, withdrew five thousand dollars, which she placed carefully in her reticule, and the three shook hands, all smiling. Giddy with the day's events.

Once they were out of the bank and on the wide sidewalk in front, Mitch couldn't wait any longer. He picked her up, laughing and spinning as she clutched his neck.

"You know," Mitch said, once he'd set her down and pressed a kiss on her forehead, "it doesn't matter. If all we had in our pockets was the money your grandfather gave us, I'd still be happy."

Genny nodded, but couldn't help smiling. "I truly don't think I would have been this happy had there only been two dollars in that account. We're wealthy, Mitch. I never, ever would have believed it. You made this all come true."

Mitch smiled, but guilt, unexpected and sharp, hit him. Hard. "I have to tell you something, darlin'."

"My, you look so serious."

"I'm not the man you think I am." When she started to speak, he stopped her. "When I first met you, when you were hurt, my plan was to stay just long enough to make certain you could get around. The last thing I wanted to do was escort some girl anywhere, never mind all the way to England. And then you showed me those letters and, well, all I could think of was getting some reward from your rich relatives so I could open my business. That's why I did it. Not because I'm a hero or a good man.

"Then something happened. Around the time we got to Sacramento and definitely by the time we got to Omaha. I started to not care about the money. It didn't matter. The only thing that mattered was getting you home."

He expected her to be hurt or angry, but Genny smiled. "You fell in love."

"I fell in love. Madly, madly in love."

"I'm glad," she said, getting up on her toes and pressing a soft kiss to his lips. "Because I fell madly, madly in love, too. Besides, I always knew you were interested in money."

He pulled back, stunned. "You did?"

"I tried sympathy, then anger, but when I mentioned my mother's jewels, that seemed to do the trick."

He grinned down at her. "You little scamp. You knew all along?"

"No, not about a possible reward. Honestly, Mitch, how disappointing." She didn't look at all angry, so he couldn't stop smiling. "I shall be very angry with you but not now. Today is too wonderful for anger. Do you think we can give some money to Tillie so she can have a grand wedding? I do like Mr. Paulings."

Mitch looked down the street and spied a hansom cab coming toward them without occupants, so he stepped forward and waved to the driver to stop. "I think you can do whatever you want with the money."

"Then I shall buy a house for us and a wedding for Tillie. And a photography studio and clothes for you. And a home in the country by a lake. I do so miss nature."

Mitch chuckled. "You certainly have thought this through. Anything else?"

"We need to set aside some money for your mother just in case her acting career takes a turn. I shouldn't like her to open another brothel, though she did seem to enjoy herself. And . . ."

"And?" The cab stopped and Mitch gave the driver the address, for the first time in his life not caring that the trip would take nearly a dollar out of his pocket.

"And we'll need furniture for the house. And clothes for the baby, of course."

"Of course," he said, helping her up to the cab. Then it hit him, what she'd said, and if Mitch thought a man could feel any happier than he had a moment ago, he learned what real happiness was in that instant. "Did you say baby?"

Genny gave him a smile he instantly recognized, for he'd been seeing it on and off for days now. She nodded, her cheeks blushing becomingly. "A baby, Mitch."

And now he knew what was behind that smile all along.

When a Lord
Needs a Lady

JANE GOODGER

Don't miss Jane Goodger's delightful Lords and Ladies series, available now wherever digital books are sold!

Lord Graham Spencer needs a wife.

But not just any girl will do. She must have the money to save his dilapidated estate and desperate tenants. So when he meets a charming American lady's maid on the beach at Brighton, the last thing he ought to do is kiss her.

Katherine Wright is hunting a titled husband.

Or at least her mother is. But Katherine can't get the memory of a most inappropriate kiss out of her mind. The handsome stranger who took her in his arms in Brighton was only a valet, but even if she is an heiress, she'd rather spend her life with him than some stiff British aristocrat.

Can true love survive two false identities, two scheming mamas, and two lavish house parties where all is revealed? It can . . .

WHEN A LORD NEEDS A LADY

Praise for the novels of Jane Goodger

"Gentle humor, witty banter, and attractive characters."
—*Library Journal* on *Marry Christmas*

"A touching, compassionate, passion-filled romance."
—*Romantic Times* on *A Christmas Waltz*

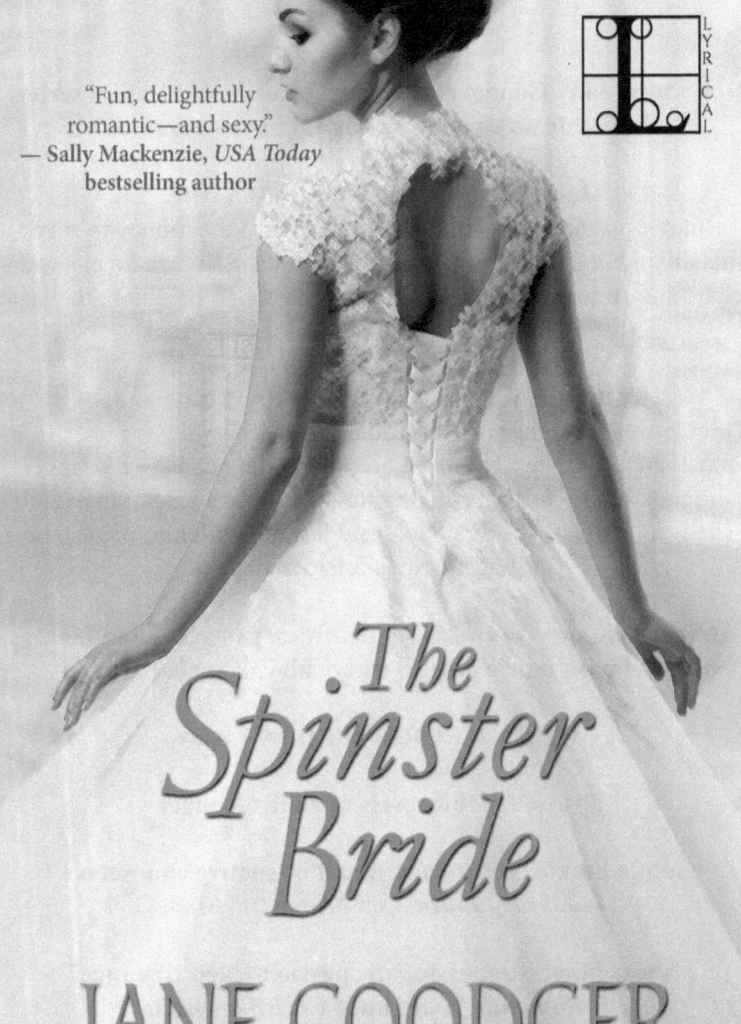

The
Spinster
Bride

JANE GOODGER

"Fun, delightfully romantic—and sexy."
—Sally Mackenzie, *USA Today* bestselling author

Mr. Charles Norris needs help finding a wife ...
For he has the unfortunate habit of falling for each Season's loveliest
debutante, only to have his heart broken when she weds another.
Surely Lady Marjorie Penwhistle can help him. She's sensible,
clever, knows the *ton*, and must marry a peer, which he is not.
Since she's decidedly out of his reach, Charles is free to enjoy her
refreshing honesty—and her unexpectedly enticing kisses ...

Lady Marjorie Penwhistle doesn't want a husband ...
At least not the titled-but-unbearable suitors her mother is
determined she wed. She'd rather stay unmarried and look after her
eccentric brother. Still, advising Mr. Norris *is* a most exciting secret
diversion. After all, how hard will it be to match-make someone so
forthright, honorable, and downright handsome? It's not as if she's
in danger of finding Charles all too irresistible herself ...

Jane Goodger lives in Rhode Island with her husband and three children. Jane, a former journalist, has written and published numerous historical romances. When she isn't writing, she's reading, walking, playing with her kids, or anything else completely unrelated to cleaning a house. You can visit her website at www.janegoodger.com.